MIDLIFE ADVENTURES OF THE FAE REALM
BOOK 1

CLAWS & COCKTAILS

TABITHA SLICK

PRAISE FOR TABITHA SLICK'S MIDLIFE ADVENTURES OF THE FAE REALM SERIES

Also from Tabitha Slick

Midlife Adventures of the Fae Realm
Claws & Cocktails
Blood & Bordeaux
Wings & Whiskey
Serpents & Scotch

YA Supernatural Academy Trilogy
Tompkin's School: For the Extraordinarily Talented
Tompkin's School: For the Dearly Departed
Tompkin's School: For the Resurrected

By Tabi Slick
The Unforgivable Act
The Detective's Nightmare
The Yuletide Killer

For all the mothers,
and the werelings they nurture.

Shadowood Forest
Shadowland
Shadowood University
Mystic City
Havenwo
Mystic Ruins
Fae Channel
Hollow Grove
Havenwood Forest
Pixie Hollow
Lunar Forest
Blood Valley
Fort Magica
The Nest
Coral Cove
Sea
Fae Roma

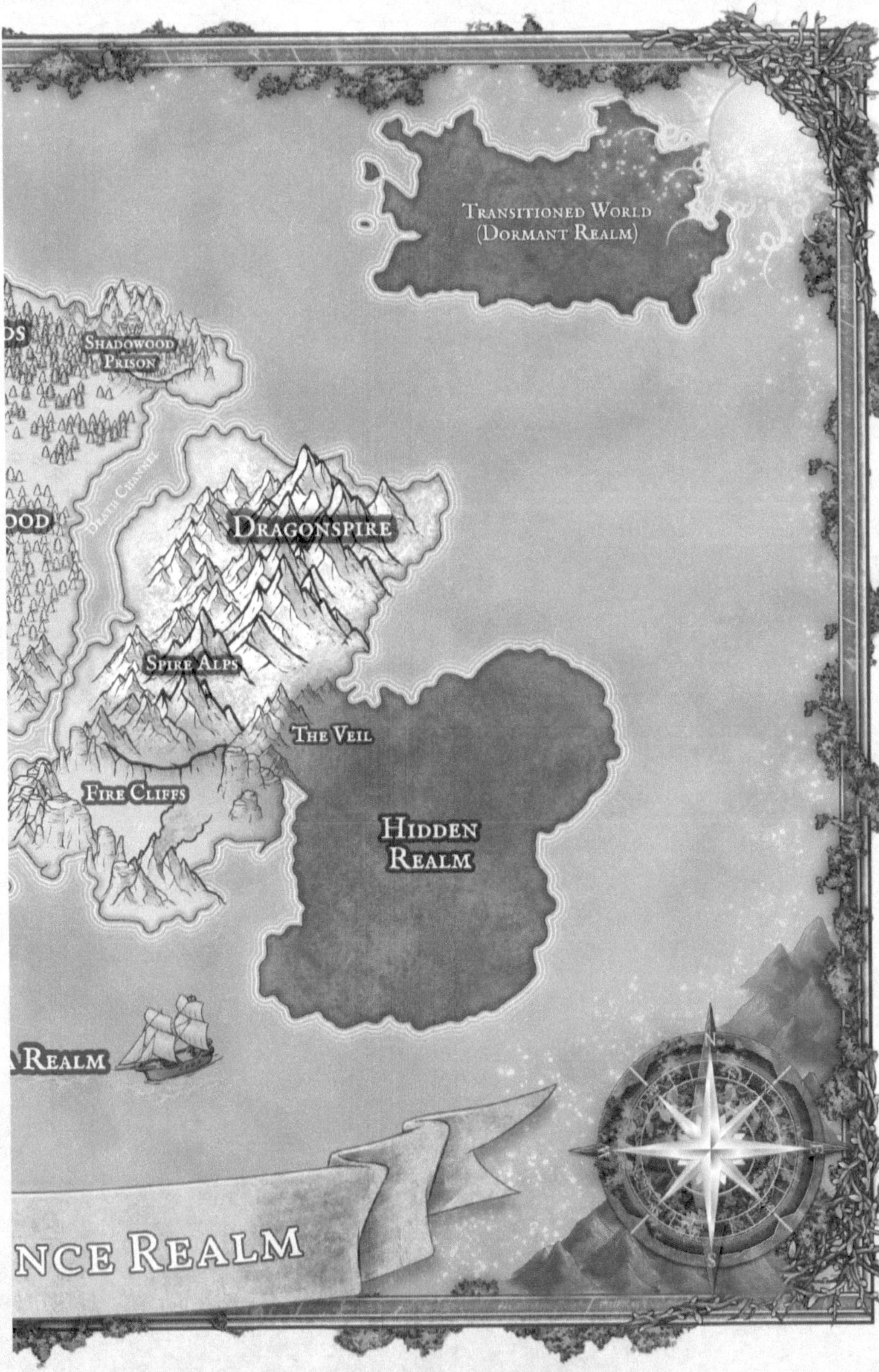

Transitioned World (Dormant Realm)
ds
Shadowood Prison
Death Channel
ood
Dragonspire
Spire Alps
The Veil
Fire Cliffs
Hidden Realm
a Realm
nce Realm

CLAWS & COCKTAILS

CONTENT & TRIGGER WARNINGS:

- Language: The story contains explicit language.
- Steamy Scenes: Includes one or more heated, romantic scenes.
- Drug Use (Off-page): Although no scenes show consumption, the story discusses a fictional drug and explores the creation of drug synthetics.
- Danger to Children (No Harm): There are intense scenes involving a mother saving her baby, but no harm comes to the child.
- Violence: Potential scenes of conflict or danger, especially related to the mother's attempts to protect her baby.

CHAPTER 1
ZERA

Zera fidgeted with the collar of her white button-down top as she sat on the play mat where her little half pixie, half wereling worked to stack brightly colored blocks on top of one another. She hadn't anticipated it being this hard to leave him for the evening while she went on a date—her first date since her asshole ex left her for some new little thing to head off into the mountains with the rest of his traitorous biker gang.

Bloody werewolf packs sucked. The alpha would always win. But at least he'd had the decency to leave her the house before abandoning them. If she were truly being honest, though, their relationship had been over long before he'd cheated and run off. She'd been too invested, following him to a new town and supporting his interests.

Then, when she found out they were going to have a baby, she knew her life would be changed forever. And it had. Just not with her now ex.

Thanks to that bloody wolf, she'd given up her dreams and quit school in order to get a job to support herself and her child.

Not that it mattered anyway. She was done with men. She didn't need the drama. The only male she wanted in her life was right in front of her, trying to gnaw his way through a plastic block. For him, she would do it all over again. She had no regrets. She loved her son more than anything in the world.

She smiled down at her son when he finally made a dent in the toy. His werewolf incisors were coming in, and it made her glad she was done with breastfeeding.

She hated the idea of not being here with him. To leave her little monster and face the real ones who hid behind masks of pleasantries and charm until they moved on to the next victim. She ground her teeth, swearing to despise whoever it was that waited for her at the fancy restaurant up in the city. She wasn't about to go through all that again and leave Cole fatherless. Again.

"Are you excited?"

Zera jumped, and her hand flew to her chest. "Jade! Don't sneak up on me like that." She shot her half sister a wary look before gazing back down at her little baby. She couldn't believe how much he'd grown. It seemed like only yesterday she'd heard his first few cries, and now he was crawling and cooing. Even talking some.

She swallowed the sudden ache in her throat at the thought of going, realizing she still needed to answer her sister. "And no. I'm definitely not excited. I might not even go."

"What? Why not?" Jade asked, tousling Cole's big head of brown curls before plopping down in the chair next to the crib placed in the middle of the dining room they'd converted into a nursery.

This home hadn't been meant to house all three of them plus a baby, but she couldn't imagine going through those early months without the help of her half sister and her wife. So, together, they'd transformed the dining room into the baby's nursery. She had to admit, her sister was good at making do.

"Because he's probably just another asshole and not worth my time." Zera stood up and, in an elegant, practiced motion, fluttered her fingers at a few creases that marred her black dress pants.

A stream of shimmering purple pixie dust poured out from her fingertips and sank into the fabric. The wrinkles vanished, as if they never existed. She was one of the few pixies left who was still able to use magic.

But now, since drug lords discovered that pixie dust could be used as a potent high, their powers were greatly diminished. Pixies had been hunted to near extinction, to the point that those who still had magic lived in fear of using it, allowing the glands within their spines to dry up altogether and causing future generations to be born without magic.

It was a wonder she even had the pixie dust to perform such a small task. But she kept hers hidden from everyone, knowing that it was dangerous to let anyone see what she was capable of. Except for her family, of course.

It was one of the main reasons she'd worked so hard in school, to learn everything she could about faeology and alchemistry so that one day she could work in a lab somewhere and develop a cure for the addiction. Or even experiment with a synthetic option, though she'd have to do that on the side, since it would fall under the illegal umbrella in the Fae Realm. Though ingesting pixie dust had been decriminalized, the process of hunting pixies and creating the drug to begin with was still, fortunately, very much illegal.

Perhaps one day she'd go back to school, but until then, she'd put her dreams of working in a lab on hold. Instead, she was a bartender at the local tavern and used what she'd learned from school to try to figure out a synthetic drug on her own. She wouldn't let her knowledge, or her dream of a world where pixies weren't hunted for their pixie dust, go to waste.

"You have to give this guy a chance." Jade's voice pulled her from her thoughts.

"Do I?" Zera asked and arched her brow. "I don't need another man in my life, Jade, and I don't know why I let you convince me otherwise."

"Because you deserve to be happy," Jade said, her face softening.

"Seriously, Zera, you need to move on, and FaeMatch has never steered me wrong. I mean, look at this hunk of faen beauty. I'm even a little turned on by him, and he's not my type."

Zera snorted.

Jade pulled the app up on her faestone—a six-by-three-inch rectangular piece of quartz—and showed the man she'd matched Zera up with. Maverick Harris, a tall, dark, and handsome sales engineer with stormy gray eyes, stared up at them. His brown hair, trimmed into a sharp crew cut, accentuated his high cheekbones and strong jawline with a hint of scruff.

He was sexy as hell—she'd give Jade that—but that didn't mean she would let herself get swept up. Looks had gotten her into too much trouble before, and she wasn't about to make that mistake twice.

She shrugged. "I don't need a man to move on. I have a healthy son, a good job as a bartender, and a happy home, and I've got you and Sloane. What more could a mom want?"

"Maybe not as a mom, but as a woman, you've got needs. I want you to have the same kind of happiness that I have with Sloane. You have to take care of yourself sometimes."

"I do... sometimes," she said.

Jade gave her a "don't lie to me" look, and Zera bit her cheek. She hated to admit it, but she really hadn't gotten a night to herself since giving birth to Cole. Even with Jade and Sloane to help. Between long hours at Haven Wolf Tavern, motherhood, and her at-home science experiments that were, so far, a complete bust, she barely had a moment to run a brush through her hair.

"Come on, it's nearly time to head out," Jade said, standing up to shoo her out. "You've got a thirty-minute drive, and you haven't even gotten ready."

"I am ready."

Jade made a face. "You mean you're going to a restaurant looking like a waiter?"

"I don't look like a waiter." Zera looked down at her white button-down and black pants and sighed. She was right again. "Well, maybe a really, really cute one."

She laughed. "Cute, yes, but not for a date night. I can't let you leave in that outfit. How do you expect to get any action looking like that?"

"Jade!" Zera's cheeks burned.

"What?"

"I don't even want or need to go on this date, and I definitely *won't* be sleeping with the guy."

Jade arched her brow. "Really? You aren't even just a tiny bit tempted by this tall, dark, and very muscly man with the dreamy eyes?"

Zera bit her lip. The thought of being wrapped in his muscled arms and feeling his breath on her neck sent a shiver of desire down her spine. She quickly shook her head, trying to push the image of their bodies intertwined in her bedsheets out of her mind. That would definitely *not* be happening.

"Not in the slightest."

Jade shook her head. "Okay, okay. I believe you. But still, let me help you. The pants are good, but the shirt must go."

She hopped up and headed down the hall past Zera's room on the right and to the primary bedroom that she shared with her wife. She returned moments later with a bright-red top with no sleeves and a plunging neckline. It obviously was one of Sloane's, since Jade owned only jeans and plaid shirts. Maybe she could borrow one of those instead?

Zera gulped. "Nope. I can't wear that."

"Why not? It's perfect and would complement your waves if you'd ever let your hair down."

She checked her bun at the nape of her neck to make sure it was still intact and rolled her eyes.

"The bun stays. Now, give me that." She grabbed the blouse and marched to the bathroom.

"You're welcome!" Jade called after her.

She knew her sister was only being nice, and there was a tiny part of her that agreed with Jade. It was more than time to have a little fun, to escape for a few hours and forget about to-do lists or sleep schedules.

But it was only a very small part of her, luckily. The rest of her was dead set on rushing through this date and getting home to snuggle up with Cole as soon as possible.

A wave of unease washed over her when she slipped the silky red shirt on. It fit okay, even though it clearly was a size too small for her, but it showed off way too much skin. Her boobs practically spilled out, not in the sexy fae-model way but in the "I've stopped breast-feeding, and now they're deflated" kind of way.

If only her pixie dust or Sloane's witchy spells could do some cosmetic-surgery magic. Unfortunately, there was no magical shortcut to fixing body issues. At least it was loose around her middle section.

Zera sighed. She was too old for this. It'd be one thing if she were in her twenties again, but those days were long gone. She tugged at the hem of the shirt, trying to make it cover a little more of her chest, but she knew it was a lost cause.

As she stepped out of the bathroom, Jade whistled and gave her a thumbs-up. "You look hot, Mama!"

She grimaced. "I need a jacket. Or a sack to cover up."

"A leather jacket and a scarf 'cause it's cold, but don't be afraid to let the girls out."

"Girls? Seriously?" She laughed. "They're more like sad, old ladies."

"Shh, don't say that! They'll hear you."

Jade laughed when she shot her a playful glare. "You're ridiculous."

"Not as ridiculous as you for thinking you don't look good in that shirt," Jade said with a smile. "Now, come on, you better get out of here or else you'll be late."

Zera checked her faestone sitting on the edge of the changing table. It was getting late. If she was going to go, she'd better leave now.

"Fine. I'll go," Zera said and took a deep breath. "But you'd better take care of Cole."

"You know I will." Jade picked up Cole, bouncing him on her hip as they followed Zera to the living room.

Zera pulled her jacket on, grabbing her purse and keys out of the cubby next to the front door. "And call me if you need anything or anything happens—"

"Zera, we'll be fine," Jade said, nudging her toward the door. "Just go have a nice date. Sloane will be home from the diner soon with food. Cole will have a nice dinner and will be fast asleep long before you come home. Promise."

Zera nodded, taking another deep breath. She knew Jade would take good care of Cole, but it still didn't make it any easier to leave him. She kissed Cole's chubby cheek.

"Okay, I'm going," she said before heading out into the evening breeze.

The sun was setting over the horizon, casting a blanket of pink and orange shadows across the endless red oaks of the Havenwood Forest that surrounded the small town. The leaves were starting to brown for winter, crunching under her heeled boots as she made her way across the gravel and into her car.

It was a tiny four-seater she'd bought used and not unlike the sedans she'd heard about from the Human Realm. Not that she'd ever been there. Only high-up fae in government could travel between the realms. But that didn't mean they hadn't brought back their technological advances and blended them with their own magical ones.

Zera started the engine and sped off through town and out onto the highway that separated the Havenwood Forest from the northern Shadowood Forest. She turned west, heading to the capital of the Fae Realm—Mystic City.

Pine trees that brushed the sky flew by her on the right, and the rainbow of browning red oaks, aspens, and birches blended together on the left, until she neared the city that stood majestic against the darkening sky.

Mystic City was the hub of the Fae Realm, the center of culture, and a place for opportunities. Zera had been living in Havenwood for a few years now, but she'd never ventured into the city before.

A thrill of excitement rushed through her veins as she maneuvered through the fancy high-rises of the west side. Bright lights illuminated the storefronts and restaurants, and the sound of laughter and conversation filled the air. The city hummed with an intoxicating energy that made her heart race with anticipation.

She had to remind herself that whatever happened, she wouldn't fall for whoever this guy was. No matter how handsome he was. Cole was her whole world, and she didn't need another man in her life. But that didn't mean she couldn't enjoy herself a little bit, did it? It wasn't every day she got to go out to a nice dinner, so she might as well enjoy it.

The restaurant finally came into view, a two-story, cylinder-shaped building with a crystal dome over the top that stood out like a beacon in the night. An elaborate sign hung above the door reading The Crystal in red text. Her stomach tied into knots. Guess this is it.

She pulled into the valet parking lot, and her anxiety spiked as she gripped the steering wheel. She couldn't do this. She didn't even want to be on this date. She'd much rather be in her pajamas, cuddled up next to their fireplace with a good romance book. At least the men in those books couldn't hurt her.

Someone tapped on her window before she could turn around. She sighed and rolled it down.

"Madame Zera?" the valet asked, his blond hair falling over his youthful eyes as he bowed. His pallid face with not a single wrinkle, on top of his fangs and fake Human Realm accent, told her he was a vampire.

There were whole nests of vampires obsessed with human blood and human customs. So, naturally, many of them latched on to not only the humans' carotid arteries but to their accents, demeanors, and fashion too.

It was even rumored that somewhere in Blood Valley, the vampire queen herself had a secret back door leading into the Human Realm, allowing her kind to lure humans in for their blood.

Not that any of these rumors had been confirmed or anything, but that didn't stop them from spreading.

The idea sent a shiver through her body.

"Um, yeah?" Zera blinked. How did he know her name?

"Your party's already waiting for you. The host inside shall escort you." The valet's strange accent was thick but not enough to cover up the sound of his fangs clicking together as he spoke.

She glanced between the valet and the entrance of the Crystal as more vamps spilled out. Well, that was just great. Her blind date had picked the worst spot possible. Vampires were notorious for their insatiable feeding habits, and even though they were forbidden to feed on unwilling parties in the Fae Realm, she didn't trust them.

Her stomach rumbled with hunger. She'd come all this way so she might as well get a meal out of the deal. She hoped he wasn't a vampire luring her here to suck her dry. Or worse.

She forced herself to shove those thoughts to the back of her mind and stepped out of the car, handing her keys to the valet. "Thanks," she called over her shoulder as she headed for the entrance.

Realizing she would likely stand out in a place like this, she decided it'd be best to mask her pixie features. With a little pixie dust and focus, she could do it. She drew in the energy from the reservoir of magic stored in a gland below the seventh vertebra, and heat warmed her body.

The dust rounded her pointed ears and subdued her lavender irises into a warm brown color. She blinked, aware of the change in color as a film spread across her vision that was hardly noticeable if she ignored it. The only problem was that, if there were any problems at the restaurant and she needed her limited supply of power, she would be unable to keep up the mirage. Ideally, she wouldn't need to use her pixie dust at all and the date would go smoothly without a fuss.

Chandeliers sparkled high overhead, casting the plush velvet chairs and marble floors underneath them in a glittery light. Zera gasped, unable to contain her awe. She had to give it to them—the vamps knew how to decorate. It was like she'd walked right into an art deco mansion.

"Welcome, Madame Zera," the hostess greeted her before she could speak. "Right this way."

How did everyone here already know who she was? It was kind of creepy. She tried not to let her unease show on her face as she followed the hostess up a giant staircase to the second floor. A waiter raced by, gripping a silver platter of wineglasses filled with what could've been wine but was most likely blood.

She shivered. This was not her scene, but she'd promised her sister she would give this date a chance. Though, in reality, the poor fae didn't have one to begin with. Whoever this guy was, vampire or not, she was determined not to fall for him.

As she and the hostess reached the top of the staircase, Zera's eyes widened as she took in the sight before her. Even more chandeliers hovered overhead, dangling dangerously high under a glass ceiling, illuminating the tables below draped with white linens and scattered across a turf of green velvet grass.

The smell of rosemary and garlic bread filled the air, mingled with something a bit more coppery that made her want to gag. Perhaps it didn't bother those who ate red meat, but Zera couldn't stand meat that was even remotely raw.

Maybe if Jade had mentioned this on the profile she'd made for Zera, then her date wouldn't have invited her to a vampire restaurant, let alone swiped yes to go on a date.

Vampires filled most of the tables, all dressed in their most elaborate attire and mingling, laughing, and drinking.

She wasn't sure which was worse, the fact that they were probably drinking blood in those wine glasses or that she was significantly underdressed. Why hadn't she looked up the restaurant ahead of time?

But it didn't really matter. All she was here for were the delicious carbs and a strong cocktail. Nothing more.

"Your date is seated over there," the hostess said, gesturing to a secluded booth near panoramic glass that offered a picturesque view of Mystic City.

Zera's breath caught in her throat when she spotted the pair of stormy gray eyes trained on her, piercing through her soul. He was even more stunning in person, tanned with broad shoulders that filled his tailored suit to perfection and a strong jawline that could cut through glass.

His sharp cheekbones made him look lethal, like a predator ready to pounce on its prey. But she was no prey, and she wasn't about to fall for this guy's charms.

Despite her resolve to loathe this man, her heart slammed against her rib cage as she navigated the tables to meet him, her heels muffled by the turf grass.

A playful smile danced on his lips as he slowly rose to greet her. "Zera, I presume?" He extended a hand to help her into the booth.

She didn't even give it a second glance as she plopped down into her seat. "Yes, but don't get too excited. I'm only here to enjoy my food and get out of here."

His eyes widened in shock as he settled in across from her. "Um... what?"

"Look, I'm going to be straight with you." She fixed him with a determined look, refusing to let herself fall under his spell. "I'm not interested in whatever game you're playing. I'm here for the food and wine and that's it. If that's not what you're looking for, we might as well end things here."

His lips quirked in amusement, his stormy gray eyes never leaving hers. "I can respect that. Although if you weren't interested in a date, then why'd you accept my invitation on FaeMatch?"

"I only recently found out that I even had a profile on there." She sighed. "My sister. She's a little... desperate to see me in another relationship, which is the last thing I need right now."

He laughed, a low rumble that sent shivers down her spine. "Well, that's a relief to hear."

Her eyebrows shot up. It was her turn to be surprised. "So you're on FaeMatch to find what? A hookup?"

She suddenly felt like she wasn't the only one in control of the conversation. His demeanor had changed, and he now had a look of amusement on his face, as if he knew something she didn't.

"No, not really," he said, leaning back in his seat. "I'm not looking for anything serious, and I assure you this date is not a hookup."

What in the bloody fae did that mean? She eyed him suspiciously, not sure what he could be up to.

Before she could press him for an explanation, the waiter materialized beside them, seemingly from thin air, causing a sudden rush of wind. Zera jumped in her seat. She would never get used to vamp speed.

"Monsieur Harris, it is lovely to see you again. Will it be the usual, or would you like to see a menu?" The waiter fixed a bored gaze pointedly at Zera, and she felt a pang of annoyance.

Just because she wasn't a regular customer didn't mean she wasn't worth the same level of respect.

"The usual for me but a menu for—" Maverick began, but she cut him off, not wanting him to assume he had control.

"I'm sure 'the usual' is fine," Zera said quickly. The waiter's impatience was like a cold draft, and she didn't want him sticking around longer than he needed to.

"Are you positive?" he pressed, looking at her with a raised eyebrow.

Zera nodded firmly. "Absolutely."

Maverick gave her a curious look but nodded to the waiter. "We'll have the usual, then. And a bottle of the Chateaux de la Nuit."

As soon as the waiter left, she turned back to Maverick, her eyes narrowing. "Don't assume you can make decisions for me."

Maverick chuckled, flashing her a wicked smile revealing totally normal, very non-vampire teeth. "Oh, I wouldn't dream of it."

Zera felt a surge of something unfamiliar and exciting. She wasn't used to a man who could keep up with her, let alone challenge her. But there was something about Maverick that made her want to push back as hard as he did.

"Tell me this," she said, trying to ignore the electricity that sparked between them. "Why would a fae who's not a vamp use this restaurant as their dating spot?"

A mischievous spark of golden lightning glimmered across his steely gray irises, as if he was enjoying the challenge of her question. "Firstly, how do you know I'm not a vampire? And, secondly, why do you presume I take all my dates here?"

"Well, for starters, your teeth lack the clacking sound that vampire teeth make when they talk," Zera pointed out, a hint of pride in her tone at her attention to detail. "And as for the second part, you seem pretty chummy with the snobby waiter who looked at me like I was this week's trash, so let's cut the crap and be honest."

"Ah, the irresistible charms of Luc," Maverick said with a smirk. "Well, for the sake of being honest, you're right. I'm not a vampire. I'm a werewolf."

It took all of Zera's self-control not to make a sour face. She almost wished he were a bloodsucking vampire. Werewolves were much worse, and she loathed the entire species.

They pretended to be loyal until their alpha called rank, then anyone else who wasn't part of the pack fell to the wayside. The priorities of the pack would always come first, even before blood. It was why she and Cole were left behind.

Fortunately, pack law didn't apply to half-breeds, so at least she would always have her son.

"I'm guessing you're not a fan of wolves?" Maverick raised an eyebrow, his gaze penetrating her own.

Zera felt a strange mix of vulnerability and defiance, not used to someone other than her sister being so direct with her. She shrugged, trying to hide her discomfort.

"I've had my fair share of bad experiences with wolves," she said with a guarded tone. "I don't trust them."

"Was this experience with an ex of yours?" he asked smugly.

"How—" she growled but stopped. Jade and that stupid FaeMatch profile. She must've mentioned it.

"Don't worry, I won't pry. Let's just say that makes two of us—on the wolf front, not the ex," he replied with a wry smile, as if they were sharing a secret. "I've had more betrayal from my own kind than you'll ever know. But some wolves are better than others. And I'm definitely one of the good ones."

"I'm sure you think you are," Zera replied, unconvinced. She'd heard similar lines before. They'd worked on her in her naive youth, but she knew better now.

Maverick chuckled and looked as if he wanted to say something, probably to change her mind, but the snub-nosed waiter returned with the wine and food, pouring the red liquid into both glasses before setting the bottle on the table and leaving as quickly as he'd arrived.

"Cheers," Maverick said with a wink.

Zera raised her glass in response and took a small sip. She sighed with relief when it was just wine, the rich, full-bodied liquid warming her insides.

"You still haven't answered the second part of my question," she said, setting her glass aside and picking up her fork and knife to dig into her meal. "About the other girls you've been bringing here."

She took a bite but froze when something raw and cold hit her tongue. She scrunched her nose and looked down at her plate. Horror swept over her as she stared at the red blob of meat in the center of her plate surrounded by toast points.

"So, I take it that steak tartare is the exception to your no-red-meat rule from your profile?"

Her eyes widened, and she quickly put her fork down.

"You knew your usual was red meat and you made me order it?"

"To be fair, I did ask if you were sure, and I didn't make you do anything. You insisted." Maverick smirked, obviously having anticipated her reaction.

"And had I known what the 'usual' actually was, I would never have ordered it."

"Perhaps next time you'll accept my suggestion of looking at the menu?" He sipped his wine to hide a laugh.

Zera bristled. "There won't be a next time. Besides, won't you be on to the next after this? Presumably taking them here for another speed date?"

Maverick studied her for a moment. Zera tried to ignore the heat that rose in her cheeks under his scrutiny.

She knew she shouldn't let herself be affected by his charm, but she couldn't help it. He was a masterpiece in a tailored suit, making her wonder what he would look like without it, and he got under her skin in a way that no one else had before.

"You want the truth?" he asked, still watching her.

"And nothing but."

His gaze intensified, and he drew closer to her. Zera could feel the heat emanating from his body, and her heart began to race.

"This isn't a date."

Zera raised an eyebrow in disbelief. "Excuse me? Then what is it?"

Maverick leaned back in his chair again, stuffing a huge scoop of the steak tartare into his mouth. He took his time to chew, which nearly drove her insane, before he finally swallowed. "It's business, Zera."

Her mouth fell open, but there were no words for the shock she was feeling. Business? What kind of business sought women out on FaeMatch?

Several shady things came to mind, and all of them made her sick to her stomach.

"How dare you solicit—"

"Please keep your voice down," he said, and she ground her teeth. The nerve of this scumbag. "And before you go and accuse me of something I'm not doing, let me tell you that we're both in grave danger."

"The only one of us who's in danger here, Maverick, is you. Not me," Zera countered, gathering her things before she scooted her way out of the booth. It really wasn't a graceful look, but she didn't care. She needed to get the hell out of there.

But before she could stand, Maverick was there, towering over her and blocking her way out. "I can't let you leave."

"Wha—" She stopped when his eyes suddenly flicked to the right in a gesture to get her to look at something over his shoulder.

Her eyes fell on a man with a razor-sharp nose, bald head, elven ears, and eyes as clear as glass who walked up the staircase like he owned the place. A posse of men dressed in black suits tailed him, fanning out once they reached the landing. They all had the same cold and calculated look in their eyes, and Zera's heart raced even faster.

"Who's that?" she asked, barely above a whisper.

"There's no time to explain."

She scowled up at him. "Make time."

Maverick sighed, muttering something under his breath as he raked a hand through his hair. "Screw it. Scoot over."

Without waiting for an answer, Maverick pushed his way into the seat next to her, his firm body pressed up against hers.

Zera tensed as he leaned in close to whisper in her ear. "The truth is... I'm a spy, my cover's about to be blown, and for the sake of both our lives, I need you to pretend to be my wife."

The whole room went ice-cold as Zera processed his words. Her thoughts raced, a torrent of emotions threatening to overwhelm her

—fear, doubt, betrayal, everything she swore she wouldn't let herself feel again. Especially not from a man.

Fear wrapped its iron grip around her sternum, and her breaths came out in short gasps as she realized this was how it would end.

Her heart clenched as Cole's face filled her thoughts and nearly brought her to tears. She was going to die, and she would never see her baby again.

CHAPTER 2
ZERA

Zera's heart beat erratically as she tried to wrap her head around what was going on. Sweat trickled down her back, her whole body suddenly hot as her fear turned to rage. Maverick's body heat only angered her more as he hovered next to her like an overbearing prick.

The nerve of this man. To think she'd ever agree to go on this date in the first place. This fake date had only put her in danger, and she didn't even get a meal out of it.

But it hadn't just put her in danger. Her son could grow up without ever knowing her. A reality that made it hard for her to breathe. Not that Maverick acted as if he knew she was a mom, but still.

And now he had the gall to ask her to pretend to be his wife. This was a mistake. It was all a huge mistake.

She glanced around, checking for the exits, but it was clear whoever was here for Maverick had all of them covered. It was too late to make a run for it now.

Her lungs felt tight and constricted. She tried to steady her breath, but panic clawed at her chest. At the same time, her stomach growled, a painful reminder that even her dinner had made her want to puke.

"Are you all right?" Maverick asked, his brows furrowed as if he was legitimately concerned about her.

She scoffed. "No, not even close. I'm pissed, scared, and starving. Are you happy now?"

She fixed him with a death stare, daring him to respond.

He shifted uncomfortably, breaking his usual controlled demeanor.

"Look, I know I messed up," he began, his voice barely above a whisper. "But please, hear me out. I didn't mean for this to happen, okay? I was supposed to be here gathering intel about the restaurant owner. That's why I've been coming here so often under the guise of a player who dates someone new every week."

"Oh, really?" Zera spat, anger bubbling up inside her. "You just use random women to cover your ass?"

"No, you have it all wrong," he insisted, leaning in as if there were any room left between them. "My partner was a Kobold goblin who could morph her features. But she decided to go into the public sector for reasons that are beyond me. That's why I turned to FaeMatch and found you." He paused, glancing nervously around the room. "We're running out of time. Gareth is getting closer."

As if on cue, Zera spotted the guy he called Gareth nearing their booth, his sickening pale complexion, sharp nose, and bald head gleaming in the low light. Another bout of panic surged within her, threatening to spill over.

"Please, play along," Maverick begged, giving her the bread-basket and cheese as a peace offering. "Then we can go our separate ways and never have to see each other again."

"Promise?"

He nodded. "You have my word."

Zera hesitated, torn between anger and fear. Finally, she grabbed a piece of bread and shoved it into her mouth, nodding her reluctant acceptance to cooperate. She didn't trust herself to speak without cursing him out and totally shattering any chance she had of getting out of there alive.

She hoped she could keep it together long enough to make it through this ordeal and back to her son. Life as a single mom was the hardest job she'd ever had, but being with Cole, watching him grow and experience life... It was the best thing in the whole world, and she didn't want to miss another second of it.

Gareth approached their booth like a predator stalking its target, and Zera's heart skipped a beat. She took a deep breath, willing herself to stay calm.

"Ah, Dane Brown." Gareth greeted Maverick with a smile that didn't quite reach his cold eyes.

"Gareth, it's been a long time, hasn't it?" Maverick replied smoothly despite the tension radiating off him.

Gareth chuckled darkly and slid into the seat across from them.

Zera's whole body tensed. Who exactly was this man? And how did he know Maverick? She glanced up at Maverick, searching for any clues, but his expression remained unreadable.

"It has, hasn't it?" Gareth sneered, plucking a fork off the table.

Zera's mind raced as the two men exchanged tense pleasantries, the sounds of Maverick's fork scraping at his steak tartare and the smacking of his lips as he digested the food grating on her every nerve.

She had to get out of there. She had to get back home to Cole. Her heart ached, and she didn't want to think about what this fae might do if she tried to run. She couldn't tell what power the elven elemental had, but he had to be powerful to make the werewolf beside her squirm.

Everything about Gareth's demeanor screamed that he killed for fun, and she didn't want to be here when that happened.

"And who is this lovely creature at your side?" Gareth asked, his gaze finally falling on Zera, making her skin crawl.

"This is my wife, Charlotte," Maverick answered smoothly, placing a protective hand on hers where they rested in her lap. It was gentle and oddly comforting. All part of his act. "Charlotte, this is an old... friend of mine."

"Well, I wouldn't go as far as calling us friends." Gareth set the fork down and wiped his mouth with the cloth napkin before resting his elbows on the table. A total power move. "Would you? Because as I see it, friends would've sent an invitation to your nuptials."

Zera swallowed hard. He knew. Somehow this Gareth guy knew they were lying. What would they do if he discovered this was their first date? Kill them? She didn't want to be there to find out, but she was way out of her comfort zone. Even with her pixie dust, there was no way she could create a diversion big enough to get them out of here without someone seeing.

"But then you're calling yourselves married, and I don't see any wedding bands." He fixed them with a pointed gaze, a dangerous glint in his eye.

Maverick's grip on Zera's hand tightened, and she could feel his tension building. She had to do something or else this man was going to kill them before they even had a chance to escape. She had to stall.

If she used just a little of her pixie dust, maybe they wouldn't notice the brief change in eye color.

With a deep breath in, she reached within the depths of what little power she had and let it wash over her. No one would notice that her magic put a few rings on their fingers, right?

When Gareth wasn't looking, she closed her eyes briefly and let the warmth of pixie dust trickle up her spine through a special nerve only pixies had that ran from where her useless pixie wings lay dormant underneath her fair skin, across her shoulders, and down to her fingertips.

She fluttered her fingers under the table, the pixie dust creating matching wedding bands for herself and Maverick. She opened her eyes, the film of subtle brown safely restored.

Gareth's gaze narrowed on her, but whether he noticed the change or not, he didn't make it known.

Maverick caught a glimpse of their new rings and frowned but quickly composed himself.

She raised her chin in pride. She didn't have to be a trained spy to play this game.

"You mean this ring?" She brandished her left hand from under the table with a forced smile she prayed was convincing.

Gareth's eyes flicked to the rings, and a slow, wicked grin spread across his face.

"Well, I stand corrected, then," he drawled, leaning back in his chair. "So you did actually settle down after all. I must confess, I knew you were engaged, but I'm surprised to hear you actually went through with it as a man of your... prowess."

Zera noticed how Maverick's jaw twitched. Gareth must've hit a nerve.

"But I stand corrected. It's such a rare occasion when I'm wrong," the elven man chuckled darkly. "We should get a proper drink to toast the happy couple and to your eternal happiness, yes?"

Zera flashed a smile in response, but inside, her every instinct screamed at her to run. It wasn't the rational part of her, though. She knew she'd be dead before she could stand.

Instead, she focused on her breath. In and out, steady and slow. She had to keep it together. It was one night. She could get through this. Maverick was a professional spy, right? He had to know how to get out of these types of situations. She was in competent hands. At least that was what she was telling herself.

"We've got drinks, thanks." Maverick's voice was tight as he replied in an attempt to shut down the suggestion.

Zera noticed Gareth's men had them surrounded now and were slowly closing in, blocking any potential escape routes. She knew they had to play along if they wanted to make it out alive. She took a sip of her drink, fully aware of the eyes on her.

Gareth's eyes sparkled with amusement. "Come now, don't be rude. Let's drink to honor the newlyweds."

He didn't wait for a response and snapped his fingers at the waiter across the restaurant. This elf must have telepathic powers because the waiter instantly ran off to fetch his order without even coming to the table.

The unease in Zera's chest intensified, and she looked to Maverick for guidance. He was silent, his eyes trained on Gareth and his expression unreadable. Yet he must've sensed her distress as his hand quickly found hers under the table, giving it a reassuring squeeze.

Zera took a deep breath, focusing on the warmth of his touch to quell the fear threatening to consume her. He might've been a prick, but she knew he was the only one who could get her out of there alive, and at least right now, he was being supportive and nice.

Not the type of qualities she was used to in a wolf.

But this was so not the time to be thinking about that. She had to focus on staying calm. Not just for her own sake but for Cole's. Moisture pricked at her eyes at the thought of never seeing him again. She wouldn't let that happen.

Bloody fae, she had to get out of there.

The snobby waiter—who'd miraculously had an attitude change since Gareth entered the restaurant—appeared beside them with three glasses of amber liquid over ice and a rosemary sprig.

"Ah, divine," Gareth said as the waiter hastily placed a glass in front of each of them before timidly retreating. "Forgefire Whiskey. There's nothing quite like the smoky, complex blend made by the dependable hands of dwarves, yes?"

There was a pointed edge to his question, and Zera wondered if there was some underlying meaning she wasn't catching on to.

"Cheers," Gareth said, lifting his glass of whiskey before taking a sip.

She followed Maverick's lead and didn't touch the whiskey.

"So, tell me," he said after downing the whole thing in one gulp, "what brings the two of you here tonight?"

"Date night," Maverick answered smoothly, his hands still intertwined with Zera's.

"Ah, romance. How sweet," Gareth mused, his tone mocking. "It seems that's been going around. Did you know a friend of mine owns this restaurant?"

Maverick's grip on Zera's hand tightened at the mention of Gareth's friend owning the restaurant, and she could sense his growing tension. Her heart raced as she remembered what Maverick said about being hired to spy on the restaurant's owner. Did Gareth know?

Zera's heart rate spiked. She had a feeling they were treading dangerous waters.

"Oh, really?" Maverick asked, his voice neutral.

"Yes, really." Gareth paused, studying Maverick for a moment before continuing. "When I heard that every week his restaurant had the displeasure of being visited by a gray wolf, I had to come see for myself. It is a rare breed of werewolves to spot outside of the Lunar Forest, seeing as how they're traditionalists and all."

Zera gulped. How had she not seen it before? The stormy gray eyes, the insistence that he wasn't like other wolves, and all the other dodgy answers he'd given her. He was part of the Lunar Brother-hood, a dangerous pack known to be in the pocket of a gang that hunted pixies down for their magic.

She yanked her hand from his. He'd lied enough to her today, and his mere touch now made her loathe the very booth they shared. Perhaps this had all been a ploy to get her pixie dust. But then, he didn't know she was a pixie yet, so perhaps that was a blessing in disguise.

She took a deep breath and tried to calm herself. She couldn't afford to panic now.

"Oh, did she not know?" Gareth asked, smirking as he looked between the two of them. "I thought for sure married couples would know such things. But I stand corrected."

Maverick opened his mouth to speak, but Gareth didn't give him a chance before he fixed Zera with a pointed gaze.

"Your husband here is a regular at this establishment," Gareth continued, his eyes darkening. "Rather... frequent visits with different ladies, wouldn't you say?"

"Old habits die hard," Maverick quipped, not missing a beat. "But I'm a reformed man now, thanks to my lovely wife."

"Ha! Wife," Gareth mused, clearly not convinced. He leaned in closer, his voice dropping to a deadly whisper. "You see, my friend who owns this place, he keeps a keen eye on repeat customers, especially those who aren't his usual clientele."

Zera swallowed hard, her mind racing as she tried to predict Gareth's next move.

"Imagine my surprise," Gareth continued, "when I saw none other than my old logistics strategist, the same one who double-crossed me, on the security footage. Quite the coincidence, isn't it?"

Zera could practically feel Maverick's muscles tense beside her, but his expression remained calm and collected.

"Coincidences do happen," Maverick replied coolly, his eyes never leaving Gareth's. "And for the record, I am married. To Charlotte."

"Of course," Gareth said, his tone dripping with sarcasm. He chuckled, a sound that made the bread she chewed turn sour. "I have to ask. Where've you been all this time? Because we both know this" —he waved his hand at the two of them—"is a sham. It's as if Dane got wiped off the face of the Realm after we... split ways."

At that moment, Maverick stiffened. Something about them parting ways got under his skin, and Zera knew there was something more to that than what they were letting on.

Maverick had only broken his stoic demeanor for a split second, but Zera noticed it immediately.

"What do you want, Gareth?" Maverick finally asked.

"Isn't it obvious, *Dane*?" He spat the name out like it was poison in his mouth. "It's what I've wanted ever since I discovered you were a mole in my operations, bringing my decades-old business to its knees. Since I found out you're actually not Dane Brown, the master logistics strategist, but rather Maverick Harris. A spy for hire."

"I don't know what you're talking about," Maverick said, but the twitch in his jaw made it clear that Gareth had hit a nerve. "I've never heard that name before in my life."

"No more lies!" Gareth waved his hand in a flourish, and the fork in front of her instantly levitated, aimed to pierce her between the eyes.

The air in her lungs froze, and her muscles locked up. She couldn't move. She could barely breathe. Her blood turned to ice as she stared at the fork and certain death.

A growl rumbled from beside her, and without warning, Maverick's whole body shuddered, shifting into his werewolf form as he lunged across the table for Gareth's jugular. He was a blur of fur, fangs, and muscle as he tackled Gareth before the elf could use his powers again, the fork clattering to the floor.

Gareth's men were on Maverick in an instant, pulling him away from their boss, who scurried out of Maverick's clutches before he had a chance to sink his teeth into him.

The restaurant descended into chaos as tables overturned and chairs crashed to the floor. Guards rushed in from all directions. Some drew weapons that sent a flurry of magical bullets while others flashed vampire fangs and werejaguar claws, and demons called upon their dark magic.

Maverick easily fought them off, swatting away the demon who'd dared drag him by his tail with a powerful swipe of his clawed paw. His wolf form dominated the room with a ferocity Zera hadn't seen in a werewolf before.

A blast hit the table near hers, and her paralysis shattered as she regained control over her body. She was going to die if she didn't move. Another blast hit the window behind her table, and it shattered on impact.

She ducked under the table as Maverick tackled Gareth, dragging the elf by his collar.

The sounds of bones cracking and spells being cast echoed

beyond the white linen. Her breath came in shallow gasps. She never should've gone on this stupid date.

She should've listened to her instincts that were telling her she didn't need a man when she had all the love she needed in being Cole's mom. Now, she was going to die while on a fake date with an arrogant spy.

She sucked at the air in desperate gulps. What the fae was she supposed to do now?

Zera peeked out from underneath the tablecloth. A druid in a brown cloak with runes tattooed across his forehead stood over Maverick's werewolf form.

Maverick howled out in pain as the druid with the forehead runes flexed his fingers, controlling a vine that wrapped itself around his wolf neck. His body shuddered as if losing oxygen, morphing back into his human form.

Her chest throbbed at the heightened thrum of her heart. If he died, she'd lose every chance of getting out of here alive. Of seeing her son again. She had no choice but to do something.

Screw it. She had to try to use her magic even if it threatened to expose what she was—a pixie who could still produce pixie dust.

"Enough!" Gareth commanded before she could make a move, his voice dripping with malice as he approached Maverick's wolf form. "You're not going anywhere."

Gareth nodded to the forehead-rune druid, who drew another pattern in the air. Maverick snarled as a table leg snapped off and warped itself into handcuffs and bound his wrists together.

Maverick's gaze met hers as he struggled against the rope tightening around his neck. She could've sworn she saw his mouth move, as if he was trying to tell her to run, but they both knew she couldn't do that.

Taking a deep breath, Zera focused on the dwindling pixie dust hidden within her, drawing up every last bit of it. She prayed it would be enough to help them escape this nightmare. She only had to distract everyone long enough for them to make a run for the exit. No pressure or anything.

She flexed her fingers, allowing the energy to surge up her spine and fill her with power. The energy pulsed down to her fingers, and she willed it to obey. As the rope around Maverick's neck tightened and his face reddened, power emanated from her hands. She aimed the magic toward the wooden handcuffs. With a bang, the wood splintered into a dozen pieces, freeing Maverick's wrists.

"Take that, you twisted piece of lumber," she muttered under her breath, leaping out from the privacy of the tablecloth. Zera's body trembled with a mix of fear and determination as she faced Gareth and his gang of fae.

She summoned all the pixie dust she could muster. The purple magic swirled around her, and she willed a shimmering illusion to life. The chaos in the restaurant blurred and shifted as the air around Maverick filled with tendrils of purple light.

The forehead-rune druid's control of the vine around Maverick's neck fell slack, since the druid was momentarily disoriented by the unexpected distraction. The other guards pivoted to attack her, but their motions slowed as if everyone had been put on pause. Even Gareth froze, except for his eyes that were locked on her like a hawk's. Shit. She guessed her secret was out. But she'd never see him again, right?

Not if she didn't escape. Luckily, her illusion hadn't affected Maverick, her only ticket out of there.

His eyes widened with a mix of shock and something else. Was that... anger? Directed at her? The glare in his eye removed all doubt that he was pissed. But she'd just saved his life. How could he be angry at her?

The pressure released from his throat with a gasp of air, he wasted zero time in taking advantage of her diversion.

Her heart raced with the realization that her magic might've bought them enough time to escape.

"Run," he barked, using the confusion to his advantage and sending a kick to the druid's shin with a nauseating crack.

Yet her feet wouldn't budge, and she couldn't look away from Maverick's skilled movements. He yanked the vine away from his neck, using it to wrap around the neck of one of Gareth's dazed guards, pulling until the guard's neck snapped. He tossed the limp body to the ground, never breaking his stride toward her.

She sucked in a breath. His movements were fluid and precise, as if killing was in his nature. She didn't know if she was more afraid or excited by his display of lethal power.

In an instant, he was at her side. He grabbed her hand, pulling her along as they weaved through the crowd moving in slow motion, dodging spells and bullets because her power couldn't slow down everything. It was only a matter of minutes or seconds before the illusion wore off Gareth and his men.

"You forgot to mention you were a pixie. With pixie dust," he growled over the cacophony, his grip on her hand tightening.

"And you forgot to mention you were a Lunar wolf who hunts my kind." She raised her chin, refusing to take his anger personally. She was the one in danger here, not him.

Besides, he hadn't divulged what kind of fae he was until she'd prodded him. She shouldn't feel obligated to tell him what species of fae she was. It wasn't his business.

A snarl rumbled from his chest. "I don't belong to a pack, and I definitely don't participate in the illegal hunting of your kind."

A wolf without a pack? Was that even a thing? He didn't give her a chance to ask the endless questions that were swarming her mind as he pulled her toward the staircase leading down to the exit.

He huffed. "What kind of pixie magic was that back there, and why didn't you run when I told you to?"

"It's an illusion. But it won't last long," she called back, her lungs straining to keep the pace as they ran. "And I kind of saved your life back there, so you're welcome."

Maverick glanced back at her with a look she couldn't quite read.

Either respect, hatred, impatience, or a mix of all three. She couldn't tell.

It didn't matter. Her only thought was of Cole and getting out of there alive.

Zera's thighs protested as they wove around overturned tables and shattered dishes at a deathly pace. She had to make it to her car. Then she could get out of there and put Maverick and all this spy business behind her.

They reached the top of the stairs as a blast of dark magic sent the chandelier shattering. Glass rained down, and they slowed to keep from slipping down the steps. Her illusion was wearing off. They needed more time. Maybe she had enough to try again.

"Wait." She stopped and focused on what little pixie dust remained within her, willing it to disorient in one final desperate move. It was all they needed.

She turned on the angry and dazed fae zeroing in on her and spread her arms out toward them as power erupted from her palms. A blinding flash of light engulfed the entire room, temporarily slowing everyone in its wake. It was the most power she'd ever used at once, and her strength slipped.

The air cracked with energy, and a wave of power rippled through the room. Maverick shielded his eyes with one hand, gripping Zera's hand tightly with the other.

"Zera?" a worried voice beside her asked, muffled but clearly Maverick's.

But she couldn't respond. Her body was numb as the magic dwindled from her. She was left with nothing. A paralyzing sensation of emptiness. And her throat burned, her legs ached, and something inside her spine twisted into a painful knot.

She'd put her magic under too much stress, and now, it was punishing her for it.

"We need to leave." Maverick's strong arms wrapped underneath hers to support her weight, seizing the opportunity her illusion provided, and yanked her down the steps along with him.

She moved her legs as fast as she could, using his support to propel her. They barged out of the restaurant and into the night. Everything became a blur, and all she wanted to do was collapse, but she couldn't give up. Not yet.

The night air whipped Zera's hair across her face as they raced for the parking garage, not stopping until they were certain they hadn't been followed.

Her breaths came in harsh gasps, her heart thumping in her ears, drowned out only by the sound of their feet hitting the pavement as they ran for their lives.

Finally, they reached the parking garage and slowed to a walk. Zera stumbled to a halt in front of her car, the distant sirens of the police as they approached barely audible over her labored breathing.

Relief and adrenaline coursed through her, leaving her heart pounding and her body trembling with the remnants of fear.

"Zera," Maverick panted, still holding her waist to support her.

She met his gaze, and his eyes searched hers, as if looking for any sign of injury or distress. As if he cared. "Are you all right?"

A laugh escaped her throat. "I'm alive, at least."

He blinked, probably not expecting her reaction, and to be honest, neither was she. She didn't know how she felt. Her muscles were tense, and her heart still beat rapidly in her chest, the thumping against her rib cage almost painful.

Maverick frowned. "Your profile said you were a pixie. How did you perform that magic?"

Zera shrugged. "I'm a very lucky pixie."

He looked at her as if he'd never seen anything like her before. He probably hadn't, since most pixies nowadays didn't have magic, and those who did would never wield it.

Especially not in front of an audience of dozens of really bad fae. Powerful fae who had nearly killed them. Her throat suddenly went dry, and that had nothing to do with the fact that she'd just performed more cardio than she'd done in forever.

Her face must've shown her panic because he reached out,

placing a gentle hand on her shoulder. "Hey, it's over now. We made it out alive," he reassured her, his voice surprisingly comforting.

Zera took a shaky breath and nodded, her body slowly relaxing.

"And I promise I won't tell a soul," he said huskily.

Their eyes locked, and she knew he would keep his promise. For a moment, she thought she saw a flare of protectiveness in his eyes, and a warmth spread through her. She'd never trusted her secret with anyone else before. Not even with her ex.

The adrenaline still surged through her veins and made her feel alive like never before. Before she could process what she was doing, she grabbed Maverick's face and pulled him to her, their lips crashing together in a passionate kiss fueled by the chaos of the night.

He hesitated for a fraction of a second before reciprocating. His strong arms pulled her closer and wrapped her in his scent, an intoxicating blend of citrus and caramel with a hint of oak like a good old-fashioned.

Their mouths moved in sync, an urgent dance of fire and need. It was as if the danger had unlocked something within them both, a connection that neither could deny.

She relished the feeling of his warmth, forgetting he was a faeboy spy, that this wasn't even a real date, and even all thoughts of being a single mother or the danger they'd escaped from. Everything melted away as their bodies molded together.

Zera's fingers tangled in Maverick's hair, pulling him closer as she surrendered. His hard body guided her to the side of her car and pressed her against it, the cool metal contrasting with the fire that blazed between them.

His hand roamed over her body, exploring every curve and dip, as if he couldn't get enough of her. With each caress, Zera felt herself unraveling, losing herself to his touch.

She broke off the kiss as suddenly as it began, her chest heaving as reality came crashing down on her. She couldn't lose control.

Especially not to this stranger, no matter how irresistible he seemed at that moment.

With a mixture of anger and frustration, she slapped Maverick across the face. His head snapped to the side, surprise etched on his features.

"You lied to me!" she hissed, tears threatening to spill down her cheeks, but she swore she wouldn't cry a drop for this man. "And you put my life on the line. For what? Because you needed a cover?"

Maverick shook his head. "Zera, I—"

"No, you don't get to talk," she choked out, moving out from his massive frame. "You invited me here under false pretenses and nearly got me killed. You're a lying piece of werewolf shit, and I won't put myself around someone like you. Not when I have a son to think about."

The color drained from his face. "You're a mother?"

"Yes. A damned good one, and we don't need a man to come save us." She lifted her chin, totally realizing she'd kept things from him, too, but her secrets wouldn't have put him in this kind of danger.

"I never want to see you again." She yanked the car door open and slid into the driver's seat, ready to get the fae out of there and finally grab some real food.

She slid into the driver's seat, and the engine roared to life as she shifted gears and sped away, leaving Maverick standing alone in the dimly lit parking garage.

CHAPTER 3
ZERA

Zera's heart raced as she drove, her mind still swirling with thoughts of the man who'd swept her off her feet and into his... Wait, scratch that. He wasn't the kind of man she should be thinking twice about. He was a werewolf. A Lunar Brotherhood werewolf, no less, and a spy. A double-crossing, lying werewolf. Even if he swore he was different.

She knew she should be grateful for making it out of there alive, but the emotional turmoil swirling inside her left her feeling raw and vulnerable.

Her body hummed with the memory of his touch, his lips on hers, his strong arms holding her close. She shivered at the thought. That kiss had ignited a fire within her she was sure only Maverick could quench. The taste of him still lingered on her lips, his touch imprinted on her fair skin.

Why had their kiss affected her so much? Why did she let herself get lost in the intensity of his touch? Zera's grip tightened on the steering wheel as she navigated the dark, winding roads leading back to Havenwood.

The night air carried a chill that mirrored the cold emptiness inside her. Maverick had awakened something inside her, wild energy far too careless for her to handle. She had to regain control over her emotions. Not only for her sake but for her son's.

She'd promised herself the next time she let herself feel this way would be to a worthy partner. Not some reckless faeboy werewolf spy who'd deceived her.

Sure, he was attractive and mysterious and piqued her curiosity. Arrogant but charismatic, a liar who made her feel things she never thought possible. But he was still a werewolf, and for that, he couldn't be trusted.

She swore she would never fall for another wolf and cursed herself for letting things go so far. Even if he claimed he wasn't like any other, she couldn't ignore his true nature.

But that kiss… It had felt so sincere, yet his intentions were anything but. Why did she have to go and kiss him in the first place?

As Zera drove deeper into the night, trying to push away the memories of their encounter, the way he'd held her close clawed at her mind, demanding attention. She had to remind herself that it was all a dangerous ruse, a way for him to gain her trust and manipulate her.

Her faestone buzzed, and she quickly answered, welcoming the distraction.

"Hello?"

"Hey, Zera, it's Quinn," the owner of the Haven Wolf Tavern's cousin said in a panicked tone. "Listen, we've got a bit of a problem. The night-shift bartender just called in sick, and now, my cousin's behind the bar, scaring off what few customers we have."

Zera smirked as she imagined the alpha of the Haven Wolf pack behind the bar. It wasn't a pretty picture. "Who let Ryker behind the bar? That man has no idea how to mix a decent drink."

"You're telling me." She laughed. "I was wondering if you could cover the rest of the shift?"

She rubbed her forehead. The tavern had been struggling ever since the great split of the Haven Wolf Pack after it was discovered that both the alpha and his cousin, Quinn—an honorary pack member—were only half-werewolf.

Like her, Quinn was a pixie, which was one of the only reasons why Zera could stand living in this small town. That and she couldn't move back to Pixie Hollow. Not after the mess she'd left behind her.

Quinn had been an integral part of the tavern and the pack, and Zera respected the alpha for standing by her. Too bad her ex wasn't part of the half of the pack who was as open-minded as the rest of the Haven Moon Pack. They'd deserted the pack and the town to form their own alliance.

So, long story short, the tavern needed all the help it could get. Guess it was going to be another long night.

"Sure. I'm on my way. Tell your cousin to stay away from the bottles."

Zera hung up the phone with a sigh. Dealing with the usual tavern drama would be a welcome distraction from her tangled emotions.

She sent a quick message to her half sister to check on how Cole was doing, letting her know she'd be a little later than expected. Jade usually didn't go to bed until late, so Zera expected a quick response asking her how the date went.

Zera didn't want to get into it, though. Not now and definitely not about Maverick. He wasn't worth the headspace.

But his scent lingered on her, making it hard to concentrate on anything else. She inhaled deeply, a mix of citrus and his unique werewolf musk filling her senses. It was driving her crazy. But he was all wrong for her. A werewolf? Seriously?

As she finally pulled into the staff parking lot in the back of Haven Wolf Tavern, Zera shook her head to clear her thoughts. She couldn't afford to let herself be consumed by the memory of Maverick's touch or the warmth of his lips on hers. No, she had a job to do, and her son was counting on her.

"Focus, Zera," she ordered herself, climbing out of her car and buttoning up her jacket to look presentable for her shift. She took a deep breath and prepared herself for the normalcy of the tavern walls.

As she pushed open the heavy metal door, Zera was immediately greeted by the sound of laughter and clinking glasses. Patrons dotted the dimly lit space, enjoying their drinks and conversations. The familiar scent of alcohol and the comforting hum of chatter washed over Zera, grounding her in the moment.

"Thank the fae you're here." Quinn towered over her, almost as tall as Maverick, and hooked her arm through Zera's. "Ryker's completely lost it."

Zera laughed. "He really needs to calm down. And hire a PR person."

"That's what I've been saying." Quinn rolled her eyes, the gold flecks bringing out the pink in her short-cropped hair. "But you know Ryker. He's stubborn."

"It's his werewolf side."

She nodded in agreement. "Oh, I almost forgot." Quinn reached into her pocket and pulled out a small leather pouch, and Zera's eyes widened.

"Is that it?" Zera asked, hoping beyond hope that it was the seedlings from a rare flower she had yet to study. She'd read in one of her latest books borrowed from the local library that in ancient times, the native mountainous fae used it to speak to their gods.

Of course, this was all deemed legend and folklore, and the flower was so rare, with it only growing once every five hundred years on the highest peak of the Spire Alps, that no one in the modern day had ever had a chance to study it, let alone regulate it. But Zera couldn't help but be intrigued by the possibility of such a rare flower, and to her luck, this was the year it was said to bloom again.

She'd searched tirelessly for any information she could find about the everfrost blossom, hoping to catch a glimpse of it in its natural habitat. But all her efforts had been fruitless—until now.

Perhaps the pouch contained the missing precursor ingredients she needed to get the same reaction she'd studied from a single cell of her pixie dust. From the shape, size, glow, and energy she'd analyzed under her portable microscope, she had yet to find the right combination to replicate it. But now she was hopeful the everfrost blossom was that missing component.

Her eyes remained fixed on the small leather pouch sitting before her, containing what she hoped were the elusive seedlings of the blue flower. Zera couldn't believe her luck. Could this be the breakthrough she had been waiting for?

Quinn handed her the pouch with a smile. "It sure is. Ryker was able to snag some when they were out on their monthly hunt."

With trembling hands, Zera carefully opened the pouch, and inside were three small seeds, each no larger than her pinky fingernail. They shone in the dim light, a deep-blue color that almost seemed to glow.

"Thank you so much," Zera said, tears pricking at the corners of her eyes. She had been searching for these seeds for years, and now, here they were, right in front of her. Perhaps there was hope after all.

"You're welcome," Quinn replied with a grin. "Now, about the bar. We really need to get Ryker to stop making drinks."

"Agreed." She laughed, following Quinn's lead to the bar where the alpha of the Haven Moon Pack stood, staring down a customer with a glare that could freeze hell over.

"What more do you want, man?" the customer asked Ryker, who gripped the edge of the polished pine bar so tightly it seemed he might snap it in two. "I gave you my card. Just run it so I can get out of this dump."

Ryker's eyes flickered between wolf gold and demon red, his patience growing thin, and Zera was certain he was seconds away from eviscerating the poor guy.

"Okay, I'm here!" Zera wrapped a black apron with pens, a notepad, and the faecoin card receiver around her waist. "I got this."

"Finally," he muttered, pushing off the counter.

He cracked all his knuckles and shot one last deathly stare at the customer before he stormed off toward the door labeled Pack Members Only. The sigil above it shimmered as he passed under it, his matching rune tattooed on his neck pulsing in response as it granted him entrance.

"See what I mean?" Quinn folded her toned arms across her chest. "He's totally lost it."

Zera had to agree. The alpha might've been the leader of the first pack to accept those outside of their own kind, but he sure didn't have the patience for customer service. Zera took a deep breath, steadying herself for what was sure to be a chaotic evening.

"Um, hello? Can I get my card?" The customer's eyebrows raised impatiently, snapping Zera out of her thoughts.

She forced an apologetic smile and retrieved the card from the register. "Of course. Sorry about the wait."

"Let me know if anyone gives you any trouble," Quinn said before heading off through the hallway after her cousin to deal with other pack matters, ideally strategizing on how to keep this place from going out of business. Zera needed this job to pay her bills.

Zera returned her attention to the customer, who was now glaring at her. She handed him his faecard, and he grabbed it with a huff, shooting one last venomous glare in the direction Ryker and Quinn had disappeared.

As the night wore on, with a practiced smile, Zera expertly mixed drinks and served the few customers who meandered in, all while trying to push thoughts of Maverick to the back of her mind. She poured a shot of fire whiskey for a homesick dwarf who reminisced about the Fire Cliffs to anyone who would listen then whipped up a colorful Fairy Fizz for a giggling satyr who'd had so many cocktails he wouldn't notice this drink didn't have a drop of alcohol in it. The drink would levitate him ever so subtly, making it harder for him to topple over in his current state, which was an added bonus.

The tavern was busier than usual, and it should have been enough to distract her. But every time she caught a whiff of a scent that even remotely resembled Maverick's caramel and citrus aroma, her heart nearly leaped from her chest. She hated how much he affected her, especially after their infuriatingly hot kiss.

She could work for werewolves, especially ones who were half-were like her son, but she would never let herself date one. They were liars, cheaters, and worst of all, disloyal to anyone outside of their pack. Maverick had failed to tell her that he was a spy until their lives were already at risk, and though he promised to keep her pixie-dust magic a secret, what about everyone else in that restaurant who witnessed what she'd done?

"Hey, Zera, can you make me one of those?" One of their usual customers pointed at a glowing orange-and-red drink in the hands of another patron.

"Sure thing," she replied, forcing herself to focus on her work.

Though she never wanted to see Maverick again, Zera couldn't shake the memory of Maverick's piercing gray eyes or his arrogant smirk. The way he'd teased her lip when he'd kissed her back. Her chest tightened at the thought of him despite how much she hated him. He was wrong for her in every way possible, and she had to keep reminding herself of this.

Zera picked up the shaker to begin making the requested cocktail, but her attention was caught by a familiar face sitting at one of the tables at the back—the forehead-tattooed druid in the brown cloak who'd nearly killed Maverick at the restaurant. He nursed a dark, frothy ale as his ice-cold gaze flitted up at her.

A slow, sinister smile curled his lips when their gazes met. Zera's breath hitched, her grip on the cocktail shaker tightening. She knew he was here for her—that part was obvious—but how had he known where to find her?

And if he were here for her—or worse, for Cole—she would move the fae realm to protect them both. But first, she needed to get out of there.

"Hey, are you all right?" Quinn's concerned voice cut through Zera's racing thoughts.

Zera glanced up as the pixie-werewolf rounded the bar. "Um, yeah. Just not feeling well. Cover me while I make a bathroom run?"

"Sure," Quinn said, "but that'll mean no more mixed drinks. Only what's on tap."

"Yeah, fine," Zera mumbled, trying to keep her composure, but fear swept over her like a blanket of dread as the druid with runes tattooed across his forehead rose from the table.

"Are you sure you're okay?" Quinn frowned, following her gaze.

The druid with the rune-covered forehead strolled toward her with slow and deliberate steps, making it clear that he had no intention of letting her go.

"Who's that?" Quinn asked.

"No one," Zera lied, backing up into a platter of mugs, sending them crashing to the floor in a loud clatter.

The noise echoed through the bar, drawing the attention of the other patrons. Zera's breaths came in rapid, shallow gasps as her heart pounded like a thunderstorm. She had to get out of there.

"Zera," Quinn repeated, grabbing her arm. "Seriously, who is that? And why does he look like he wants to rip your head off?"

Zera swallowed hard. Quinn had no idea how right she was.

"Just a creepy guy from earlier tonight."

"Say no more." Quinn turned to face the forehead-rune druid.

Without warning, she flicked her hand toward the dangerous man, who had reached the bar. Purple light sparked from her palms, wrapping around his wrists and locking him in place.

Zera's mouth fell open. She thought she was the only pixie who still had magic, and Quinn wasn't even full pixie. How was that possible?

Quinn shot her a look of warning. "Go! Get out of here! I won't be able to hold him long."

She had no idea why Quinn would help protect her, especially since she had no reason to and didn't have a clue what this druid was capable of. But Zera didn't have time to question her luck.

"What about the customers?"

"I've got it. I'm the alpha's cousin, remember? Now go!"

With a grateful nod, Zera bolted toward the tavern's back exit, her heart pounding in her ears. She could feel the druid's gaze burn into her as she slipped through the door, praying that Quinn could hold him off long enough for her to get away.

Outside, the cool night air offered temporary relief from the chaos inside. Thank the fae gods Quinn had been there to help, though Zera hoped Quinn wasn't harmed because of it.

The distant crashing of more glass signaled that Quinn was doing her best to keep the druid occupied, but Zera knew it wouldn't last forever.

A cold sweat broke out on Zera's forehead as she sprinted through the dark parking lot, her pulse pounding like a drum.

"Come on, come on," she muttered, fumbling with her keys while keeping an eye on the back door of the tavern.

Her hands shook as she tried to steady herself and focus on making it to her car. She should've parked closer.

A metal crash echoed as the back door slammed open, followed by the crunch of boots on the gravel parking lot. Zera's gaze jerked back to the tavern, and her heart felt like it was stuck in her throat as the druid stepped out into the night, his creepy smile still plastered on his rune-covered face.

"Running won't save you, little pixie," he called after her, drawing shapes in the air. His fingers traced intricate patterns, and within moments, a ball of fire formed in the palm of his hand.

Zera cursed, panic setting in as she tried to reach for her inner pixie-dust magic. But she was still drained from casting her illusion at the restaurant earlier, and nothing happened.

In desperation, she threw herself behind the nearby dumpster as the druid hurled the fireball toward her. The flames licked the edge of the dumpster, scorching the metal but missing her by mere inches.

"Is that all you've got?" she shouted back, hoping to buy herself some time.

As the druid prepared another attack, Zera scrambled to her feet and made a break for her car, parked a short distance away. She somehow got it unlocked and dove inside as another fireball whizzed past her, singing her bare shoulder. She'd left her coat in the tavern, but there was no way she was going back inside to get it.

Why was this rune-covered druid after her? And how did he know she would be here?

Another red-hot fireball slammed into her car so hard the glass cracked but didn't shatter. Not yet. If she didn't move, this druid would kill her, and she wasn't about to let that happen. The only thing she could think of was getting home to Cole. Alive.

She started the engine, slammed her foot on the accelerator, and peeled out onto the open road.

Her eyes flitted to her rearview mirror, at the druid somehow keeping up with her. The spiral flames hovered above the druid's palms, a stark contrast to the dark night that surrounded them. Was he *flying*?

Her knuckles turned white as she gripped the steering wheel tighter. She would never be able to outrun this fae. She needed help —and there was only one person she could think of who might be able to save her.

"Bloody arrogant werewolf," she hissed, cursing herself for even considering calling Maverick.

He was the last person she wanted to rely on. She never wanted to speak to that lying wolf again. But what could she do?

Her mind raced as she tried to think of a plan, one that didn't involve working with the enemy.

She weaved through the empty streets of Havenwood while monitoring the rearview mirror. The druid was relentless in his pursuit, and it was clear his power was limitless. He could probably do this all night, but even now the heavy weight of sleep threatened to drag Zera down.

It was late, and her eyelids grew heavy, her focus wavering as exhaustion seeped into her bones. She couldn't afford to lose control now, not with the druid still on her tail. But she knew she couldn't keep driving like this.

She glanced down at her faestone tucked in a cup holder. Deep down, she knew it was the only solution, and if it meant getting back home safe and sound to see her son again, she would do it.

Metal screeched as the druid's magic collided with the rear end of Zera's vehicle. The force of the impact jolted Zera forward in her seat, and she struggled to maintain control of her car. The trunk erupted into flames, but her car remained drivable.

"Damn it!" Her heart raced as adrenaline coursed through her veins.

That was it. She had to call Maverick. It was the only option, but would he even help her after she'd left him the way she had? She shook her head, trying to clear away the lingering doubt and uncertainty. She'd saved his life, right? As far as she was concerned, he owed her. He was her last hope, even if he was a cocky, lying son of a werewolf.

She snatched her faestone out of the cup holder and navigated through the FaeMatch app to find his number. Her heart thumped wildly, as if trying to break free, drowning out the sound of screeching tires and the howl of the wind outside her car.

The screen blurred before her eyes, but she found his number and hit Dial, praying that he would answer.

"Maverick," she said as soon as he picked up, not giving him a chance to say hello. "It's Zera."

"Oh, I know." Maverick's voice was bored, and was that a hint of... annoyance?

Zera's grip on the faestone tightened, frustration and desperation intertwining within her.

"I need your help."

"I thought you never wanted to see me again?" he teased, his voice dripping with sarcasm. "And that I'm a... how did you put it? 'A lying piece of werewolf shit'?"

Zera gritted her teeth. She didn't have time to deal with Maverick's games or his wounded pride.

"Look, Maverick," she snapped, her voice laced with urgency. "I don't have time for this. Right now, I need you—"

"I guess I am rather irresistible," Maverick's deep voice interrupted her, sending a shiver of desire down her spine. She shoved her feelings down and replaced them with rage.

"Listen to me!" Zera hissed into her faestone, her heart pounding in her chest. "I'm not calling you because I want to see your smug face again. You owe me for saving your life, and right now, I need your help."

Maverick sighed. "Fine. What's going on?"

"That druid who tried to kill you is after me," she explained, her voice shaking with fear. "He followed me to Havenwood and nearly set me on fire at the bar. He's still chasing me, and I don't know how to lose him."

"Whoa, whoa, calm down," Maverick said, his tone shifting from playful to serious and focused. "Tell me what happened."

"Does it matter? He's chasing me right now, and he's trying to kill me!" Zera shouted, frustration evident in her voice. "I've shared my location with you. Now, help me."

"All right, listen carefully." Maverick's tone took on a commanding tone. "First, we need to make sure he can't track your car. Take a sharp turn and drive in the opposite direction from where you were heading."

Zera obeyed, her tires squealing as she whipped around a corner. She glanced in her rearview mirror, but the druid was still hot on her trail.

"Okay, now what?" she demanded.

"Take the next left, and then get off the main road," Maverick instructed.

"Got it." She took the turn so quickly, she was sure the druid hadn't seen her.

"Drive for two miles until you reach a bridge. Cross it. There's an abandoned cabin out there on the right side. Park behind it, and kill the engine."

"And then what?" she cried, the blood draining from her face. "Wait for the druid to slit my throat and eat it for dinner?"

"Just trust me. I know what I'm doing," Maverick reassured her, his voice laced with a confidence she didn't feel. "I'll be there as soon as I can."

As she imagined him rushing to her aid, a swarm of anxious butterflies fluttered in her stomach. She took a deep breath and forced herself to push away those feelings.

"You're almost there, Zera," Maverick murmured into the phone. "You're doing great."

She crossed the bridge, and her eyes darted around, searching for this abandoned cabin that felt like a really bad idea. She'd be a sitting duck out there with no one to hear her scream.

"I think I lost him." She checked the mirror again. The pitch black that surrounded her was a surprising comfort.

"Good. Stay on the course for now until I get there."

She checked the time on the dashboard. Cole would be up in a few hours, and she had to be there. To make sure he was okay. Her chest tightened at the thought of her son being home unprotected, her maternal instincts kicking into high gear. Jade might be home, but it wasn't the same. Zera couldn't be out all night. She needed to be with Cole.

She let out a frustrated sigh. "I need to get home. I have to be there for my son."

"I know, Zera. I promise we'll get you home, but for now, I need you to get to the cabin."

"And do what? Wait for the druid to catch up with me and set me on fire or conjure up another ivy to wrap around my neck this time?"

"Trust me, it's not safe to go home right now. Just follow my directions to the cabin, and we'll figure this out together," Maverick urged, concern lacing his words.

Zera gritted her teeth, anger flaring up inside her. "I don't have to take orders from you, Maverick. You got me into this mess, and I'll decide how I'm getting out of it."

"Please, listen to me," Maverick pleaded, his usual arrogance momentarily absent.

"Sorry, but Cole is my first and only priority right now, and I can handle myself." With that, Zera hung up the call, her resolve hardening.

Bloody arrogant wolf. She'd gotten herself out of plenty of dangerous situations before without Maverick's help. Granted, they were less life-or-death and more dealing with unruly customers at the tavern, but still. She could handle herself. Besides, the goal was to lose the druid, and he'd helped with that, hadn't he? She was safe now, and it was time to get home.

Despite the reassurance that the druid was no longer following her, a wave of nervous energy still washed through her veins as a sudden thought occurred to her. If the druid was able to find her here, how many others from Maverick's world could get to her?

Damn it, Maverick, she thought, gripping the steering wheel. Why did you have to involve me in all of this?

She glanced in the rearview mirror, paranoia creeping in. As she drove back into town and pulled onto her street, every passing car seemed like a potential threat, every pedestrian a potential enemy.

Zera's heart raced, the weight of her responsibility as a mother pressing down on her. She needed to protect Cole from the druid and from anyone else involved in Maverick's undercover work. She cursed him for not only bringing danger to her doorstep but for also making her question everything she thought she knew. That after one night, one unfortunate fake date, this damned werewolf spy had turned her world upside down with his lies, his arrogance, and those infuriatingly captivating eyes.

But now was not the time to dwell on Maverick. Zera needed to focus on getting home and ensuring that her son was safe. She would deal with the fallout from tonight's disaster at the tavern later

—after she'd put some distance between herself and the chaos that seemed to follow Maverick wherever he went.

As Zera pulled onto her street, Zera's heart lodged in her throat. The familiar sight of her modest home lay ahead, but instead of the comforting glow of the porch light, everything was dark. A shiver ran down her spine. They never left that light off. Jade would never turn that off. Something was wrong.

"Stay focused, Zera," she whispered, steeling herself for whatever might be waiting for her at home. "You can handle this."

With a determined nod, Zera parked the car and raced for the front door. If anyone was inside—if the druid had somehow found her home and was there to hurt her baby—she was prepared to fight with all her might.

Her adrenaline pumping, she reached for her keys to the front door but stopped in her tracks. It had been left ajar. That was when fear dug its claws into her chest and squeezed. Someone was in her house.

Panic seized her, and she stormed inside, welcomed by the messy living room.

"Hello?" she called out, her voice a hoarse whisper. "Jade? Sloane? Is anyone here?"

No answer. Zera held her breath and crept down the hallway toward the makeshift nursery. She grabbed a lamp from a nearby end table and inched her way to the kitchen that led to the dining-room-turned-nursery where her son slept.

Movement in the darkness made her stop dead in her tracks. She wielded her lamp as a weapon. Whoever it was in her house did not know the force they were about to reckon with.

"Got it!" a voice from somewhere outside shouted.

Just as she was about to strike, all the lights flickered on, and she stood face-to-face with Sloane, her eyes wide and a bat raised above her head.

"Oh, thank the bloody fae it's you." Zera let out a deep sigh, relief flooding her bloodstream. "The front door was left open. I thought you were an intruder."

"Well, I thought you were one too! I didn't think you'd be home tonight," Sloane said, lowering her bat. "And of course it's me. Who else would be here?"

"You've no idea." Zera sighed with relief.

Sloane frowned. "Weren't you on a date?"

"I—" Zera began but was quickly cut off by Jade's voice from the front porch.

"It was only a tripped breaker and—uh... What's going on here?"

Zera whirled around to meet Jade's curious stare, her brows furrowing as she glanced between the bat in her wife's grip and the lamp in Zera's.

"Nothing. Just a misunderstanding." Zera waved it off, setting the lamp down. "How's Cole doing?"

"Still sleeping soundly, last I checked." Jade shrugged. "The power went out and set off the alarm. Luckily, the little one's sound machine drowned it out."

"Good." Zera ran a hand over her hair, undoing the bun at the nape of her neck that was starting to unravel.

Her faestone buzzed, but she didn't bother picking it up. She already knew who it was. But she didn't want to talk to Maverick, and what would be the point? He'd helped her lose the druid, and that was all she'd needed. Now she was going to forget about him, and things could return to normal.

"Anything we should be worried about?" Jade asked, glancing at the phone as it rang again.

"Nope. A wrong number," she lied, not wanting to get into the fact that her date was a liar who'd put her in danger just by having dinner with her, and, oh yeah, she'd nearly gotten killed by a flame-throwing druid. "I think I'll check on Cole before calling it a night. Good night."

She gave them both a reassuring smile as she passed them on her way to the kitchen.

"Are you sure you're okay?" Jade asked.

"Yeah, I'll be fine," Zera called over her shoulder. "I'll see you all in the morning."

It'd been the longest night of her life, and she was hoping to put all of this fear behind her. The sight of the front door ajar, the thought of someone breaking in here, it was all too much.

She had to keep reminding herself that it was all a false alarm. The breaker had a glitch. No one who shouldn't be in the house was here.

With a wave of her hand, she activated the monitor that hovered over the kitchen counter next to the door they'd installed to close off the nursery-slash-dining room. Cole's crib flickered on the screen, and his little form was bundled in a sleep sack. Zera smiled, her heart melting at the sight of him sleeping safe and sound.

She reached to turn off the monitor but stopped. A dark form reflected off the kettle on the counter next to her. From his sheer size, she knew it wasn't Jade or Sloane. She knew, from the sound of the TV in the living room, they were both on the couch, watching their favorite reality dating show.

A second later, thunder cracked, and all the lights went out. Again. Lightning flashed, casting an eerie glow that illuminated a man with a rune-covered forehead. Recognition washed over her like a tidal wave. The druid had found her, and she was dead meat.

CHAPTER 4
MAVERICK

THE CLICK OF THE FAESTONE BEING HUNG UP ECHOED IN MAVERICK'S EARS, A defiant punctuation to Zera's last words that still resonated through the tiny bare-bones loft he owned on the outskirts of Mystic City. It wasn't much, but it was quiet, and the neighbors didn't ask questions when he came in at all hours of the night, covered in dirt and blood. The perfect place for a spy.

"I can handle myself," she'd said with a mix of determination and exasperation. He stood motionless for a moment, the cool blue light from the city's neon skyline filtering through his windows and casting a spectral glow on his chiseled features.

"Handle yourself? You're about to walk straight into a trap," Maverick muttered to the empty room, his voice laced with irritation and something that resembled panic. He couldn't believe he was about to go save a pixie, let alone get himself so worked up about one. What was it about Zera that stirred this primal reaction within him?

From his past, he knew pixies were nothing but tricksters and deceivers and not to be trusted. Hell, after being captured, stripped of his fertility—though, luckily, not his ability to perform, just reproduce—and tortured by a gossamer of pixie warriors when he was only a wereling, he loathed the entire species.

Not because he couldn't reproduce. No, the pixies had probably done him a favor in that department. But the fact that they'd attacked a near child. He'd been too young to go through that. It'd messed with his head and changed him in ways he still didn't understand. Their glares of various shades of purples and pinks still haunted his dreams. And it was all because of his inexplicable attraction to a certain pixie. The one who'd deceived him to begin with.

Perhaps, deep down, it was why he never wanted to become alpha and refused the alpha blood that still simmered within his veins. He hated his own kind for using his loyalty as a weapon and despised pixies for their deceit and violence, even though he knew it was deserving. Pixies had been hunted for decades by his very own pack, who had sold themselves to the elves. Elves thought themselves the superior species and got rich off the backs of wolf packs and pixie dust.

Yet even though he understood their hatred, it still didn't mean he wouldn't avoid pixies at all costs. Especially because even to this day, pixies held too much power over him. Zera was the proof of that.

He should loathe her for what she was, and on some level, he did. But there was something about her that seemed different, and it wasn't because she had pixie dust. It was partly the fact that, at the restaurant, she'd stood by him and saved his life. Even though she knew he was a werewolf, her worst enemy. Even though she'd made it clear she loathed his species with a passion, perhaps as deeply rooted as his for pixies.

And then there was that kiss. An obvious mistake on both their parts, all thanks to the adrenaline high, but it was...

Maverick growled. He couldn't think about that right now. Hatred for pixies or not, his inbred duty to protect innocent lives kept him from ignoring Zera's plea for help. Bottom line, he had to save her, and that was that.

His keen eyes flicked to the array of weapons and gadgets scattered across his workspace—his dining room table that doubled as his work desk, thanks to the unpredictable hours of his spy work. He never knew when the next mission would come, so he liked to always be ready.

He grabbed his harness, which bristled with hidden compartments, and stuffed it with an assortment of high-tech tools. A pulse shackler, his favorite knife, and a compact shock grenade joined the growing arsenal within, preparing him for anything, unlike the total fiasco at the restaurant.

Gareth never should've figured out his true identity. How could this have happened? Not even Mystic Dynamic Solutions—the company acting as a front for a competing arms-dealing gang that had hired him to collect intel on Gareth—had that information. The only ones who knew his real name were himself, his old partner, Zera, and the faen government.

There was no way Gareth could've found out his true identity, unless he was more connected than Maverick gave him credit for.

A frustrated growl rumbled deep within his chest. He didn't have time to obsess over Gareth right now. Zera was in trouble, and he had to act fast if he was going to catch her in time.

He still couldn't believe Zera hadn't followed his instructions. The plan was foolproof, if only she'd gotten to the cabin. Now, the druid was probably already at her house.

He ripped off his button-down shirt, quickly shucking his shoes and socks as he prepared to shift from man to werewolf. It was the only way he'd make it in time.

"Zera, you stubborn pixie," he grumbled, snatching up the leather harness.

As he strapped it onto his muscular torso, the frustration seemed to seep into his veins, fueling an almost electric surge of adrenaline. With swift precision, he checked his gear, all while his mind raced with a hundred scenarios for what he might find when he got to her.

In the midst of his preparations, Maverick's senses shifted, heightened by the urgency of the situation. The transformation was as involuntary as it was necessary. His body knew what needed to be done, even if his heart rebelled against the idea of Zera or her child in danger because of him. Bones cracked and reformed, muscles bulged and expanded, black fur sprouted along his arms and down his spine. Within moments, the man was gone, replaced by the imposing figure of a werewolf—piercing eyes now glowing with a primal intensity.

He could hear the distant thrum of the city's heartbeat, each car and engine and late-night partier calling out to him in a cacophony of sound.

The scent of rain on concrete filled his nostrils, mingling with the faint trace of Zera's unique fragrance—a sugary blend of lilac and determination—that he had committed to memory from the moment she first sat down at the restaurant.

He had never met a woman like her—strong yet gentle, fiery yet soft, and with a stubbornness that could rival his own. The way she'd declared she was only there for the food sent his lip curling in a smile. But then he remembered how she'd accused him of being a faeboy, as if he'd use FaeMatch just for a hookup. Though, to be fair, how was she supposed to know he was actually a spy and his partner had abandoned him?

Maverick shook his head, attempting to concentrate on the current task. Whether Zera realized it or not, she needed him now more than ever, since she went and decided to take matters into her own hands.

"What was she thinking?" The growled thought came unbidden, a reminder of his lone-wolf tendencies clashing with the protective instincts that Zera seemed to evoke in him.

Maverick took a deep breath, allowing the scents of the city to guide him, his ears perking up at the slightest disturbance.

"Time to track a pixie," he snarled, the sound more guttural than human. And with one last glance at the urban jumble he called home, Maverick leapt from the balcony, his powerful legs propelling him forward into the night.

He would find Zera and her family, no matter what dangers lay ahead. Because despite his chaotic nature and his self-imposed solitude, there was nothing that could stop him—not when it came to her. He was ready to do whatever it took to make sure Zera and her son were safe. These feelings weren't something he'd expected or wanted, but there they were.

Not that he'd ever admit to them. As a spy, he couldn't afford to share his life with anyone. He'd learned that the hard way.

Maverick's senses were on fire, every nerve ending tingling with the urgency of the situation. The storm clouds above mirrored his own worry. Rain began to lash down, slicking the streets with a sheen that reflected the chaotic energy pulsing through his veins.

"Zera," he whispered into the night, her name a talisman against the darkness swelling around him. With each step, his sense of smell grew sharper, her scent drawing him closer.

Even if she hadn't shared her location with him, he could find her. That was how strong he was. It was why he'd been next in line as alpha, but to his father's disapproval, he couldn't accept. He loathed the blind loyalty and the old ways of the Lunar Brotherhood, and in the end, he'd rejected them as harshly as they'd rejected him. He was better off without them. On his own as a spy for hire.

But now that his identity was out there, his future was at risk. Not just his but Zera's too. He would fix this.

Like a shadow among shadows, Maverick moved with an agility that belied his size, his werewolf form blending seamlessly into the night. His ears twitched at the faintest sounds ahead—a muffled whimper, a baby's cry, the rustle of movement, the sinister murmur of voices.

They were close, and it sounded like the baby was present, which meant using the shock grenade was out of the question. He'd have to use his more covert weapons.

"Damn it." The curse was a low, frustrated growl, barely audible over the pounding rain. Just like he'd predicted, she had walked right into the druid's trap, and it was up to him to spring her loose.

The small home loomed ahead, its windows darkened, its aura one of foreboding rather than sanctuary. Maverick could hear them inside—the druid and a posse of Gareth's fae guards—and his heart raced, not with fear but with the primal urge to fight, to protect.

Easy there, he coached himself, pressing against the wet wall beside the front window. Stealth over strength.

He knew better than anyone that brawn wasn't always the answer. It was about being smart, being one step ahead. And right now, as the sound of Zera's soft attempts at comforting her frightened baby reached his ears, Maverick's resolve hardened like steel.

"Mommy's here." Zera's voice was laced with both love and panic. "It's going to be okay."

Maverick's chest tightened in response, his wolfish heart feeling an unexpected twinge at the vulnerability in her tone.

Let's make it okay, then.

With a silent prayer to whatever faen goddesses watched over wayward werewolves and stubborn pixies, Maverick slipped through the unlocked door, a testament to the druid's arrogance that he hadn't considered someone—or something—like Maverick.

The first fae guard with demon features didn't even see him coming. A swift, precise takedown, and the demon slumped, unconscious before he hit the living room floor.

A cry from the kitchen jerked Maverick's attention to the hallway. A growl ripped through his chest when the sweet scent of pixie blood flooded his senses. They were torturing innocents.

Maverick's muscles coiled as he launched himself forward with a burst of raw power. His paws padded silently against the linoleum floor, leaving behind faint traces of moisture from the demon's blood dripping from his claws.

He slid to a stop when he reached the kitchen as the druid snatched a little baby from Zera's hands.

"No!" she screamed, reaching for her baby, who had a head of chestnut-brown waves, but it was no use. Her wrists were zip-tied together so tightly to cause circulation issues.

His eyes remained on the child in the murderous druid's grasp, and his rage strangled all thoughts of stealth. All he saw was death.

"Give him back, you bastard!" Zera's voice was raw with terror and fury as she strained against her bindings, her pixie magic flickering in and out from distress.

The druid's cold laughter echoed through the kitchen, a chilling contrast to the baby's wails. "Ah, but this little one is our new leverage. My boss sent me to find you, the pixie with pixie dust, but to come back with you *and* the child? They'll make billions, and it'll be all thanks to me," he crooned, eyes gleaming with malice.

Maverick counted a dozen other thugs in the darkened room, their weapons in holsters and their faen abilities relaxed or otherwise masked. They weren't expecting anyone to barge in, much less a werewolf of his skill.

Two other women, both tied up beside Zera, exchanged a glance that spoke volumes of fear and resolve. It was obvious they were family. They wouldn't give up without a fight.

Maverick's pulse thundered in his ears, his instincts screaming for blood. He wouldn't let the druid hurt the little boy. Not if he had anything to say about it.

"Please," Zera cried, "take me, but leave my baby out of this!"

Ignoring her please, the druid turned his head, sniffing the air, sensing something amiss. "It appears we have an unwelcome guest," he mused, tightening his grip on the child.

With no time to lose, Maverick sprang into action, teeth bared and claws extended, leaping onto the nearest fae thug. The guard went down with a gurgled scream, fear emanating from him like a pungent perfume.

"Get him!" the druid ordered, but his companions were already scattering, tripping over themselves to flee from the feral beast that tore through their ranks.

Maverick's movements were a blur of black fur and fury, each connective strike fueled by the desperate cries of Zera and the little boy's whimpering sobs. The room reeked of sweat, fear, and the coppery tang of spilled blood.

The thunder outside muffled their screams as, one by one, he devoured them or chased them out of the house and into the storm, leaving a path of destruction in his wake. Their various faen abilities were met with his own primal strength, and in that moment, he felt invincible.

"Stop him!" the druid roared, his hold on Cole unyielding. Zera screamed again, straining to get out of her restraints to save her son.

The druid waved his hand in an intricate pattern around the baby and magicked a crib of vines that enveloped the little one, sending the crib hovering high above the chase before turning on the werewolf.

Maverick bared his teeth in response, his wolf form making him even more menacing. Now that the baby was out of the way, he didn't give the druid a chance and launched himself into the air.

He dove for the druid's neck, his teeth and claws stretched out, ready to rip and tear.

The druid, sensing the danger, cast a protective shield around himself and the vine crib. Maverick slammed into the shield and rolled onto the floor with a snarl. He picked himself up, crouching to try again when the shield evaporated.

The demons who'd remained circled from behind the druid, flinging fireballs at him, but Maverick was too fast and dodged them all. Spells of imprisonment flung toward Maverick from every direction, trying to contain him, but they bounced off him as if they were merely the wind.

What made an alpha wasn't his ability to overthrow the previous leader of the pack, but his blood. Yes, alphas could rule without being part of the bloodline of alphas but not in the Lunar Brotherhood. It was what set him apart, but it was also what made him want to rid himself of all things that reminded him of the pack life. He would never live that life again.

"Stand strong!" the druid cried as more demons deserted him in a puff of black smoke. "His defenses are weakening!"

Maverick chuffed. That was what the druid thought. He could do this all night. A vampire zipped across the room to the back door, but Maverick plunged his claws into his back before he could escape.

"Traitors!" the druid bellowed, his hands flinging out more spells—each one missing Maverick by an inch.

Maverick dispatched the last of the minions with a swift, crunching blow to the throat, leaving only the druid standing in the blood-splattered kitchen. His piercing eyes locked on his foe, prepared for the final confrontation.

The baby wailed from his prison crib, the druid standing between them.

"Shh, shh, Cole, baby, Mommy's here," Zera cooed, her voice breaking as tears streamed down her cheeks. She still struggled with everything she had to free herself. A maternal persistence that triggered his own primal nature to protect.

Maverick smacked his lips and squared his shoulders, facing the druid head-on. The druid grabbed Zera and yanked her in front of himself as a shield.

"Any step closer, and I'll use this dagger." The glint of a blade pressed against Zera's throat brought Maverick to a halt.

Get your slimy druid hands off her, Maverick's wolf snarled.

But the druid couldn't hear his thoughts, only the menacing tone of his growl. The druid's gaze hardened on him, daring him to make a move.

Zera's panicked eyes locked on his werewolf form. Fear washed over her, and he didn't think she recognized him. This would take a human touch if he was going to save her.

He exhaled, his werewolf letting out one last growl before melting into his human form, the black fur that blanketed his body retreating until he was towering over the druid. He was strong, but Maverick was stronger.

"Zera… It's okay. I've got you," he said, his voice a guttural promise of protection.

Shock flickered across her face for a second until recognition struck her. "Save Cole," she whispered, and he could sense that she handed over every bit of her trust to him in that moment.

He gave her a firm nod, focusing on the druid.

"You think you can save her? Or the child? It's all over now." The druid sneered, lowering the blade a fraction in response. He was trying to save face, posturing as if he still had some control over the situation.

Maverick didn't give him any more time to gloat, though. Instead, he grabbed his pulse shackler from the harness strapped to his chest and pulled the trigger, aiming for the narrow bit of forehead exposed from behind Zera. The weapon was powerful but could be used only once, so he couldn't miss.

The women screamed as blue-white light surged from the gun and hit its target with precision. The druid stumbled back, pushing Zera forward and into Maverick's arms.

Another cry wailed, and the crib fell toward the floor as the druid's magic vanished. Maverick's heart quickened with fear, but he didn't let that deter him. Maverick reached out and grabbed the falling crib inches from the floor. The baby inside was crying, its face red and teary-eyed. After setting the crib down, he ripped off the zip ties around Zera's wrists before she stumbled to the floor next to the crib.

"Cole!" she gasped, scooping him up.

"Are you both okay?" Maverick asked, checking both of them for any sign of external damage.

She nodded, holding her boy close and placing endless kisses on his chubby cheeks.

Relief flooded him as he watched the two reunited. The boy turned his head, his gaze landing on Maverick, and he stopped crying.

Maverick's chest constricted at the pair of innocent lavender eyes that focused on him, stirring the alpha blood within him. The instinct to nurture and protect kicked in with a force he could feel almost physically. It was an irrational part of being a werewolf that he couldn't free himself from even if he wanted to.

The muffled protests of the two other women still bound and gagged drew Maverick's attention, and he shook off the wolf instincts to focus on what he did best—cleaning up other people's messes.

"Who the fae is this guy?" One of the women, whose lavender eyes matched Zera's and who had hair cropped close to her scalp, asked once her gag was removed. Great. Another pixie.

She nodded toward the druid, whose body lay frozen on the kitchen floor. The pulse shackler kept him in an immobile state, but it wouldn't last for long.

"Someone you don't want to know," he said, moving on to the woman at her side and working until everyone was unbound and intact.

The buzzed-haircut pixie rubbed her wrists as she stood and helped the second woman up.

"Maverick, how did he know where I lived?" Zera asked.

He met her panicked gaze as she bounced the little boy on her hip. A toothless grin spread across his face when he spotted Maverick, for reasons unknown.

Maverick grimaced. "He followed you home from the restaurant. It's why I told you to wait for me at the abandoned—"

"And like I told *you*, I lost him," Zera snapped. "The druid was long gone when I started home, and it was like he was already here."

The lavender-eyed pixie with the buzzed haircut gasped. "You're the guy from Zera's FaeMatch date."

It wasn't a question.

"Is he really?" asked the second woman, who wasn't a pixie. He couldn't tell what kind of fae she was. Her corkscrew curls and dark complexion glowed in the moonlight that wafted in from the kitchen window. The storm must've broken. "What's he doing here, and why would he have a military-grade weapon on him?"

"More importantly, why did these guys want to capture us, and what does it have to do with you?" The buzzed-haircut pixie fixed Maverick with a skeptical look, as if to suggest he was one of the bad guys.

Maverick sighed. "Listen, I don't have time to explain, but you should leave the room. All of you."

He didn't want them to witness his interrogation. Especially not Zera or her son. It could get messy, even with the druid immobilized.

"And you should put some pants on," the woman with the curls said and muttered something under her breath. She waved her hand, and then he was clothed in sweatpants and a shirt that would probably be large on any of them, but the fabric strained against his muscles with an uncomfortable amount of tension. So she was a witch or a mage.

The buzzed-haircut pixie burst out laughing. "Sweatpants? Really, Sloane. You couldn't spring for menswear?"

"It's not like I had the time to conjure up a whole new outfit." The other woman, called Sloane, smirked but gave the buzzed-haircut pixie an affectionate grin.

"Jade, Sloane, just stop," Zera snapped, drawing their attention. "How can you all think about clothes right now? This intruder was the same one who attacked me on my date and followed me to my place of work, and now, my family is in danger. My son." Her voice broke as she held her son closer to her chest, tears brimming in her lavender eyes.

"Let's go, ladies," Maverick growled, the timbre of his werewolf form still lacing his words with a ferocity that was not entirely human.

With stern nods, the women shuffled out, leaving him and the incapacitated druid in the midst of the upturned kitchen.

Once they were safely beyond the kitchen doors, Maverick

turned his attention back to the druid, who was starting to regain control of his faculties. He would have to move quickly.

He crouched over the druid, a storm of frustration broiling within him. His instinct, that primal drive to protect, had surged to the forefront, fighting against the calculated coolness required of a spy. He was torn between the desire to rip apart the druid who dared threaten Zera and Cole and the knowledge that his duty was to remain in control of his emotions, to deceive, to wear masks that protected them all from his profession.

The arrogance he wore like armor clashed with the raw vulnerability of caring for someone else's life—especially that of an innocent child.

"Are you going to just stare at him or what?" Zera's voice cut through his inner turmoil, sharp and laced with irritation.

Maverick glanced over as Zera marched into the room and folded her arms across her chest, bringing his attention to her commanding presence. For someone so short, she had an aura of power that could put even the most confident of men in their place. A trait he found himself drawn to.

"You can't be here," he said, rising to his feet. He noticed the child wasn't with her but heard his coos in the living room, where he was with the other women.

Zera glared up at him. "Oh, aside from this being my kitchen, I will not let you be the only one doing the questioning here."

"This is my business."

"In my house." She cocked head to the side. "That makes it mine."

It took all his energy not to crack a smile. She had guts. He liked that. Instead, he stepped into her space and crossed his arms, the fabric of the too-small sweatshirt straining against the movement.

Her eyes flitted over his massive arms, and for a second, he thought he saw a flicker of desire, but it was quickly replaced with anger.

He leaned in closer, ignoring how her sugary aroma sent his

senses reeling. It was nothing like the bitter stench of rotting dewdrops of the pixies who'd tormented him. "This is what I'm trained to do."

She lifted her chin in defiance. "I'm not leaving until I get answers."

The druid grunted as he strained to move, his body beginning to break the bonds of the pulse shackler. It wouldn't hold much longer, and it was clear Zera wouldn't budge.

Maverick sighed and gave a reluctant nod before turning his attention back to the druid, who now glared up at him from where he lay helplessly on the floor.

"Who sent you?" Maverick asked, his voice low and steady. "Because even Gareth doesn't have the power to know my identity. Not after the way I heard his competitors squeezed him dry."

The druid spat in response, his eyes flickering with hazy magic as he fought against the dwindling effects of the shackler.

"You're going to make this harder for yourself by not talking." A growl rumbled from Maverick's chest as his canines elongated, indicating how close he was to unleashing his true power.

His wolf claws extended, threatening to rip out the druid's throat as he leaned over him. "I can smell the lies on the tip of your tongue. It's only a matter of time before I sniff them out and discover the truth."

"I don't have to tell you anything." The druid sneered.

Maverick's jaw clenched. This wouldn't be easy, but the druid would talk. There were ways, and Maverick was exceptionally gifted in the department of torture.

"I'll give you one last chance to answer."

"This is taking too long." Zera pushed Maverick aside and grabbed the druid's collar in her small fist while the other hand sparked with the glow of soft purple light. "Tell me who you work for? How did you know where to find me?"

Maverick had known pixies could be fierce even without magic, but Zera was far more dangerous.

The druid's eyes widened in shock as the purple magic forced its way through his nostrils and air passageways, seeking the truth. His body jerked as he tried to free himself, not just by the pulse shackler but from Zera's pixie magic. It was obvious from the way his face reddened that the pixie was inflicting pain, and the druid's body quivered in response.

Maverick watched in stunned awe—aroused at the sheer sight of her interrogating someone who was more than double her size. She was fearless, and her pixie power was far greater than any he'd ever witnessed before. It was true what they said about the fury of a woman scorned, but that was nothing in the face of a mother's wrath.

"Who sent you?" Zera repeated, her voice low and menacing.

The druid's body writhed in agony and his lips moved, but no sound came out. As the seconds ticked by, Maverick could hear Zera's breath coming in harsh gasps, her body shaking with the effort of draining whatever remained of her pixie dust. She was pushing herself too far.

A light sheen of sweat beaded across her forehead, while the druid's eyes rolled back in his head as his body struggled against the combination of pain and restraints.

"Zera, stop." Maverick moved to her side. He knew she could easily kill the druid or, worse, burn out herself if she didn't. "Let him speak."

A gust of magic lifted her brown waves off her shoulder, and pure malice was in her eyes. He rested his hand on her shoulder, and when her eyes met his, she blinked with realization.

With a flash of purple light, Zera finally released him from her hold. The druid's body slumped to the floor, unconscious.

"Maverick!" she gasped, running a hand through her hair as she stumbled back. "I didn't know... I didn't know it would hurt him that much."

Maverick grabbed her arm to steady her and help her find a nearby chair.

"It's fine. You saved us time," he replied, more concerned about her than he was for the druid, who struggled to breathe. "We can still get some answers from him."

After making sure Zera was okay, he focused on the druid, who was starting to wake up. He used Zera's move, fisting a chunk full of the fae's collar, but his grip lifted the druid up far enough that only his tiptoes scraped the floor.

"Who sent you?" Maverick whispered, his tone lethal. His nostrils flared, taking in the scent of fear mixed with blood and pain.

"Gareth…" The druid trailed off, and his head lolled to one side.

Maverick slammed the druid's head against the kitchen cabinet, yanking his attention back from the brink before he passed out.

"Explain," Maverick growled, pressing his clawed fingers even harder against the druid's neck to remind him who was in control.

Blood trickled from small cuts on his own hand, but it only fueled his determination further.

The druid coughed violently before speaking between gasps for air. "Gareth… is a pawn in a much bigger game."

Illegal arms dealing, drug trafficking, fae trafficking—they were all games played for profit. Some Maverick could look the other way from, but others he couldn't.

As a self-employed spy for hire, he chose which jobs he took. Which games he chose to support. Some he could. Some he couldn't. He had control. But now, his control was slipping.

Maverick's eyes narrowed at the realization that Gareth might not be the one trying to kill him. That the druid might be an accomplice to a much bigger threat out there that could crush Maverick like a pawn.

But it was the only reality that made sense after what had happened in the restaurant and now this.

"Names," he commanded, pressing his claws deeper into the druid's bronzed skin. "Give me names."

"I would rather die."

Maverick narrowed his eyes, a cruel smile playing upon his lips.

"Then perhaps you will. Give me a name, or I will make you wish for death."

"I'm not afraid of death," he said in a rasp. "They know where you are now. Where the woman with pixie dust is. My job is finished."

Maverick's heartbeat came to a rapid halt as the druid's words sank in, and a chill swept down his spine. It was all a diversion so that the druid could cast whatever spell he had left in his arsenal and send word back to whoever was bankrolling Gareth's new venture. He'd had no intention of escaping this.

"You're not going anywhere until I've—" Maverick's growl was cut short as a sudden fire erupted and engulfed the druid until he was only a flurry of ash raining down on the kitchen floor.

As the last embers faded away, Maverick stared at the ashes in disbelief. The druid had played him. He clenched his fists in frustration, knowing that time was running out.

A slow, burning anger simmered inside him. He knew what he had to do. He swallowed hard. As long as Gareth and whoever he was now working for were alive, Zera's life and the life of her son were in danger.

"What do we do now?" Zera asked, her voice quiet with both shock and fear.

Maverick looked down at her, wanting in that moment to pull her against his chest to comfort her but thinking better of it. He told himself it was only his wolf talking, but something deep within him said it was anything but.

He took a deep breath, trying to remember his training to keep his feelings in check. Zera wouldn't like what he knew they had to do, but it was the only way for him to do his job. For him to keep his past from hurting any more innocent lives. To keep her and her child alive.

He'd let her out of his sight once before, and it had nearly cost her life. He wouldn't let that happen again.

"You and I? We hunt," he said firmly. "And we make them pay."

CHAPTER 5
ZERA

Zera scooped up a forkful of creamy pasta, blowing on it to cool it down before offering it to Cole. He sat perched in his high chair, which she'd moved into his nursery to protect him from the heated debate in the kitchen, his eyes wide with anticipation and hunger as he waited for a bite of his favorite meal.

The soft, warm light from the butterfly lamp perched on his dresser bathed them both in its glow, creating a cozy and intimate atmosphere that Zera cherished.

"Here comes another bite," she cooed, guiding the fork toward his open mouth.

He giggled with delight as he took a big bite, smacking his lips happily. Zera smiled at the pure joy on his face, feeling her heart swell with love for her little boy.

Feeding Cole was her favorite thing in the entire realm. Sure, it was messy and tedious, and sometimes none of the food would get in his mouth, but these were the brief, blissful moments when she could forget about everything—her responsibilities, her fears, her doubts—while she focused on her son, who was growing up much too quickly.

As she continued to feed Cole, the heated discussion from the kitchen intruded on her peaceful bubble. Jade's voice rose above the others, her tone sharp and argumentative.

"Absolutely not! It's too dangerous." Jade's voice pierced through the open doorway, as if there weren't a good distance between the kitchen table and the nursery, followed by Sloane's calmer, firm tone. "Maverick, you can't seriously expect—"

"Zera must go with me. There's no other way," Maverick said, his voice firm. "And Cole... He'll be safer in Pixie Hollow."

"So will she!" Jade snapped, but the undercurrent of concern in her voice was clear even through her frustration. "Look, I know we can't just stay here waiting for this Gareth guy and whoever he's working with to come here and catch us off guard. But why can't Zera come with us?"

Her words were punctuated by her fist slamming against the table.

"Jade, please," Sloane interjected. "I agree the situation is less than ideal, but we must keep calm in order to make a solid plan."

"I won't be making any plans before he gives us more answers. We don't even know who he really is."

"Who I am is irrelevant. The only thing that matters now is this," Maverick said, his deep, commanding voice holding a note of authority that demanded attention. "Now that Gareth knows about Zera and her powers, he will stop at nothing to capture her. Whoever was stupid enough to partner up with him has made him even more deadly than he was before. Anyone in his way will wind up dead."

Zera's heart clenched at the name—Gareth. The name itself felt like a cold hand closing around her throat. She could still hear the elf's harsh whisper ringing in her ears. It was the voice of nightmares.

With every fiber of her being, she knew she had to face him, to protect Cole from the shadows that sought to ensnare their little family. Gareth and whoever he was working for would never find out about her son, and she would make sure that whoever knew of her pixie dust wouldn't live to breathe her secret to another living soul. Even if that meant killing the wolf who got her into this mess in the first place.

Zera looked up from Cole, her eyes landing on Maverick, who lounged against the fridge next to the nursery's doorway. His massive frame nearly blocked her view of Jade and Sloane taking up space around the kitchen table.

It would be a pity to kill him, but if she had to, she would do it. No one meant more to her than her son. A werewolf stranger with a nice face couldn't change that.

Maverick's eyes flicked to hers, an electric current humming between them. Something in the way he looked at her, like he was reading her from the inside out, made her shiver in anticipation. Shit. He really did have a nice face.

She jerked her attention back to her son, cursing her traitorous heart for the uptick in rhythm she knew Maverick heard.

"Then we'll hide," Jade said. "Like you said, we should be safe in Pixie Hollow. It's not like anyone will go looking for Zera in the one place she's not welcome anymore."

Ouch. That stung. It was one thing to know she would never be able to go back to her homeland because of the lamest decision she'd ever made. Even if it had led her to create the best thing in her life—Cole. But it was so much worse hearing it spoken out loud by her half sister.

"Of course he'll look for her there," Maverick said with a sigh. "It's her last-known location, aside from this one. He'll know anywhere she's been for the last ten years, and from what I can tell, the list isn't very long. He will come for her, he will find and kill his way to her, and if Cole is anything like his mother, then he'll take him too."

Zera's face hardened. Like hell she'd let anyone get to Cole.

"Right now, Zera is his only target. That and his intent to kill me," Maverick continued. "And I intend to keep it that way. I only ask that you all trust me."

"Trust you?" Jade scoffed. "We don't even know you."

"It's the only way to keep everyone safe." The tone of Maverick's voice was calm, but Zera could sense the urgency. "I won't let anything happen to her or her son."

Zera gulped. For a faeboy, this werewolf seemed to care a lot. Maybe it was merely a sense of obligation, but she pondered why he was going out of his way to help them. Perhaps he was right. Maybe separating until the Gareth situation was handled would be best. She would do anything to keep her boy safe.

She gazed down at Cole, whose face was smeared with pasta sauce as he grinned up at her, blissfully unaware of the danger that loomed over them.

He held out his chubby little hands for another bite.

"Of course, baby," she replied, swallowing the lump in her throat as she spooned up more food for him.

As much as she yearned to keep Cole safe, the thought of leaving him behind shattered her heart. But she couldn't let her fear get in the way of what she knew she needed to do.

She hated the idea of working with a werewolf, especially an arrogant faeboy spy, but deep down, she knew it was the best chance she had to protect her son.

With her mind made up, she placed the spoon on Cole's empty plate.

"Give Mommy a minute, okay?" She leaned down and pressed a tender kiss to his forehead, inhaling the sweet scent of the shampoo that still lingered in his full head of brown curls. "I love you more than anything in this realm, Cole. You know that, right?"

Her little one responded with muffled coos, his mouth still full.

"Promise me," she choked out, her eyes filling with tears. "Promise me you'll be brave and strong and, no matter what happens, know that Auntie Jade and Aunt Sloane got you, okay?"

Cole's tiny brow furrowed for a second, but he nodded as he shoved the spoon of food back into his mouth. Whether it was a nod because he understood her or was just exploring his neck muscles, it didn't matter. To her, it meant he knew, and that was all that mattered.

"Good." She gave him one more kiss on the top of his head before, reluctantly, she pulled away. "I'll be in the kitchen."

He gave her a toothy grin and waved his free hand, oblivious to the weight of her decision.

Steeling herself, she rose and stepped lightly across the room, pausing at the door that separated her from the argument so she could keep a watchful eye on Cole.

"Enough," Zera declared as she entered the kitchen, her voice steady despite the tremor in her soul. Jade and Sloane turned to her, their expressions a blend of relief and dread. Maverick stood near her like a dark sentinel, his piercing eyes locking on to hers.

"I will go with Maverick."

Jade rose from her chair to protest, but Zera raised her hand. "Let me finish. I'll go with him like he suggests while you and Sloane go back to Pixie Hollow with Cole. Maverick's right that it's the only way to ensure my son's safety. I won't put him in any more danger."

"But you'll be going with a total stranger," Jade declared for the umpteenth time, heat rushing to her cheeks. "For all we know, he could be leading you straight to the fae who's trying to steal your pixie dust, and then Cole will be left motherless."

"This total stranger saved our lives," Zera said, surprising even herself by standing up for a werewolf. "As much as I hate to admit it, trusting Maverick is the only way to ensure Cole doesn't end up without me. Besides, I'd imagine a mission like this shouldn't take us more than three, four days tops. Right?"

Maverick shrugged. "I won't promise and underdeliver but maybe a week or two. As long as there are no unforeseen complications."

Zera drew in a deep breath and nodded. One to two weeks. She could do that, right?

She shook off the dread that threatened to take control of her. She didn't have time for her anxiety. There was no other choice but to move forward. "See? A week or two isn't so bad. Especially if it means we're all safe and reunited at the end of this. And if you need to reach me, I'll have my faestone."

Maverick cleared his throat, gaining her attention. "Unfortunately, you won't. We have to assume our devices have been compromised, since I'm guessing they were both present at the restaurant."

Zera bit her lip, not liking the sound of where this was going.

"We'll all need to get rid of them before we leave."

She swallowed hard and shot a look of concern to Jade and Sloane, who both shared the expression she imagined was etched into her face.

"But then how will we know…" Sloane let the question hang in the air.

An awkward silence fell over the room.

"Don't worry," Maverick reassured them. "Our first takes will be tracking down untraceable faestones and shipping them to whatever location you all decide on."

"Aren't those incredibly illegal?" Jade asked, her eyes widening.

"Yes," Maverick said nonchalantly. "But so is everything else we've witnessed tonight."

Jade rolled her eyes, and Zera had to mimic her actions, feeling the tension in the room ease slightly.

"Okay, say you somehow get your hands on these illegal, untraceable faestones," Jade said, "though I wouldn't even know where to look in the first place for them. What happens if we get caught?"

Zera's stomach clenched. It was a fair question. Could she really leave with some faeboy wolf she hated and barely trusted for several days or, maybe, weeks and risk losing her freedom? What if the Fae Police or, even worse, the Faen Bureau of Investigation caught them using untraceable faestones and forced them to answer to the Fae Tribunal?

Panic settled in, making her cold straight down to her bones. She wasn't a spy. She didn't have the kind of skills Maverick must've had to slip by undetected. She was just a single mom. A pixie with pixie dust, sure, but still a mom working to make ends meet.

Maverick must've sensed her unease and pushed off the refrigerator he leaned on, coming to stand next to her, his calming scent filling her nose— a mix of warm caramel and citrus.

"You won't," Maverick answered, his confidence unwavering. "I'm a trained spy. I know how to cover our tracks and make sure we remain undetected. The only thing you need to worry about is staying safe until we can take care of this problem and reunite Zera with her son."

Jade looked to Zera. The wary look in her eyes made it clear she didn't like the idea, but what other choice did they have? If they stayed, they'd be dead. If they followed Maverick's plan, then at least they'd have a fighting chance.

She looked back into the nursery at Cole, who was still playing with his spoon, sending food flying everywhere. Her chest ached at the thought of not being with him every day but better that than dead. Besides, he'd be safe with his pixie and witch aunties.

"All right, Maverick," she said with a decisive nod as she turned back to face the group. "I'll go with you. But only if Cole goes to Pixie Hollow."

Her words fell like stones into the silence that ensued.

"Zera—" Sloane began, but Zera raised a hand to stop her.

"Jade, I need you to both promise me you'll keep him safe." Her gaze flickered to her half sister, seeking the unspoken vow only siblings could understand.

"Of course," Jade said, her usual whimsy subdued by the gravity of the request. "You know I'd fight off an entire legion of trolls for him."

"Good," Zera exhaled, allowing herself a momentary smile. "Because you might have to."

"Are you sure about this?" Maverick's voice held an unexpected gentleness, throwing her for a second. "I don't know about whoever he's working for, but I know Gareth won't hold back."

"Neither will I," she replied, her voice laced with steel and something else—a fiery determination that even she hadn't known simmered within her.

"Then we'll leave at dawn," Maverick stated, his glance briefly softening as he looked toward the nursery. "We'll need to get moving. Coyotes will be sent to sniff everything out. If they get a single whiff that Cole ever existed here, then we've already failed, and that's not an option."

"Agreed," Zera replied.

"How are we supposed to do that?" Jade asked with a baffled expression.

"Just pack up your things, only the necessities," Maverick said, moving toward the nursery. "Leave the rest to me."

Zera shared a glance with her half sister and Sloane before rushing after Maverick.

Cole should've been asleep, but instead he was cooing to his spoon, fully awake and not showing any signs of tiredness. Her baby stopped when Maverick walked into the room, his eyes locked on the giant werewolf and his brows quirked before he burst into a huge smile.

"Looks like someone's made a new friend," Maverick said with a grin as Cole giggled and reached out for him.

"Seems so," Zera said, her smile soft but her emotions raging with a strength she couldn't quite understand.

It filled her heart to see her son express his happiness and delight at meeting new people. It also made her heart ache that there really was something Cole needed that she could never be. A father figure. But those weren't important, right?

She swallowed the lump in her throat and pushed the emotions aside. Of course she was everything he needed and more. She was a boss.

"I can hold him while you pack. If you want," Maverick offered.

Zera had to hide her surprise at the unexpected offer, giving him a curt nod. A spy deliberately volunteering to hold a baby?

"Thank you, that would help," she said, turning her attention to the task at hand, packing up Cole's things.

They had to leave it as if he never existed. Moisture stung her eyes at the unbearable thought. This would prove harder than she anticipated.

"Okay, little man, let's give your mom some space to work," Maverick cooed, his voice an odd mix of gruff and gentle as he scooped up Cole with surprising ease.

She watched in awe as Cole instantly relaxed in Maverick's arms. Cole began to coo when Maverick made faces at him and rocked from one foot to the other, as if he'd done this a thousand times before.

Zera shook the foolish thoughts that were rolling into her head. Like wondering if he would make a good partner, that perhaps there was something more to him than just a faeboy spy who used her as cover then caused her whole world to come crumbling down. Again.

She huffed. He didn't deserve the headspace.

Instead, she focused on packing up Cole's things, knowing that whatever she didn't take would wind up destroyed. She attempted to ignore the pain in her heart as memories overwhelmed her of each stained onesie, every chewed toy, and all the mismatched socks.

As much as she tried to avoid it, her attention shifted between packing and Cole, who giggled when Maverick tossed him into the air or flew him around the room like an airplane. She watched them from the corner of her eye, momentarily captivated by the unexpected tenderness that radiated from this rough-edged man. It was as if he'd had years of experience caring for babies.

She quickly reminded herself that it was more likely due to his supernatural instincts as a werewolf than any past with children. Werewolves were notorious for breeding large families. The larger the family, the more powerful the pack. She wasn't about to inflate his ego by acknowledging his innate wolf abilities.

She gritted her teeth, hating that she actually loved it. That it made him all the more attractive. And very much unattractive, both at the same time.

"You're staring," Maverick said, sparing a quick glance at her. He flashed a smile that sent heat rushing to her cheeks.

She rolled her eyes and zipped up the diaper bag. "Don't flatter yourself. You're holding my child. Of course I'm going to keep an eye out."

Maverick chuckled. He lowered Cole into his little seat on the floor and proceeded to play peekaboo, eliciting even more laughter from her little one.

She was going to miss those sounds. They were music to her ears. She would do anything for her son—swim across the Death Channel, scale the Spire Alps, even brave the flames of the Fire Cliffs. She'd sacrificed so much for him, and she would do it all over again and then some.

Yet somehow the thought of being away from him was nearly unbearable. Zera let out a heavy sigh, and she zipped up the diaper bag. She had to muster up the courage, suck it up, and be brave because if she didn't, the alternative was unthinkable.

Jade and Sloane entered the nursery, their suitcases rolling themselves and following behind Sloane with her witchy powers, the tension in the room palpable.

"We can take it from here," Sloane said, her voice steady and reassuring.

Zera nodded and swatted away a sudden tear. She wasn't ready to leave the room, to face the emptiness of her own, but she knew she had to if she was going to be ready. "Make sure to get Cole's green blanket. He won't sleep without it."

"We know," Jade chimed in, her chaotic energy somehow soothing in that moment. "Green blankie, extra cuddles, and maybe a new adventure. Cole's going to love Pixie Hollow."

Sloane reached for the bag Zera was packing. It easily slipped away as she let go. The same thing she would have to do with Cole in a few hours.

"We'll pack his things and put him to bed," Sloane promised.

With a heavy heart, Zera retreated to her modest bedroom,

where her belongings lay scattered. She moved quickly, her mind racing through a mental checklist of necessities to keep from focusing on the inevitable goodbye that lay ahead.

A few changes of clothes—practical, not flashy—were folded neatly into her bag. Her bartending aprons and uniform, usually vital, were left untouched; they'd serve no purpose on this mission. But her home lab kit with the new seedlings from the rare blue ever-frost blossom that Quinn brought for her experiment to find something, anything that had similar properties to pixie dust? Perhaps she'd have more time for this while she was playing spy.

She packed up the home lab into another bag, promising herself she wouldn't give up on her project no matter how crazy things got, and then continued with the rest of her things. Each item she chose was a silent testament to her resolve—a sturdy pair of boots for the journey ahead, a small collection of healing herbs, and a locket given to her by her mother the day her pixie dust had emerged, a reminder of her dwindling powers. She never wore it, but she was never without it and always kept it in a place of importance in her room.

It was a symbol of the promise she'd made to her late mother that she would always keep her pixie dust a secret, and up until today, she'd done just that. She guessed it was too late to worry about broken promises. She tucked it into her pocket and moved on to her dresser.

Zera's fingers brushed against a photo frame on her nightstand, a snapshot of Cole laughing, his eyes sparkling with mischief. She hesitated before tucking it into the side pocket of her bag, a talisman to remind her of what she was fighting for.

"Are you absolutely sure?" Maverick's voice pulled her from her thoughts.

"About leaving my son? No. About stopping Gareth and whoever else is hunting me and other pixies for our pixie dust? Absolutely." Zera zipped up her bag with finality. "This isn't only about us anymore. It's bigger than that."

Maverick nodded, understanding etched into his crisp features. "I'll protect you with my life, Zera. We're in this together."

"Let's hope it doesn't come to that," she replied, slinging her bag over her shoulder. Her senses sharpened as she prepared for the unknown, her mother's intuition merging with the instincts of a pixie.

She could do this. She had to.

"Jade put Cole down for a nap," Maverick said when she turned toward him. He leaned against the doorframe, his arms crossed over his chest.

Zera felt a pang of guilt at the thought of uprooting her son's life, but she knew he was in good hands with his aunts. If all went according to plan, she'd be reunited with him in no time at all.

"Thank you," Zera said sincerely. She took a deep breath and squared her shoulders.

"All set to pack up?" Maverick asked, extending his hand for her bag.

"Ready as I'll ever be." Zera handed him the bag.

His eyes flickered to her ears, and he grimaced. She frowned, unable to fight the sudden feeling of self-consciousness. He'd been different ever since discovering she was a pixie, which Jade had obviously left out of her FaeMatch profile. Would that have changed anything? Had her profile mentioned that she was a pixie, would Maverick not have initiated a non-date with her?

She hated the pang of disappointment—although he was a werewolf, and she hated them to their very core. But she had a reason to. Not just because of her ex but because many wolf packs were known to hunt her kind. They were the reason only a few pixies had power anymore.

Still, she didn't like the thought of werewolves being prejudiced in return. A double standard, but it was what it was.

"You should get some rest."

She shook her head. "We only have a few hours, and there's still so much to do."

"I'll take care of it," Maverick insisted, the usual gruffness in his tone replaced with something else. Something sweet, as if he actually cared about her as more than just a liability to his cover. As if he hadn't shown his visible disgust for her kind.

She caught his eye, and the tenderness that had been there before quickly vanished, replaced with the ice-cold resolve that had come to define their relationship.

"Rest up. Tomorrow, you'll become Mrs. Brown, and you'll definitely need your energy." With that, he gave her a curt nod and backed out of her room with her bag, leaving her alone in the uncomfortable silence.

As if she could sleep now.

THE NEXT MORNING, they were all up before dawn, fed, and ready to go. All remnants of Cole had been removed from a house devoid of personal touches, as if it were a model home ready to be put up for sale.

Zera's heart beat wildly as she considered what lay ahead, but she knew she couldn't afford to waver—not with so much at stake. She gripped the box she carried out to the waiting car a little tighter.

Sloane waved her hand, and the waiting trunk popped open before she magicked the luggage inside. The bags flew into the trunk and arranged themselves into a neat row.

Catching Zera's glance, she gave her a somber nod. Somber was the theme of this morning. No one seemed to be in good spirits except for Cole, who was blissfully content playing games with Maverick on the porch.

Cole, with his tousled brown hair sticking up in all directions from sleep, was perched beside Maverick, eyes wide with curiosity at the bright stuffed animal Maverick was playing with.

"Beep! Beep!" Maverick moved the stuffed animal in front of Cole. "Oh no, Agent Shadow set off the alarm. Quick, we need a distraction." Maverick glanced conspiratorially at Cole. "Think you can handle that, partner?"

Cole grinned and laughed at the high-pitched voice Maverick used, and Zera soon joined in.

Maverick caught her staring again and flashed her a crooked smile, scooping her son up and walking over to meet her where she stood next to the waiting cars.

"Your son's got some serious covert-ops potential." Maverick grinned, winking at her, his usual bravado softened around the edges.

"Thanks, I think?" Zera chuckled, setting the box she carried on the ground beside them so she could hold her son.

"He's a great kid," Maverick said with a sincerity that struck a chord within her.

"Careful there, Mr. Spy," she teased as he handed Cole back to her. "You might find yourself on permanent diaper duty."

"A mission I'd happily accept." Maverick's words slipped out quickly, as if he'd spoken before thinking about it.

Their eyes locked for a moment, the air between them thick. Had she heard him right? Had he really just said that? She didn't know what she could trust anymore. All she could think about was her skyrocketing heartbeat. Maverick dipped his head, his lips hovering dangerously close to Zera. If she leaned in, their lips would meet.

Maverick cupped her face with his free hand, caressing her cheek with his thumb. Zera's breath hitched, and she didn't dare move an inch. She couldn't believe how easily he affected her, how a simple touch from him could make her body feel alive.

A car trunk slammed shut, breaking the spell between them. The pain and desire in Maverick's gaze morphed into a look of mild disgust, sending Zera's heart plummeting.

Zera stepped back and desperately tried to catch her breath. What was it that made him both seem attracted yet at the same time repelled by her?

A bloody mind game of an arrogant wolf, perhaps. The thought left a sour taste in her mouth.

"We're all set," Jade called, rounding the car. "Guess it's time to say our goodbyes if we're going to make it to Pixie Hollow before dark."

Zera swallowed hard, holding Cole close. "Okay, baby. Be good for your aunties, all right?"

She pulled him into a hug, and his laughter tore at her heartstrings. It would be a while before she would hold her son in her arms again, but she promised herself it wouldn't be that long. She would do whatever she needed to in order to get back to him safe and sound.

"I'll see you soon," she whispered into Cole's ear, praying to the fae it would only be a few days, though she knew this would depend on how good of a spy Maverick really was.

"Ready?" Maverick asked, his voice tight.

"Can we ever really be ready for this?" Zera replied, mustering a weak smile but never once taking her eyes off her son.

If these were the last few moments she had with her baby boy, then she would spend them cherishing every little wrist roll and chubby cheek.

Cole reached for her nose and giggled. He had no idea how much she was going to miss him during this mission or the danger she most likely would face, if the incident at the restaurant was any indicator of what might happen. He simply knew that he was loved, and that brought a certain comfort to her heart.

"It's time," Maverick said softly.

Zera nodded, and with one final kiss on Cole's forehead, she loaded him into his car seat, which waited in Sloane's car. She looked up at Sloane in the driver's seat. "Keep him safe, will you?"

"With my life." Sloane gave a sad smile. "But we'll see you soon."

"See you soon," Zera repeated, praying to the fae that was true.

She straightened in time to be pulled against Jade's chest, her half sister's strong arms wrapping around her. "Promise me you'll be safe."

Zera gripped the fabric of her sister's shirt and nodded into her shoulder.

"And be careful with that one." Jade nodded toward Maverick, who was now busy emptying the things she'd just packed from her car.

Zera frowned. What in the fae realm was he doing?

"Zera, promise me."

She looked back at her sister, who had a worried expression on her face.

"Of course. I promise I'll be safe and careful. You don't have to worry about me with Maverick."

"Good," Jade said, hopping into the open passenger seat. "I'll talk to you as soon as Maverick ships us those faestones."

"Oh!" Zera exclaimed, holding Jade's door open as her mom brain suddenly warped into overdrive. She went through a laundry list of things that popped into her mind. "Remember he only likes his blue sippy cup with milk when he wakes up, the green one for before naps and bedtime and—"

"Zera, we've got this," Jade said with an understanding smile. "Just take care of yourself. We'll take care of the rest."

She nodded, unable to vocalize another somber goodbye. With one final glance at Cole, Zera shut Jade's door and stepped away.

The engine roared to life and drove off, taking with it everyone she loved in this realm. A pang of sorrow swept over her and threatened to take control of her limbs. She wanted to fall to her knees, to weep. But that wouldn't help bring them all back. She had to keep her emotions in check. If not for her sake, for Cole's.

"Let's go," Maverick said, walking up and handing her a backpack that definitely didn't belong to her.

"What's this?"

"Your things," he said, pulling on an identical backpack onto his shoulders. "I moved them into this one. It'll be better. More agile."

"Uh-uh... How'd you get them so quickly?"

He gave her a look that said she wouldn't want to know.

"Okay, new backpack. Got it." She took the bag and unzipped it, checking to be sure everything was in there. Her heart stopped in panic when she didn't see her most valuable item. "Where's my home lab kit?"

Maverick frowned. "You mean the chest that took up more space than necessary, filled with vials, a microscope, and a bunch of other doodads?"

"Yes, that."

"I left it in the car." He shrugged. "You won't need that stuff."

"Like bloody fae I'm leaving here without it," she huffed over her shoulder and marched right back to the car.

She pulled the hard-shelled chest that took up an entire section of her suitcase out of the car and set in on the ground. It definitely wouldn't fit in the backpack, but she'd use her pixie dust to magic it down a few sizes to fit. Anything to not be parted with her third true love—science. Third, because her first true love was her son and second was the rest of her family.

"What's the deal with all this... science stuff anyway? I thought you were a bartender, not a scientist." Maverick, suddenly next to her, leaned against the trunk of her car.

"It's... only a hobby." She took a deep breath, bracing her hands on the chest as the heat of her pixie dust rushed up her spine. She hoped it was enough to do its magic. "Something I love to do in my free time."

He raised an eyebrow, clearly not buying her explanation. She couldn't blame him—it wasn't exactly a common hobby for a bartender.

But the truth was, she had always been fascinated by science. Even before she knew about the pixie-dust crisis. Growing up, she would spend hours poring over books about faeology, dreaming of one day becoming a true scientist or a biologist. But life had obviously taken her down a different path.

"Well, you won't have much free time where we're going," he said with a shrug, a look of awe briefly flitting across his otherwise-stoic features when purple magic absorbed the chest, shrinking it down to the size of her palm.

"I can't afford to leave it," she said, and she stuffed it into a pocket of the backpack before standing. She pulled the straps over her shoulders and adjusted the weight. It was surprisingly light. "So... what about my car?"

"It stays."

Her eyebrows shot up. "What? Why?"

Maverick turned to face her, his massive frame towering over her. "Because if we take it, then it'll look like you're on the run. Which you're not, right?"

"Right. So we're walking to Mystic City on foot?" she asked, bewildered. "Because my pixie wings can barely carry me across my living room, let alone carry a giant werewolf like yourself. No offense."

"None taken." He smirked, and she gritted her teeth. So much for not feeding his overinflated ego.

She sighed and followed him down the road, trying to keep up with his brisk pace. "Where to now?"

"To get you a new identity." He shot her a crooked smile, and his eyes glinted with mischief. "It's time you truly became Mrs. Brown."

Zera swallowed hard. Her heart skipped a beat as she realized what this meant. She tried to be afraid or angry about what this would entail, but she wasn't. To her horror, and one she would never admit to, the prospect of pretending to be someone else actually sounded like... fun.

CHAPTER 6
ZERA

All thoughts of fun vanished when they hopped on the bus out of Havenwood, scattered with passengers lost in their own thoughts as the vehicle trudged along the winding road to Mystic City.

Reality had sunk in, a sudden wave of nausea rolling through her at the fact that she was seated next to a werewolf spy and at the prospect of going undercover to chase down a dangerous elven arms dealer. This was ludicrous. She'd absolutely lost her marbles.

But perhaps that was a good thing. After all, that same elven arms dealer had sent hit men after her, endangering her son and family. She hardened her resolve. She would go to the end of the realm and back to protect her little pixie-wereling, and if she couldn't find the fae who did this in the Fae Realm, she would fight her way into the next. Somehow.

She clenched her fists as panic rose within her, constricting her air passageways at the thought of what might've happened if Maverick hadn't arrived when he had and at the lengths she would go to protect her child. There wasn't anything she wouldn't do for Cole, but that didn't mean her stomach didn't churn with dread at the thought of it.

"Does it ever get easier?" she asked Maverick, who sat with her, tucked in the far back, away from prying ears.

"What?" He arched a brow at her.

"This feeling like my insides are about to burst at the thought of going undercover."

"I've never heard of it," he said, his lips curling into a smug grin.

She scoffed. "Okay, faeboy. I get it. You're this hotshot spy who knows everything, so what would you have to fear?"

He smirked. "Who said I know everything?"

"Probably only you."

His muscled arms, which took up most of the seat, shook with laughter at that, and Zera smiled back. She had half expected him to mansplain spy techniques or agree that he actually knew everything. Her ex never would've let her get away with making a joke like that. She lived in fear of being wrong, of saying anything that would make her ex lecture her on how she shouldn't say wrong things. It was like a weight had been lifted from her, a relief that left her heart fluttery.

"In all honesty, I understand your fear. I've felt it too." He shrugged. "Eventually, all of this becomes like second nature."

"Oh." She wondered how long that would take. Probably longer than she was willing to play a spy's pretend wife. "So, tell me about this Dane Brown."

She might as well get started working on getting to know Maverick's alias, right? It was only a matter of time before she would have to get into character, and as of yet, she knew nothing about her fake husband.

"All you need to know is that he's a high-stakes logistics consultant." He paused, his piercing eyes flicking to Zera for a moment. "I worked for Gareth on a job securing a weapons shipment coming in from the Human Realm."

Zera gasped. "You've been out of this realm? But how did you get that kind of clearance? I didn't think you worked for the government."

"I don't." Maverick pointedly ignored her other question, perhaps for plausible deniability.

"Okay, guess I don't need to know that, but answer me this," she said, taking the hint. "Why would Gareth go to so much trouble going after a consultant who only worked on one job for him?"

His jaw ticked.

"Unless it was more than one job?"

It ticked again. She was onto something.

"And how did he figure out your name? Perhaps whoever he's working for now gave it to him?"

"Impossible," Maverick muttered under his breath. He tapped his fingers against the armrest. He was growing restless.

Zera knew she had struck a nerve and decided to press on for good measure. He was the only reason these fae thugs even knew her pixie dust existed and were out to kill her too. She had the right to probe for answers.

Leaning in closer to Maverick, Zera locked her gaze with his intense stormy eyes. "Tell me the truth, Maverick. What aren't you telling me?"

Maverick's gaze hardened, his steely resolve shining through when he finally spoke through clenched teeth. "He should never have been able to figure out my true identity. Not unless he was helped by someone more powerful than the company who hired me."

"And who was that?"

A flicker of hesitation passed over his face, and for a second, she thought he was done divulging his secrets.

He sighed, rubbing his suddenly tired eyes. "Mystic Dynamic Solutions, a shell company used as a front for an illegal-arms-dealing operation. Gareth was barely competing with them, but they wanted a monopoly, and they got it."

Zera sat in silence for a moment as the bus made another stop in a neighboring village on the border between Havenwood Forest and the northern Shadowlands. Crisp auburn leaves flaked off the stems of the red oaks that filled Havenwood Forest, standing out like a golden beacon against the wall of forest green pines that lined the Shadowlands.

"What lengths do you think Gareth would go to so he could ensure his survival after this company came after him?" she asked.

Maverick looked down at her in surprise, as if the question never occurred to him.

"My guess is, he'd go to plenty," Maverick said, his deep baritone rumbling with a weariness that defied his age.

Or at least the age she thought he looked, which was roughly mid-thirties, as the subtle speckles of gray in his otherwise-deep-brown hair suggested.

She was similar in age but was lucky enough not to have spotted a single gray hair in her own hair yet.

"But enough about Gareth." He gazed back out the window of the bus as the pines flew by, his voice resigned. "You should be focusing on your cover. When we arrive in Mystic City, we'll need to sell your alias to everyone around us. From the moment we arrive, you'll no longer be Zera."

Her heart skipped a beat at the thought of becoming someone new. "What do I need to know about Charlotte?"

Maverick chuckled, a flicker of amusement crossing his otherwise uninterested expression. "Nothing."

Heat flared in Zera's cheeks at his response. She had expected some guidance, some insight into the life she was about to step into. After all, she wasn't the one who was the professional spy.

Instead, he dismissed her, as if her question was trivial and her concerns insignificant. Anger swelled inside her, fueled by his condescending demeanor.

"What do you mean 'nothing'? I'm about to be impersonating another fae. I should at least know something about them."

Maverick turned on her, fixing her with a hard stare that reminded her of the look he'd given her when he saw her as a pixie for the first time at the restaurant. Anger.

She frowned. What did he have to be angry with her about? It was a fair question. And hadn't he been the one to make a move on her just hours earlier? Not that she should've wanted him to and not that she would admit she did, but he had no reason to be this cold to her. He was the Lunar werewolf, after all. A predator of her kind.

She'd grown up on the stories of the big bad wolf from the Lunar Forest, who hunted the pixies for sport and sold off their pixie dust to the highest bidder. It was why pixies had made it an unspoken rule never to interact with werewolves.

But she never bought into all that. Not all wolves were bad. At least she'd thought that when she was younger. That was when she'd mistakenly told herself her now ex was different because he wasn't a Lunar wolf, which meant he was good. She'd been wrong then. She wouldn't be wrong again, which was why she had to get a grip on her feelings. If only to prevent another heartbreak.

"Just be as much like yourself as you can," he finally replied. "A good alias is always in some way the truth."

Zera raised her eyebrows. "Is that the case with your faeboy ways? Or your pixie-hunting ways?"

He glowered at her. "I'd never hunt your kind."

"But didn't Gareth say you're a Lunar Brotherhood wolf?"

"I used to be. Once."

She frowned. "I thought all wolves belonged to a pack, and yours definitely is the worst. At least for my kind, that is."

"Like I told you at the restaurant, I'm one of the good ones."

"You're different, I'll give you that," she said with a shrug. "But I'm not sure if you're good yet."

"Even though I saved your life?" He arched a brow at her.

"I saved yours first."

Maverick rolled his eyes and looked away, leaving Zera to stew in her curiosity. But she was too old to care. They were both adults and could choose whichever lifestyle they wanted. Hers was taking care of her son.

She sighed, her thoughts drifting back to Cole, Jade, and Sloane.

Were they okay on their journey? She couldn't wait to get her hands on a faestone to talk to them but worried about the delivery process.

"Once we have the faestones forged, how long do you think it'll take to get them to Jade and Sloane? Won't the normal post flag them?"

Maverick cleared his throat, keeping his voice low. "Yes, if we used the normal post sender. But, like you said, they wouldn't make it past the Fae Channel, damn gnomes."

Everyone knew gnomes were responsible for the universal postal system. Their underground tunnels and speed made them perfect for the job. If only they weren't controlled by the Fae Tribunal that governed the Fae Realm. Even if they didn't include a return address, they would still be putting Jade and Sloane—and her son—in unnecessary danger.

But if they couldn't send anything through the normal channels, how would they ever get the faestones to them?

"It won't be as instant as shipping with the postal system," Maverick continued. "But there are other ways to ensure their delivery is discreet."

"And what exactly does that mean?" Zera pressed, feeling a mix of frustration and concern.

Maverick's lips curled into an impatient smile. "If I told you, then it wouldn't be discreet."

Zera huffed, crossing her arms over her chest. She hated not knowing all the details, but she had to trust Maverick for now.

The landscape changed as they neared the city. The trees turned into towering skyscrapers made of steel and glass, stretching toward the sky like giants reaching for the sun that beamed down on them—a dazzling display of supernatural diversity and danger.

Zera's heart raced as the bustling business district engulfed them. Fae of all kinds milled on the crowded sidewalks during the lunch rush. Vampires with their sharp fangs sipping their blood coffee, plumpish dwarves with full beards groomed into braids, elves with their sharp noses, bald scalps, and long ears—even longer than hers.

It was a convergence of all faen species working alongside one another, as if there were no difference. As if vampires, elementals, and shape-shifters weren't in a social war with one another. As if class meant nothing and here everyone worked together for a common purpose.

But everyone knew deep down it didn't matter what the cover looked like. Only upper-level elementals like the elves, demons, and even pixies like herself made it into government. She'd never had the desire to go into politics, especially when elections were a far cry from fair. It was a problem everyone avoided to keep the peace. Zera wondered how long that would last.

"Remember to stick to the plan," Maverick said softly as the skyscrapers and nicely dressed business fae fell away.

The bus turned down a long stretch of dilapidated buildings, each one with a neon sign or two advertising services and products she wasn't quite sure were legal. This wasn't the fancy west side where Maverick had taken her the night before or the business district. This was the underbelly of Mystic City.

"We're here as a husband and wife on a date," he said softly as the bus squealed to a stop. Zera's stomach churned, the reality of their mission setting in. "Follow my lead."

Zera nodded, securing her backpack before taking a deep breath to steady herself as they disembarked. Outside the bus, the stenches of sweat and urine filled the streets. A homeless glucksboten—a goblin faerie with the power of luck—with tattoos under his eyelids, pointed ears, and short stature held out his shabby top hat for faecoin in exchange for his luck, though everyone knew it was a trick. Luck went both ways, and if one gave him a penny, they could find themselves losing their livelihood just as easily as winning the lottery. It was a fool's game.

She still felt sorry for him as a troll with large gauges and a spike through his nose knocked the glumorgeist to the ground with his fat belly.

Maverick weaved a path down the sidewalk and took a turn down a narrow alleyway that was far less crowded. He didn't let go of her hand, even though there was barely anyone around, save for a scantily clad dryad with vibrant green irises who meandered by and a few stark, skinny junkies, their bones nearly visible through their purple skin as they came down from their pixie-dust highs, from the looks of the swirls in their eyes. Whatever fae they'd been before they got hooked was unrecognizable, and they lay about useless in homeless groups.

Bile rose up in her mouth. She wanted to vomit and scream at them all at the same time. She wanted to curse them for what they did to her kind, not to mention what they did to themselves.

But she had to remind herself that, even if she did that, users would still use as long as dealers were still dealing. It didn't matter if the Fae Tribunal had already made it illegal. It didn't change anything. The only thing that would stop it was if the supply completely ran out and her kind ceased to exist. There had to be a better way. A way to end this without more death.

She balled her hands into fists and forced her eyes to look away.

"Did it make you happy when your kind hunted mine?" she asked, her voice tight.

Maverick glanced over his shoulder at a deteriorating fae, pity in his gaze. "Not one bit. And I never joined them."

"How?" she prodded. "You are a born Lunar wolf. Grew up in their ways. Haven't you all had some decades-long deal with an elf gang to supply them with enough pixie dust to last generations?"

He ground his teeth. "One of the many reasons I refused to participate."

She frowned and studied his features. He was telling the truth. Perhaps there was more to this arrogant faeboy werewolf after all. "But wouldn't they have rejected you for insubordination? I've never heard of a wolf breaking pack law."

"*I rejected them.*" he said, fixing her with a stare that said he was finished with the topic of his old life before masking it with one she couldn't quite figure out. He took her hand in his. "Now, let's sell this married thing, shall we?"

She rolled her eyes but didn't remove her hand. She didn't mind the warmth. It kept her focused on the present instead of the endless worries that kept creeping in.

He held her close, dodging a homeless junkie who swiped at their ankles. By the size of the fae, she was sure had the junkie not been under the influence, it would've been a fair fight. But because of what the addiction had done to the junkie's body, leaving deep holes in their spidery legs and bat wings, they were no threat to them anymore. Even if the fae wanted help, she'd heard on the news that the addiction treatment centers were overrun and heavily underfunded.

For the addicts, there probably was nothing she could do, not without going back to school, but for her people... she had to find another way. Create a competing drug, perhaps, that didn't involve hunting and killing pixies. An added bonus would be if it were less devastating on the users. But as of yet, she hadn't made any progress toward this. No combination of herbs or enchanted elements resembled the compounds she'd studied in her own pixie dust. When she figured this out, it would change everything.

On the other hand, it would be better if everyone just stopped putting bad things into their bodies, but if fae were going to use anything to chase a high, they might as well use what wouldn't kill them and the innocent pixies who were hunted for it. For that, she'd keep experimenting.

They came to a nondescript building nestled at the end of the alleyway. A neon open sign flickered above a crusty window with peeling letters stuck to it reading Bar. She couldn't imagine this place ever being as classy as the Crystal.

Maverick paused in front of the bar, a hand on the door, and whispered, "You should do whatever you did to your eyes and ears when I first met you. Yours will draw too much attention."

Understanding what he met, Zera reached for her pixie dust within. There wasn't much magic left inside. She'd used more than she'd ever had before these last few hours and didn't know when her power would be back to full capacity. She would have to stick close to Maverick.

When the brown film across her irises was safely in place, Maverick took one last look around to ensure they weren't being followed before he yanked the door open and they entered the seedy bar.

Gritty darkness enveloped them, punctuated by the flicker of cigarette lighters and candles on every table. A haze of blue smoke hung in the air, making everything look like it was underwater. The smell of stale beer and body odor made Zera's stomach turn.

Maverick guided her closer to him, as if to protect her, and she didn't fight back. Even though she worked in a tavern, this place felt entirely different. It was darker, more dangerous, and the atmosphere was thick with an eerie tension that sent shivers down her spine. Perhaps it was just that she was here under false pretenses, but either way, something didn't sit right.

"Stay by my side," Maverick whispered in her ear, his breath warm against her skin. Despite her reservations about him, the closeness provided a sense of security she couldn't deny.

She nodded, unable to speak as they moved through the dimly lit space. Though it was still early in the day, the bar was already filled with patrons, all in various stages of drunkenness. Zera couldn't help but feel out of place, her clean clothes and straight posture giving away the fact that she didn't belong here.

Supernatural beings of all shapes and sizes were scattered across the room, some hunched over tables nursing their drinks while others engaged in heated conversations. A group of goblins laughed raucously in one corner, their hooked noses snorting up the thick smoke that hung in the air. Across from them, a pair of vampires sat in silence, their red eyes gleaming with hunger while demons played a heated game of cards and a rowdy group of werewolves howled and drank malt beer from chipped mugs.

Bone cracked as a monstrous, scale-tatted dragon shifter stretched and eyed them both warily as they passed by. Maverick didn't have to remind her to stay close. She was practically glued to his side and tried not to make eye contact. Dragon shifters were known to be dangerous, and if he could shoot fire out of his mouth like the sigil branded on his neck suggested, then Zera definitely didn't want to draw more attention to herself.

The bartender, a snake shifter with slits for pupils and a forked tongue that jetted out at random intervals, leered at Maverick when they reached the counter. "What'll it be?"

Maverick smirked back. "Forgefire Whiskey on the rocks, and my darling Charlotte here will—"

"She'll have the same," Zera cut in, her cheeks heating up at the sudden nickname.

She ignored Maverick's look of warning. She hated others speaking on her behalf, regardless of the situation, and she was certain she would regret consuming anything else this unclean, fae-forsaken dump had to offer.

"She'll have the same, then." He tossed his faecoin card onto the wooden surface. "Keep the tab open, and tell Quill that Dane's here. He'll know why."

The snake shifter grinned, showing off rows of glistening, jagged teeth. "Coming right up."

When the bartender was well out of earshot, Maverick wrapped a strong arm across her shoulders and leaned into her, pressing his whole body against her.

"I thought I told you to follow my lead," he growled, his breath hot on her ear.

"I am," she replied, her voice barely a whisper as she turned into him. Their eyes met. "Would anyone believe a strong, lone faeboy wolf like yourself would ever marry a pushover?"

Maverick's eyes narrowed, a faint glimmer of amusement tugging at the corners of his lips. His eyes roamed every inch of her face, as if he was both committing it to memory and searching for any signs of deception. Zera held her breath, hating her traitorous eyes that flitted to his lips, remembering the kiss they shared.

She hated that she was drawn to this man, this werewolf, but couldn't help it. There was something about him that made her heart race and her pulse quicken. It almost made her forget what he was. Who he'd grown up as despite his claims that he had never supported his birth pack to begin with. His promise that he was, in fact, different.

Her ex had ruined her trust in werewolves, making her swear off them forever. But here she was, sitting next to one, feeling a pull toward him that she desperately tried to ignore.

The bartender's irises flickered black before a glass materialized in front of her, a single ice cube glistening within. Amber liquid filled the glass from the bottom, as if the counter itself were the bottle.

"Who are we meeting, exactly?" Zera asked, inhaling the smoky blend of grains infused with heat from the forges off the Fire Cliffs, the land just south of the Spire Alps belonging to the dwarves.

"Someone who'll help us get everything we need," Maverick explained, his eyes scanning their surroundings with practiced ease. "He's reliable and discreet, which is exactly what we need."

She followed his gaze, looking for exits in case they needed a sudden escape. There was only one, and it was blocked now by the dragon shifter who still eyed her over the rim of his frothy beer mug.

"Sounds like we're in good hands, then," Zera said, her voice light as she tried to hide the nervousness that still gripped her. She took another sip of her drink, the hot liquid doing its magic in easing her tense muscles.

Maverick leaned in closer to her, his lips nearly brushing her ear. "Don't worry, Zera. I'll always protect my *wife*," he whispered, barking that last word in a stark reminder to get back into character as his fingers trailed circles along her fair skin.

Goose bumps swept down her arms, the touch too intimate. Zera suppressed a rush of emotions that threatened to overwhelm her, the conflicting desires swirling like a tempest. Maverick's words, laced with possessiveness and protection, resonated deep within her, stirring something she thought she had buried. Something she'd only been foolish to allow herself to feel once before.

She bit her tongue until her eyes watered to keep her mind from going down that path. Maverick was only a means to an end. She would follow him to Gareth, use whatever magic she had to end him and whatever thugs were targeting her to protect her son, and then she'd leave him like the heinous Lunar Brotherhood wolf he was, pack deserter or not.

"Kiss me," he said huskily. His lips were too close to her ear. "Look at me, and kiss me."

She clenched her fists under the table, fighting the urge to show her true feelings. It was only the charade they'd agreed to, right? She had to play his wife. A wife would kiss him now. In front of all these fae. But it wasn't the fact that she was forced to play his wife that tormented her. No, it was the fact that every fiber in her being wanted to kiss him. Wanted to put her hands on him. Wanted his hands on her. She wanted it more than anything. She was a fool. She should loathe the ground he walked on simply because of who his family was, what they'd done to her kind, and because he was an arrogant faeboy.

Yet he was sticking his neck out for her as much as she was for him. Both of them were risking something to gain something even more important. Their lives. Their freedom. Hadn't he also vowed to protect her and her son? That was who she was here for. That was who she was fighting for.

Glancing around the seedy bar, with floors that stuck to her shoes with each step, she noticed it wasn't just the dragon shifter who eyed them now. A few other curious fae patrons had taken an interest in their whispered conversation and watched them, their eyes narrowed.

Taking a deep breath, Zera turned her gaze toward him, the film of brown tenting his steely gray eyes. Her pixie dust was still low, but she had enough to keep her disguise. She hoped it would last long enough.

The hunger in Maverick's eyes startled her. No one had ever looked at her with such longing, and whether it was part of his cover or not, it matched her own desires. It was a dangerous game they played, one that blurred the lines between reality and pretense. But she had no other choice. Maverick was her only ally, the self-proclaimed lone wolf.

Her lips claimed his with a fierce desperation, the taste of urgency mingled with a bittersweet surrender. She would play the part of his wife. She'd be Charlotte until she could be Zera and be reunited with her son once again.

The taste of Maverick, a mixture of whiskey and something wild, flooded her senses, igniting a fire within her that she would never admit to. It was only a cover. At least that was what she told herself. His arms stroked her back, pulling her closer, deepening the kiss as his tongue danced with hers. Slowly at first but then harder as desire coiled tightly within her, threatening to consume all rational thought.

"Well, look who the troll dragged in," a voice purred behind them, deep and velvety smooth.

It was a voice she wanted to drown out with a simple flick of her wrist, but she knew better. If she wanted to stop Gareth, bring down whoever was after her, and finally be reunited with her son, she had to follow the plan. She had to become Charlotte Brown.

CHAPTER 7

ZERA

MAVERICK LET OUT A MOAN, AND HIS TEETH PULLED AT HER BOTTOM LIP, AS if reluctant to pull away. Zera's heart skipped a beat, the rhythm of their charade momentarily shattered by the interruption.

She pulled away, and one look at Maverick told her the kiss had been planned. She forced her breathing back into a normal pace, cursing herself for forgetting the line. It was all for show, and she should be happy about that.

Zera followed Maverick's gaze as a tall man approached them, his wild curls tied back in a casual bun. He wore nothing but a vest that exposed a tattooed serpent that wound its way from his tanned stomach to his left temple and leather pants that hugged his thighs like a second skin.

"I hate to interrupt such a moment between newlyweds," he said, his eyes flickering demon violet in the low light. "But when I heard the infamous Dane was here inquiring about my services, I had to come myself."

"Quill. It's been a long time." Maverick kept a protective hand on the small of Zera's back as he shook the demon's hand with his free one.

"It has. It's good to see you again, old friend," he said as his knowing gaze fell on her.

Zera had a feeling he knew something they didn't, but she couldn't figure out what or why. There was something off about him, and she wasn't sure if she could trust him.

"This is Charlotte," Maverick said with a smile, pulling her hand into his and placing a gentle kiss on her knuckles. "*My* Charlotte."

The power that rippled off this demon made her cringe inwardly. Suddenly Maverick's advice of sticking to "mostly truths" made sense. She didn't want Quill knowing who she really was. But her heart still raced, and she hoped the demon couldn't hear it. Their role-playing had officially begun, but she wasn't ready to be Charlotte Brown. She didn't have a clue what she was doing.

"Congrats. May the fae bless you." Quill barely gave her a bored glance before he turned and nodded toward a doorway at the back she hadn't noticed before. "Follow me."

The demon led the way past the bar to the doorway she was certain hadn't been there. A green snake with intricate demon sigils for scales was etched on either side of the doorframe.

"Hold my hand," the demon said, reaching both of his hands out.

Zera didn't ask the question of why that bubbled up her throat. She had a feeling this demon wouldn't care, and if she were truly married to Maverick—or his alias, Dane—she didn't think Charlotte would even care to ask. She would probably be used to all of this.

They both took hold of the demon's hands and stepped through the threshold. Maverick ducked under, his height brimming the doorframe. The air rippled around them as they passed through, and her skin prickled. The sigils. It must be a way to keep outsiders from entering or even seeing this passageway, same as the one at Haven Wolf Tavern.

She exhaled when they made it through the ward unscathed. A long staircase illuminated by violet lamps welcomed them, matching the demon's eyes.

Quill flashed her a wry grin, as if sensing her unease. "This way."

They descended the gritty steps that spiraled down, each step farther into darkness, until they finally reached a dimly lit room that smelled of ink and sulfur. Shelves lined the walls, filled with various tools and materials, and at the center of the room was a large, cluttered worktable.

"Welcome to my lair," Quill said as he waved his hand to indicate the chaos surrounding them.

Zera's eyes darted around the room, taking in the peculiar pieces of machinery that lay about on random tables, tools she'd never seen before but instinctively knew held immense power. The largest one tucked in the corner caught her eye, an industrial piece of equipment with crystals and runes cut into it. Each symbol glowed in various colors, as if waiting to activate whatever operation it triggered. She didn't have a clue what it did or how it was operated, but she had a feeling it was incredibly illegal to own, let alone use.

"And this"—Quill motioned to the giant machine she eyed—"is my masterpiece. My life's work. The Ethereal Forger."

"Humble as always, I see." Maverick chuckled, tossing his backpack on a tiny couch pushed against the only remaining wall that wasn't littered with equipment.

Zera followed suit, setting her stuff down, and tried to look at ease, even though her heart raced with a mix of awe and apprehension.

Quill's persistent grin deepened, and his violet eyes flickered. "Don't pretend like you're not always impressed with my work, Dane Brown. It's why you've worked all these years undetected, though rumor has it you've gone sloppy and let someone discover your true identity."

"Not sloppy. Just betrayed, and I'd like to know who," he growled, his eyes narrowing at Quill.

His bushy blond brows vanished into his curls. "You think I did this? You're my best customer. Really, my reputation alone keeps me in business, and that would shut me down for good. Besides, I never knew your true identity from the start."

Maverick sighed. "You're right. It's hard to know who to trust these days. I had to ask."

"Of course." Quill gave him a pitying *tsk* before shrugging it off. "Well, I assume you need papers for her, a coin card, accounts, and a new faestone?"

"Yes. And it needs to be untraceable."

"Naturally," Quill shot over his shoulder as he meandered to his Ethereal Forger.

"And I need three faestones this time."

"Three?" He whistled as he pressed his hand against various runes on the forger, which whirred to life. "My prices have increased since the last time you had me create your identity, Dane Brown."

"You always do good work for me," Maverick said with a smirk. "Have it charged to my tab."

Zera noticed he didn't ask for the exact total, but she wasn't entirely sure she wanted to know what the going rate was for illegal identifications and untraceable faestones. It couldn't have been cheap. But it would be worth it to be able to video chat with Jade and Sloane and to see Cole again, hear his coos and baby talk. Even if it was just through a lens.

Her heart ached as she wanted to be there to cradle him in her arms until he went to sleep. She didn't even know what time it was, since there weren't any windows in this deep cellar-like lair, but she was pretty sure it was nearly late afternoon. Jade would probably be making him something to eat before starting the bedtime routine. She didn't know what she would do with her evening without her little one to care for.

Guilt hit her like a wave and flooded her with doubt. She knew she'd had no choice but to leave Cole with Jade, the only person she would trust to take care of him while she did what needed to be done to ensure their safety. Still, the thought of not being there for him made her insides churn.

As Quill worked, Maverick took up a space near a giant cabinet as far away from her as possible. She frowned. So much for keeping up their role-playing. Why did he get to pick and choose when they were to stay in character?

The charged silence between Maverick and Zera filled the room, thick as the enchanted fog that often rolled through Havenwood from the north. Zera's gaze flickered to him unintentionally, catching a glimpse of those piercing, storm-filled eyes that seemed to see right through her. She quickly looked away, feeling an unbidden warmth spread across her cheeks. What was she, some pixie teen hyped up on hormones? She had to get a grip. Some type of control over these feelings that betrayed all reasoning.

"Almost done, Charlotte," Quill murmured, his voice pulling Zera back from the brink of whatever dangerous precipice she found herself teetering on when it came to Maverick.

"Charlotte?" she repeated, the name foreign on her tongue.

"Your identity," Quill said with a finalizing tap on the Ethereal Forger in front of him before he snapped his fingers and an image fluttered above one of the runes. "Charlotte Brown, elf-born elemental from the Lunar Forest with a clean slate."

Zera ground her teeth at the mention of the Lunar Forest, just south of her hometown in Pixie Hollow. It was a forest she knew well but one pixies, for obvious reasons, didn't dare venture into. But she guessed if she was to be playing wife to a Lunar wolf, with a pack or not, she might as well embrace it.

She leaned in, scrutinizing the image of herself, now sporting brown eyes instead of her usual lavender. Of course, not even Quill knew she was a pixie. Or did he? He seemed to pride himself on deception. Perhaps he was only pretending not to know Maverick's true identity. But right now, he was the only one helping them, so if Maverick trusted him, then she guessed she would have to as well.

Her heart raced at the thought of becoming someone else, temporarily or not. The intricacy of the holographic seals and the flawless forgery of the governmental Fae Realm insignia were impressive. Quill had outdone himself.

"Quite the craftsman, aren't you, Quill?" Maverick quipped from behind her, leaning against the cold stone wall, arms crossed. His nonchalance grated on her nerves.

Did he not realize she was having to step into the shoes of someone else entirely? Did he care that even this paper separated her further from the only person who mattered to her?

She cleared her throat, shaking off her sudden emotion before the moisture that threatened to brim her eyes spilled. If she let her guard down in front of this demon, her brown film covering up her pixie irises would slip, and she couldn't risk that. There were too many who already knew she had pixie dust. She didn't need to add to that list.

"Let's hope your untraceable faestones are half as convincing," Zera retorted with a forced casualness, her eyes meeting Maverick's for a fleeting moment. She thought she detected a bit of pride, but it was quickly masked back into his look of indifference.

"Please, this is what I do," Quill sneered as he moved to the worktable, waving his hand again, and suddenly, an envelope appeared in a puff of violet smoke on the table in front of him. "Everything you need—faestones, documents—all of it is in here."

Zera reached for the envelope, her fingers brushing against Maverick's as he also extended his hand. The brief touch sent a spark up her arm, igniting something dangerous within her chest. She withdrew swiftly, letting Maverick take the envelope and tuck it under his arm.

"Thank you, Quill," Maverick said, checking the envelope to ensure it was all accounted for before handing Zera her ID and faecoin card.

She tucked the documents in her backpack before slipping her arms through the strap, matching Maverick's smirk with a challenging lift of her chin. Inside, though, her thoughts were a whirlwind. This man, who annoyed her to no end, somehow managed to stir a flutter in her stomach that she couldn't quite quell.

But she had more important things to focus on. Her son. His safety. Zera reminded herself of these priorities as she followed

Maverick's confident stride out of Quill's lair to the staircase, the weight of her new identity resting on her shoulders.

"Oh, I wouldn't leave that way if I were you," Quill's voice purred behind them.

They both froze. Violet smoke puffed in front of them as Maverick's image displayed itself out of thin air and New Bounty flickered in bright-red letters across his face.

"Looks like you've got a bounty on your head," Quill said, appearing beside them. "Ooh, and it looks like it's a juicy one meant for both of you."

"What does it say?" Maverick demanded when his image vanished in another cloud of smoke.

Quill fixed him with a firm stare. "It says it's offering one million faecoin for one Dane Brown, logistics strategist—you, obviously. But it also mentions an additional million for his pixie companion with pixie dust. Alive."

His gaze shifted to Zera, and she gulped. "You didn't mention she was a pixie."

Maverick stepped in front of her, blocking Quill's path to her. "You've never needed to know before."

The room fell quiet again, both men debating their next move.

She cleared her throat, trying to deflect from the panic that threatened to set in. "Well, at least they want us alive."

And at least they didn't use a picture of her. There was still a chance she could get out of this.

Quill's gaze moved to hers, and Maverick reached his arm to block his path. "Make a move for her, and you're dead," Maverick growled.

"Dane, do you really think I would stoop so low?" He arched a blond brow at him. "You're my customer. In my bar, under my protection. You can trust me. Besides, I make more than that in a week. I have no intention of getting into the bounty game."

He turned and strolled back to his worktable. Maverick kept his eyes glued to every move the demon made, and Zera couldn't blame him for his concern.

"Now," Quill continued, "the fae upstairs will all have seen this notice by now, and I can't make any promises for them."

The dragon shifter and his probing eyes flickered in her mind.

"How do we know this is real?" Maverick asked.

Quill tilted his head. "Dane, when have I ever been anything but honest?"

Maverick didn't respond but had a look as if he knew Quill was telling the truth. Even if he wasn't, could they risk going upstairs with all of those fae ready to pounce in order to get their bounty?

"Whoever's after you isn't messing around," Quill said, his voice carrying a hint of concern. "These bounties don't come up often, especially with that kind of price tag. You must have really pissed someone off."

Zera's heart thumped erratically as she tried to process the gravity of the situation. There were no other exits that she could see down here. How did Quill expect them to leave?

"Gareth," Maverick said, finally taking a breath and running a hand through his dark, crisply cut hair. "We had a run-in with him at the Crystal. Tried to kill... Charlotte because of her pixie dust. She's a walking target if anyone finds out, so please—"

"I won't tell a soul. You have my word," Quill said, his voice firm and his gaze steady. "Rumor has it that Gareth's gotten himself in bed with a much bigger kelpie."

"Who?" Maverick prodded, gripping the straps of his backpack so hard his knuckles turned white.

Quill shrugged. "That I don't know, but I heard he's looking to get into the drug business now that his arms dealing has fizzled out, though I wouldn't put it past him to be expanding now that he's got a sugarfae who can bankroll him."

Maverick's jaw twitched, glancing between Quill and the bounty that flickered on a monitor behind him. "How many have access to this alert?"

"Other than everyone upstairs?" Quill arched a brow. "Anyone on shadowcom, which is anyone who's anyone in this business nowadays. Really, Dane, are you still determined to work old-school?"

"I prefer not to be tracked more than I am already," Maverick grumbled.

Zera could practically see the gears turning in his head.

"How can we get out of here?" he finally asked the demon, who watched them carefully.

His violet eyes flickered like jewels, and the moment he snapped his fingers, a second winding staircase appeared behind him.

"You can take my emergency exit," he said with a lazy yawn, as if the whole world weren't about to crash through the walls around them.

Maverick nodded, his gaze flicking over to Zera. "We need to move."

Zera nodded, fear making it difficult to move. Her feet felt glued to the floor. She tried to even her breath, her hand going to her mother's locket in her pocket. It seemed to bring her the calm she hoped for.

"And we'll need a car," Maverick said, taking her hand in his before turning back to Quill.

"Obviously." Quill snapped his fingers again, and a set of shiny keys materialized out of violet smoke. "You know where it's parked. I'd suggest you hurry, though. They'll likely suspect you to take the back exit."

"I appreciate it," Maverick replied, taking the keys before rushing to the stairs.

"Never a dull day in the life of Dane Brown," Quill drawled lazily behind them. "Oh, and don't forget your card."

They stopped at the foot of Quill's secret staircase and turned as Maverick's faecoin card flipped through the air with a snap and landed in the wolf's outstretched hand. Zera shuddered to think how powerful this demon's machines were if he had the power to make things appear like that.

"Your tab's been closed." The demon flashed Maverick a devilish grin before glaring down at Zera. "Oh, and pixie?"

Zera met his tense violet eyes, apprehension crawling up her back.

"Please do avoid all government buildings. The Fae Tribunal's security is the only one my IDs can't fool, and I'd rather not have to deal with the mess of relocation."

Zera nodded, a motion that was beginning to be her signature right now.

"Come on, let's get out of here," Maverick said and guided their way up the stairs and out of the underground lair.

A rush of cool night air greeted them as they emerged from the concealed doorway. They must've been down there for hours, since it was already nightfall. She drew in a deep breath, filling her lungs with what she hoped to be fresh air after being stuck in that stifling lair. She immediately regretted it as the scent of wet asphalt mingled with decaying garbage filled her nostrils. It must've rained.

She zipped her coat up against the wind. The alley was deserted, save for the distant echoes of Mystic City's nightlife spilling into the shadows. Maverick took point, striding ahead with a confidence that Zera begrudgingly admired.

A siren in the distance sent her jogging after him.

"Where to next?" she asked, hoping beyond hope it would be to send the untraceable faestone by whatever secret means Maverick had planned to Jade so Zera could finally video chat with her boy.

This was the longest she'd ever been away from him, and the thought of how long it would be before she could hold him again was beginning to send her mind into a spiral of worry and longing.

Maverick held up his forefinger in response, a cue that someone might be listening. Zera glanced over her shoulder at the nondescript building behind them but saw no one.

He led them to a car parked at the corner of the street. How he knew which one the set of keys belonged to was beyond her.

"There you are," a gruff voice hissed from the shadows. "Thought you two ran off without giving me a shot at your sweet little heads."

Zera swallowed hard when the dragon shifter stepped out from behind the car they were headed for, his nasty tattoo gleaming in the moonlight. His eyes flared as they met hers, and she knew in an instant that he might not kill her, but she would be nearly dead if they didn't get out of there soon.

"Get behind me," Maverick gritted out, his hands balled into fists as his wolf muscles bulged.

Zera's heart hammered against her rib cage. He didn't have to ask her twice. The dragon shifter from the bar, with the intricate tattoo that seemed to write on his nearly iridescent skin, stood between them and their only means of escape. His presence sent a primal warning through her, every instinct screaming at the danger he posed.

"Planning on taking us in for that bounty, are you?" Maverick's tone was deceptively casual, but Zera could feel the coiled tension in him ready to spring.

"Thought you'd never ask," the shifter growled, the smirk on his face not reaching his cold eyes.

The silence that followed was electric. Zera could almost feel Maverick's wolf senses sharpening, his body preparing for the inevitable confrontation.

"Zera, take the keys," Maverick whispered without moving his gaze from the dragon shifter, whose eyes flashed with fire. "And when I say run, you run straight to the car, got it?"

"I will, but next time I'm joining you," she muttered, hating that he had to fight her battles for her. She wasn't used to men doing that, but she wasn't used to life-threatening fights either.

"Stubborn pixie," he murmured, a trace of admiration in his voice.

"Bloody arrogant faeboy," she shot back, and she could've sworn she saw the hint of a smile.

Maverick's stance shifted imperceptibly, and Zera knew it was about to happen. Time seemed to slow down as the dragon shifter took a menacing step forward, scales rippling down his arms. He opened his mouth, the faintest hint of flames dancing at the edges of his graying lips.

"Run!" Maverick barked, and Zera's body responded before her mind could argue. She darted toward the car, her minimal flight powers giving her speed an extra boost.

Behind her, the sounds of violence erupted—a snarl, a roar, the unmistakable sound of flesh hitting flesh. She reached the car, the door unlocking the moment she was close, and she slid into the driver's seat and locked the doors behind her.

She tossed her backpack in the rear seat, sparing a glance at Maverick, who landed a solid hit, but the dragon shifter wasn't going down without a fight. The thought to leave, to head south for Pixie Hollow sprang to mind, and her fear made it tempting. But she couldn't leave Maverick, not when he was fighting for their lives and definitely not with a bounty on her head. She would never survive.

"Come on, Maverick!" she yelled, but he couldn't hear her.

She watched in horror as the dragon shifter's powers increased, spraying fire at Maverick. Smoke plumed in the air from the heat. Maverick dodged the fire at the last second, trying to find a way to defeat him. Movement behind Maverick caught her eye, and she suddenly realized the dragon shifter wasn't alone. Maverick was caged in.

"Drive!" she heard Maverick shout, his voice strained.

She hesitated, torn between the urge to flee and the desire to aid him. But as the brawl grew more vicious, she knew what she had to do.

With a deep breath, she reached for her pixie dust. Only a glimmer was left, but maybe, just maybe it would buy him enough time. She let the trickle of power swirl up her spine, and she fluttered her fingers at the figures standing behind him.

Purple sparkled at their ankles as invisible bands tied their feet together, immobilizing them as they were about to launch themselves at Maverick.

He didn't even look when they all toppled behind him as he dodged another burst of fire. The dragon lashed out with flame after flame. Maverick dodged each attempt, getting closer to the dragon shifter with each lunge. Scaly wings slid from the shifter's back as he prepared to shift into full-on dragon form. The dragon shifter lashed out in one last attempt.

Maverick propelled himself into the air, shifting into wolf form in the blink of an eye. His jaw clamped down on the dragon shifter's scaly neck, a growl reverberating through his chest.

The dragon shifter shrieked in agony, its fiery breath dissipating into feeble wisps of smoke. Maverick's grip tightened, teeth sinking deeper into the thick flesh as he refused to let go until victory was secured.

Zera blinked. The dragon shifter stopped moving, but his posse still writhed against her trap, trying to get a swipe at Maverick. His bloodied wolf face shadowed over the dying beast as he howled a triumphant cry before sliding back into his human form.

She started the engine and unlocked the door for Maverick.

The commotion from the other fae in the street reached a fever pitch, and she knew her bindings were wearing off. They screamed for his death, swearing to slit their throats. Her heart lodged in her throat as she noticed him limp toward her, dodging a lightning whip that lashed out from the darkness.

"Go!" Maverick's voice cut through the stillness, his form still partially shifted, fur bristling with aggression.

He all but collapsed into the passenger seat, sweat dripping down his broad chest, which peeked out from his shredded clothes. There was no sign of his backpack, but perhaps it didn't matter. At least they had their lives. And her home science lab. She longed for a quiet moment to unpack her home lab and actually try to create the controlled conditions for the everfrost blossom, which would prove difficult, but it would be a welcome change from everything she'd experienced in the last twenty-four hours.

"Drive," he growled, his stormy eyes still swirling with wolf rage, and he slammed the door shut.

Zera didn't need another word. She pushed the pedal to the floor, the car's tires screeching as they peeled away from the alley and the defeated dragon shifter and his posse behind them.

"Are you okay?" she asked, glancing at Maverick's rugged profile, looking for signs of injury.

"I'll heal," he grunted, shifting back into his fully human form. It was true—he would. But as Zera drove through the night, the tightness in her chest eased a little because they were both still alive. Alive and together, despite everything.

CHAPTER 8

MAVERICK

The first rays of sunlight filtered through the curtains, casting a warm glow over the living room. Maverick stirred on the couch, his sleep-addled mind slowly registering where he was. His penthouse in the heart of the city, a place he inhabited only when he was Dane Brown.

He'd hoped to never return to that oversized one-bedroom, two-story glorified apartment with its rooftop garden, infinity pool, and balcony. The place wasn't him. Decorated with costly, useless figurines that he'd been told by the decorator were priceless. Paintings, worth fortunes that held no meaning, scattered along any available wall that wasn't ceiling-to-floor windows. It was the home of a cold, calculating logistics strategist, not the lone werewolf in his heart.

The quiet life Zera led in Havenwood with her son sounded much preferable. He envied the simple days she must've enjoyed living in a home that wasn't a cover or basically a military base ready for missions. He wondered what that would be like, to live a life in which the only things he had to worry about were getting to work on time and caring for his family. An ordinary life for an ordinary were-wolf. But that wasn't his life.

He stretched out his limbs, the soreness from yesterday's events reminding him of the reason he was here playing a married man.

His eyes followed the stairs leading up to the bedroom occupied by Zera, who'd saved his life last night, a fact that still intrigued him. She could've driven away when they were attacked, left him to fend for himself. But she didn't. Instead, she used her pixie magic to save him despite barely knowing him.

If she hadn't used her pixie magic to trap the dragon shifter's buddies, he would have certainly been outnumbered.

Sure, he probably would have put a dent in them, but they were strong, and he didn't doubt that they would have brought him down eventually. He hated to think about what might've happened to her if he'd failed.

But neither of them had failed, and she had stayed despite his background that stirred something inside of him. The urge to suppress those feelings gnawed at him, but even he knew it wouldn't be easy.

Then there was the bounty on their heads. He scratched his head, knowing this would only make their mission to find Gareth and his current employer more difficult. He was probably the one who had put the bounty on their heads in the first place. Perhaps it would've been smart just to let one of the bounty hunters bring them to Gareth and be done with it. But something told him if any of the bounty hunters caught them, they'd be lucky to remain alive.

That, and Maverick refused to be caught on someone else's terms. Their best shot at survival was finding Gareth on their own. At least then they'd have the element of surprise.

Maverick rolled off the couch, his muscles protesting as he stood up. As much as he wanted to dwell on his thoughts, he needed a distraction. Making breakfast—a mundane household chore that usually helped him clear his mind—seemed like a good idea.

He moved around the kitchen with practiced ease, even if he

hadn't been here in months. It was a room that was a constant no matter where he lived, and all he needed were a few ingredients and a functioning stove.

Opening the refrigerator—which was stocked, thanks to the request he'd made of his newly set-up faestone—he grabbed what he needed and prepared their meal. The sizzling sound of eggs frying and the aroma of coffee brewing filled the spacious penthouse, offering a sense of normalcy in an otherwise-chaotic situation.

The sound of a door opening followed by footsteps upstairs caught his attention, and Maverick turned his head in time to see Zera emerge from the staircase leading to the bedroom and rooftop garden. Her hair tumbled over her shoulder in loose waves, her lavender eyes sparkling with a mix of amusement and curiosity. The simple sight of her struck him like a bolt of lightning, leaving him momentarily lost for words.

"Good morning," she greeted, a hint of a smile gracing her lips. "I didn't expect to wake up to the smell of breakfast."

"Morning," Maverick rumbled, trying to sound nonchalant as he busied himself with flipping the eggs in the pan. "Figured we could both use a decent meal before we get on with our day."

"Thanks, I appreciate it," Zera said, moving closer to the kitchen counter.

As she leaned against the counter, watching him cook, Maverick was acutely aware of her presence. It was unsettling and exhilarating at the same time, leaving him unsure of how to react. But for now, he focused on finishing their breakfast because that was a task he could handle without losing his bearings.

"How'd you sleep?" He had been happy to sleep on the couch while she took the primary bedroom. This house never felt like his anyway, and the spare bathroom had the essentials.

"Good. It's quiet," she said with a yawn as Maverick plated the eggs and poured coffee into two mugs. "So, what's the plan for today?"

The steam danced through the air, creating a cozy atmosphere despite the uptight decor. Even the furniture was made of cold, sleek metal that seemed too pristine for everyday use. Somehow, even years of spy work had made him feel more like an imposter with each case, and despite what he'd told Zera about it getting easier, it didn't. It just got... different.

Maverick took a sip of his coffee, savoring the rich, bitter taste. His eyes flitted to Zera as she seemed to do the same. He set his mug down and sighed.

"Well, first I need to get this faestone shipped to Jade's address down in Pixie Hollow," he explained, his voice steady as he tried to keep his focus on the task at hand.

A hard feat to do when Zera moved her toned legs up to her chest, as if curling her whole body around the mug. Maverick's gaze involuntarily followed the graceful curve of her body, his mind momentarily veering off course.

Zera caught his lingering look, and her eyebrows shot up in mock surprise. A playful smirk tugged at the corners of her lips, betraying her amusement.

"And by shipping the faestones, you mean...?" She twirled the stirrer in her coffee absently, the movement sending ripples through the dark liquid.

Maverick cleared his throat, quickly averting his gaze and regaining his composure. "By means that won't raise suspicion."

"But you won't tell me how?"

"No," he said with finality, digging into his food. "You just focus on the mission."

She didn't need to know he was planning on giving them to a clan of were-chameleons who specialized in smuggling almost anything past the border guards without raising suspicion. He had a feeling she would be hesitant to trust any were-fae, even if they weren't like the pack he'd fled from.

He'd already made the arrangements. They were to meet him in the downstairs bar at eleven on his way out. He doubted she would even notice the transaction.

"The mission of being your wife?" she teased, throwing him a kiss and biting her lip before popping a piece of bacon in her mouth.

He nearly choked on his food. The seductive undertones in Zera's voice caught him off guard. He coughed, attempting to regain his composure as he avoided eye contact with her.

"Being Mrs. Charlotte Brown is part of the cover story," he replied, his voice slightly strained. "Which you'll have to commit to during our main objective today."

He dared a glance at Zera and masked how his heart quickened at her playful demeanor with a look of indifference. She already thought he was a bloody arrogant faeboy. Might as well act like one.

"Oh?" She arched her brow. "And what's that?"

A smug grin crept onto Maverick's face as he realized she was the type of woman who liked to be in control, and here in his world, she had to play by his rules, and it made her... nervous. Just like being around a pixie made him. He leaned back against the counter, exuding an air of self-assured confidence.

His voice dripped with amusement as he responded, "We're going to get you fitted for war."

"War?" Zera's eyebrows furrowed in confusion.

"Don't worry about it," Maverick replied, his jaw set in a cocky manner. He knew the mysterious would put her on edge, and he enjoyed seeing her squirm a little. "You'll see soon enough."

Zera glowered, but to Maverick's surprise, she didn't prod him on the topic as they finished their breakfast.

"And how's your... hobby coming along?" he asked, hoping to distract from the lingering tension between them.

She shrugged. "I think I've been able to recreate the right conditions for the seedlings I brought."

"Oh?" He hadn't the faintest clue what sort of plant was so important that she had to bring it with her along with a whole science lab, but she'd stubbornly refused to leave it at home. "And what are those?"

"You really want to know?" She arched her brow.

"Sure."

"Well," she began, leaning forward with excitement, "first, I had to consider the natural habitat of the everfrost blossom." She noticed his confusion. "It's a rare flower that blooms only once every five hundred years in the Spire Alps."

"So it will only grow in a very cold, snowy climate?" he asked.

"Exactly, and with plenty of sun, which the south-facing windows in the room upstairs provide," she said, the light in her eyes drawing him in. The sheer passion in her voice was intoxicating. "But I needed to figure out the snow and temperature situation without setting your thermostat to arctic levels."

"I appreciate that." He chuckled. "Were you able to figure it out?"

She nodded, beaming from ear to ear. She was devastatingly beautiful in her element. "My home lab kit isn't much, but it's adaptable. I used my compact glass terrarium as the base and enchanted ice crystals to create a perpetual winter inside. I've got the first seedling growing now."

He couldn't help but admire her. She was smart, resourceful, and determined, but she was a distraction. He needed to stay focused on the mission and not on the naughty ways he wanted to worship her.

Maverick cleared his throat and forced himself to look away from Zera's radiant smile. "That's impressive," he said, trying to sound nonchalant. "So, how does a pixie bartender wind up with such a... unique little hobby?"

"It's not just a little hobby." Her face soured, and Maverick marveled at how beautiful she still looked when she was mad at him. Perhaps even more than when she wasn't. "And, if you must know, I have a degree in faeology and alchemical sciences. Sort of."

"What do you mean 'sort of'?"

"It's a long story I'd rather not get into right now," she said with a grimace. "When do we head out?"

Maverick smirked at her abrupt change of topic, unable to resist the temptation to tease her. "Oh, don't worry, Pixie Professor. I'm sure we'll have plenty of time during our tasks today to engage in lengthy discussions about your 'sort of' degree."

Zera shot him a glare that he took as a challenge. The glint in her eyes only fueled his desire to push her buttons even further.

The tension between them grew with every exchanged glance and snarky retort. Despite his best effort, Maverick found it increasingly difficult to deflect and conceal his growing attraction for Zera. Her wit and independence both fascinated and infuriated him, making it impossible for him to get anything done.

Even after breakfast, she demanded to wash her own dish, though he insisted on doing it for her. She said something about it being the least she could do after he'd made the breakfast or some other excuse.

Her stubbornness would be the bane of his existence, though he had to admire her tenacity. It had only been twenty-four hours since she'd been separated from her son, and she was worried about doing the dishes.

Once they were ready to go, Maverick led the way out of the penthouse and down the elevator to the lobby. His plan to hand off the faestones to the were-chameleons worked perfectly. Zera was too busy explaining to him how, as a mom on a single income, she didn't have the luxury of eating out at the Crystal like he did or living in a rich penthouse like his and how it must be nice to live the faeboy lifestyle. Little did she know this wasn't him at all. Perhaps she would one day see that, but right now his truth wasn't important.

They arrived in the fashion district in minutes, and Maverick reveled in Zera's continued confusion, the anticipation of what was to come only adding fuel to their already heated dynamic.

"A clothing store?" she asked skeptically when he ushered her into the upscale boutique.

Maverick leaned in close, savoring the way it caused an uptick in her heart rate even though she wouldn't admit to it.

"If I'm such a faeboy," he whispered in her ear, "isn't it time you started dressing like my fae-woman?"

The remark awarded him a sarcastic side glance from Zera as she shoved him back. "You wish."

He chuckled, holding the door open and allowing her to enter first.

Inside the boutique, mannequins displayed the latest fashions, and soft music played in the background. But it wasn't the usual fashion they were on a mission for. He approached the statuesque woman behind the checkout counter with fiery red hair, slicked into a pile of curls on top of her head.

"Dane!" She greeted them with a warm smile when she looked up from her work. "It's been too long."

"It has," he replied, grinning as he wrapped an arm around Zera's waist. No time like the present to get into character. Though Felice was an acquaintance of his alias and he trusted her to protect her own, he didn't trust her with Zera's secrets. "This is Charlotte, my wife."

"It's a pleasure to meet you, Charlotte," Felice said, her siren voice melodic and enchanting, as she extended a slender, bejeweled hand to Zera.

"Likewise," Zera replied, shaking her hand politely.

Felice flicked her gaze over Zera appraisingly. Maverick smirked at the way Zera squirmed under the scrutiny. He knew the siren could probably see right through their ruse, but she wouldn't pry. Dane had given her too much business for her to ask questions.

"Let me show you some of our more exclusive collections," Felice suggested, leading them farther into the store.

"Are we really going clothes shopping?" Zera asked, her voice barely above a whisper.

"Not exactly." Maverick gave her an amused look. "The siren does design ordinary clothes, but her exclusive collection involves weaponry. Magic that will help you defend yourself during our missions."

She gawked at him. He just laughed and continued through a more private section in the back of the boutique.

Maverick took a seat on a luxurious couch beside the dressing room while Zera examined the clothes Felice had chosen for her, each piece stylish yet laced with hidden weaponry. He admired how Zera handled herself even while posing as his wife. She was strong, independent, and a devoted mother—traits he found himself envying, especially since he would never have that life.

Then he remembered she was a pixie. A con artist. Even if she did seem different from the pixie who'd tricked him when he was younger, he knew deep down she would always deceive him in the end. It was his curse. That and the curse of being the only lone wolf in a pack world.

But then, Zera had saved his life many times, hadn't she? And she had every reason to hate him, yet she still had his back. Perhaps there was hope that maybe this could be real.

"Will this actually protect me?" Zera asked skeptically, holding up a sleek black dress with a low-cut back he was certain would hug her like a glove.

"Trust me," Felice assured her with a knowing smile. "Each piece is designed to be both fashionable and functional."

As Zera disappeared into the dressing room to try on the clothes, Maverick took the opportunity to speak privately with Felice.

"So... how have things been around here?" he asked, hoping to ease into the questions he really wanted to ask.

Felice gave him a withering look. "Please, Dane. You insult me with small talk?" The siren knew all too well why he'd come here. It was one of her many gifts. "Let's skip the formalities and get to what you want to know."

Maverick shifted forward in his seat. "Do you remember when I came to you the last time?"

"I remember you were on an intel mission with that—oh, what's his name—Gareth, the arms dealer?"

He nodded. "That's the one. Well, he attacked me and my wife while we were at dinner the other night."

"He's back?" Her eyes widened.

"You didn't know?" he asked, shocked that someone like her, who had ears everywhere, hadn't heard.

She shrugged. "It's never come up."

He chewed his lip in thought. If Gareth was back, wouldn't he have made more noise about it? Unless whoever he was working for now was keeping a low profile. Maverick couldn't shake the feeling that there was something bigger at play, something far more dangerous than Gareth alone.

"But," Felice began, her fingers tapping absently on the rack of clothes beside her, "rumor has it that there's a bounty on your head."

Maverick looked up to meet her piercing gaze. "Have you heard anything about it? Do you know if Gareth's behind it?"

Felice shook her head. "Only rumors, nothing concrete. People are talking, but no one seems to know anything for sure."

Maverick frowned at the lack of information. He needed something more substantial if he was going to track down Gareth. "What about anyone he might've been in contact with after I put him out of business?"

"After that, Gareth went dark. No one heard from him." Felice thought for a moment before she said, "But there are whispers of a new player taking over, someone with his talons in everything—drugs, weapons, fae trafficking, money laundering, even the government. He's making quite a name for himself. Might be worth looking into."

"Do you have a name or know where I might find a lead? Someone who could make an introduction?"

"He goes by Kraven. There's a gala tonight, hosted by a notorious underground figure. It's a gathering of the city's most influential criminals, the perfect opportunity to dig for information. I can get you an invitation."

Maverick raised an eyebrow, impressed by Felice's seemingly endless connections. "Sounds like just the kind of party we need. Thank you."

"I should warn you, though. Kraven should not be underestimated. His power in the Fae Realm is ever growing, his influence formidable, and he's dangerous. Did you hear about the bodies found in the Shadowood Forest?"

"You mean the fae that were found skinned alive?"

She nodded, and a chill ran down Maverick's spine. He'd seen the news about it a few months ago.

"From what I hear, that's what happens to fae who cross him, and the authorities won't even dare question him," she said, her grave expression conveying even she was scared of him. "So if I were you, I'd be careful."

"I will take that under advisement," he said, grateful for the information.

The siren gave him a nod as a gesture of acknowledgement as Zera emerged from the dressing room, dressed in one of Felice's creations. In that moment, he had eyes only for the pixie. The form-fitting black gown accentuated her curves and flattered her figure, leaving him momentarily speechless. The black fabric was so dark it seemed to change colors with each movement, from hellfire red to midnight blue, making her appear as enchanting as the night sky itself.

Her fair skin peeked out from the lace that wound up her arms in a floral pattern from her wrists up to her shoulders before plunging down to a daring V-neckline. The bodice hugged her curves in all the right places and accentuated every enticing contour of her body before flowing into a floor-length skirt that swirled with every step she took. A slit ran up the side of the skirt, revealing just enough of her toned leg to make his heart skip a beat.

"Wow," he breathed out, unable to stop himself. "You look incredible."

"Thanks," Zera replied, her cheeks turning a rosy pink. She was clearly pleased by his reaction. "Your friend here does know what she's doing. But I'm pretty sure this is the least practical of all the clothes, and how in the world do the weapons in this thing work?"

A bell chimed at the front door to the shop, gaining Felice's attention. "Why don't I give you two newlyweds some privacy? Dane, I trust you remember the basics of how my fashion works."

Maverick nodded before she disappeared out the small doorway separating the main clothing store from the private showroom and dressing room.

He barely noticed her leaving, his eyes still roaming Zera's figure. When she turned, it nearly knocked the breath right out of him. The fabric stopped at her shoulders, leaving her back bare and exposed all the way down to just above the curve of her lower back, where the intricate lace design continued, a tantalizing sight that sent a delicious shiver down Maverick's spine.

"Right." He stood up and came to join her in front of the mirror, her exquisite reflection looking back at him intently.

"May I?" he asked, lifting his hand to prepare to show her how to activate the few magical defensive weapons that were standard in all of Felice's clothes. But who knew what other secrets a dress like this contained?

"Of course," she said, and he heard her hold her breath.

He kept his eyes on hers while his hands roamed over her body, delicately caressing her skin as he slipped one arm around her to support her waist while the other trailed the delicate fabric down the length of her sleeve, stopping at her wrist.

"When you move this hand in a figure eight"—he demonstrated, moving her wrist in the motion—"a small-yet-effective shield will form around you. It can deflect minor spells and even physical attacks."

Tension coiled within him when he watched her breath visibly hitch in response as energy rippled from the sleeve of her dress. Her jaw dropped in awe as a shimmering, translucent barrier formed around her body for a moment before dissipating when he moved her wrist in the same shape, only in reverse.

"And here"—he laced his fingers through hers and pulled her hand up to her chest—"if you press the heel of your palm against your sternum, the dress will release a burst of light, temporarily blinding your enemies and allowing you to escape or strike back."

"Strike back?" She leaned into him to look up and meet his gaze, her warmth making him harden against her.

He could feel the electricity between them, a magnetic pull that seemed to intensify with every passing moment. His heart raced as he gazed into her eyes, and he saw her vulnerability mingled with a fierce determination. Was it possible for her to fall for a werewolf again? For her to trust him despite who he was born as? Could she accept him for who he was and not be defined by his past?

He shook these thoughts and the primal instincts within him out of his mind. They didn't have time for that. Especially with the echoes of a confrontation coming from the front of the boutique. He knew Felice could handle herself, but it didn't sound like he and Zera had much time.

"With this," he said, finally removing his hand from her waist and moving her right arm in a circular motion so that a dagger perfectly weighted for her size appeared from the sleeve and slid into her hand.

"Oh no." She pulled her hand away from his, but the dagger followed her. She opened her palm to drop it and gasped when the weapon stayed glued to her. "How do I get rid of it? I don't know how to use this thing, and I'll get us both stabbed."

He met her panic with a smirk. "You're in luck, since your pretend husband here is a spy. I'll show you how to use it and the others."

"Others? You mean there are more of these things?" She nearly shouted in frustration as she turned on him, the fabric of her dress swirling around her. "I'm a bartender. I can whip up a mean Moonlit Mule or even a Nightshade Spritz, and I have some rudimentary knowledge in faeology, so... there's that, but I'm mostly just a mom, so if you need a quick diaper change, I've got you. I'm definitely not you. I'm not a trained assassin!"

"I'm not either. I'm a spy."

"Same difference!" she retorted. "This is insane!"

He chuckled at her fiery spirit. It was both endearing and amusing. "I know it seems overwhelming, but trust me. I'm the best at what I do."

She scoffed. "I'm sure you think you are, bloody faeboy."

"It takes one to know one." He shot her a wolfish grin then turned serious. "These weapons are not just for spies. They're tools to protect ourselves and those we care about, like your son. Don't you want to learn to better defend yourself, if not for you then for Cole?"

Zera looked at the dagger in her hand, and he could sense her uncertainty. Finally, she took a deep breath and nodded, straightening her shoulders and meeting his gaze in the mirror. "You're right. I should know how to do this. But how can I... put it back? Do I have to use my pixie dust?"

"No. Tap your pinky finger on the hilt three times. It should vanish."

She did as she was told, and the dagger melted back into the dress.

"Incredible," she whispered, her eyes widening with amazement. "Is there anything else I should know?"

Maverick hesitated for a moment, his eyes searching hers in the reflection. The thump of her heartbeat reached his ears, the rhythm somehow drawing him closer.

"There's one more thing," he finally said, moving his hand to the side of her hip. "If you slide your hand into this hidden pocket"—he carefully ran his hand along the slit of her dress—"you'll find that it'll launch a tiny enchanted smoke bomb that will render vampires and shape-shifters powerless for a short period of time."

"Not elementals?" she asked, a shudder escaping her lips when his fingers briefly touched her thigh.

"Only your shield will work against them," he breathed, not daring to move.

Her eyes flickered down to his lips, and before he thought better of it, he pressed them against hers, his tongue demanding entry. She opened to him, and he welcomed the taste of her desire. Somehow her leg wound up in his hand, wrapped around his waist, and her hands were tangled in his hair, pulling him closer.

Perhaps it was the dress, or perhaps it was the danger that lurked just beyond those walls. Whatever it was it made him forget the differences he knew still lingered. The prejudices and anger for each other's kind. What would confusing the line between their fake marriage and their very real bitterness toward each other do to their already fragile alliance? To their mission?

Maverick groaned, pulling them apart.

Her eyes filled with relief and a hint of longing.

"What's wrong?" she asked, her hands still wrapped around his neck.

"Zera," he whispered, stroking her chin with his thumb. "We can't do this."

"We can," she said breathlessly. "After all, we are married now."

She teased him, pressing her breasts against him.

He growled. It wasn't how it was supposed to be. He wouldn't cross a line, even to retain their cover. Fake relationship or not, once they did this and the heat of the moment was over, what would be left?

No, he couldn't do this. But it was tempting.

"We shouldn't," he said. "We have a job to do."

She stared at him, biting her lip, and his eyes nearly burned with the intensity of his desire for her.

"But I want you."

Maverick groaned, his body reacting to her admission. It was all the wolf within him needed to hear. He slid his other hand around her standing leg so she straddled his waist as he carried her into the private dressing room. Their kiss deepened, and the scent of her arousal hit him hard, igniting a fire deep inside him. He needed to touch her, to feel her come.

"Fae gods, Zera. You'll be the death of me," he murmured against her ear when she pulled the curtain shut behind them.

Desire and lust flashed in her eyes, and he kissed her again. This time, he didn't hold back, his tongue diving deep, tasting and exploring every corner of her mouth as his hands traveled up the slit of her dress and caressed between her thighs. She gasped into his mouth as his fingers brushed the coil of heat radiating from her core, causing her to arch into his touch.

He didn't care if she deceived him in the end, if her saving his life was a ploy to get what she wanted. She could have it. All of it and more. He would bend to her beck and call, kneel before her, and worship her body like the queen she was.

Outside the dressing room, Felice's siren song rang out from the front of the boutique at a decibel only his ears could pick up, warning them of the danger approaching. In his passion-filled haze, he barely registered it.

But then shouts neared and snapped him back to reality. He heaved a frustrated sigh as he pulled them apart. She breathed heavily against him, and he ached to fulfill her needs, wouldn't rest until he ensured she was completely satiated. But now was not that time.

"Wh-What was that?" she stammered, still breathless, her lips swollen from his touch. He would claim them again.

"Nothing good. Stay behind me," Maverick whispered, his voice low and urgent. He could sense the fear in Zera building as she nodded, her eyes wide with concern.

He led the way out of the tiny dressing room into the private showroom at the back of the boutique. There was only one entrance. They'd have to fight their way out of there, then.

"Have your shield ready," he warned Zera, praying that she didn't have to use it.

They inched their way toward the main boutique in time to see a group of suspicious-looking shoppers push past Felice, even though she insisted the store was closed. Maverick's instincts kicked in, and he recognized the threat immediately. As the intruders ignored Felice, she gave Maverick a look of warning. She needed them to stall. This gave him an idea.

Without warning, Maverick pulled Zera back into the dressing room and pulled the curtain shut around them once again, pulling her close against his firm body. His muscles popped as the wolf within primed for action.

"What are we doing? Shouldn't we fight?" she asked, her voice shaking slightly.

"*We* aren't doing anything yet," he said, his tone low. He looked deep into her eyes, seeing the fear and confusion reflected back at him but also the trust and desire that burned like a wildfire. "Zera, I'm sorry we have to do this, but I can't let them hurt you. I'll make sure they don't get close, but I need you to trust me and activate that shield."

She hesitated, her eyes darting back to the curtain and then back to him. "Okay, but be careful."

He brushed his thumb across her cheek, and her eyes briefly closed at the sensual touch. Then his face hardened as he focused on what he had to do. "I will be. Now, stay here, and don't make a sound."

With a deep breath, Maverick swiftly exited the dressing room and prepared to devour whoever attacked first. He could feel the adrenaline pumping through his veins, and he allowed the beast inside him to surge forward. His vision became narrowed and his hearing sharpened as he waited for the first intruder. Whoever they were didn't stand a chance.

CHAPTER 9
ZERA

Zera's heart raced within her chest, quickening its pace as if it wanted to break free. She stood alone in the small dressing room, feeling trapped and vulnerable. Warmth still coiled within her, a reminder of her heated moment with Maverick.

What was she thinking, letting herself get physical with him like that? It would only complicate their situation.

Oh, yeah. Because she was a woman with needs, needs that hadn't been met in way too long.

"Get a grip, Zera," she whispered to herself, taking a deep breath to steady her nerves. But as she did so, her thoughts wandered back to her past experience with werewolves, and she questioned her feelings for Maverick.

He was a born Lunar Brotherhood wolf, hunter of pixies and her kind. It was because of his werewolf pack that pixies feared to use their pixie dust, allowing the gland to dry up and causing future generations to be born without it at all. She was one of the lucky ones. So how could she trust someone like him, let alone feel anything more than contempt for him?

Even if he wasn't from the Lunar pack and was one of the others who didn't care about pixies or involve themselves in the pixie-dust drug game, was she being foolish in thinking he was different from other werewolves who obeyed pack law above everything else? The way she had been with her ex? She didn't want to make the same mistakes twice. She'd learned her lesson once. But still, there was something different about Maverick. Perhaps it was that he was a lone wolf or something else entirely, she didn't know.

What she did know was that their mission relied on them both having clear heads and blurring the line between reality and fiction. What was real was that she was a pixie, and he was a werewolf from a pixie-dust hunting pack. They despised each other for obvious reasons, and they would never work. One of them would likely kill the other, and it wasn't going to be her. She was done being walked all over by wolves.

But then, she remembered how he'd saved her, her son, and Jade and Sloane from danger, putting his own life on the line. Didn't that prove that he was, in fact, different, like he'd said? A part of her wanted to believe him, but another part remained guarded, fearful of what might happen if she let down her defenses.

She pressed her fingers against the cool wall of the dressing room, raking her fists through her tousled hair in frustration. She needed to focus on the mission at hand and not get distracted by her confusing emotions.

Maverick's piercing eyes and the intoxicating citrus and caramel scent still lingered on her lips, filling her senses and making it hard to gather her thoughts. The way his fingers knew just what to do, stirring a fire within her core that she knew he'd be able to ignite again with a single touch. She was a woman with needs, after all, and if she was here playing married to a handsome man, why shouldn't she enjoy all the perks that came with that?

"Ugh, why is this so complicated?" she muttered, but her words were quickly silenced when she heard a commotion outside the dressing room.

The sounds of scuffling and raised voices snapped Zera out of her reverie, forcing her to put those thoughts aside. Her instincts kicked in, and she focused on staying hidden. like Maverick had instructed.

She looked down at the dress she wore, remembering the shield function Maverick had shown her. The faeologist in her wondered at how it all worked, how the magical properties had been built into the fabric and invisible to the naked eye.

With her left hand, she traced a figure eight motion, activating the dress's shield. As it shimmered to life around her, she felt a sense of determination surge through her. She was a mother, a survivor, and she would not let anyone or anything harm her.

The shield now surrounding her, Zera braced herself for whatever might come next. A siren scream rang out, so loud she saw the sound waves ripple against the barrier protecting her. It was as if the sound came from underwater, muffled yet still making her freeze out of fear of bringing attention to herself.

Zera's heart raced, and tiny droplets of sweat glistened on her brow as she listened intently. Whatever fight ensued beyond the dressing room, she got the sense that Maverick's wolf form was putting up quite the struggle. The snarling and growls grew louder, echoing through the air, intermingled with the cries of pain from the assailants. But there were still others that sounded as though they were putting up a good fight.

"Where is she?" one of them hissed, loud enough for her to hear from where she hid.

Her grip tightened on the edge of her dress, her knuckles turning white as she struggled to maintain her composure. A grunt of pain followed by a whimper of agony pierced through the chaos. Maverick. He was in trouble. She had to do something. She swallowed hard, her mouth suddenly dry.

She clenched her fists, wishing she could help but not knowing what to do. Her thoughts were soon interrupted by the sudden, violent yanking open of the dressing room curtain, exposing her hiding place.

"Found you, little pixie." The assailant greeted her with a slow smile, revealing jagged teeth.

Her eyes locked on the two slits for pupils, and something clicked inside her mind. It was the bartender from the seedy bar who had served them drinks. The snake shifter.

"It's you!" She gasped, blinking in disbelief. But he worked for Quill, didn't he? Had Quill sold them out?

She didn't have time to process this as the snake shifter grabbed her by the hair and pulled her out from the sanctuary of the dressing room and into the private show room that was now torn apart by the ongoing battle. The air crackled with energy as she stumbled, her shield dissipating upon contact with the assailant's grip. Fear and anger twisted in her gut.

"I'm no pixie! Let me go!" Zera cried out, fighting the urge to use her pixie dust. She had to maintain her cover for as long as possible.

"Shut up!" the snake shifter snarled, tightening his hold on her hair while the other gripped her shoulder so tightly it made her eyes water.

Zera's heartbeat echoed in her ears as she searched for Maverick amid the chaos. Fear clawed at her insides, but she refused to give in. She knew she needed to stay strong for Cole, even if it meant fighting back against this snake who smelled like sulfur.

She swallowed a bit of bile that rose up at the stench, fighting against the snake shifter's grip with each step as he nearly dragged her to the front of the shop. Racks of clothes and mangled hangers scattered across the floor, some torn and trampled under the weight of the ongoing fight.

Felice battled a fae with pointed ears, red blood dripping from the fae's earlobe. Felice's siren scream earlier must've busted eardrums. But the snake shifter showed no effect, probably because snakes had more subdued hearing abilities. It must've made this shifter less susceptible to the siren's power.

Finally, her eyes met Maverick's as he fought the other two attackers with bleeding eardrums. His body shuddered, rippling back into his human form. His face twisted in fear and anger, as if he knew he wouldn't be able to get to her in time as the snake shifter pulled her to an emergency exit on the side of the store.

"Zera!" Maverick shouted, his voice strained. He landed a vicious punch on one of them, sending the fae stumbling back into a pile of broken mirrors. But the distraction gave the other attacker precious seconds to dodge Maverick's counterattack and to land a fierce kick to his chin.

Maverick hit the ground with a thunderous smack. Panic surged through Zera. She had to do something, anything to escape this snake shifter's grasp.

The dress. It had weapons. How did she activate the dagger? Or the other ones? She swiped her hand in the formation she thought activated the dagger, but instead of triggering the intended weapon, a cascade of tiny firecrackers burst from her dress, creating a color-ful-yet-ineffective display.

"Damn it!" she muttered under her breath. What the bloody fae was that useful for?

They were nearly to the door, and she knew as soon as they were out of Felice's boutique, she was done for. The snake would shift or use whatever magic he'd used to make her drink appear the night before and teleport them far away from Maverick. Or maybe the snake shifter couldn't move anything larger than a cocktail glass. She didn't know, but she didn't want to find out.

Either way, if she didn't figure something out soon, she would lose any chance of getting out of this alive. She'd never see her son again. The numbing thought made it hard to breathe and threatened to send her into a spiral of despair.

No, she wouldn't let this snake win. She tried again. This time, a small cloud of glittering smoke puffed out, obscuring her vision momentarily but doing nothing to deter the snake shifter.

As he tightened his grip on her hair, sending searing pain through her scalp, Zera knew she was running out of options. She had to find the right weapon or risk being taken away by this vile creature. Determination fueled her actions as she swiped her hand once more, praying this attempt would finally free her.

The circular motion produced the black dagger. Relief washed over her as she used the self-defense moves she'd learned after too many close calls at Haven Wolf Tavern when someone out of town got a little too handsy.

She stomped down hard on the snake shifter's foot, twisting her body to the side, and sliced the dagger across his arm. A sharp cry of pain echoed in the small boutique as the attacker's grip loosened, and he released Zera, stumbling backward.

"You stupid pixie," the snake shifter hissed. His forked tongue jetted out and licked his wound. The ooze subsided, and he raced for her.

She backed away as fast as possible, but he was too quick, and that stupid dress kept getting in her way. She needed pants.

"Move, pixie!" the snake shifter said with a hiss, shoving her against the door.

Behind her, Maverick roared, "Get your filthy hands off her!"

His voice was laced with a primal rage that sent shivers down Zera's spine. He made quick work of the remaining bounty hunter fae, his sudden determination and muscular form overpowering them with ease. The intensity in his stormy eyes never wavered from the snake shifter who had held her moments before.

As he dispatched the last fae, Maverick's gaze locked on Zera and the snake shifter. The air around them crackled with tension, and she knew he was coming for her. His determination to protect her was evident in every move he made.

In a swift motion, Maverick closed the distance between them, grabbed the snake shifter by the collar, and threw him against the wall with a resounding thud. The impact left the attacker dazed and struggling to regain his footing. Maverick slammed his fist against the snake's jaw, and the bone cracked under impact.

"Stay down and don't move if you want to live," Maverick

snarled, his words dripping with menace. He towered over the snake shifter, asserting his dominance.

A wave of gratitude washed over Zera, who still clutched the dagger that now dripped with black snake blood. Despite the pack Maverick had been born into, he'd saved her. Again. That had to mean something.

"Are you okay?" Maverick asked, turning his attention back to Zera. His expression softened, concern etched across his handsome features.

She nodded shakily, feeling her heart race as she met his gaze. "I am now."

He smirked. "See? You didn't need to be trained to use that dagger. You're a natural."

She gave him a wry grin, but despite her nerves that ran on overdrive, she was pretty proud of herself for taking that guy down. The rush of adrenaline was exhilarating, and she felt a new sense of confidence within her.

"Well," Felice said, pulling their attention to where she tossed glowing red cuffs on the wrists of the other attackers, who lay either unconscious or dead—Zera couldn't tell which—in the middle of her destroyed boutique. "At least I won't have to go hunting for dinner."

Felice smirked, and Zera's eyes widened. She didn't want to know what the boutique owner meant by that.

"What about him?" Zera asked, nodding toward the snake shifter, who groaned but failed to rise.

Maverick looked at the fallen shifter, his eyes narrowing. "He won't be going anywhere."

Felice tossed Maverick a set of cuffs, and he swiftly secured the snake shifter's hands behind his back. The shifter hissed in pain and glared at them.

"Why don't you just kill me like the others?" he snarled.

"Oh, we will," Maverick growled. "But first, we need you to give us some information."

With a nod from Felice, they led him down a dimly lit corridor behind the checkout counter to her office, where a small-but-sturdy cell awaited.

"Get in," Maverick ordered, his voice cold and unwavering. The snake shifter hesitated for a moment before complying, slithering into the cell with a snarl.

"Feel free to keep him here alive for the night," Felice said as she locked the door behind him. "But anyone here tomorrow will be my breakfast."

She waltzed over to her desk, as if that was a completely ordinary request, and busied herself with paperwork, well out of earshot.

"I thought sirens only ate fish and other aquatic things, not fae," Zera said, suddenly uneasy about being here.

"Her husband is a wendigo," he said with a shrug. "He doesn't get out much."

Zera shuddered, not wanting to know how a siren and a wendigo ended up together.

"Who sent you?" Maverick asked the snake shifter.

His forked tongue jetted out, and he flashed them a jagged-tooth smile but made no attempt to respond.

Maverick banged his fist on the bars, shaking the cell. "I'd suggest you start talking because, as you heard, you have a limited amount of time left. Does Quill know you're here?"

The snake shifter's eyes flickered black, and Zera got the sense he was trying to conjure his way out of there.

Maverick raised a brow, folding his arms across his muscled chest. "Stop stalling, or I'll deliver you to the wendigo myself."

"All right, I'll talk," he hissed, desperation laced in his voice. Death by wendigo didn't sound like a fun way to go.

"Good choice." Maverick narrowed his eyes. "Who sent you?"

"No one," the snake spat. "I wanted to make a name for myself and take a shot at the bounty on your head."

"And did Quill tell you where we were?" Maverick prodded.

The snake shook his head. "He barely comes out of his lair to pay us."

Zera let out a puff of air. At least that meant her identity and their faestones hadn't been compromised.

"Then how'd you track us?" Zera asked, unable to shake the feeling that something was off.

"Your scent," he hissed, twining his forklike tongue around his lips. "It led me here."

The way the snake's narrowed pupils zeroed in on her, like she was a rat to eat, sent a chill down her spine.

"Don't even dare to look at her," Maverick growled. "Or you'll find your eyes gouged out. Now, tell us something useful."

The snake let out a hiss, clearly not enjoying the threat, but his shoulders slumped in defeat. "Fine. After the alert for the bounty on your heads, I got a tip from a buddy of mine who used to run with Gareth's crowd. Said he knew who put the bounty on your heads and would double the bounty if I brought her to the gala for the underground fae."

Zera's pixie ears perked up in interest, but she quickly let her magic round them back out to maintain her disguise despite her pixie nature already being discovered. She might as well practice her control. She had a feeling she was going to need it a lot in the coming days.

"Is that right?" Maverick asked, a hint of skepticism in his tone.

"Swear on my scales," the snake shifter insisted. "And I can get you in. Just promise me my freedom."

Zera and Maverick exchanged a glance as they weighed the pros and cons of trusting their attacker.

"That's not up to me to decide." Maverick nodded toward Felice, who was now hanging custom blouses on a rack to roll out into the boutique.

A security screen behind her revealed the entire shop had been restored to its previous state.

"I can hold him here until you two can verify his information at the gala," she called, not looking up from her work. "If he's telling the truth, I'll let him live. If not, well…" Her voice trailed off, leaving the consequences understood.

"Deal," Maverick agreed, looking back at the snake shifter with a steely gaze. The tension between them was palpable, but for now, they had a common goal.

"Deal," Zera echoed, her thoughts racing with the prospect of attending the gala and getting closer to taking down Gareth and this mysterious "sugarfae," as Quill had called them.

Despite the fear and uncertainty that lingered in her heart, she knew that together with Maverick, they stood a fighting chance. And maybe they'd find something more along the way.

ZERA AND MAVERICK returned to his penthouse, the weight of their mission heavy on their minds. Zera glanced around the luxurious space, lost in thought as she considered their next move. They needed to draw out Gareth at the gala that night, but there was one pressing issue.

"What is it?" Maverick asked, as if sensing her unease.

She sighed. "It's silly, really."

"Tell me," he said as they made their way to the living room. The expanse of the city skyline could be seen through the wall of windows that lined one side of the room.

He stood much too close, his scent enveloping her senses, taking her back to their heated moment in the dressing room. Her eyes fluttered shut for a moment as she tried to focus.

"It's… my dress." She flushed, feeling foolish for even bringing it up as she looked down at the tear in the slit of her dress. "It must've gotten ruined during the attack, so I don't have anything appropriate to wear, and I definitely didn't pack formal wear."

Maverick didn't move an inch, but his presence was still overwhelming. He raised an eyebrow, a small smile playing at the edges of his lips.

"Is that all?" He chuckled softly. "Well then, it's a good thing Felice had some clothes delivered to the room upstairs. I'm sure you'll find something suitable there."

His nearness reminded her of how close they'd come to crossing a line. Maverick seemed to sense her thoughts, and he hesitated, waiting just within reach. It was as if he was seeking her permission to finish what they'd started.

She took a shaky step back. "Thank you, Maverick. I'll go take a look."

As Zera climbed the stairs to her temporary room, she felt a magnetic pull toward Maverick even as she tried to resist it. Her resolve, however, remained steadfast. This was not the time to let emotions cloud her judgment. They had a dangerous adversary to face, and they needed to keep their heads in the game.

Entering the room, Zera found a few garment bags laid out on the giant king-sized bed. Her jaw dropped. Not only did she have a gown that wasn't ripped, but she had options. She'd never dreamed of ever wearing anything as fine as the gown she had on, let alone having her choice of multiple gowns. How much did all of it cost?

Something told her that she didn't want to know.

A little overwhelmed, she began the process of hunting for a gown fit for a gala. She opened bag after bag, some filled with more practical garments while others held gowns worth probably more than her car.

She finally settled on a royal blue gown made of velvet that caught her eye—elegant yet fierce. The best part about it was it had pants hidden underneath the sleek skirt like a secret layer, providing both practicality and protection in a moment of danger. A likely scenario, since they were about to go to a party filled with the Fae Realm's criminal elite.

She just hoped the weapons woven within it worked similarly to those in the other dress.

Later, as she descended the staircase back into the living area that overlooked Mystic City, she found Maverick waiting for her.

The setting sun cast shadows across one of the two sofas he sat on that framed a giant marble coffee table.

He rose and met her at the foot of the staircase. The striking silver tuxedo he donned clung to his muscles in all the right ways and nearly made her falter on the last step.

"You look…" His eyes swept over her, and her breath caught. "'Stunning' doesn't even begin to describe you."

She smiled, tucking a curl behind her pointed ear. While they were in the apartment, she didn't bother masking her pixie features, though now that her pixie-dust supply seemed to be back to one hundred percent, she didn't see why she bothered. But there was something freeing about being herself with him.

Their eyes met, and for a moment, the unresolved tension between them threatened to engulf them once more. But it would be a mistake. A part of her knew she could trust him, at least with her life, but with her heart?

She had to be more careful and knew she had to address it before they left for the gala.

"Listen, Maverick," she began, her voice steady despite the nerves churning inside her. "About earlier… in the dressing room."

He looked at her, waiting for her to continue, but there was an unmistakable undercurrent of anticipation glinting in his wolf-gray eyes.

"I think it'd probably be best for both of us if we kept our relationship to what it is—an amicable partnership to bring Gareth and whoever he's working for down—and then go our separate ways at the end of this." Her words were firmer than what she felt but crystallized by the thoughts that had been swirling around in her head since their heated moment.

Maverick's expression softened with disappointment, but he nodded. "I understand. And I respect your boundaries." He paused for a moment before adding, "By the way, Jade should have received her faestone by now, so if you need to make an untraceable call to her, you should be able to."

Her heart swelled with gratitude, not just for the faestone but also for his understanding. She'd been terrified about this moment. History told her men didn't take kindly to rejection, but Maverick was different, and she was starting to see that. But mostly, it was because of the faestones.

"Her information is already saved," he said, pulling the rectangular quartz out of his front pocket and handing it to her.

"Thank you," she said, overwhelmed with relief. He had no idea how much this meant to her. "Can I call her now?"

He checked the time and nodded. "You should have a few minutes."

Zera swiped through the familiar settings of the faestone, pulled up the information labeled Jade, and clicked on her image. Her half sister's reflection popped up on the screen. As Zera tried to reach Jade over video chat, her heart raced with the anticipation of getting to see Cole again.

She made her way to the windows of the penthouse, the cityscape of Mystic City glittering below her.

The faestone finally beeped when a connection was made, and she bounced on the balls of her feet, excitement bubbling within her. Magic did only so much for the signal out in Pixie Hollow.

"Zera!" Her half sister's voice rang through the device, and her image appeared as they switched to video chat. She held Cole up to the screen, his chubby cheeks and bright eyes instantly filling Zera with warmth and joy.

"Hey, Jade! And there's my little man!" Zera cooed, reaching out to the screen as if she could somehow caress her son's face. "How are you both doing?"

"Great! Cole's been perfect," Jade responded, beaming. "We're at Dad's old place. It hasn't changed a bit."

A pang of sadness struck her at the mention of their father. He had never understood her independent nature. The need to leave on her own. Especially when she left with her werewolf ex. She had questioned her decision numerous times. But then Cole wouldn't be here, and he was everything to her.

"But enough about us." Jade's voice cut through her thoughts. "Look at where you are,"

"Yep, this is the place," she said, letting the faestone scan over the lavish open-concept living room and kitchen beyond, where Maverick had retreated, out of earshot.

Jade whistled, and Cole giggled in response, trying to grab her nose. "Looks swanky. And how's it going with the hot wolf spy?"

"Jade!" Zera hissed, turning a deep shade of red and taking another step closer to the windows. She prayed Maverick's werewolf hearing hadn't caught that. "It's not like that. We're strictly partners here on one mission. To catch the guys who are hunting me."

"Uh-huh, sure," Jade teased, her gaze sharp and knowing. "I can read your face like an open book, Zera. Something happened between you two."

Zera chewed her lip. Jade was too perceptive for her own good. Zera couldn't deny there was a connection with Maverick. That much had been proved back in that dressing room. But there was too much at stake right now, and she wouldn't risk anything with him.

"Okay, fine," Zera relented, avoiding Jade's eyes. "We... had a moment. But it won't happen again."

"Why not?" Jade inquired, genuine curiosity etched on her features.

"Because he's a werewolf. Like my ex. And he's a Lunar Brotherhood wolf, to be more precise," Zera explained, her heart heavy with the truth of their conflicting natures. "Or at least he used to be. You know what that means for us."

"What do you mean 'used to be'?"

"He's a lone wolf." She shrugged. "He said he rejected their ways, so his pack kicked him out, which I didn't think was possible, but maybe there's something different about him."

Jade's eyebrows furrowed, her lips pursing in contemplation. After a moment, she spoke up, her voice filled with conviction.

"Look, Zera, I know what the Lunar Brotherhood has done to our kind. But think about this: if Maverick was really after your pixie dust, why would he save your life and stop that druid from taking you? He could've fooled us all if that were his true intention."

Zera paused at that. She hadn't expected Jade to mirror her same thoughts, let alone voice them. It was true. Maverick had saved her more than once, and there was something about the way he looked at her that made her believe he genuinely cared.

Whenever it mattered most, at least. There were other times when he seemed to change entirely, and the only thing left was the arrogant werewolf faeboy.

But even when he was being the caring lone-wolf spy, the weight of history and the danger they faced threatened to smother any chance of them exploring their connection further.

"Maybe you're right," Zera conceded, a hint of hope flickering within her. "But we have bigger things to focus on right now."

"Fair enough," Jade agreed, giving her a reassuring nod. "Promise me you'll be careful, okay?"

"I will," Zera assured her.

"Hey, is that Zera?" Sloane's cheerful voice came from somewhere in the background. She peered around from behind Jade, her head of corkscrew curls and cheerful smile coming into view. "Wow, girl, you look hot. Where are you going?"

Cole lit up when he spotted her, and she playfully waved at her little boy. Zera's heart swelled with love. Though she knew he was safe with Jade and Sloane, she just wanted to be there with him.

"We're headed to a gala," she replied, her nerves beginning to unravel. "It's some fancy party for elite crime lords or something."

"Oooh, sounds exciting," Sloane exclaimed.

"Maybe? We'll see. I'm hoping to be done with all of this soon."

"Don't worry, sis," Jade said, bouncing Cole as the sudden evening fussiness ensued. Zera was surprised he was even still up. "You've got this."

"Thanks," she said with a small smile. As they said their goodbyes, she knew that no matter what happened between her and Maverick, her family would always be her top priority. Which was exactly why she was going to the gala that promised to be as dangerous as Felice's boutique, if not more.

With a sigh, Zera hung up the call and made her way over to the kitchen.

"Everyone okay?" he asked, nodding to the phone that was still in her hands.

She nodded, suddenly feeling the weight of her decision of having to leave Cole. She missed him more than she could possibly put into words.

"You'll see him again. In person," Maverick said huskily, somehow knowing the fears that swirled around in her mind. "I'll make sure of it."

She knew it wasn't a promise he could guarantee, but there was a certainty in his eyes that filled her with hope.

Zera took a deep breath, trying to steady her nerves. She knew that her operation at the gala was crucial to their mission, and Maverick was right—she wouldn't let her personal fears get in the way of their objectives.

"When do we go?" she asked, slipping the faestone into the hidden pocket in one of the folds of the royal blue velvet gown.

"Now, the chariot awaits," he said, offering her his arm.

She raised her eyebrows. "The chariot?"

"Please, Zera," he said with a wink. "This is a gala for the most elite in all of Mystic City, and your date is the formidable Dane Brown."

Zera laughed so hard she snorted as she slunk her arm around his muscled forearm. "All right then, Dane Brown," she teased. "Let's go make our presence known."

CHAPTER 10
ZERA

The night sky was a dark canvas, illuminated by the glow of neon lights and punctuated by the twinkling stars above. Zera had never been in a chariot before, but the glass dome of the sleek vehicle allowed her to take in the dazzling cityscape. The city felt mystical and alive, with secrets waiting to be discovered in every shadowy corner.

Maverick and Zera sat in silence in a chariot made of glass. Zera admired the twinkling light from the overhead lamps that floated along the road as they followed the procession through the gate. Finally, they arrived at the stone mansion, which stood out among the surrounding skyscrapers like a historical reminder of the early Fae Realm from centuries past. The extravagant gala was in full swing, with throngs of people climbing up the front staircase leading to a massive entrance.

As they came to a stop, Maverick jumped out and extended his hand to help Zera down. Their fingers brushed, sending a shiver down her spine.

"Ready?" he asked, his storm-filled eyes catching hers for a brief moment before she nodded in response.

She looped her arm into the crook of his muscled forearm and joined the line.

"One more thing," Maverick whispered, causing a sinking feeling. "Upon entering, we'll have landed on neutral territory. A spell will magically bind us to the promise that we won't hurt anyone while we're here and they us."

Zera's eyes widened, but relief washed over her. Otherwise, the bounty on their heads alone would've made them prime targets.

The line moved quickly, and they soon found themselves in the grand entrance of the castle that had been transformed into a magnificent art gallery that boasted a luxuriousness reserved only for the elite. The walls were adorned with intricate tapestries depicting heroic battles, and the floors were made of polished marble, reflecting the soft glow of candlelight. Chandeliers dripping with jewels of all colors cast dazzling reflections.

The scent of roses and jasmine filled the air; the floral arrangements were a feast for the eyes as they climbed the walls like ivy. A subtle-yet-intoxicating aroma wafted from Maverick, somehow intensifying the vibrancy of the atmosphere. Zera felt a sense of awe at everything that surrounded her.

Together, they followed the enormous hall through a long corridor that opened to a ballroom with even more artwork, ivy floral arrangements, and echoes of a great party.

"Wow," Zera whispered as her wide-eyed gaze swept over the art pieces displayed along the walls. "It's... breathtaking."

"Stay focused," Maverick reminded her gently, his voice a low drawl that sent warmth curling through her body. His tux was a second skin, outlining each muscle and making it hard for Zera to remember why they were here.

"I'm always focused," she retorted playfully, giving him a sidelong glance. "Just appreciating the view." She let her gaze linger on him for a moment longer before turning back to the artwork.

He chuckled, a low rumble that made her stomach flutter. "If I didn't know any better, I'd think you were flirting with me, Zera."

Her cheeks warmed, but she shrugged nonchalantly. If she was at a ball undercover as a married woman, she might as well enjoy it. "And if I am?"

The corners of his mouth twitched upward in a smirk. "Then I'd say you're doing a good job. But we should try to keep things on track. Stick to the mission."

He was right. She had to stay focused. Besides, hadn't she been the one moments before telling him they needed to stay professional?

She shook off the inappropriate thoughts that threatened to make her full-on pull him into the next dark corner they passed and bring her wettest dream to life. And if the dressing room incident was any preview, she knew Maverick could do just that and more.

"Right. Focused." She licked her lips, shaking off the distracting fantasies and the awe-inspiring wonder of this place.

As they mingled among the guests, Zera could feel the weight of gazes upon them. She tucked a strand of her hair back to ensure her ears were still rounded and the brown film concealing her pixie identity was in place. She couldn't risk revealing herself. Not in a roomful of crime lords and thugs.

"Remember, we're just a normal married couple here," Maverick murmured into her ear as they made their way toward the center of the ballroom lined with endless artwork from floor to ceiling.

"Yes, because being married to a werewolf spy—"

"Logistics strategist," he corrected with a teasing grin.

"Right, 'cause that's totally normal." She rolled her eyes but tightened her grip on his arm when they passed by two druids with matching runes tattooed onto their foreheads.

"Our target goes by the name of Kraven," he said in a hushed voice. "He's supposedly a hotshot around here, so expect him to have a strong following of guards."

"Got it," she replied, an odd mix of nerves and excitement bubbling within her. She could do this. After all, she had the best logistics strategist by her side, whatever that meant.

"Also, I heard he's behind the recent fae murders, though to my knowledge, it's gang related and not random. Still, stay close."

She gulped. The news had said that the bodies had been skinned alive. A shudder ran through her, but her fear wouldn't help her right now.

Shaking off her fear as best she could, she took on the role of a confident and poised woman. It was like those espionage shows she and Jade had watched late at night growing up until they fell asleep.

The lively music from the string quartet of fairies filled the ballroom as Maverick and Zera began to navigate their way through the crowd. While she tried to concentrate on their mission, she stole glances at Maverick, admiring the ease with which he blended into the high society. It was almost as if he had been born for this life—a stark contrast to her own humble origins.

The guests whirled around them, their opulent attire and sparkling jewelry adding to the already mesmerizing display. Zera caught glimpses of conversations and snippets of whispers that hinted at the dangerous undercurrent coursing through this elegant facade.

Zera marveled at the way Maverick effortlessly charmed those around them, his smile disarming and his words dripping with charisma. He was a werewolf of many talents, seamlessly adapting to any situation. Zera struggled to keep up with the intricate dance of lies and deceit they were engaged in, but Maverick had proved capable, and she trusted that. All she had to do was keep calm, keep holding on to his arm, and keep a small flow of pixie dust flowing to shield her features.

If anything, Maverick assured her that all of the features of her black dress worked the same way they did in all of Felice's creations, so if she had to defend herself, she wasn't at risk of exposing her pixie dust in a roomful of killers.

"There," he whispered in her ear, resting a hand on the small of her back that sent a jolt of electricity through her.

Zera's heart raced as she followed Maverick's gaze. Her eyes landed on a tall figure with silver hair and piercing blue eyes that cut through the dim light like shards of ice. It must be Kraven. He stood near a roaring fire, speaking to a woman who was practically drooling into her champagne glass over him, her eyes fixed on his stunning face. But it was a mere distraction from the guards surrounding him, who were strapped with weapons and looked as menacing as they were impeccably dressed, their expressions cold and unyielding.

"That's sure a lot of firepower for a party on neutral territory," she murmured back, feigning a laugh as she pretended Maverick had just whispered a joke.

"Rumor has it Kraven's the new ringleader of the criminal underworld," Maverick said, pulling her against him when Kraven's gaze flickered across them. "Of course he's allowed more protection than the rest of us."

The crime lord looked away as someone else came to introduce themselves. He seemed to be very popular with the ladies, and she could see why. He was a gray fox, if she ever saw one.

"Is he dangerous?" Zera asked as they continued to mingle in the crowd.

"Very," he replied, his voice barely audible above the symphony of voices and the string quartet as the fairies continued playing a traditional faen anthem.

Maverick's grip on her waist tightened suddenly as a man in his mid-to-late thirties approached them, holding a wineglass filled with what looked suspiciously like blood. He donned a polished red suit that complemented his obsidian complexion that glistened with a mesmerizing sheen.

"Dane? Dane Brown?"

She cringed when his pearly teeth clacked together, revealing sharp incisors. Definitely a vampire.

"Sebastian," Maverick greeted the vamp with a genuine smile, but there was a strained undertone she didn't understand. "How's life in the Fae Realm's very own hell?"

The vampire named Sebastian nearly keeled over with laughter. "Ah, good old Dane. You never did get why I entered to compete for the vampire queen's court, did you?"

Now, she got it. Sebastian belonged to the queen as one of her many consorts. In addition to the rumors of the vampire queen having a back door to the Human Realm, there were other well-founded whisperings that vampire fae traded their freedom for access to said back door. No one could prove it, and no one in the consort ever broke their silence on the matter.

"Seems like a high price to pay," Maverick replied, his eyes narrowing as he studied the vampire. "But I suppose it has its perks."

"Indeed, it does," Sebastian said with a smirk. "I've seen things most can only dream of, and the queen's favor is not without its benefits."

Zera watched their exchange closely, trying to pick up any subtle cues from Maverick that might signal danger or an opportunity for gathering information. She knew she had a lot to learn about navigating these treacherous waters, but she was determined to keep her wits about her and stay focused.

As they spoke, Zera felt the weight of the numerous gazes upon them. The luxurious ballroom was filled with all of the elite criminals of the Fae Realm and their associates, all dressed in their finest and exuding power and influence. Yet all of them seemed to orbit the gray fox—Kraven.

Whispers of his power in the underground community met her ear, from money laundering to drug trafficking, which meant only one thing. Kraven was a pixie murderer. Zera realized then that she was a mouse in a lion's den.

"And this must be your wife," Sebastian said, his crimson gaze taking in her appearance.

"It's Charlotte," Zera said, giving him her hand. He placed a kiss upon the top of her hand. She refrained from visibly cringing when his fangs grazed her skin. "And how do you two know each other?"

"I see Dane hasn't told you about me, eh?" Sebastian chuckled.

"Figures, given the gossip that he ratted out our old boss, Gareth. Probably why there's a bounty on your head."

Maverick's jaw twitched, but he made no response.

"Hit a nerve, did I?" Sebastian taunted, taking a step closer and making a growl rumble through Maverick's chest. "Good thing I was already on my way out. Otherwise, I'd be one of the many fae here just counting the ticking seconds until midnight."

"Bounty? Midnight?" Zera asked, fixing her expression with a look of confusion, hoping no one heard the way her heart stopped beating for a second.

"The time when neutrality ends. That's when this place will plunge into chaos, and all bets are off." The vampire laughed and fixed his gaze on Zera. "And stop pretending like you don't know anything about the bounty on your head. Everyone knows you must be the pixie under Dane's protection."

Zera forced a small smile, trying to maintain her composure despite the growing unease in her gut. The weight of the room suddenly felt suffocating, as if the air had thickened.

"I'm afraid I don't—" she began, but the vampire cut her off.

"Don't insult me." He flashed her a fanged smile before looking up at Maverick, who bested him by a few inches. "I was quite surprised when you settled down, and who knew it'd be with a blushing pixie bride? Sounds like a payday, if you ask me."

Every muscle in Maverick's body rippled at Sebastian's words, and Zera thought for sure he would pounce on the vampire right then and there.

But instead, he took a deep breath and grasped Zera's hand in his. "Come, Charlotte," he said, leading them away. "Let's get a drink."

She shot Sebastian a final look as they zigzagged their way toward grand windows that lined the great hall where refreshments were being served. Trays floated away from a drink station, but Maverick didn't stop for any of the flutes it held. Instead, they stopped at the source, and he grabbed the whole bottle of champagne from the bucket.

"Is that true about the neutrality thing? Do we really only have until midnight?" she asked, watching him as he popped the cork.

A waiter eyed him with a scowl but made no move to stop him.

"Here," Maverick said, handing her a glass and pouring the golden liquid with practiced ease. "Never trust a glass someone else has poured here."

"Oh." It was all she could say with every nerve in her body in overdrive. She sipped the champagne, its bubbles tickling her nose. She noticed Maverick's eyes linger on her lips for a moment before he caught himself and looked away.

"And yes," he said with a grimace. "About the midnight thing."

Zera gulped, rethinking this whole gala thing to begin with. Why was she even here?

Maverick downed the rest of his glass and set it down on the nearest table.

"Let's split up," he growled, something in his eyes darkening. "I need to settle this thing with Sebastian."

"Wait, what?" Zera's voice trembled with concern as she reached out and grabbed Maverick's arm. "You can't leave me here. I'm dead meat in this place!"

"It's barely nine. You'll be fine," he said, barely looking down at her as he brushed her off and beelined through the crowd to wherever that vampire was.

She frowned. Something wasn't right. He wouldn't leave her like this, not when her life was at stake. Would he?

She mulled over her options as she set the champagne down next to Maverick's. What would she do if he never came back? How would she get back to the penthouse?

It grew suddenly very hot in the bustling ballroom. Zera's anxiety rose, and beads of sweat formed on her forehead. She felt flushed and buzzed all at once, but she'd had only a few sips of the champagne.

She leaned against the table, gripping it with one hand while discreetly fanning herself with the other.

"Here," a deep, velvety voice said from behind her. A silk handkerchief appeared in front of her face, and she hesitantly took it. "You look like you could use this."

"Thank you," Zera murmured, dabbing at her forehead so her makeup wouldn't smudge. She turned to face the stranger who had come to her aid and found herself locking eyes with the tall and dangerously handsome gray fox. His sculpted features were undeniably attractive, but there was something about him that also made her feel uneasy.

"Are you all right?" he asked, genuine concern lacing his voice. "This palace can be overwhelming for some."

"Y-yes," Zera stammered, trying to regain her composure. "I'm fine. Just feeling a bit... off."

"Allow me to introduce myself," he said, extending a hand, which she hesitantly accepted. "My name is Kraven."

Skinned. Alive. The words repeated in her mind as she stared at his deceptively kind face, but his eyes gave way to something far more sinister.

"Charlotte Brown," Zera replied, somehow remembering her cover identity. She couldn't shake the nagging suspicion that there was more to this man than met the eye. She couldn't even get a read on what kind of fae he was. It was like there was something blocking anything about him.

"Ah, Charlotte." Kraven's lips curled into a smile that made Zera shiver, though she couldn't tell if it was from fear or something else entirely. "How intriguing."

Her eyes jerked in the direction Maverick had disappeared, praying to any fae god who would listen that he'd come back soon. She didn't like how this man was making her feel.

"You don't usually come to these, do you?" he asked, taking a sip from his whiskey tumbler.

She shook her head. "What gave it away?"

"I have a knack for... knowing things. Things about people anyway."

"I'm just here with my husband," she said with a thin smile.

Kraven looked around. "And where is he?"

She swallowed hard, fighting the sudden urge to tell him about the fight Maverick had with Sebastian. But why?

A wave of heat washed over her once more, and she briefly closed her eyes.

"If I had a wife as beautiful as you..." His voice was too close to her. She opened her eyes to find him leaning into her space. "I would never let her out of my sight."

A shiver ran down her spine. Attractive or not, this man reeked of power and control. It was unsettling and not in a good way. It made her skin crawl, but somehow she couldn't get herself to move, like he had this invisible hold on her.

"Here, let me get you a drink," he said, reaching for a long-stemmed martini glass on a platter floating by. The glass glistened with clear liquid, a single olive inside.

"I'm good, thanks," she said, folding her arms across her chest, as if to physically keep the truth of her pixie heritage and pixie-dust magic locked within her.

What was it about him that made her want to both run like hell in the opposite direction from him and divulge all her secrets at the same time?

"It's a shame," he said, two martini glasses suddenly in hand, and before she could stop herself, she took one from him.

"What is?" she asked, taking a long sip of the drink. The clear liquid burned her throat, but she held back a cough.

"What Gareth has put you through," he said, his eyes swirling with rose gold as he focused on her.

An inexplicable urge to open up to Kraven washed over her, and before she knew it, she had divulged everything—her true identity, her relationship with Maverick, their mission to stop Gareth and whoever he was working with or for, and even her pixie dust.

"Such a fascinating tale," Kraven mused, his eyes gleaming with interest. "And here I thought this party was going to be dreadfully dull."

Zera blinked, shocked by her own sudden lack of restraint. Why had she revealed so much to this stranger? She shut her mouth. Maverick had been gone for five minutes, and already she'd blown her cover. At least she hadn't mentioned her son. But something about this didn't feel right. Like she wasn't herself. Then her jaw dropped.

"This is you!" she gasped. "You're making me say these things."

A sly grin played across his face, which was smooth despite his graying hair that was swept into an impeccably stylish pompadour.

"My dear," Kraven said, his voice laced with amusement, "I merely encouraged you to speak your heart's deepest desires. You did the rest."

Zera's heart stopped for a breath as realization dawned on her. Kraven was no ordinary fae. He was one of the rarest, in fact. He was an incubus, using his powers to manipulate her emotions and extract information. No wonder he was rising to the top of the crime underworld so quickly.

Panic surged through her veins as her mind raced with thoughts of protecting Cole and warning Maverick about Kraven's true nature. She needed to get out of there. Where was Maverick anyway?

"But I do mean it," he said, his head tilting as he appraised her. "It's a real shame to waste such beauty for something so fleeting."

He reached for a strand of hair that fell into her eyes, but she swatted his hand away. One of the many women nearby gasped, unable to fathom standing up against him. It was probably stupid of her, but she wasn't about to let this incubus get any closer to her.

"Ooh, you are a delightful thing, now, aren't you?" He chuckled and ran a hand through his ridiculous hair. "Such a waste, indeed."

"That's rich coming from you," she spat, and he arched a gray brow.

"And why's that?" he asked.

"Among the many criminal organizations you control, one includes the murdering of my kind," she hissed, not bothering anymore to keep to her cover. He already knew who and what she was. "You're a pixie murderer, and the only thing keeping you from killing me for my pixie dust is this stupid neutrality thing. Unless these laws don't apply to me?"

The grin vanished from Kraven's face, melting into a scowl as he stepped within a hair's breadth from her. His eyes flickered with anger, the amusement replaced by a dangerous glint. Zera stood her ground, refusing to let fear swallow her whole. She had come too far to back down now.

"I only provide what is craved." Kraven seethed, his voice dripping with venom. "If there were any other way of supplying what my customers desire, I would do it. But as it so happens, there is no such alternative. That's the way of life. Supply and demand."

Her throat went dry, and she was suddenly unable to speak. Kraven gripped her arm with an ice-cold hand and added, "You are no exception, and when the clock strikes midnight, I won't be able to stop every single one of my hit men from coming after you. You'll be just another supply of pixie dust, a means to an end. I wish it were different, but that's how it works."

She gulped, getting the message. As long as there were those who sought out the illegal drug, there would be fae monsters like him profiting from it, and there was nothing she could do about it.

"Excuse me," she muttered, yanking her arm from Kraven's icy grip. "I need to find my husband."

"Of course," Kraven replied smoothly, as if he hadn't threatened her life only a moment earlier. "But remember, Charlotte, I'll be watching like a seductive shadow under the steel titan's watchful gaze."

She furrowed her brows in confusion. What did that even mean? She hoped it wasn't another one of those incubus powers. Still, she shivered at the promise of being watched and at the way he said her cover name as if he had just whispered a threat into her ear. Zera forced herself to maintain composure, refusing to show any sign of weakness or fear. She knew that if she let a sliver of doubt enter her mind, Kraven would exploit it ruthlessly.

As Zera navigated the crowded gala in search of Maverick, she could feel the weight of Kraven's gaze on her back. It was as if every step she took, every breath she drew brought her closer to her death. The air seemed thick with danger, and Zera knew that her survival—and that of Maverick—hung by a thread.

"Where are you, you bloody stubborn faeboy?" she whispered on a shaky breath.

It wasn't only Kraven's eyes she felt on her. Everyone around her kept glancing at the giant clock on the back wall, ticking down the seconds to her doom. Why had she and Maverick come here? They hadn't gotten any closer to finding out where Gareth was hiding or where they might be able to find him. This had been a total disaster, and now she was entirely alone, surrounded by monsters who would kill her for her pixie dust as soon as the clock struck midnight.

Shouts and screams echoed from the glass balcony doors, and she picked up the pace. Fae shoved their way inside, escaping whatever madness had erupted outside. Zera's heart raced, and she knew that Maverick was somehow involved in this commotion.

"Excuse me!" she called out, pushing her way through the panicked crowd.

It was like treading against a current. She finally reached the balcony, the brisk night air hitting her face as she pushed her way onto the stone terrace. Her breath caught in her throat when she saw Maverick standing at the center of it all. There, amid the chaos, Maverick stood in full werewolf form, his giant black wolf towering over Sebastian. His venomous teeth were inches away from sinking into the neck of the vampire, who hissed against the alpha's grip.

Shit. Maverick was about to break the law of neutrality. What would happen to him if he did so? Just by being in this mansion, they were magically bound to obey. She didn't know what the consequences would be, but she knew they would be life-threatening if he killed the vampire.

"Stop!" she screamed, her voice barely audible over the shrieking wind and the gasps of the onlookers.

Maverick's wolf eyes, swirling with rose gold, jerked to her, and the fear clouding her mind began to dissipate as she realized that this must be Kraven too. He must've manipulated Maverick's emotions back in the ballroom, causing him to lose control. This wasn't the Maverick she knew. This was the puppet being controlled by a ruthless incubus.

"Please, Dane. Don't do this," she pleaded softly, her eyes locked on his while she prayed he would still respond to her, even though she was forced to avoid using his real name. Since Kraven already knew their true names, though, what did it matter?

The massive black werewolf chomped his giant snout, pawing Sebastian like he was merely prey. And if what Maverick had told her about alpha-born werewolves was right, he was just that. It didn't matter how powerful of a fae one was or how immortal. His bite could kill.

Finally, something flickered in Maverick's werewolf gaze, and the snarling beast hesitated for a moment, as if considering her words. She could see the conflict within him, the struggle between his innate ferocity and the man he truly was.

"Remember why we're here?" she asked, raising her hands as she carefully approached him. "You're my husband. We're here to enjoy a gala. That's all."

The alpha werewolf's stormy eyes looked down at the vampire, as if to accuse Sebastian of taunting him.

She took another step forward and a deep breath. "Yes, Sebastian said some stupid things. But he didn't mean any of it. Right, Sebastian?"

"R-Right." Sebastian nodded profusely.

Another step, and she closed the distance between them. She carefully stroked Maverick's wolf behind the ears, his soft fur hot and comforting to the touch. It was like being curled up with a blanket next to a roaring fire.

"See? All is right. Now, let's let everyone get back to enjoying the party," she said, her tone soft and reassuring.

Slowly, agonizingly, Maverick's wolf form began to shrink, and the fur receded back into his body as he stepped away from Sebastian. His suit hung in shreds, barely covering his body as bits of muscle reformed, reconstructing his human figure. Maverick's eyes, once wild and feral, regained their familiar storm as he stood before her in his true form. Maverick released a low growl as he fought against the lingering instincts of his werewolf self, struggling to regain control.

With turmoil etched on his face, he battled between human reason and animalistic instinct. She reached for his hand and grasped it. His fingers trembled, but he finally held her hand, the beast within subdued.

Sebastian shuffled to his feet, brushing off his suit as he shot Maverick a dirty look. "I'll be seeing you later, Dane."

Maverick's grip tightened on her hand at the threat, but he didn't move when Sebastian backed away into the throng of spectators who had gathered to witness the near-violent spectacle.

"Zera," Maverick whispered, his voice hoarse and filled with regret. "I'm so sorry. I didn't mean to leave you in there. This is all my fault."

"It's okay. Kraven manipulated us both. He was testing us, testing you," she whispered urgently. "But we should be careful. He may know about our mission now."

She was beginning to understand why everyone in the ballroom seemed to orbit him. He was a power to reckon with.

Maverick glanced around the crowded balcony, as if assessing their situation. Dozens of bystanders kept an eye on them under the guise of enjoying the night air.

"We need to get out of here," he said, his jaw set. "But you won't like it."

She followed his gaze to the corner of the balcony where a vine-covered trellis met the side of the building. "Um, no. I'm not going to climb down that rickety old thing. Especially not in this dress!"

"Oh?" Maverick cocked an eyebrow, a smirk playing on his lips as he took in her appearance. Guess he was back to his bloody faeboy humor.

"Would you rather take your chances with another round of Kraven's games or trust me to keep you safe?" His voice held a teasing edge, but the undercurrent of concern was unmistakable.

Zera rolled her eyes dramatically but couldn't suppress her own smile. "Fine, but if I tear this gown, you're on seamstress duty."

He chuckled, the sound rich and grounding. He reached out, brushing a loose strand of hair from her face with a tenderness that belied his brute strength of moments earlier. Maybe there was more to this conceited faeboy wolf after all.

"Deal," he murmured. His hands found her waist, lifting her effortlessly onto the trellis, as if she weighed no more than a feather.

She grasped the wooden lattice, her heart fluttering—not out of fear from the descent, though from the breeze she felt the height and didn't dare look down, but from the proximity to Maverick.

"Look! They're getting away!"

The angry voice of someone from the balcony snapped her out of the moment. Maverick looked over his shoulder and quickly leapt onto the trellis beside her, making the whole thing quiver under the weight.

"Come on, we need to go. Now!" he growled, beginning the descent at a dangerously fast pace.

That was when she made the mistake of looking down. She gulped. The darkness below her seemed to go on forever.

"Right," she breathed, the dizzying drop making her head spin.

But she trusted Maverick.

Closing her eyes, Zera took a deep breath, steadying herself as she began to climb down.

The trellis creaked with every step, the wood groaning under their combined weight. Zera's chest heaved with every breath as she focused on her grip and each foothold, desperate not to slip.

"You're doing great." Maverick encouraged her, his voice steady and comforting as he climbed down below. "Just a little bit farther."

If anything happened, he would catch her. He'd saved her time and time again, and she trusted he would do it again.

Finally, they reached the ground safely, their hearts pounding to the beat of the fae above them rushing to the edge of the balcony to see their demise. Vampires hissed, their fangs glinting in the moonlight, and witches muttered curses under their breath, as if they all were hoping to get a chance to stab a pixie once midnight struck.

Zera's legs trembled as they landed on the grass, but relief overwhelmed her. The sooner they got out of there, the better.

CHAPTER 11
ZERA

Zera awoke with a start, the silk sheets tangled around her legs like some stubborn vine. She felt like she'd been climbing down that nightmarish trellis all night. The memory of the disastrous gala ran through her mind, each scene replaying like a twisted movie reel.

She shuddered at the cacophony of laughter from the ballroom that still echoed in her mind. Monsters. They were all monsters in there. But she was safe and sound now.

The sun's rays bathed the luxurious silk sheets spread across the massive king bed as she blinked away the remnants of her restless dreams. She brushed the sleep from her eyes, her gaze falling on the royal blue gown strewn on the floor, right where she'd left it, and her mind raced back to the disastrous gala.

She shuddered at the danger they'd faced and escaped by a hair's breadth. As she thought of the previous night's events, her heart pounded, threatening to leap out of her chest. A chill ran down her spine as Kraven's sinister smile and gleaming blue eyes haunted her thoughts.

Ugh, she had to get moving. Otherwise, she would be useless for the rest of the day. With a determined sigh, she swung her legs over the edge of the bed, threw a kiss to her mother's locket, which she'd put on her bedside table for luck, and pushed herself up, her pixie-like frame tense with apprehension.

Her feet touched the plush carpet, and she reveled in its softness, a rare indulgence for someone used to the bare wooden floors of her small house. A house that wasn't even truly hers, that her ex could come and commandeer at any time.

She tried not to think about that, though. It was the only home she had, and without it, she wouldn't be able to raise her little boy. It was a blessing and a curse.

She padded across the room, her thoughts still swirling with the events that had transpired at the ball. As much as she wanted to focus on her son, Cole, and the life she was fighting to protect, Zera couldn't ignore the growing connection between her and Maverick. Somehow, despite their differences, they fit together like two pieces of an intricate puzzle. A puzzle that, if she were being honest with herself, terrified her to pieces.

Her reflection in the floor-to-ceiling mirror in the bathroom caught her eye. Her brown waves were a tangled mess, and the remnants of last night's makeup did little to hide the exhaustion lining her face. Zera shook her head, shutting the bathroom door, eager to enjoy the shower that was the size of her entire bathroom at home and to wash away the stress and grime from the night before.

"Time to get myself together," she whispered as she turned on the hot water that instantly sent a hazy mist of steam twisting through the air.

As Zera slipped under the torrent of water, the heat enveloped her, soothing her muscles and washing away the tension that had built from the late night. She let out a content sigh, leaning against the cool tiles behind her, closing her eyes and soaking in the calmness of the water from the shower that filled the room with white noise.

Finally, she had a moment to herself. With the warmth and privacy, she let her mind drift back to her first encounter with

Maverick. The way he smirked at her. The playful glint in his eyes when he tormented her with his arrogant remarks.

"He really doesn't give a bloody fae," she murmured to herself, running a frustrated hand through her mass of tangled waves, letting the water rinse out the soap.

This whole situation was the polar opposite of how she'd imagined her life going. It felt like a fairy tale gone wrong, a single mother lost in a world of espionage and danger. A world where she really didn't belong but was forced to fight alongside a werewolf, a species she despised, and not just any werewolf but one from the Lunar Brotherhood pack—her sworn enemy.

But somehow, despite how much Maverick got under her skin, Zera couldn't deny the chemistry that sparked between them. It was like fire and ice coming together, creating a beautiful dance of contradictions. Each encounter only fueled the growing flame within her, making it harder to resist the pull.

Zera knew she had to keep her distance, for Cole's sake. A man like Maverick would only bring more trouble into their already-complicated lives. but every time she looked at him and felt his gaze on her, she felt her resolve slipping away.

She sighed, knowing that the tension between them wasn't going anywhere anytime soon. She needed to finish this. To kill Gareth and stop anyone else who came for her and her family.

The water gradually cooled down, and she knew it was time to face reality once again. The reality that last night's efforts were futile and they weren't any closer to finding Gareth and whoever his collaborator was than they had been before the gala.

Shutting off the water, she grabbed one of the plush towels and wrapped it around her body, noticing how the thick fabric caressed her skin. She made her way through the bathroom to the closet, still unable to wrap her mind around the extravagance of the penthouse.

It was larger than her entire house back home and had enough closet space for an entire department store. Her keen eyes spotted several outfits hanging on the rack from Felice's boutique, waiting for her to try them on. They must've cost a fortune, and after checking several tags, she verified they were all in her size. But they weren't just any clothes. Their fabrics exuded a rich softness she'd never experienced before, the structure solid yet relaxed enough that she would be comfortable wearing them while tending to her plants and experiments. The closet even contained a lab coat, protective eyewear, and gloves.

Tears welled in her eyes. Maverick had bought all of them for her? She couldn't remember the last time she'd gotten new clothes in her size. She'd had her clothes from before pregnancy, but those definitely didn't fit anymore, and she'd gotten a few items for work, but nothing felt right. Everything fit... wrong.

But between the gowns from yesterday—which must've cost a fortune—and this, she'd never felt so seen and cared for. Maybe he did care after all. It made her wonder what a rogue spy for hire even made. Probably a lot more than what a bartender in a small country town did. Perhaps she needed a job change.

This is ridiculous, she thought. A single mom bartender turned spy? Absurd.

Grabbing one of the more practical items, a pair of comfortable pants and T-shirt that felt like a cloud was caressing her skin, she descended the stairs. The scent of hot coffee and a savory breakfast greeted her as she reached the bottom of the stairs. The open living room had been transformed into a gym, with a giant fighting mat in the center and a rack of weights and various weapons on racks next to the wall of windows.

Maverick stood in the midst of it all, leaning against glass as he peered out across Mystic City's bustling downtown metropolis. His chest was bare, and he wore only black fitted leather pants that somehow looked like they would accommodate any movement. No doubt a work of Felice's doing. They hung low at his bones that were still visible from his grueling training regimen. The sunlight kissed his tanned, sculpted chest, highlighting every muscle and contour of muscle. Zera's breath hitched at the sight, her heart pounding.

Whether he was arrogant or not, she had to appreciate the raw beauty before her.

"Morning, Zera," he said, his stormy eyes reflecting the sun as they locked on her when she approached. There was intensity in his gaze that seemed to read her every thought, leaving her feeling both vulnerable and intrigued. "I was thinking we'd start your combat training today. Maybe it'll help clear our heads before going over last night."

Zera's heart clenched at his words, a sudden tightness taking residence in her chest. She drew a deep breath, the steam from the shower lingering in her lungs like a phantom echo of the fear simmering beneath her resolve.

"Uh... sure," she replied, trying to hide her nervousness. She'd never considered herself a fighter. She knew a few self-defense moves, sure, and she had made an impact against that snake shifter at the siren's boutique, but true combat training was something else entirely.

She thought of Cole and the night the druid had nearly killed him, and she balled her hands into fists. Learning how to defend herself and her son from dangers they might face was essential. Plus, she couldn't deny the allure of being trained like a spy by a true spy.

"Great," Maverick said, a hint of a smile playing at the corners of his mouth. "You look good."

His eyes raked over her with appreciation. Heat crept up Zera's cheeks, and she bit her lower lip, trying to suppress the surge of desire that bubbled within her. She didn't want to admit how his compliment affected her, how his lingering gaze sent a shiver of electricity through her veins, awakening a hunger she hadn't felt in years.

"Thanks," she finally said, heading for the kitchen for a mug of coffee. Liquid energy would be necessary if she was going to face off with the massive beast of a wolf that towered over her.

He took her lead and joined her at the kitchen counter, where a pot of steaming black nectar awaited. "We'll begin with what you know first, the basic self-defense techniques you displayed yester-day. Then we'll move on to more complex maneuvers," Maverick said, pouring himself a cup of coffee as well.

The morning light streamed through the wall of windows, casting a celestial glow over the makeshift gym. Zera sipped her coffee, the bitterness a stark contrast to the overwhelming sweetness of the situation. Here she was, a single mom accustomed to the rhythm of caring for everyone else, now not only being cared for but about to step onto a mat and learn the art of combat. It was a surreal moment, one that Zera never thought she would experience in her lifetime.

"Are you okay?" Maverick asked, his voice barely above a whisper.

She jumped, looking over her shoulder where Maverick stood next to the couch that had been pushed up against the wall. She real-ized she'd been staring at a shelf full of various-sized daggers perched next to the weights. She hadn't even noticed when she'd moved from the kitchen.

Luckily, her coffee mug was nearly empty. Otherwise, she was sure she'd spill it on the row of leather belts. And was that a... a toothbrush?

She couldn't fathom what any of those things were useful for.

"Yeah, it's just... a lot," she admitted as she looked at the assorted weaponry. The gleam of knives seemed to mock her, a reminder of her naiveté in this dangerous new world. Maverick's world.

Maverick approached, his presence reassuring and intimidating. "It can be," he agreed, his voice low and steady. "But remember, you're not fighting against the weapons or the training. You're fighting for something—someone—far more important."

Zera nodded, feeling the truth of his words resonate within her. Cole. This was all for his safety. She set her mug down on a nearby end table with determination.

"Let's do this," she said, her mind made up.

Without another word, he led her to the center of the mat, his movements fluid and deliberate. "Let's start with your stance," he instructed, demonstrating a balanced position. "Good foundation is key."

As she mirrored his pose, she felt an unfamiliar sense of power coursing within her veins. With each pivot and block that Maverick guided her through, she could feel herself transforming, her confidence building like a fortress around her heart. Despite the fear that showered her thoughts, there was also something invigorating about learning to fight. Each jab and kick released pent-up anxieties and doubts, leaving behind a growing certainty of her own strength.

She had a long way to go, though, as Maverick pinned her to the mat with ease, his muscles flexing as he held her in place. Citrus and burnt wood surrounded her. She struggled beneath him, trying to will her aching muscles to push back—to break free.

But despite her best efforts, she couldn't escape his grasp. Maverick's grip tightened slightly, his eyes locked on hers with a mixture of intensity and amusement.

"Where are all those self-defense moves now?" He cocked his dark brow at her.

She scowled up at his smug face. "They didn't exactly have us practice getting pinned down by a trained werewolf spy," she huffed in frustration.

Zera strained against his hold, determined to prove that she wasn't completely helpless.

"No?" Maverick chuckled, the sound vibrating through his chest and sending a tantalizing shiver down her spine. "Too busy pouring cocktails at that wolf tavern you work at?"

She narrowed her eyes at him. *Arrogant faeboy.*

He must've read the insult on her face because he laughed even harder.

"Stop it," she said, shoving him again. It did nothing. It was like trying to push a mountain. Her mouth deceived her, and she cracked a smile.

"Listen," he said, his deep, masculine voice somehow still soft and comforting. "Everyone has a weak spot. Even me."

"Oh, really? The great lone wolf turned rogue spy admits to having a weakness?" She gawked in jest.

He rolled his eyes. "Everyone has a weakness. Yours is your self-doubt."

"Gee, thanks," she muttered with a mock-appreciative tone, feeling a pang of annoyance mixed with a touch of truth.

Maverick was right. She had always struggled with self-doubt, constantly second-guessing her abilities as a pixie and as a mother. It was hard not to, especially when her responsibilities weighed heavy on her shoulders.

And it didn't help matters when the man she'd loved, the one who'd supposedly loved her, completely abandoned her and his own son.

She blinked the tears that threatened to rise. Not because she missed him but because of the fact that neither she nor her son had been worthy enough to stick around for. But she knew without a doubt that Cole was. He was worth more than her life and deserved better. She knew it, but she hated the little voice inside her head that whispered that her son might deserve better than her. That she wasn't good enough or strong enough to protect Cole when it truly mattered, and she loathed herself for sometimes believing that.

You're more than good enough. Her body froze. It wasn't a thought she expected to hear, and it didn't quite sound like her own, but it was enough to jar her out of her self-deprecating thoughts.

"Believe it or not, Zera," Maverick said, releasing her as he stood up and offered her a hand. "Even the best of us have a weak spot."

Zera took his hand warily, rising to stand beside him. His grip, firm and warm, seemed to ground her spiraling thoughts, sending an unexpected jolt of energy through her. She quickly withdrew her hand, trying to ignore the lingering sensation.

"All right, so how do I find this 'weak spot'?" she asked, crossing her arms over her chest. Her heart was still pounding from their close encounter, and her cheeks were flushed.

Maverick's trademark smirk returned as he folded his arms. "Ah, that's the million-faecoin question, isn't it?" he mused. "It's not something you can see. You have to feel it, sense it. It's more about intuition than physical or even magical strength."

His words rang true, making her think of their unspoken connection. The way Maverick seemed to understand her on a deeper level. The way he encouraged her and pushed her to the limits. It made her want to push herself harder too. To prove to herself she was capable of more, as Maverick seemed to think.

"Let's go again," he said, the intensity in his eyes sparking a fire within her.

Zera's eyes locked on his. An unmistakable hum filled her body when his lips parted into a crooked smile, as if he was challenging her.

She was there to learn, to protect herself and her son, but there was something else between them, a spark that ignited every time their eyes met. But she didn't have time for that. She needed to train, to master everything Maverick had to teach her because there was no way Gareth, or whoever, could come into her life and threaten her son and her family without her putting up a fight and defending them.

"All right, but this time you won't pin me. I'm going to find your weak spot," she declared, her own determination evident in her voice.

Maverick chuckled. "Let's see it, then."

She rolled her sore shoulders and squared off against Maverick once again, this time more focused than ever. As they circled each other, Zera let everything go. Everything she'd ever believed, thought, or felt, leaving only intuition and instinct in the wake. She focused on everything Maverick had taught her so far—the precise movements, the calculated strikes, and the art of anticipation. She observed his every motion as she countered them, analyzing his body language for any sign of weakness.

As they continued to spar, their movements seemed to become more synchronized, as if they were dancing. Maverick was patient with her, guiding her through the moves with a steady hand. His touch was firm yet gentle, instilling in her a sense of safety she hadn't felt in a long time. Despite the seriousness of their training, he often wore a playful grin, especially when he pinned her down and she finally managed to sense his weak spot—a small ticklish spot on his side. Zera burst into laughter as she wiggled out from underneath him. Maverick's laughter joined hers, the sound filling the room and creating an atmosphere of pure joy.

"Okay, okay, you win," he said, his voice resonating with pride. "How'd you know that would work?"

Zera caught her breath, still giggling as she sat up. "Pixie powers," she teased, her voice brimming with playful confidence. "We have our ways of uncovering secrets."

"Oh, do you now?" he taunted with a wickedly handsome grin.

She wiped the sweat from her brow. "That, or I made a mental note of your reaction when I brushed by you earlier. It was a lucky guess."

"Lucky or not, you're a quick learner."

She smiled at his words, feeling a warmth spread through her once again. It was then that she heard it again—or thought she heard it.

You're beautiful when you smile like that.

The voice this time was undeniably Maverick's, but his lips hadn't moved. Or at least she hadn't seen them move. She blinked at him, a wave of confusion washing over her. Had he said that out loud? Or had she imagined it?

Before she could dwell on it further, Maverick cleared his throat and continued their training. But Zera couldn't shake off the incident. Every time their hands brushed or their eyes met, she wondered if he felt it, too, the inexplicable bond between them.

During a particularly intense sparring session, Zera stumbled back, gasping for breath. Maverick stepped forward, concern etching his features. *Shit. Are you all right?* His voice echoed in her mind again, soft and soothing. She looked at him, her eyes wide. He hadn't opened his mouth.

This was no coincidence, and the sudden gut feeling within her that was too foreign to be her own confirmed that he thought so too. But why hadn't he said anything? And why did he seem as surprised as she was?

Maybe she was wrong. Maybe she'd only imagined it. "Again," she said with a firm nod when he looked like he was going to suggest a break.

Her breath was ragged, her muscles sore from repetitive movements, but she pushed through it, determined to prove to herself she could do it. But more importantly, despite the fear and doubt, she wouldn't back down. She would face this and whatever else came her way, for her son, for herself, and for her future.

Zera dodged one of his strikes but only by a second.

Lucky, she thought.

You're skilled, a voice whispered in response.

"What did you say?" she asked and frowned at Maverick, who mirrored her expression.

"I didn't say anything," he said, sending another round of punches her way, each one faster than the next. She was getting better at not getting hit.

"But I heard you," she pushed back, her voice rising in frustration.

"I swear, Zera, I didn't say anything," Maverick insisted, his eyes wide with sincerity.

The room fell into an uncomfortable silence as they both tried to understand what was happening.

"You didn't just say 'you're skilled'?" she asked, her voice growing weak at the thought of the alternative. What if he hadn't said it out loud but he was now in her head?

She'd heard rumors of deep connections made between fae that allowed mates to communicate through their bond. They were common among werewolves, dragons, and other shape-shifters. Sometimes among vampires, but that was less common, and never, ever with elementals like pixies.

All humor drained from Maverick's face, his jaw clenched as if he was holding back something. "No, Zera, I didn't say that."

Something in his tone conveyed there was something else, but the look in Maverick's eyes told her he was done with the conversation.

"But..." She trailed off.

"Enough." Maverick dropped his stance. "We're both tired. Let's call it a day on the training front, okay?"

Zera's frustration bubbled to the surface. He was avoiding what had just happened, what she'd heard in her mind. It hadn't been her voice, and if she could hear his thoughts, then that meant something. This realization made her even angrier, though a part of her was intrigued by it. As much as she wouldn't mind the idea of a romp in the sheets with this broodingly handsome spy, the idea of being tied to an arrogant faeboy werewolf was unthinkable. How responsible would that be?

"Are you going to pretend like nothing happened?" she snapped, unable to let it go.

"Zera, we don't have time for this," Maverick said firmly, refusing to continue training. "Let's get some water."

Her dry throat ached, and questions rumbled in her mind. She didn't get a chance to ask them, though, as Maverick made a beeline for the kitchen. Hint taken.

"About last night," he said, tossing one of the bottles of water to her before sitting down at the island. "We should go over everything we saw and heard."

Zera reluctantly followed him, emotions swirling within her. She took a seat across from him, clutching the cold bottle in her hands, trying to focus on the task at hand.

"Fine," she agreed, taking a deep breath to calm herself.

As they discussed the events of the gala, her newfound connection with Maverick weighed upon her. She knew they needed to focus on their mission, but the thought of their potential bond lingered in the back of her mind, clouding her thoughts.

She would have to confront it eventually, but for now, she needed to concentrate on their mission and the danger that awaited them. It was the only way she could protect her son and herself from this dangerous world they'd become entangled in.

"What did he say exactly?" Maverick asked her for what seemed like the hundredth time.

"I think that was all." She shrugged and winced. Every muscle screamed at her, and she knew she'd be paying for that workout tomorrow. "He said something about Gareth and being sorry about what he did, offered me a drink I didn't want but somehow still drank, and then I spilled everything to him. Or at least everything aside from Cole, thank the fae."

"And there's nothing else you can think of? Anything out of the ordinary?" he asked, his desperation apparent. She knew he wanted the night not to have been a bust, but it was beginning to look like it had all been a waste of time.

Her stomach rumbled.

Zera shook her head. "I've told you everything I remember."

Maverick sighed heavily, running a hand through his tousled hair. "All right," he conceded, his voice barely above a whisper. There was a hint of disappointment in his tone, and she felt a pang of guilt. They had both hoped for more from the gala, but it seemed like they were back to square one.

"I'm sorry," she murmured, reaching across the table to lightly touch his hand. It was an instinctive gesture, an attempt to offer comfort in the face of their shared disappointment. He looked at her, surprise flickering in his eyes before it was replaced by a soft warmth. He turned his hand around, his fingers curling around hers, giving a reassuring squeeze.

"Don't apologize, Zera," he said, his voice gentle. "I should be the one apologizing. For putting your life at risk. For using that bloody FaeMatch app. I was a fool to think it wouldn't have consequences."

The sudden sting of tears took Zera by surprise as Maverick's apology struck a chord within her. She blinked them away, refusing to let them fall. She couldn't afford to let her emotions get the better of her, not when they were in the midst of a dangerous game. She had to stay focused.

Still, his words meant something to her, and she took them to heart. Perhaps he wasn't a complete faeboy after all.

"Can you ever forgive me?" His eyes pleaded in an uncharacteristic way, filled with genuine remorse.

Zera could feel the sincerity radiating from him, casting a new light on their situation. Maverick wasn't just some arrogant cold-hearted werewolf and spy. He was a man who had made mistakes and was taking responsibility for them, a trait she found to be one of the sexiest a man could have.

That and a good set of abs, which Maverick had in spades.

She finally nodded, squeezing his hand back. He was trying to help her, to make it right, at least. She could forgive him. Thoughts of her son flooded her mind as she remembered who she was doing all of this for. A sudden tension replaced the calm as she wondered what would happen if they failed. They knew Gareth was out there looking for her, looking for a way to hurt them both. What if they didn't find him before he struck again?

"Hey, we'll figure all this other stuff out," he promised, as if sensing her fears.

His reassurance did little to quell the storm of worry brewing inside her, but she appreciated his effort. And his apology.

Mate.

The word filled her mind, but she squashed the thought before it could solidify. She didn't want to think about that. She just wanted to finish their mission and get back to her life with her son.

They sat in silence, their hands absently entwined on the table, each lost in their own thoughts.

Suddenly, her stomach grumbled even louder than before, breaking the silence. She blushed, quickly pulling her hand away.

"Sorry," she said, wincing at the interruption.

Maverick chuckled and cocked an eyebrow, his sweet demeanor vanishing into a smirk. She guessed the arrogance was back. "Hungry?"

"A bit," she admitted, not caring to be embarrassed as she realized she hadn't eaten anything since last night.

Maverick stood up from the table, his smirk widening. "Well, lucky for you, I happen to have connections in all the right places. How about I whip us up something to eat?"

Zera raised an eyebrow, a mixture of curiosity and skepticism crossing her face. "You can cook something other than eggs and coffee?"

He shrugged. "I'm full of surprises."

It took Maverick no time at all to grill a couple of grilled cheeses made with a fancy cheese and sliver of pesto. As he cooked, he went on about the cheese and how it came from goats raised in the mountains of the Lunar Forest that were fed only moonlit-infused grasses —or some other fancy-sounding process.

She didn't care. If it tasted as good as it smelled, the goats could've been fed moonlit unicorns for all she cared.

He returned to the island with the sandwiches and bowls of soup, a comforting aroma filling the room. Zera stifled a moan when she bit into the cheesy deliciousness. The flavors melted together in a symphony on her tongue, causing her eyes to flutter closed in purse bliss. Maverick's cooking skills were definitely unexpected, but she was certainly enjoying them.

She opened her eyes to Maverick watching her, that smirk painted across his lips.

"Enjoying it?" he asked, a mischievous glint in his eyes.

Jerk, she thought but nodded, too hungry to formulate a retort.

Maverick leaned back in his chair, appraising her with a playful gaze, as if he'd heard her thoughts. She swallowed hard, hoping he hadn't. The last thing she needed right now was to find her fated mate, especially if it was a werewolf spy.

"How did you learn to cook like this?" she half moaned.

He shrugged. "You have your little experiment upstairs. I have this. It's therapeutic for me."

She nodded, understanding the need to have an outlet for stress and anxiety. Zera took another bite of her grilled cheese, savoring the flavors that danced on her taste buds. Maverick's mention of her pixie-dust experiment was a reminder that her first seedling had failed in the budding stage. She only had two more seeds to attempt. One of them had to work. It just had to.

"What are you doing up there anyway?" he asked, taking a bite of his own food.

She took a sip of water. "Well, you know why I'm being hunted, right? To harvest my pixie dust."

Maverick's expression hardened, but he nodded.

"I've been trying to come up with an alternative."

He frowned. "You mean, to grow pixie dust?"

"No, that's not possible, but there is a potential to create a synthetic."

Maverick's eyes widened in surprise, and he set his sandwich down on the plate. "A synthetic version of pixie dust? Is that even possible?"

Zera nodded. "I believe it. If I can ever perfect the conditions to get the everfrost blossom seedling to grow." Excitement bubbled from her chest. "I've been researching and experimenting with different combinations of enchanted elements, trying to replicate the essence of it. It wouldn't create magic, but that's not the goal. The goal is to mimic the euphoric properties that make pixie dust so profitable for drug lords. Plus, they have the added bonus of not being deadly for consumption."

"What about the legality of creating such a synthetic drug?"

"Well, you're a rogue spy, and I'm a pixie with a bounty on her head," Zera replied with a wry smile. "I think we've already established legality isn't really our top priority."

"Fair point." He chuckled and leaned back in his chair. "Have you ever considered finishing your degree?"

A pang of regret tugged at Zera's heart as she thought about her unfinished degree. "I used to dream about finishing it, working in an official laboratory somewhere conducting groundbreaking research," she admitted, her voice laced with nostalgia. "But life had other plans for me, and if I had to do it all over again, I would. My son is the best thing that's ever happened to me."

Maverick only nodded, and the topic was never brought up again. He must've sensed how hard it was to talk about what she had to give up in order to make room for what she had now. But it was worth it. She loved Cole more than anything, and she wouldn't even think about what life might've been like without him. He was the best part of her, and that was that.

With each passing day, a rhythm began to emerge between them. They trained each morning until her muscles felt like jelly, followed by Maverick's famous cooking. Then she spent the remainder of the day working on caring for her everfrost blossom seedling or studying the other ingredients she'd begun to accumulate for her experiment. Maverick used his spy skills to find any sign of where Gareth could be hiding out while at the same time avoiding bounty hunters.

It was the main reason they rarely left the penthouse, not that she minded. If she lived the rest of her life without being in another ballroom full of pixie killers, she'd be okay with that.

But her favorite part about their routine was ending the day on the phone with Jade and getting to wish her little baby sweet dreams. He was growing up too fast, and she couldn't wait for all this to be behind her so she could be reunited with her son.

Maverick's voice, which she'd thought she heard in her mind, never returned, and it was a topic she learned to avoid.

CHAPTER 12
ZERA

Zera's fists sliced through the air, her breaths coming out in pants as she practiced her jabs and crosses under Maverick's watchful gaze. The living room turned training room was bathed in the soft glow of the afternoon sun, casting long shadows across the floor. Through the wall of windows, downtown Mystic City stretched out before them, its skyscrapers gleaming like a cluster of silver needles against the blue sky.

"Keep your guard up," Maverick instructed, his voice smooth and steady.

Zera's eyes never left his, the intensity of her determination evident in their locked gazes. She gritted her teeth and pushed herself harder, sweat beading on her brow as she sought to improve her skills. Maverick countered her moves with ease, but she refused to let it discourage her. She'd done harder things than this. At least that was what she kept telling herself.

"Again," he commanded, and Zera obeyed without hesitation.

Her footwork had grown more agile over the past days, weeks, or however long they'd been holed up in that penthouse. She was tired and ready to go home but not until the mission was complete. Not until Gareth was out of their lives once and for all. Especially after she learned her house had been burned to the ground. The blow was devastating, but she couldn't let it consume her. She had training to do, and she was getting damn good at it.

She lunged forward, flexing her right hand as her knife, aimed at Maverick's chest, appeared in a puff of smoke from the sleeve of her fighting leathers, but he easily dodged it and trapped her arm in a lock. With a flick of his wrist, the blade went flying across the room. Zera cursed under her breath and attempted to break free from his grasp. He chuckled and tightened his hold on her.

"Your moves are getting predictable," he teased.

Zera glared at him, knowing he was right. She needed to switch up her tactics if she wanted any chance of beating him. She took a deep breath and focused all her energy on finding an opening in his defense.

Suddenly, she saw it. A small gap in his stance that she could exploit. She quickly twisted her body, breaking free from his hold and landing a solid punch to his gut. Maverick stumbled back, surprised by her sudden burst of strength.

Zera took advantage of the momentary distraction, grabbed her knife off the floor, and lunged at him again with renewed determination. This time, she was able to land a few fake strikes before he disarmed her.

But she still didn't give up as they continued to spar. She kept fighting, using every move and technique she had learned from him or had taught herself. Her unwavering resolve to keep getting up every time she fell down propelled her forward. She would never let herself feel weak, powerless, or unloved, like she had during those first months postpartum.

The dark memory of feeling so underwater flooded her mind. She had barely been able to keep things together as she juggled taking care of Cole and working at Haven Wolf Tavern while surrounded by people who didn't seem to understand or really see her struggling. But somehow she had persevered, drawing strength from her love for her son. Now, that same fierce determination fueled her desire to be better—for herself, for Cole, and for whatever future awaited them.

And finally, after what felt like an eternity but was only a few minutes, she managed to pin Maverick down on the floor and hold her knife to his throat.

"Break," Maverick called out, tapping the mat on the floor where she straddled him.

"Break so soon?" She cocked her head to the side. "You're getting too easy."

A wholehearted laugh rumbled through Maverick's chest, one she hadn't heard in a little while, and his dark eyes sparkled with amusement. The look sent a shiver of anticipation down her spine.

"Easy? Far from it," he said, his breath warm against her cheek. He sat up, picking her up by the thighs and setting her on the mat beside him, like she barely weighed a thing.

A sudden disappointment filled Zera's chest as Maverick released her, breaking their physical connection and reminding her that he was still avoiding the unspoken bond between them. She'd hoped for a little more, a lingering touch or perhaps even something more. She knew she should fear being with another werewolf, letting herself be vulnerable like that, and maybe a part of her still did.

But he wasn't a wolf, slave to his pack. He was a fae of his own making, and she respected that. He continuously proved how different he was from anyone she'd ever known, devoting every waking minute to her training and relentlessly pursuing the arms dealer who, it seemed, had turned drug lord and was a threat to her and her son.

And he seemed to be drawn to her, too, judging by the way she'd caught him admiring her physique while she trained or helped clean up from dinner.

She couldn't deny the chemistry between them, and she found herself eagerly anticipating their next training sessions. But there was a nagging doubt in the back of her mind. Would they ever be able to truly be together? Would their different species and backgrounds always keep them apart?

Despite these doubts, she couldn't help but feel safe and comfortable around him. He had become a constant presence in her life for these past weeks, someone she could rely on during this chaotic time. And as much as she tried to resist, she found herself falling for him more each day.

His cooking helped. Each morning they'd wake up with a protein smoothie. Lunch was light, but then at dinner, he would whip up an amazing dish, tapping into some magic to create flavors she'd never experienced before. She could tell he enjoyed it, too, from the way his eyes would sparkle as he presented each meal to her. It was a small thing, but it spoke volumes about him and his priorities. He was surprisingly homey for a spy. Not that she'd met many spies, but she imagined them being far colder and more detached, always on the move and never forming real connections.

But he was different. He had a warmth to him that drew her in, making her feel safe and protected. And it only strengthened the connection she knew was growing between them. Yet, as was typical these days, Maverick kept his walls up, refusing to let her in since she'd brought up his voice she'd heard in her mind. It hadn't happened again, and she was starting to think she'd imagined it.

"Your progress is impressive," he said, rising and stretching his hand out to help her up. She stifled a frustrated sigh as she tried to keep from admiring his glorious pecs. At least his chivalry hadn't been locked away, like his feelings seemed to be. "You have a natural gift for this."

A small smile played on her lips as she straightened and wiped the perspiration away with the back of her hand. "Was that a compliment?"

"Maybe," Maverick replied with a smirk, his arrogance making a brief appearance. "But you've earned it. Your dedication is truly paying off."

Zera felt her cheeks warm at the praise, but she quickly refocused her mind on the task at hand. She knew she couldn't afford to let anything distract her from her goal of becoming stronger and more self-assured, not even Maverick's confusing behavior or his striking good looks. A feat that was getting harder as the days went by.

"Let's move on to more-complex weapons training," Maverick suggested, walking over to a chest filled with an array of enchanted weapons. "As you know, your clothing isn't only for show. It's been designed to conjure various weapons that can be seamlessly incorporated into your movements. The dagger is just one of them."

"Yes, I know. Shields and defense weapons on my left, daggers on the right," Zera said, approaching the chest with a sense of anticipation. She was beginning to enjoy learning to use all these weapons. It was like opening a new set of measuring beakers and experimenting with a new element every day.

"There's a third category where you can conceal your own weapons," Maverick began and offered her a sleek silver staff adorned with intricate markings and symbols. "I think this one will suit you."

She gawked at its height. It was nearly as tall as her, stopping at shoulder height. She raised her eyebrows at Maverick. "A stick? You shouldn't have."

"It's not a stick. A staff." He laughed when her face twisted in even more confusion. "Just... take it."

The storm in his icy eyes hinted at something deeper, some distant pain perhaps, and though she couldn't feel him through the bond she knew they had, his tone conveyed to her that this weapon in particular meant something.

She finally took the stick in her right hand and gasped. Warmth and energy rushed up her arm and spine simultaneously like the surge of her pixie dust, only it seemed to come from the staff like it was an amplifier. She felt stronger, more focused, and like her power was limitless.

Without thinking, she flicked her wrist, and two blades shot out from either end of the staff.

"See? You're a natural." He shrugged nonchalantly, but she wasn't listening. Wind rushed through her ears like the sound she played Cole to hush him to sleep. She looked up, but the sliding door to the balcony was closed, and the curtains were still. Where was the breeze coming from?

Whispers reached her ear as if the staff was speaking to her. Her eyes jerked down the weapon that glowed faintly in the setting sun. A symbol near her grip caught her eye—two circles in a pike formation with a smaller circle connecting them in the center. She'd heard the legends of the Whispers as a young child, but they were folklore. Ancient pixie warriors trained in battle with their blades of terror and would slaughter those who kept secrets from them. But it was just a story parents used to scare their children not to lie.

This couldn't be one of those weapons because pixies hadn't actually been warriors in ancient times. They'd been servants or farmers who tended the fields with the other nature fae, and even today in the modern age, they were mostly clerks in various wildlife and forestry offices. Important but overlooked by society and definitely not in positions that required much higher education.

That was why she strove to be different. To set her own path. Not that it had worked out so well for her on that front, since she was a bartender. Perhaps one day she'd go back to school and finally graduate with a faeology and alchemistry science degree. But until then, she would have to make do with serving drinks when she stopped playing spy and got back to her reality.

"Where did you get this?" she managed to gasp, but she couldn't bring herself to look up. She felt a pull toward the design, like it was beckoning her to come closer.

"That's a long story," Maverick whispered from somewhere far away.

The whispers grew louder and more urgent, as if guiding her movements. She followed their lead and raised the staff above her head before bringing it down in a sweeping motion, letting the blades slice through the air. A ripple of her power surged out in purple waves.

Confused but intrigued, she repeated the motion and again felt the surge of energy. With each swing and thrust, she felt connected to something primal yet foreign.

A growl erupted from Maverick's throat as they sparred more fiercely than ever before. It was as if they were dancing together, their bodies moving harmoniously with each other's desires and needs.

She could feel her control over the power growing with each movement, as if it was connected to the staff in some primal-yet-foreign way. The staff seemed to amplify not only her strength but also awakened desires she thought long buried beneath single motherhood and heartbreak.

The whispers began to form words, guiding her in a language she didn't understand but somehow knew how to follow. Then they changed. The whispers urged a new dance, a new path, but it felt wrong. It wasn't her movement, and suddenly what the whispers asked of her, she wanted no part in.

A breath for a breath, it whispered to her. *Take what they stole from so many before you.*

No, she wouldn't do it. Couldn't.

Traitor! it hissed as her movements with the double-bladed staff grew more and more intense. *You call yourself a pixie? Pathetic. Only blood will do.*

The whisper faded, but the hold on her only tightened. She tried to stop, to break free from whatever curse this staff had put on her. Though she was a pixie, this energy wasn't made for her. She wasn't a murderer, and what the staff whispered to her wasn't to kill out of self-defense or to protect her child from Gareth; it was slaughter. And it was coming for every last wolf.

"Zera," a familiar voice shouted at her, but it was so distant she couldn't tell where it came from.

She struck the air again, only this time a scream sliced through the silence, piercing Zera's ears. The sound was filled with pain and desperation.

"*Zera!*"

Suddenly, Zera found herself on top of Maverick once again, his handsome face twisted in pain. She blinked once, twice, confused at what might've happened. She knew something wasn't right. He was at eye level, and his arms were struggling with something between them. Her gaze followed his, and bile rose up in her throat as she saw the source of his agony. The blade at the end of the staff had pierced through his torso. Crimson blood stained his shirt and dripped onto the floor.

Horror swept over Zera, her heart pounding in her chest as she dropped the staff. The whispers silenced in an instant.

"Maverick!" she cried, rushing toward him. Panic flooded her senses as she tried to process everything. Zera's eyes filled with tears as she frantically searched for something to help him.

"Stay still. I'll call for help!" Zera's voice shook, but Maverick grabbed her wrist, stopping her from reaching for her faestone.

"I'm okay," he said with a grunt, but the look in his eyes told a different story. Zera could see the pain and fear lurking within his storm-filled gaze.

"But—"

"I said I'm fine," he growled, shoving her hand away as he managed to get to his feet. "I'm a werewolf with alpha blood in my veins. It'll heal in no time."

"You're an alpha?" The contents of the egg salad she'd had for lunch churned in her stomach, and suddenly she didn't feel well. Being a Lunar Brotherhood wolf who'd abandoned his pack was one thing, but he had the alpha bloodline. That changed everything. It made him even more dangerous than she'd thought. At least that explained how he'd been able to reject the pack and live to tell about it.

And she'd nearly killed him. An alpha without a pack. But how?

Her throat went dry when she looked down at the silver staff that still glowed on the floor, beckoning to her.

"What the bloody fae is that thing?" she demanded, whirling on Maverick, who hobbled over to the nearest chair. She just watched, since the arrogant, stupid wolf rejected her offer to help him. Too much pride for his own damn good.

"I told you. It's a staff."

She folded her arms and scoffed. "That's no staff. Or a stick. It's alive. It breathes the same energy as my own pixie dust, but it wanted me to kill you."

He made no response, letting out a grimace as he slumped against the cushion and peeled back his hand, which was covered in his own blood. The wound was already stitching itself back up.

"What is it?" she demanded again. She wouldn't take his silence for an answer. He had to say it.

His eyes met hers, as if to say she already knew, but she didn't want to say it first. Didn't want to even think of it as a possibility.

"It's a Whisper's staff," he said, and she shuddered as the walls of her reality shattered all around her. "The ancient pixie warriors fashioned the double-bladed weapon only they could wield to enhance their own powers against the Lunar Brotherhood. A way the universe kept everything in balance. For a time. Until the Lunar Brotherhood alpha bloodline grew in numbers and strength, nearly making them extinct."

She shook her head. "But the Whispers are only a legend. These weapons don't exist because that would mean..."

Her eyes flitted between the healed wound in his chest and the storm raging in Maverick's gaze.

"I could've killed you," she gasped.

He nodded. "One inch to the right, my heart would've stopped."

"Why won't you tell me where you got it? And what happened to its wielder?" Zera's voice shook, a mix of anger and fear coursing through her veins as the haunting tales she'd grown up on of the Whispers came rushing back. If he had this staff, then he must've killed the Whisper pixie who'd wielded it. The legend, if it was true, was that the blade could only be separated from a pixie warrior if they were bested in battle or if they gave it willingly.

Maverick's jaw hardened as he checked his wounds and wiped the blood on the shirt he'd left on the arm of the chair. "It doesn't matter."

"It does to me," Zera insisted, reaching out to touch the intricate engravings that lined the length of the staff. They glowed faintly in response to her touch, as if recognizing her pixie magic.

"I don't want to talk about it." He stood when she tried to press him on the matter. "Trust me. The less you know, the better."

She ground her teeth. He was keeping secrets from her, and he had the nerve to tell her to trust him.

"Trust goes both ways, you know," she said, following him to the kitchen island, where he turned on the sink to clean up. "I've trusted you so far. When every instinct in my bones screams that I should run, I trust you. But you keep secrets from me. How long do you think that'll keep my trust? We're supposed to be partners, Maverick!"

His jaw clenched twice, but he made no response. He wasn't going to budge on where he got the staff. Fine. She would try a different question, then.

"Why would you give me a weapon like that if you knew it could kill you?"

"I was just... testing a theory out." His words were hesitant as he continued to wash the blood from his hands.

She raised an eyebrow, unconvinced. "A theory? About what?"

He paused for a moment before turning off the water and drying his hands on a nearby towel. "A theory about the staff, but it doesn't matter. We have bigger issues at hand. Like Gareth and the bounty on our heads."

"Fine," Zera snapped, frustrated by his evasiveness. "If that's all that matters to you, then so be it." With that, she stormed up to the bedroom, determined to distance herself from the infuriating werewolf spy. He could keep his secrets. She didn't want them anyway.

As she entered the room, she tried to distract herself by focusing on her everfrost blossom. She knelt down beside the small plant budding in the protected terrarium pushed against the south-facing window for optimal sunlight. She meticulously documented each detail of progress she perceived, her heart swelling with hope and anticipation for it to bud.

The potential breakthrough the everfrost blossom could bring once she extracted its properties and studied its elements excited her. She knew it could be the precursor for her plans to create a synthetic pixie-dust drug, which would ultimately save her people from being hunted.

But this was the second attempt, and if it failed, she had only one remaining seed, one final chance to extract its elements. No pressure, she reminded herself as she carefully watered the plant and monitored its growth. She couldn't afford to make any mistakes this time.

The last time, she had gotten too excited and added too much fertilizer, causing the plant to wilt and die. It had been a painful lesson to learn but one that taught her the importance of patience and precision in her work.

As she continued observing the everfrost blossom's progress, she couldn't help but think about the staff and all the secrets Maverick was keeping from her. She couldn't help but feel a growing resentment toward him. Despite everything he'd done for her and her son, all that he continued to do, he'd kept vital information from her and put their partnership in jeopardy. The weight of their secrets and the tension between them left her feeling emotionally drained.

Checking the time on her faestone, Zera realized it was six p.m. in Pixie Hollow—time for her daily call with Cole before Jade tucked him into his crib. Eager for a brief respite from the tension and unanswered questions swirling in her mind, Zera stepped away from the terrarium and the makeshift lab that took up most of the space next to the bed. She clicked her sister's image.

"Hey, Zera," Jade's voice came through the faestone, warm and familiar. "How's everything going?"

"Could be better," Zera admitted, forcing a smile that turned genuine as soon as Cole's face appeared on the quartz screen. Her heart swelled at the sight of her son, his lavender eyes bright and curious even through the small screen. It never failed to amaze her how much love she felt for him and how seeing his face could momentarily chase away her frustrations and concerns.

"Mama!" Cole exclaimed, his little voice bringing moisture to her eyes.

"Oh, baby! How I've missed you," Zera cooed, dabbing her eyelids.

Jade held the faestone up to Cole as she caught Zera up on his day—how he ate, napped, and all the things. She was amazing like that. Zera listened intently, taking it all in. She tried to ignore the ache it caused in her chest. She missed the normalcy and business of life with a little one. She couldn't wait to get back. To put all of this mess with Maverick, Gareth, and the rest of it behind her. She wasn't made for the spy life.

"Any new updates on when we'll be able to go back to Havenwood?" Jade asked when Zera said good night to Cole before Sloane took him for a bath.

"No." Zera paced back and forth in the spacious bedroom, gazing out of the window that showcased the city skyline to the south and the opposite window that overlooked the penthouse's balcony to the north.

"And what about finding Gareth?" Jade prodded, her voice laced with concern.

Zera's pacing came to a halt as she caught sight of Maverick on the balcony. He stood there, engaged in some conversation on his faestone, his expression tense and focused. Zera sighed before answering her sister.

"Things aren't going well, Jade," she confessed. "We haven't been able to find many contacts. The one promising lead we had took us to that fancy gala, but Gareth wasn't there, and no one was willing to give him up. It's like someone's paid everyone off."

"But I thought the last job Maverick took shut him down? Where would he have gotten the money?"

Zera shrugged. "He has to be bankrolled by someone new. Maybe it's them, whoever they are. I think it's this guy named Kraven, though."

Jade frowned. "Who's that?"

"This very powerful, very evil fae I never want to cross paths with again." She shuddered at how easily he'd manipulated her at the gala. The way he'd slithered into her mind like a snake. She never wanted to be that close to death again. Not even if she had the Whisper's staff, which reminded her of her current issue with the arrogant wolf who was keeping secrets from her. She clenched her fists, trying to push away the nagging feeling of betrayal.

"What else is wrong?" Jade asked, sensing a change in her tone.

Zera closed her eyes for a moment before replying. "It's Maverick. I found out he's not just a Lunar Brotherhood wolf, but he's of the alpha bloodline."

Jade's eyes widened for a moment as realization set in. "Wow, that... explains a lot. But are you really that surprised? I mean, it'd explain how he was able to leave the pack. They're not beholden to the pack the way betas and the rest of them are."

"True." Zera took a moment to gather her thoughts, her gaze still fixed on Maverick as she absently ran a hand through her ponytail of thick waves.

Not knowing how much she should share, she decided against bringing up the Whisper's staff to Jade, who'd probably think she was crazy anyway. However, Zera still had a lingering suspicion that the staff was somehow connected to Maverick's evasive behavior about the deepening bond they shared.

"You know, Jade, I'm starting to think that maybe he's keeping things from me on purpose, that he might have a hidden agenda."

Jade was silent for a moment before she responded. "Maybe he does. But to be honest, he's proven to be trustworthy when it comes to your safety. Hasn't he?"

"Yes, he has," Zera agreed. "It just bothers me that he's keeping things from me. It feels like he's not being entirely honest about everything, which makes it hard to trust him."

"Well, maybe you need to confront him again. If you two are going to work together effectively and beat this Gareth guy once and for all, there needs to be trust between you."

Zera nodded, knowing Jade was right. But for now, she decided to put that conversation on hold. It was late, and she didn't have the energy for it.

"I'll give it a try. Good night, Jade. Give Cole a kiss for me," Zera said, forcing a smile.

"Will do. Good night."

After hanging up, Zera changed into something more comfortable and headed downstairs for dinner. Maverick had prepared the meal, setting the table with candles and fine dishes. It would have been romantic if not for the secrets he kept and the connection he avoided. The tension was palpable as they ate in silence, occasionally brushing against each other as they reached for the various dishes.

The accidental touches sent sparks of electricity through Zera's body, hinting at the sexual tension between them. But her anger toward Maverick prevented her from giving in to the desire that simmered beneath the surface.

When dinner was finished, Zera retreated to her bedroom, feeling restless and agitated. She couldn't shake the feeling that Maverick was hiding something important from her, and she knew she wouldn't be able to sleep until she confronted him about it.

As Zera lay in bed, she vowed to herself that tomorrow would be the day she demanded answers from Maverick. About everything. She wouldn't let their growing connection be overshadowed by secrets and mistrust any longer. With that resolution in mind, Zera closed her eyes, hoping sleep would come and bring her some peace before the confrontation that awaited her.

SLEEP CAME SLOWLY but eventually wrapped her in soft, flickering light. Candles filled every inch of the penthouse living room surrounding the training mat. She stood in its center, dressed in her leathers and strapped with every weapon imaginable humming against her skin, ready to be called to the surface.

"Turn around," Maverick ordered.

She obeyed to find Maverick towering in front of the wall of windows, the candlelight reflecting off the glass behind his tanned, chiseled chest. His stormy eyes pierced right through her as he stepped closer, his muscles rippling with each movement. She sucked in a breath as the scents of his sweat mixed with worn leather and oak engulfed her senses. It brought back memories of their first meeting and the stolen moments of pleasure that had followed in the parking garage, fueled by toxic adrenaline following their near-death escape from the restaurant and Gareth's men.

She hesitated, her heart pounding and her breaths coming out shallow. She could feel the heat of Maverick's gaze on her, as if he was searching for answers she didn't have. But the truth was, she didn't want to hide anything from him. She only wished he would open up to her in the same way.

"Zera," he whispered. Even the way he spoke her name made her unravel at the seams. "Trust me, I want to tell you... need to tell you everything."

"Then why don't you?" she asked, her voice echoing, acutely aware she was still dreaming but not wanting it to end.

His hands were at her waist in an instant, pressing her flush against his rock-hard body, and she couldn't resist tangling her hands in his hair. Their gazes locked, and time seemed to stand still. Maverick's eyes held a hunger that matched her own, a desire to be closer.

"Because I'm afraid of this." His hot breath against her ear sent her eyelids fluttering. "Of what we might become if we give in to this bond between us."

His grip loosened against her waist, as if to let her go, but her grip tightened against his shoulders in desperation. She needed this—his closeness, his tanned skin pressed against hers. Then his mouth lowered to her neck, tasting her with a soft tenderness that left her breathless.

With a swift movement, he swept her off her feet and lowered her to the mat. He hovered above her for a moment, his gaze delving into hers, as if looking for consent. She pulled him down hard against her.

"No more distance," she said, gasping as she felt him hard against her.

His growl vibrated through her core as arousal flickered in his eyes, and then his lips were on hers, sending her toes curling. His lips were warm and tender as they caressed hers with surprising gentleness, his hands tracing down her sides in a smooth motion, stirring up goose bumps. Her lips moved in perfect sync with his. The scent of his skin mingling with the smell of leather and an old-fashioned cocktail drove her insane with want. Her body arched underneath his weight, inviting him to take more control.

But he didn't. Instead, he continued to tease her lips and neck. She moaned softly against his mouth, longing for him to continue but also wanting more. Her mind was filled with questions about the Whisper's staff, their mission, and their connection. She needed answers, but he wanted this more. His fingers explored farther south to her hips, where they caressed her gently as he sucked lightly on the sensitive skin between earlobe and neck. Her legs wound around his waist instinctively as she pulled him closer once again—craving his touch even more now that he had given her a taste of what was possible between them. Even in a dream.

"Please," she whispered against his lips while arching into him once more.

She wanted all of him right there on the mat beneath the flickering candles that surrounded them both, making everything glow golden in the night skyline outside the windows that lined the north wall of the living room.

"Again," he commanded her, and they were standing on the mat, their bodies too far from each other. She blinked, her mind trying to catch up with the sudden change. Her body was still coiled tightly from the lingering passion.

What had he asked?

Then something cool and familiar materialized right into her palm. The Whisper's staff. No, this couldn't be happening. She didn't want it. She looked back up at Maverick in desperation as they circled each other like predators ready to pounce. Zera's heart raced with panic as he closed the distance between them.

"Do it again," he ordered. The hilt of the blade pressed against his bare chest so hard blood should've trickled out. This time, it was aimed directly at his heart.

Tears stung her eyes as she struggled to balance her desire for Maverick and comprehend the situation. Her heart screamed for him to stop this. She didn't want this weapon. Despite the familiar power it contained, it wasn't hers. Deep down, she knew it too. There was something dark and hideous that lived within that thing, and in that moment, she knew it wanted to kill Maverick.

But it was just a dream. She gulped air in desperate bursts. Just a dream.

"A breath for a breath," Maverick hissed, but it wasn't his voice. It was the Whisper, and with a gush of wind, all the candles flickered out.

Zera shot upright, and the dream vanished as she woke up back in her bed, the Whisper's staff in hand.

CHAPTER 13
MAVERICK

Maverick paced the length of the penthouse balcony, the city lights below doing nothing to illuminate the darkness shrouding his search. It'd been a week. A week and still another dead end. Gareth's trail had gone cold, and Maverick's frustration simmered.

He winced as the bruise in his chest still throbbed where Zera had stabbed him with the Whisper's staff, a reminder of how truly stupid he'd been in giving it to her. But he had to know, to test whether the pixie wielded the weapon or the weapon wielded the pixie. From Zera's terrified and shocked reaction, he'd gotten his answer.

It didn't change things. The pixie warrior who'd tricked him had still stripped him of his fertility and nearly killed him. If he hadn't taken the pixie out, using all of his strength and stealing the staff in the process, he might not be alive. But Zera wouldn't understand that even if he tried to explain it. She would only hear that he'd taken a pixie life, and then she would leave, going back to Pixie Hollow to hide, and Gareth would be sure to find her. She would be dead before she could even understand the truth. Maverick clenched his fists, his nails digging into his palms. He couldn't let that happen.

His gaze kept flitting up to the north-facing window of the bedroom he'd dreamed they'd shared last night. She'd whispered about no more distance, and their bond had ignited in a passionate embrace. He hardened at the mere memory of the dream, and he wished it'd been real. The taste of her sugar and lilac skin still lingered on his tongue, as if it'd been more than a dream.

Maverick's thoughts were abruptly interrupted by the sliding door opening behind him. He turned as Zera stepped out in a warm purple sweater that made her lavender eyes pop. His heart stuttered at the sight of the fitted leathers she'd paired the sweater with that hugged her every curve and ignited a fire within him.

"Any luck?" she asked. Her brown waves tied back into a loose bun revealed her pixie ears that came to points, and her sultry eyes glimmered lavender in the glow of the golden lamps dangling above them. Something was on her mind. He could sense it.

Maverick shook his head, jaw clenched, wishing he had better news. "Nothing. All my contacts are still not talking."

Zera nodded, as if she expected that. She barely made eye contact, and it was killing him. She cleared her throat and said, "My everfrost blossom finally sprouted a bud."

"Oh, really?" Maverick's eyes flickered with intrigue, a hint of a smile tugging at the corners of his lips. He could tell she was just making small talk, but at least it was something. The silent treatment she'd been giving him ever since he'd brought up the Whisper's staff was killing him. "You've been tending to that thing for a while now. I was starting to think it was an elaborate ploy to avoid me."

The stoic mask she wore to cover up her true feelings vanished, replaced with irritation and something else. "You're one to talk about avoidance. Who's the one who changes the subject whenever I try to talk about this bond between us or hearing each other's thoughts?"

Maverick winced at her words, the truth of them cutting through his defenses. He had been avoiding the topic of their mental connection, the possibility that they were... He couldn't even form the word in his mind. He couldn't acknowledge it or the depth of their bond. She was a pixie. She would deceive him in the end, even if she hadn't killed him with the Whisper's staff. He had to avoid the topic as long as possible, to stay focused on the mission to ensure both her and her son were safe. There was no way she would ever understand, though, but he'd come to terms with that the moment he'd decided to test her.

"It was a test, wasn't it?" she asked, hurt and anger reflecting in her eyes as she looked up at him.

That damned bond. It would be the death of him if he didn't keep it in check.

His gaze hardened. "I don't know what you're talking about."

"Liar," she muttered.

"Zera, please," he said, his eyes begging her to drop the subject. "It's probably just a side effect of spending so much time training. We need to keep our focus on finding Gareth. Our safety depends on it. Your safety depends on it and your son's."

"You really care about our safety?" She scoffed, waving her hand, and the silver double-bladed staff with the intertwined circles—the mark of the Whisper—appeared in her hands.

She chucked it at him, and he stepped back out of instinct, letting it clatter at his feet.

"That's what I thought." She sneered at him, so angry yet still so beautiful, even with the way her eyebrows crinkled when she was mad. "It wants you dead, and I could've killed you."

He shrugged. "If you'd wanted me dead, you wouldn't have missed my heart."

"How do you know that?"

It was a probing question. She was baiting him for information that brought up a past he would rather forget. But Zera was here, and so was he. She'd passed the test. Didn't that mean something? That he could trust her with the truth?

But even though he did, he wasn't ready to share that story with anyone. It was too painful and would bring back things he didn't ever want to feel again.

Instead, Maverick chose to deflect her question with a playful smile, hoping to lighten the tension in the air. "Because I'm a spy, remember? I'm paid to know these things, and you should work on your aim," he teased, his voice laced with a hint of amusement.

Zera's eyes narrowed. She was clearly unamused by his joke. "You're afraid."

He froze, the memory of his dream still fresh in his mind.

"Afraid of what we might become if you open up," she pressed on when he didn't respond, and he wondered if he might still be dreaming. She'd said the exact words he'd only dreamed of telling her. "You're so scared of truly letting yourself be vulnerable, even for a second, to admit that there's something more to all of this that you're keeping from me."

He couldn't believe it. She must've shared his same dream. But how? It wasn't possible. Even if it were, it would be too dangerous for them both to even consider it. It would only bring more hurt and distrust. Besides, it was impossible for him to bond, for him to have a connection with anyone because of his naiveté as a young wereling. Considering any other scenario was just a waste of time.

Maverick took a step closer to Zera, his piercing eyes searching hers for understanding. He could see the hurt and the anger but also the desire in her gaze, the longing for something deeper than what he was capable of. Something deep down he knew he wanted but could never have.

"Zera, there are things in my past that... haunt me," he admitted softly, his voice laced with the weight of memories. "Things that I've done... things that I regret. I won't jeopardize your safety and definitely not the safety of your son for whatever you might think is between us. It's not possible."

"What would a Lunar werewolf care about my safety, let alone my son's?" she snapped.

Her words cut sharper than his favorite knife. She already knew he'd rejected the Lunar Brotherhood pack and its evil ways. Wasn't that enough? Wasn't it enough that everything he'd done since then was to make things right? He lived alone now, his life forever changed as he carved his own path. She should understand the struggles of living such a life.

But the hurt wereling within him, still angry and afraid of opening up again like he had back then, made him keep his mouth shut. Everything he did was to be a different werewolf from one belonging to the pack he'd been raised in. But had he actually ever said it? He thought he'd made it clear at the restaurant, but that felt like so long ago, he didn't even know anymore.

"Why am I even here, huh?" She waved her hand at the penthouse, taking a step toward him, her arms loose at her sides, ready to block or throw a punch like he'd taught her. "There's a bounty on my head because of you, and I'm here training and literally waiting for plants to grow while my son wakes up every day without me. Do you have any idea what that's like? What it means to make sacrifices for one's child?"

He balled his hands into fists, his wolf rippling beneath the surface of his skin. "I will never know what that means, thanks to your kind."

The ache in his chest threatened to consume him as he locked eyes with Zera, her pixie-like form trembling with a mix of anger and hurt that mirrored his own. He'd never thought about being a father, of having children of his own, until the choice was taken from him. She would never know that kind of pain just like he would never know hers. Didn't need to.

Thanks to those damned pixies many years ago, he would never be anyone's mate. That was okay. He'd accepted that by now, and it was, indeed, a favor they'd done for him. But he'd never questioned any of it until he met her. Zera had gotten under his skin, and he cursed himself for letting his emotions get the better of him. It only made him sloppy.

She frowned. "What do you mean by that?"

"It doesn't matter." He shut his mouth before he said too much. He brushed by her, picking up the Whisper's staff on his way, and headed for the sliding glass door. He'd had enough of the not-so-fresh city air.

"Yes, it does," she pushed as she followed him. He could feel her rage coiling behind him, desperate for an outlet. They'd been stuck in this penthouse for far too long.

He marched straight to the chest that held the staff's case, ready to be done with it. Even if the staff might be the only way to kill Gareth, it wasn't worth it.

"Don't you dare walk away from me!" she shouted after him as he secured the staff and buried it deep within the chest. "Explain what you meant back there."

Maverick avoided her gaze as he pivoted toward the rack of weights with every intention of distracting his mind from the reeling memories he didn't want to repeat. Perhaps he could banish the memories by working out.

The cool steel of the weights was a welcome reprieve from the heat that boiled under his skin, but his shoulders grew taut when she neared. "Drop it, Zera. It's not important."

Zera flew in front of him, blocking him from the weights. Her eyes flashed with anger. "It clearly is important if it's got you this upset."

Maverick scowled. "You're the one accusing me of not caring about you or your child. That I'm just some Lunar Brotherhood wolf. A killer. That's what you think of me, isn't it?"

She shut her mouth, and he pressed on. "It doesn't matter that, like you, I left everything behind me. I left to be a better person than my ancestors. This is me living up to that promise I made to myself all those years ago. Why or how I left has nothing to do with you."

"And what about the Whisper's staff? Does that have anything to do with me or my kind?" She folded her arms across her chest, her lavender eyes dimming.

He swallowed the lump in his throat. "It's ancient history, and like I said, it doesn't matter."

"And what about how we're connected? Our bond? Why are you avoiding this?"

Because she was right. He desperately wanted there to be a chance between them, but he knew that wasn't possible. The idea of confirming that terrified him. It made him feel too... exposed. He couldn't let his guard down, not when Gareth was still out there hunting them. Especially not with her. If he was truly being honest, he feared that if he truly let her in, let himself feel anything for her, that she'd used it against him. Just like they all did. He couldn't afford to believe she might be different. He didn't have anyone else, like she did with her son, her half sister, and even her half sister's wife. At the end of the day, she had a family worth fighting for. If he didn't protect himself—his life—he'd have nothing left.

Maverick took a step back. "Zera, you have to understand that my life is dangerous. This bond you think is between us, if there is one, it complicates things even more. I can't let myself open up to you because it puts everyone in danger."

She seethed up at him. "Coward." She spun on her heel and stormed up the staircase to the bedroom above. The door slammed with a finality.

He raked a hand through his hair, frustration and anger coursing through him. He was about to follow her when a sudden knock at the penthouse door stopped him. It was probably for the best that they kept some space between them.

With a deep breath, Maverick checked the monitor next to the elevator door. Quill stood in the center of the small elevator and glanced up at the camera. Maverick pressed the button to open the door, and Quill waltzed in with a casual air about him. The forger's hands were shoved in the pockets of his jean jacket, his blond curls loose. But there was something off about him, an urgent energy that lingered in his otherwise nonchalant features.

"Quill." Maverick greeted him, trying to conceal the turmoil inside him. "I'm surprised to see you. What're you doing here?"

"Come to collect you for that bounty," Quill said with a teasing chuckle when Maverick glared at him. "Always so serious, aren't you?"

"And you're not funny, as usual." Maverick smirked, ushering him inside. "I didn't order any new documents."

"No, you didn't," he agreed, resting his elbows on the kitchen island and then frowning at the makeshift gym that now took over the living room. "Are you hosting a Fight Club and didn't tell me?"

"Every Wednesday night." Maverick rolled his eyes. "Come on, enough of your demon theatrics. Just get on with it. What do you want?"

Quill's eyes glimmered violet. "Oh, well, word on the street is you're looking for Gareth, and I've got some news on that front."

Maverick's interest piqued at the mention of Gareth. He leaned against the counter, studying Quill's face for any sign of deception. "What kind of news?"

"The kind that may help you get his attention," the demon replied with a sly smile.

"How?"

"By jeopardizing his deal that's going down tonight." Quill snapped his fingers, and a bluish little baggy materialized in his hands. "I snatched this off a mouthy little siren in my bar. She claims it's pure pixie dust and that there's more where that came from."

Maverick took it, examining its contents. "Not laced with anything?"

"Apparently not," he said with a shrug. "And tonight, Gareth plans on securing the hottest nightclub in the city as a distribution channel. Rumor has it he already has the Crystal and dozens of other locations. The nightclub is his final foothold, though I'm told it's just a formality. The owner's probably the true brains of the operation anyway."

But Maverick stopped listening as his mind raced with this new information. If it was true, then Quill already had a source for his pixies and Zera was just an afterthought. Icing on the cake, perhaps. That, or Gareth was bluffing and his drug was actually laced with other, more common elements to buy him time until he found her.

But even if Gareth tapped her dry, she wouldn't have enough to satisfy the demand for such a high-quality product. The sheer number of pixies it would take Gareth to make a product that was one hundred percent pure pixie dust would put pixies into extinction. The death toll would be catastrophic, and Maverick couldn't let that happen.

"Which nightclub?" Maverick asked through gritted teeth. It was a risky move, especially with the bounty on their heads, but if he could disrupt Gareth's drug deal, it would undoubtedly draw the arms dealer out into the open and finally put an end to him.

"It's called the Inferno Lounge. Have you heard of it?"

Quill chuckled when Maverick growled. Everyone had heard of that nightclub by now. It was one of the many establishments owned by that bloody incubus Kraven, who seemed to be popping up everywhere with his bloody mind control. Maverick didn't need to look up the address; he knew where it was all too well. He'd taken a couple of odd jobs from a few clients there, but the whole place reeked of dark energy, and now that he knew who owned it, he understood why. It was the devil's den, and in order to rustle Gareth's feathers, he would have to go right smack-dab into the middle of it.

Maverick's heart pulsed with hope. It was the first potential lead on Gareth since the gala, and Quill was here delivering it on a silver platter? What was the catch? He eyed the baggie, wary of Quill's ulterior motives. Old friend or not, the demon had a reputation for being unpredictable, and Maverick couldn't afford any more surprises.

"What do you want in return for this information?"

"Consider it a favor." Quill straightened as he prepared to leave but not before tossing two new IDs on the counter. "For your cover tonight. You'll need to glamour yourselves to avoid that pesky bounty Gareth has on you."

Maverick shook his head. "This is too much. I already owe you for the car."

"Keep it. I already have a replacement." Quill paused at the door to the elevator in thought before tossing over his shoulder, "But I wouldn't turn down a photo of you chained to that pixie bride of yours in Kraven's nightclub."

"Excuse me?" Maverick's eyebrows shot up.

"Oh, did I not mention that it's dominatrix night at the Inferno?" Quill feigned a look of innocence, but Maverick had a feeling he knew exactly what information he'd divulged. "No men are allowed to enter without an escort, so you'd better bring Charlotte."

Maverick stared at the forger's back as he left, the thought of asking Zera to such an event causing a jumble of conflicting emotions inside him. Even if they weren't on fighting terms, the thought of Zera in nothing but strips of leather and weapons... A shiver of desire ran down his spine. This wasn't even his kink, and yet the sheer mental image of her going into that club sent a surge of heat through his veins.

Zera would never agree to it, though, especially in her current state of frustration with him. But maybe she would if it meant getting closer to Gareth and saving the lives of countless pixies.

He stood at the bottom of the staircase, his hand gripping the polished wooden railing. His eyes flicked up to the darkened hallway leading to the primary bedroom, and he hesitated. He knew he had to try, and it would probably mean opening up about everything. Even the parts he wanted to bury deep inside him. But he needed her, and they were now out of time.

"Here goes nothing," he muttered under his breath, mentally preparing himself for what lay ahead as he took a step forward.

He prayed to the faen gods that it wouldn't lead to two steps back.

CHAPTER 14

ZERA

Zera paced the bedroom, her heart pounding with frustration and anger. It felt like this had become a daily ritual—train with Maverick, argue with Maverick, then pace the giant bedroom while avoiding him altogether.

She cursed the carpet beneath her feet. It was his. Everything in this room was—save for her makeshift lab and plant that had made as much progress as Maverick's efforts on the Gareth front—and it just made her angrier. She replayed the infuriating conversation with Maverick over and over in her mind. How could he avoid her questions like that, refusing to admit there was something more between them? And then he had the nerve to test her with the Whisper's staff without even telling her why or how he'd gotten it in the first place. He could've gotten them all killed.

"Damn him," she muttered under her breath, her lavender pixie eyes flaring.

A flicker of fear rippled through her every time she thought about that Whisper's staff and how it had appeared in her hands this morning after that dream. She knew Maverick had dreamed it too. She'd felt it through the bond the instant she quoted him, and his face had said as much. A bond he refused to acknowledge, for fae only knew why. Maverick had ensnared her, asking her for her trust, yet he didn't seem to trust her when it mattered most.

Trust was earned, not given, she reminded herself, taking a deep breath. But hadn't he earned that each and every day since Gareth had sent those men to kill her and her family? How often had he gone out on a limb to save her?

She huffed. It didn't matter when he kept the truth to himself. But something he had said earlier kept popping up, making it hard to stay mad at him. It was after she accused him of not knowing what it was like to sacrifice for your child. She regretted saying that and calling him a coward the moment the words left her mouth, but she was so angry they'd slipped out before she could stop them.

But now, in the quiet of the serene bedroom cast in the evening glow of the setting sun that trickled in through the surrounding windows, his words echoed in her mind. That thanks to her kind, he would never know what it was like to be a father. What could have possibly happened to him at the hands of pixies that left such a deep, festering wound?

He was a Lunar werewolf, after all. They hunted pixies like her. What could they have done to him that would scar him so deeply?

Zera couldn't help but feel a twinge of guilt for her harsh words and assumptions. She knew what it was like to be judged based on her kind, and yet she had done the same to Maverick. It must have been difficult for a werewolf to live alone, rejecting his own kind. There had to be more to his story, and she wanted to know.

These questions tumbled around in her conflicted mind, anger warring with curiosity and guilt. She owed him an apology, but she needed answers too. Before she could make up her mind about how to approach the situation, a soft knock at the bedroom door startled her.

"Come in," Zera called out, her voice wavering ever so slightly.

The door opened slowly, and Maverick stood at the threshold, looking apprehensive. The sight of his nervousness filled Zera with a mix of tenderness and frustration. Even though they had been through so much together, why did it still feel like he was holding back? Was there any way they could move forward if he continued to keep secrets from her?

"I'm ready to talk," he said finally. "All I ask is that you listen to the very end first before making any judgments or decisions."

Zera nodded, not daring to utter a word for the fear that he might change his mind. She motioned for him to sit next to her on the bed, and he did so.

He sighed, running a hand through his hair, his eyes flickering with a mix of sadness and regret. "First, I must explain how I know that the Whisper's staff will only kill if the wielder wishes it. To do that, I must start at the beginning.

"The Whisper's staff belonged to a pixie. A warrior," he admitted, his voice laced with a hint of vulnerability, yet his expression was unreadable.

"But pixies aren't warriors, and the Whispers are just a myth," she said, unable to keep quiet. Perhaps waiting to speak until the end had been too big of an ask for her to agree to.

She didn't care. It wasn't true. Whispers were a myth, and to believe any differently... Well, it would mean something terrible had happened because they didn't exist anymore.

He chuckled bitterly. "That's what they want you to believe." He took a deep breath, apparently bracing himself for what he was about to reveal.

"I was barely sixteen when I met her, a magical girl with shimmering wings who danced between the cedar oaks of the Lunar forest," he began, his eyes locked on hers.

"She called herself Seraphine, and she was the most beautiful fae I'd ever encountered. I would sneak out of the mountains where our pack lived just to watch her dance. When I finally got the courage to speak to her, she nearly vanished out of fear, but she stopped when I said to her, 'In the tapestry of fresh morning dew, none reflect—'"

"'The sun's radiance quite like you,'" she gasped, completing his quote. "That's from *A Tale of Eramir and Alandria,* a famous pixie fairy tale passed down the generations. It was my favorite as a kid. But how did a wolf like you know about this story?"

"As a child, I met a traveling librarian who passed through the mountains on his way to Pixie Hollow from whatever trade route he'd taken. He left me a book each time." He smiled, his gaze distant, as if reliving a fond memory.

"I read fantastical stories that challenged me and expanded my horizons, and I realized the way my family lived... It wasn't right." He scowled and looked off into the distance, the cityscape darkening in the setting sun. "The one that convinced me the most was that book of pixie folklore. A tale of undying love that I'd never witnessed before, one that I craved. 'A Tale of Eramir and Alandria' changed me forever."

He paused before saying, "It still amazes me how words from so long ago can inspire such change. Even in a wolf like me, who was conditioned to a life of blood and hatred. How many books had it taken to persuade me that I could be more than a drone in a murderous pack? That I could do more and that my life could mean something?"

She felt the hopelessness in his words. The unspoken admission that he now believed these books had given him a false hope.

"That was just the beginning," Maverick continued, shaking his head. "Seraphine and I met every night for a year, and I proposed. I was a stupid boy in love with a snake. She told me she would say yes but that I had to come back to her village and ask her father for permission first, and I went. I never questioned her."

Zera swallowed hard, having a bad feeling of where this might go. If the folklore of the Whispers was true, then she would be leading him back to her gossamer. He nodded, as if he saw the light bulb turn on in her head.

"They captured and tortured me for days. Weeks, even. All by the hand of Seraphine. The girl who supposedly loved me," he growled, the betrayal evident. "They wanted to use me as leverage against the

Lunar Brotherhood, to return the alpha's heir alive in exchange for the rest of the pack. But they didn't know my pack already found me to be a traitor with my books. I was a pixie sympathizer to them and bait to the pixie warriors."

His laugh was hollow, the sound tinged with pain. "Funny, isn't it? How love can blind you to the truth. How we can be so willing to sacrifice ourselves for someone who would turn against us without a second thought."

Zera's heart clenched at the pain in his words as she realized how deep his wounds were. She wanted nothing more than to reach out and comfort him, but she wasn't sure if he'd welcome her touch. Instead, she managed to whisper, "I'm so sorry."

"Don't be," he said, his eyes darkening. "I'd witnessed Seraphine kill innocent after innocent in front of me with that damn Whisper's staff. I pleaded with her to stop, that this wasn't her, and that's when she said to me that the staff will only let the wielder kill when it's desired of them. She demonstrated all of it. She paraded a pixie and another kidnapped wereling in front of me. I'm sure you can guess which of the two survived. She wanted to torment me and knew that my heart had grown soft. It didn't matter. No one would come for me. Instead, they took—"

He stopped, moisture suddenly misting his eyes, but he blinked, and it was gone, replaced with a hardness that made Zera's heart ache. She could see the walls he had built around himself, and she understood why he kept her at arm's length. Maverick had been through unimaginable pain, and love had become a dangerous territory for him. She finally knew what he meant when he said that he would never have a chance to be a father, thanks to them. Because the Whispers had taken that ability from him.

Swallowing back her own emotions, Zera reached out cautiously, her fingertips brushing the back of Maverick's hand that gripped the edge of the bed so tightly his knuckles turned white.

"That was the first time I shifted," he said, his voice even quieter as his hand relaxed against her touch. "I mean, truly shifted and felt the full power of who I was. I killed them all. Stole the Whisper's staff from her as she looked at me with shocked, wide-open eyes. I barely escaped with my life. And then I wept. I was a child without a family, without a home. I had given everything, and in the end, I was alone."

Zera sucked in a sudden breath. She wanted to tell him it didn't have to be that way. That he didn't have to be alone. Having a faeological child didn't make one a father. Shit, her own ex had one, and he'd up and deserted Cole before he'd ever met him.

But the moment escaped them, and Maverick cleared his throat, pulling his hand from hers.

"Anyway," he said, his voice realigning with the present, "I needed to know if you could wield it because Gareth knows all of my tricks from when I worked with him, but you? You could be the surprise we need to finally end him. I just needed to know if I could trust you not to kill me in the process. I figured if you killed me here in the penthouse, at least I would know Gareth couldn't kill you, and you'd have your faestone to get in touch with your family."

He paused, taking a ragged breath. "But I should've told you first, and for that, I apologize to you sincerely. I promise I won't keep anything from you. Our partnership depends on trust, and I owe you that."

Zera's anger for him testing her dissipated, replaced by a profound sense of sorrow for the hardships he had faced. She bit her lip, hesitating for a moment before speaking. "Maverick, I had no idea about any of this. I'm so sorry. I didn't mean what I said before. You've sacrificed so much for me and my son. Even with me being a pixie, though I'd understand if you never wanted anything to do with me again."

His conflicted emotions reflected in his gaze. "That's just it, though. I know what I was born into. What my own blood did to pixies for decades. My story, it doesn't change the long history of injustices inflicted upon your kind."

"No, but your wounds are just as valid," she said firmly. "I didn't mean to stir up those old wounds."

He looked back at her, his piercing gray eyes still guarded but tinged with a flicker of hope. "I know you didn't. But I wanted you to understand why I tested you. I probably should've told you first. I promise I'll work on improving my bad communication skills."

She chuckled at his extreme understatement, but his promise filled her with hope that perhaps there was still a chance for their bond. He'd bared his soul to her, opened himself up in a way no man had ever done before, and she found him even more attractive than before. Her eyes wandered down his strong jawline to his lips as she remembered the taste of them against her own. Lips that were capable of doing such tempting things to her.

"Now," he began, a hint of a smirk gracing those perfect lips as if he'd known what she was thinking. She jerked her gaze to meet his knowing eyes. "We should focus on what's important—stopping Gareth."

"Have there been any updates on that front?" Zera asked, acutely aware of how close he was sitting to her. "I heard voices downstairs earlier."

Maverick's eyes sparkled mischievously as his smirk widened. "Oh yeah, that was Quill from the bar. He gave me a lead on where Gareth might be tonight. Apparently, he's securing the last location in his distribution network."

Zera raised an eyebrow. "Really? The forger just happened to have this information now? You don't think that's a little suspicious?"

Maverick shrugged. "I trust Quill. He's never let me down yet."

"Do you think it could be the chance we need to finally take Gareth down?" A flicker of hope sparked within her as she imagined finally being free from the constant threat of Gareth and being reunited with her son.

Maverick chuckled, allowing his usual cocky and infuriating

demeanor to surface once again. "Oh, it's definitely a solid lead. But"—he paused as if savoring the moment—"there's a catch."

Of course there was. Demons always had a trick up their sleeves. Zera crossed her arms and regarded him with suspicion. Whatever lead Quill had given him had put Maverick in an obnoxious mood.

"What do I have to do?" she asked, staring him down.

"First, you must agree to join me. Agree, and we should be able to save hundreds, if not thousands, of pixies from Gareth's clutches. The choice is yours." He gave her a nonchalant shrug, but the look on his face told her he was trying to keep from laughing. What was she about to get herself into?

"Fine. I'm in," she said, not really having a choice in the matter because she would do anything to finally end this. "Now, tell me what I have to do."

"All I can say is that things are about to get... interesting," Maverick replied cryptically, his lips curling into a devilish grin as he stood from her bed and waltzed toward the bathroom and dressing room.

She rolled her eyes. "Can you just tell me already? And what are you doing in there?"

"Finding you appropriate attire for tonight," he called, his voice echoing off the marble bathroom floor before he disappeared into the closet.

"Wait, what?" She hopped off the bed and marched to the closet, where Maverick held a black garment bag that was significantly smaller than the rest.

She froze, eyes glued to the garment bag. "What's in the bag?"

"Trust me, you're probably going to hate this," Maverick warned, his grin widening even more. "But I promise it's necessary for the mission. Think of it as... an undercover operation as Charlotte."

He unzipped the bag. When she laid eyes on the outfit, she suddenly regretted everything.

CHAPTER 15

ZERA

An hour and an entire bottle of hairspray later, Zera and Maverick stood outside the nightclub, the pulsating bass of music seeping through the cracks in the door. Zera couldn't believe he'd convinced her to come here, especially with her looking like this.

"I hate this," she hissed, pulling her coat closer around her against the evening breeze. It was starting to smell like snow.

"Your heartbeat would suggest otherwise," Maverick retorted, and she scoffed. The sheer arrogance of this wolf.

Yet her heartbeat only fluttered with excitement. Damn wolf hearing. They were in line to enter the nightclub, freezing their bits off to get into a club she didn't even want to set foot in. It was bad enough this mission of theirs was making her stand out in the cold, but what she had to wear made her even more uncomfortable.

But from the looks of other women around her, she was in the minority, as far as that went. A vampiress glared at her when she made eye contact and flashed her fangs, her hand on her porcelain hip as though uncaring that the bitter wind nipped at her exposed flesh. Zera's leather skirt and matching bustier were almost modest in comparison.

Zera withered farther into her coat, wishing she could go back to the penthouse. She never should've squeezed into the little skirt that barely covered her ass. As soon as she put it on, she'd nearly ripped it back off. She wanted to swap it for a nice comfortable pair of sweatpants instead. But Maverick had been adamant that the outfit would ensure their survival. They had to blend in with this crowd, though she wasn't sure if it was worth it. Even the leather bustier she wore seemed to squeeze the air out of her lungs. At least he had to wear an outfit too.

She glanced back at the giant werewolf that stalked behind her, letting her eyes graze his bare chest and the leather pants that hung low and tight against his thighs.

"Keep looking at me like that, and we won't make it to the lounge," he said huskily.

"And what are you going to do about it?" She winked and gave the flimsy chain that secured his choke collar to her wrist a little tug.

Why not have a little fun while they were catching bad guys? She never got out, and when she did, it was usually to order to-go fries at the Haven Wolf Tavern. Not to party it up at one of Mystic City's hottest nightclubs.

He growled, his hot breath hitting her ear from behind her as his hands grazed her bare hips just above her panty line.

She rolled her eyes. "You should've worn a coat."

His brow arched. "And miss an opportunity to tempt you?"

"You're so full of it." She laughed and playfully shoved him back, and his deep chuckle sent a shiver of anticipation down her spine. "So, I'm guessing this is your scene?"

"Not at all," he said as the line moved forward. He flashed her a cocky grin. "But I'm a spy, so I can blend."

"Oh, right. I almost forgot." She was certain that wasn't true. Someone with his good looks couldn't possibly blend in anywhere.

"Speaking of blending in," he said, his tone switching back to business, "there's no neutrality here, so if the glamour wavers even for a moment and someone recognizes either of us, then—"

"It'll be utter chaos. Yes, I know. Don't worry, our glamours are intact." She glanced up at him just to be sure. "You know, I think you might look hotter with your new face."

He smirked. "So you admit that I'm hot?"

"I didn't say that."

"But you do."

"Oh, stop being so... you," she grumbled, and his smile only grew wider.

The last pair in front of them entered the nightclub, where pounding music and flashing lights spilled onto the streets. The bouncer, a troll with a cigar crammed into his cheek and smoke puffing from his snout, flicked his eyes over Zera and Maverick. He eyed her with suspicion, and it wiped the smile right off her face. She replaced it with her best scowl as she showed him their IDs.

Her glamour work did the trick, both on the IDs and on their faces. She'd given Maverick a full beard and honey-brown eyes, the simplest ways to change a face. Then, for her, she'd chosen violet eyes because she could probably pass for a demon. She used a gold band to hold her now-black hair in a high ponytail. Her face was a little more heart-shaped too. Even if someone here had been at the gala, they would only think Maverick and Zera looked similar to a couple who had been there.

The troll handed her the IDs back and ushered them inside. She stepped through the door.

"Just as I suspected," Maverick whispered from behind her.

"What is?"

"There's an enchantment on this nightclub," he said, nodding to the red lettering on the walls on either side of them. "It's dominatrix night, so women run the show. This spell ensures it, so you'll have to take the lead on things."

She gulped as she took in the crimson writing. She could do this. She could take charge and exude a commanding presence, right?

"Coats," Maverick breathed softly into her ear, nodding toward the fairy checking coats in.

Zera nodded. She led the way to the coat check and reluctantly removed her coat. A breeze from the entrance hit her bare skin, leaving goose bumps in its wake, but the nightclub was warmer than expected. She scanned the nightclub, a twisted labyrinth of pulsing lights, leather-clad bodies, and the relentless thump of the music. At least she wouldn't be the only one with her ass hanging out.

She handed her coat to the fairy, her fingers trembling slightly before she led the way farther into the nightclub.

"Remember what the plan is?" Maverick asked while the music pulsated in their chests.

Zera nodded, her mind racing to recall the details. They'd gone over it multiple times, but now that they were inside the club, her nerves started getting the best of her. But she knew the plan. Once they spotted Gareth or one of his associates approaching the owner of the nightclub, that was when they would create a distraction to disrupt the deal. It was simple, clean, and efficient. Zera could handle it. She had to.

"Should we get drinks?" she asked.

"You tell me, boss," he said with a wink.

Oh, right. She was in charge. "Drinks, it is."

They moved to the bar, weaving through the crowd, bodies pressed tightly together. She ordered them both a cocktail and hoped the liquid courage would ease her nerves. A tall, slender fae she couldn't identify sat next to her, tentacles wrapped around a male with elven ears and spiked blue hair. They barely took a breath between kisses. Beyond them, a pair of werejaguars were in a similar embrace. That was when she realized she and Maverick would have to get a lot more physical to blend in.

Fortunately, their drinks arrived quickly. Zera took a sip of her cocktail, the fruity concoction providing a refreshing distraction. Maverick stood, glued to her side, taking it all in.

"No sign of Gareth or the bar owner yet," he whispered in her ear as she fidgeted with the ridiculous skirt. "And you look sexy as hell."

She flashed him a crooked smile. Perhaps she was emboldened

by the drink or the sensually charged atmosphere, but Zera gently pulled the chain that bound them together closer to her and leaned in, her voice dripping with playfulness. "Is that your spy training talking, or are you trying to get on my good side?"

"It's whatever you want it to be," he said, his storm-filled eyes heavy with desire.

It took all of her self-control to peel her gaze from Maverick's. He was incredibly seductive when he wanted to be, and he was right. He could blend in anywhere.

She took in the dance floor, her gaze searching for Gareth or anyone she recognized from the restaurant. No one stuck out to her in the mass of bodies that swayed, moving in time to the thumping beat of the music. Vampires, demons, fairies, and even a satyr here and there flocked to the dance floor, their movements intoxicating. The heavy scent of alcohol, sweat, and perfume filled the air, heightening Zera's senses. She could feel the energy coursing through the crowd, their collective desire for release and escape palpable.

The call to move, to join the dance, was strong. She spotted an opening on the dance floor.

"Let's dance," she suggested.

"Lead the way," Maverick replied, a playful smirk on his face.

While she and Maverick joined the dance, their bodies moved in sync and a surge of adrenaline rushed through her veins.

Maverick's hands found their way to her hips, his warm fingers once again playing at the edge of her leather skirt. Zera couldn't help but let out a small gasp as she felt the heat from his touch spread through her body. The music pulsed around them, drowning out any other thoughts or distractions.

As they danced, a sense of freedom and release washed over Zera. Here, in this crowded club filled with fantastical beings, she could forget about her responsibilities and just be in the moment. Maverick's presence only added to that feeling, his playful energy and smooth moves keeping her fully engaged in the dance.

Their bodies moved closer together until there was barely any space between them. A spark ignited between them as their eyes locked, and she felt her heart race at the unexpected intensity. She wrapped her arms around his neck, enjoying the warmth and firmness of his chest and biceps. Their eyes locked as they moved in rhythm.

"Try not to get too lost in my eyes, Zera," Maverick teased.

"You wish," she retorted, forcing herself to focus on the task at hand.

But as she tangled her hands in his hair, he leaned down, and his lips grazed her neck, making that an impossible task. She let her eyes wander the club while he proceeded to kiss the sensitive skin below her ear.

"See anything?" he asked between kisses, making it hard for her to concentrate.

"Not with you distracting me," Zera managed to breathe out.

Maverick chuckled against her skin, the sound sending shivers down her spine. His lips trailed a path of fire along her jawline, causing her mind to blur and her body to melt into his arms.

Zera's eyes flickered up. That was when she spotted the balcony and who occupied it. She tensed under Maverick's touch.

"You didn't tell me the owner of this nightclub was Kraven," she hissed, and Maverick smirked, his lips still dangerously close to her skin.

"Well, where's the fun in spoiling all the surprises?" he whispered.

Her jaw clenched. "Fun? Like it was fun when he mind whipped you into breaking the law of neutrality at the gala? Or dug out all my secrets with merely a single question?"

How could Maverick not be taking this more seriously? If Kraven was the owner who Gareth was making a deal with, then their cover was already blown. He probably already knew they were here. She watched Kraven on the balcony, where his eyes scanned the crowd below. His gray hair was swept away from his stone-cold features, a constant reminder of what he was capable of. Zera remembered how his mere presence urged her to confess her deepest desires. How quickly he'd gotten every bit of information from her that he wanted and even some he didn't. It was no wonder this fae was the leading crime lord of Mystic City's criminal underworld. She should've known that a club like this would be his.

Kraven's ice-blue eyes suddenly met hers, as if he could see right through her, and her skin crawled at the violation. He knew.

"Damn it, Maverick," Zera whispered urgently, her heart pounding. "We have to do something before he exposes us."

"Relax, Zera," Maverick murmured, his hands on her waist as they continued to dance. "If he knew who we really were, he would have acted by now. Just keep up the act, and stay close to me."

"I thought you had to do what I say in here," she said, glaring at the wolf, who, despite the desire in his eyes, kept his hands strictly at the top of her waist.

"I do, but we have to wait for Gareth and his posse to show up," he replied before flashing a mischievous grin. "And as of yet, you haven't given me a command. So until then, I can still enjoy the view."

Zera huffed in frustration, her mind racing for an alternative plan. None of their scenarios had involved Kraven specifically, so there were a thousand ways this could go wrong. They could lose their chance at stopping a deal that could save thousands of pixies and potentially take Gareth down. That was, if he ever showed.

"Fine," she said through gritted teeth, trying to ignore Kraven's intrusive stare from the balcony. She could feel his eyes on them. "But if this goes south, I'm blaming you."

Maverick gave a low chuckle. "Fair enough."

As the music continued to pulse around them, Zera couldn't help but feel like a ticking time bomb. Each second that passed brought them closer to potential disaster. It was nearly midnight, and Gareth still hadn't shown up.

The music changed, a slow and sensual beat filling the room. She pulled Maverick closer, using his touch as a cover as she stole glances at the balcony. Kraven's gaze never wavered, and she wondered how long they could keep up this charade. The choke collar connecting her and Maverick grew heavier with each passing moment.

"Listen," she whispered urgently, leaning close to Maverick's ear. "I have a plan. Come on."

She didn't wait for him to argue. His raised eyebrows showed his surprise. It was risky, but it would work. It had to. With a firm tug on the chain, Zera led Maverick through the crowd toward the staircase leading up to the balcony.

"Zera." His grip on her hand stiffened when he saw what she was about to do. But if the spells written in red that covered the black walls and reflected off the dance floor had any bite to them, there wasn't a thing he could do to stop her.

"Please," he repeated when she didn't respond, and she whirled on him.

"I told you I have a plan, and you're going to have to trust me," she bit out, pointing a finger at his chest. She barely reached his collarbone, and he had to dip down to hear her whisper. "I did, and look where it got me? You had me come here without all the information. Now, you're going to have to do the same."

She unhooked the cuff at her wrist, wagging it in his face before she hooked it on a knob of the railing. "Stay put until I get back."

This was his mess, and she was just cleaning it up. But that was what moms did, right? Sat back, watched the mess so another human being could learn, and stayed there to wipe everything up. A thankless job but one she was good at and desperately wanted to get back to. Playing spy was fun and all, but she missed her baby, and if Gareth wasn't going to show up, she wouldn't let this opportunity go to waste.

As she approached Kraven, Zera's mind raced with possibilities. She knew she had to be cunning and use her wits to outmaneuver the incubus crime lord. She also knew she had to get to the point before he dug into her mind and exposed even more of her secrets. Cole had to be the furthest thing from her mind. If Kraven got hold of that information, that she had a son who could be used against her, who knew what would happen?

"Kraven," Zera called out, feigning confidence as she approached the imposing figure. The crime lord lounged on a plush velvet chair, and all around him sat scantily clad women vying for his attention. His eyes locked on Zera's, and she felt a shiver down her spine.

He'd be in her mind in a matter of seconds if she didn't keep her thoughts shut down, so she worked on steeling herself like a shield.

"Step back," a security guard in a black suit wearing an ear mic said, stepping into her path. His eyes flickered gold, and a wolfish growl emanated from his chest when he sniffed and smelled her pixie scent.

Why hadn't she thought to glamour her scent too? It was a rookie mistake but one she couldn't fix right now.

"Can you make me?" She flared her violet eyes, daring him to make a move or question her demon facade. She placed a hand on her hip, eyeing the giant guard like he was a beetle she could stomp out.

Kraven laughed. "Let her pass."

The second he stepped aside, she was face-to-face with the incubus crime lord. There was no turning back now. She had to own this.

"And who do we have here?" Kraven asked, his voice dripping with curiosity.

"Rumor is you're striking a deal with Gareth. I'm here to offer you a better one," she replied boldly.

Kraven raised an eyebrow, clearly intrigued. "Oh?"

"I've developed a synthetic that could rival the real thing. A competitor in the market, but more importantly, it's safer and much harder to trace." She had to clamp her hands down at her sides to keep from fidgeting with her ponytail, a tell of nervousness she didn't know she even had until Maverick pointed it out during one of their training sessions.

"And why would I trust you or your product?" he asked, clearly not convinced. "Especially when you come to me as a lie, Charlotte."

She swallowed hard. Of course he saw right through her glamour. What could she do now?

"You see, I know everyone who enters my nightclub"—he peeled himself up from the velvet seat, his black suit a sharp contrast to his silver hair—"and what their intentions are, and though you are in charge tonight..." He took in her leather skirt, which had inched up her waist, exposing even more of her bare legs, and her boobs, which were practically spilling out of her bustier.

She felt ridiculous and violated by his lingering gaze.

"I already know why you are here tonight, so tell me, why should I care about your little offer?"

Her mouth went dry. She hadn't thought this through. What could she say to make this crime lord switch and turn Gareth's deal down? Especially for a product she didn't even have a working recipe for? She'd made a horrible mistake, and judging by the way the werewolf security guard's claws poked out of his fingers, she was about to pay for it.

CHAPTER 16

ZERA

ZERA DARED NOT MOVE AN INCH ON THAT BALCONY AS SHE STARED DOWN THE face of pure evil incarnate without an answer. If she didn't give Kraven a good enough reason why he should listen to her deal, then she was as good as dead. But then an idea came to her. A sliver of hope produced by a chance moment shared at the gala.

"Are you a man of your word?" she asked, squaring her shoulders with a newfound confidence.

Kraven frowned, clearly confused by her sudden change in topic. "Yes, I believe I am. But what does that have to do with anything?"

"And did you mean what you said when you told me you only provided what was craved? That if there was another way to meet your demand that you'd do it?"

"Supply and demand." He nodded in acknowledgement. "But you weren't supposed to remember that little detail. A magic unique to pixies with pixie dust, I suppose."

A calculating smile spread across Kraven's face that terrified her to her core. "But what's stopping me from taking you right now and delivering you to Gareth myself?"

Zera's heart slammed into her rib cage. She couldn't afford to show her fear, not when everything was at stake. With a deep breath, she mustered up her courage and met Kraven's cold stare head-on.

"Nothing," she said boldly. "But if you do, then you're ruining your chances of making more money and influence than you could possibly imagine and an opportunity to expand into a new territory."

"And which territory is that?"

"Havenwood," she said, her voice steady despite the tremble in her hands.

She knew she was counting her eggs before they hatched, thinking the Haven Wolf Tavern owner would agree to working with Kraven. But the tavern owner had skin in the game. His own cousin was a pixie, and bureaucracy hadn't made their problem any better. She was sure she'd be able to convince him to get on board.

"Haven Moon Pack turf?" Kraven's smile faded, replaced by a look of interest. "No one's been able to establish a foothold there. It would likely eliminate all other competition."

"Exactly." She didn't move an inch while he seemed to contemplate her proposal.

But one never knew for sure with the incubus, and if this went south, she would be dead, and there would be nothing Maverick could do about it, since she'd made him wait at the bottom of the stairs.

"All right, you've convinced me," Kraven said finally, and Zera let out a breath. "If you can deliver this synthetic pixie dust as promised and secure relations with the Haven Wolf Pack territory, I'll reject Gareth's deal. But know this, Charlotte, if you fail to deliver or try to deceive me, there will be fatal consequences."

Zera nodded, understanding the gravity of Kraven's words. She glanced back at Maverick, who stood watching her intently from the railing, his expression a mixture of concern and rage. But he couldn't argue with her decision. She was in charge tonight.

"I'll be in touch." Kraven waved his hand in dismissal.

He didn't have to say it twice. Zera turned to leave, but before she could reach the bottom of the stairs, Kraven's voice stopped her in her tracks.

"By the way, Charlotte," he drawled from where he leaned over the balcony railing, his voice somehow carrying over the loud music and the crowded dance floor. "I should tell you that I already canceled my meeting with Gareth before you made your offer. Now, you've given me an even better deal."

Her stomach twisted into knots as she realized the gravity of her situation. She'd just promised a dangerous crime lord she would deliver a synthetic pixie-dust drug she didn't even have, to say nothing of the means to reproduce it in mass, and offered up her tavern boss's territory as a new turf for him. The weight of her decisions pressed down on her, making it difficult to breathe. She was in far deeper than she'd anticipated, and Kraven hadn't even needed her intervention.

Trying to hide her panic, Zera let her eyes land on Maverick's muscular build and captivating, piercing eyes. He stood right where she had left him, concern etched on his face. With a burst of adrenaline-fueled speed, she grabbed his hand along with the chain cuff, and they darted out of the club.

Maverick followed without hesitation. His werewolf hearing had probably picked up everything that went down between her and Kraven, and he was pissed. But she couldn't worry about that right now. She just had to get out.

"Zera," he said once they were outside.

"Please, save it, okay?" she asked, not breaking her speed when he tried to pull her to a stop. "I know what you're going to say. That you think I was reckless, that I jeopardized our whole mission, that I—"

"Completely astound me?" he whispered, tugging her toward him, and this time she didn't resist as he pulled her closer. His other hand cupped her chin, tilting her gaze to meet his. "That was... incredible."

"You think so?" she asked, her nerves in overdrive. She didn't know if he could sense that she'd lied to Kraven about the synthetic pixie dust, but if he did, he didn't give it away, and she didn't have the energy to tell him and dampen the mood. Not with the way he was touching her.

"Absolutely," he said, but there was an underlying tone of worry in his voice. "But what exactly happened back there? You actually did it? You created a synthetic pixie-dust drug?"

She hesitated. She didn't want to confess her lie in the hopes of not adding to his concerns. She swallowed hard and nodded. "Yeah, I got something," she whispered, hoping her voice wouldn't betray her.

"That's amazing!" Maverick's eyes widened, and he pulled her into an embrace. Though she knew she should feel safe in his strong arms, guilt gnawed at her insides. "I know how hard you've been working on that in between training. I'm proud of you," he murmured into her hair. "But we need to be careful now. Kraven isn't someone to mess with."

"Trust me, I know," she muttered, her mind racing through the potential consequences of her decision. She couldn't help but think about Cole, her precious son who she would do anything to protect.

As they walked to the car in silence, Zera's thoughts kept spiraling. She knew she should come clean to Maverick, but the fear of his reaction and the uncertainty of their situation held her back. They had grown so close, yet there was still so much they didn't know about each other. And despite their pasts and differences, the thought of losing him—whether from her lies or from the dangers lurking in the shadows—threatened to shatter her heart into pieces.

She hadn't realized how far she'd actually fallen for Maverick until that moment. It took all of her energy to keep her thoughts from reeling from this realization as they drove back to the penthouse.

Upon their arrival, the door clicked shut behind them, and Zera went to the kitchen cabinet for a glass of water. She tried to avoid

Maverick's stare as she went to fill up a glass. She sighed, rolling her shoulders as she tried to stretch the tense knot that had suddenly formed on the drive over.

Maverick leaned against the door, his piercing eyes studying her carefully. "Are you okay?" he asked gently. "You seem... off."

Zera hesitated before nodding, still grappling with her decision to keep the truth from him. Maverick had been so supportive, standing by her side and even revealing the truth about his past and the Whisper's staff. He'd been vulnerable with her in a way she could tell wasn't easy for him after she made him relive unthinkable hardships because of the Whispers. How could he still care this deeply when he'd been hurt by her own kind? How could she be so drawn to him when his kind had tormented her people?

That was when it clicked. They were more than the faen species that made them up. They were more than their own kind. They were different, and how deeply they cared set them apart from everyone else, making them their own.

"You were incredible back there, you know," Maverick said, his voice soft and earnest. He didn't move from the doorway, but his eyes lingered on her lips as she sipped her water.

Guilt weighed heavily on her chest as she glanced at him, trying to read his thoughts. She set the glass down, preparing to come clean.

I love you.

The thought drifted through her mind, so clear that it felt like a whisper in her ear. She froze. "What did you say?" she asked, her heart pounding wildly.

"I didn't say anything." Maverick's gaze searched hers. "But what did you hear?"

"You... you s-said," she stammered, her emotions a whirlwind of confusion, hope, and fear. But she must've been mistaken. "Nothing. Never mind."

She turned away from him, dumping the rest of her water into the sink. She shouldn't want for him to have said what she thought she'd heard, but she did.

"Zera." Maverick's voice was a warm balm against her chaotic heart. She felt him move closer, his breath ghosting over the nape of her neck. The air rushed out from her. She closed her eyes, trying to process the words that echoed in her mind. *I love you.*

"What did you hear?" he purred against her ear, his hands resting gently on her shoulders, his touch as light as a feather that sent goose bumps in its wake.

Her pulse quickened, fear and hope battling within her as she whispered, "You said that you loved me."

"Ah, that." Maverick paused, and she could almost feel the weight of his gaze on her. "I didn't say it, Zera. I thought it."

The room seemed to shrink around them, their proximity heightening the intensity of the moment. Zera's mind raced as she struggled to comprehend the implications of his admission. He had never admitted to their connection so boldly before, avoiding it as if he was afraid of it, but somehow, that fear was gone. Perhaps they'd both been changed by Kraven's nightclub.

"Wait," she said, her voice cracking in disbelief. "You thought it?"

Maverick's thumbs traced circles on her shoulders in a soothing motion. "Yes, I thought it."

"But you said before that I couldn't have heard your thoughts."

"That's because of what that meant," he said, his breathless voice in awe as if he was admitting this to himself as much as he was to her. "It meant that on some level you love me too."

"But how?" Zera gasped. She turned around to find him so close she had to crane her neck up to look into his pensive gaze.

Their eyes locked in an electrifying moment of possibility. Maverick's eyes held a mixture of vulnerability and desire, mirroring the emotions coursing through Zera's veins.

"Because I'm a werewolf," he said finally, his eyes searching hers. "Only a mate who loves them back can hear their thoughts. You didn't know?"

She understood the underlying question. He wondered if she'd had this type of connection with her ex. The werewolf who deserted her and her son. The truth was, she was in love at first, and then he changed, or perhaps she changed once she realized she was going to have a child. Either way, he showed his true colors when he cheated on her. Yet, even though they were in love once and shared a good chunk of their lives together, she'd never felt this way with him. The connection she had with Maverick was so different from anything else, so intimate it made everything else pale in comparison.

"This doesn't have to change anything if you don't want it to." He pulled back, his eyes searching hers, pleading for an answer.

"Does it scare you?" she asked quietly, searching for any hint of regret or hesitation in his expression.

"Of losing my heart again? Yes," he admitted, a small smile tugging at the corners of his lips. "But like you, I've never had this bond before. Never felt so connected with someone that I'd risk it all."

She understood the feeling. He must've heard her unspoken response. "But this... this bond between us, what does it mean?"

"It means that there's something real between us, something I'm willing and ready to take a chance on."

His words sparked a fire within her, burning away the guilt and uncertainty that had plagued her since their return to the apartment. For the first time in her life, Zera felt truly connected to someone, bound by a love and a bond that transcended the physical realm.

Her mind raced through all the things that could keep them apart—his past, her past, her being a mom, his job—but through their bond, she knew how sincerely he meant the words, that no matter what, he was there for the long haul, and suddenly, their differences didn't matter. She knew she didn't want to lose him. That she loved him. She realized that she had for a while now, and she was willing to take that chance with him.

"I love you too," she said, her voice barely above a whisper. She licked her lips, biting her lower one as she did so. "And I want you. Now."

A growl rumbled in Maverick's chest as he pulled her closer, capturing her lips in a kiss that was gentle yet urgent. He tugged on her lower lip, as if to express just that. It told her he knew exactly what he was doing and knew how to take care of her. Zera responded eagerly, her hands roaming his well-muscled chest, feeling the heat of his skin beneath her fingertips. Their passion rose steadily, the bond between them growing stronger than ever. It was almost as if they didn't have to speak to know what the other one wanted, which was true. The thought sent a shudder of anticipation down her spine.

Without breaking away from their kiss, Maverick scooped her up in his arms, and her legs straddled his waist. He carried her as if she weighed nothing around the kitchen island and toward the training mat in the center of the living room. Maverick gently lowered her onto the soft surface, his muscular form hovering above her, his hips settling between her thighs. Heat rushed through her veins, her body yearning for more of his touch.

Her eyes locked with his, which were filled with desire and determination.

I won't last long with you looking at me like that. He moaned, his thoughts bursting through their connection. *And I want to take care of you. Thoroughly.*

Is that a promise? She grinned, tugging on his leather pants.

Maverick chuckled, his lips brushing lightly against hers. "Absolutely," he whispered, answering her thoughts.

The heat between them ignited as they moved in sync, their limbs entwining like vines reaching for a shared source of light. Maverick's hands were at her hips, her waist, her neck. They traced lines of desire and danced across her collarbone, dipping into the hollow of her throat, a gesture that sent shivers through her body.

"Your skin is so soft," he murmured, his breath hot against her ear. "Like moonlight on silk."

Zera laughed, a sound both nervous and delighted. "Leave it to a spy to come up with such poetic descriptions." Her laughter gave way to a soft gasp as Maverick nipped playfully at her neck, his teeth grazing her sensitive skin.

"Maybe I have a hidden talent for poetry," he teased, his hands continuing their exploration. "But only when it comes to you."

He claimed her lips again before his lips followed the line along her collarbone he'd traced with his hand. Each kiss sent a wave of pleasure in its wake. There were no more words, just touch. Just this.

As Maverick's mouth traced a fiery path down her body, Zera found herself lost in the sensations he evoked. His fingers worked their magic, deftly unfastening her bustier. She sighed with relief when she was finally freed of the constricting garment, and Maverick sucked in a breath, his eyes filled with heat and love for her.

"Fae, Zera," he whispered, admiration lacing his voice. "You're breathtaking."

Zera's cheeks flushed at the compliment, but the feeling of vulnerability quickly dissipated as he continued to shower her with tender affection. He took his time trailing kisses along her neck, his hand finding her breast before he took it in his mouth. A moan escaped her lips as heat coursed through her body, fueled by his gentle-yet-passionate touch.

His hands shifted, replaced by his mouth as he moved lower, kissing every inch of her stomach down to her hip bones. She arched in anticipation when he paused at the soft skin near her thigh, his vow of wanting to take care of her echoing in her mind.

He looked up at her, his mouth inches away from her heated core, as if he was thinking the same thing. His lips parted into a crooked smile as he kissed her thighs instead. A devilish thing to do, but it elicited a laugh from her.

"Maverick," she pleaded, arching up into him again.

It's all part of my plan. To make you moan my name as you come to me again and again.

The promise had her coiled so tightly, she nearly exploded from the sheer anticipation alone.

But Maverick, ever the master of patience, deviated from his plan with a sudden, tender kiss to her other inner thigh. He traced the curve with his tongue, his eyes never leaving hers as he teased her. Each caress brought her closer to shattering against his touch.

"Please," she whispered, her voice barely audible as she gripped the edge of the training mat, her knuckles turning white.

Maverick finally relented, his lips finding their way to the sensitive bundle of nerves at her core. His tongue swirled with just enough pressure to make her toes curl, and Zera's eyes rolled back in ecstasy. He worked his magic on her body as if it were his own, as if he understood precisely how to bring her pleasure beyond anything she had ever experienced before.

Heat coiled within her again, threatening to consume her entirely as he licked her over and over, completely shattering her control. Her hips rolled to the rhythm he set against her with his tongue. Her body trembled as he pushed her closer and closer to the edge until she screamed his name as waves of pleasure crashed through her, leaving her breathless. While her body trembled, Maverick held her, anchoring her to reality as she floated back down to earth.

As the tremors faded, Zera opened her eyes, finding Maverick's gaze locked on hers. He had a smug, satisfied grin on his face before he leaned up to kiss her again, as if to tell her he wasn't done with her yet, but she needed him whole inside her. Their lips met. Fiery. Hungry. Passionate. He pressed himself against her as they kissed, his hardness evident, and she tugged him closer.

"Patience," he whispered as he pulled away from the kiss, his breath warm with citrus and strong whiskey. "I want to enjoy you."

Zera moaned as Maverick slipped a finger into his mouth, wetting it before teasing her opening until he entered her, stroking her at a rhythm that brought the coil of heat to an all-new high she hadn't known existed.

She bit her lip, trying to contain the overwhelming desire that made her heart beat faster.

He groaned at the sight, his voice low and husky. "I love the way you bite your lip like that."

Maverick's expert touch sent her spiraling into ecstasy once more. She arched her back and cried out in passion. Zera was lost in the sensations, consumed by the heat of their connection. When she came back to earth once more, Maverick removed his fingers, trailing teasing circles up her body. His touch was electrifying, making her skin tingle as he moved higher. She felt a warmth inside her that she'd never experienced in her life, and it wasn't just physical. It was deeper than that, and she never wanted to let go of it.

Their lips met again, hot and desperate. Zera needed him now.

Zera swiftly moved her body, her muscles flexing as she quickly used a maneuver he'd taught her during one of their training sessions to gain leverage on him. With surprising strength, she had him on his back, straddling him as she climbed onto his lap.

"Who taught you that?" Maverick asked, laughing in shock, his eyes wide with surprise and admiration.

"Must've been some hot spy I know," she replied with a playful smirk, leaning down into his chest before guiding him inside her, which efficiently turned his laugh into a moan of his own.

It was his turn for his eyes to roll back as she took him in whole, riding him. He thrust against her, sending wave after wave of pleasure through her whole body. He coiled underneath her, his hands at her hips as his face tensed in a way that told her he wouldn't last long.

He hardened even more inside her until he pumped once, twice, and then his body shuddered beneath her, sending her over the edge one final time. He cried out her name, the sound of it filling her with a wild and heady sensation. She collapsed into his arms, their bodies slick with sweat and their chests heaving as they struggled to catch their breaths. They lay entwined, Maverick's strong arms wrapped around Zera. Home. She felt at home in those arms.

Whatever tomorrow brought—all the unknowns—it didn't matter. She knew she could face it because they were together. Wholeheartedly and honestly together.

A small echo in her mind reminded her of the synthetic pixie-dust issue, but it flitted away as sleep encroached. Everything else could wait until the morning.

CHAPTER 17
ZERA

Zera's eyes fluttered open as the first rays of sunlight peeked through the curtains. She nestled deeper into the warmth beside her, breathing in Maverick's familiar scent of oak and citrus. His arm draped over her bare waist stirred memories of their passionate night together. They must've found their way up the stairs to the bedroom at some point last night.

Panic flared in her chest. The everfrost blossom.

She eased out of Maverick's embrace, grabbed a pair of sweats and a shirt that must've belonged to him because it was huge, and tiptoed across the room, dread mounting with each step. She pushed the drapes the rest of the way open to bring more light into the room. Sunrays beamed across the table she'd turned into her lab and positioned in front of the window for maximum sun exposure.

She nearly cried. There it was, the once-vibrant flower drooped in its wintery terrarium, petals shriveled and brown.

Only one seed was left.

Zera clutched at her hair, pacing in circles. She was dead. No, worse than dead. If she didn't develop and bring the synthetic pixiedust drug to Kraven, he would make an example of her. Images of fae strung up by their wrists, flesh peeled from their bodies, flashed through her mind. The work of the incubus to those who crossed him. He'd turned down the meeting with Gareth, and somehow, she knew it was because of her offer. He must've had a seer in his gang.

"Good morning," Maverick murmured from the bed.

She turned and gazed at him, his godlike muscles glowing in the morning light and reflecting off his glorious pecs. How could she tell him she'd lied after he'd been so open with her about his past? That she didn't have a working synthetic pixie-dust drug like she claimed. She didn't even have a live plant to study for the missing element for her precursor.

"Zera? Are you okay?" Maverick asked when she didn't respond, concern etched into his handsome features.

"Uh, yeah. Fine," she lied, forcing a smile. "Just need to use the bathroom." She yanked the curtain closed before she hurried across the room, her mind racing. She had to figure out what had gone wrong with the plant. It couldn't have been lack of sunlight, and she'd already taken the temperature into consideration. Perhaps elevation? It was a good theory, but they were in the penthouse. Surely, that was high enough.

She splashed cold water onto her face, taking a deep breath to calm her nerves. She glanced at her faestone on the bathroom sink. They'd been out late, and she'd missed her evening routine of calling Jade. She would try to reach her later.

A heavy sigh escaped her. She needed to tell Maverick the truth about her predicament, but fear of his reaction held her back. Would he understand? Or would he see her as just another lying pixie?

"Zera?" Maverick called softly from the doorway, his boxers straining against the vee of muscles leading all the way down. "Is everything all right?"

She looked at him in the mirror, forgetting she hadn't closed the door. For a moment, she thought she saw a hint of vulnerability in his eyes. It made her heart ache. She swallowed hard, her throat suddenly feeling dry.

"I... I need to talk to you," she managed to choke out, her voice barely above a whisper.

Maverick leaned against the doorframe, his triceps rippling as he folded his arms across his massive chest. "What's wrong?" he asked gently.

Zera took a deep breath, steeling herself for what she was about to say. "I lied to you, Maverick," she began, her words tumbling out in a rush. "About my progress with the everfrost plant. I haven't actually been able to extract its elements to study them to see if they're a precursor for my synthetic pixie dust because the plant keeps dying."

He didn't say anything, so she kept going.

"Last night, I thought that when Gareth didn't show up that I could distract Kraven from even considering Gareth's deal with a better one. Then at least we could keep Gareth from getting Kraven's business, even if Gareth didn't arrive when we were there. Then we could use Kraven to get to Gareth somehow while I finished developing the synthetic.

"I had to do something. Gareth was never going to show up, but I didn't think it all the way through. I was just thinking we had to do something. My son needs me back, and I will do anything to finally go back to the way things were. We need to take Gareth down by any means necessary. I need to be with my son again, and I'll do anything. But then last night happened, and you were so... happy. I didn't want to ruin the mood."

She stopped, running out of breath. A myriad of emotions flickered across Maverick's face—confusion, disappointment, and finally, betrayal. A storm raged in his eyes and bore into hers. Zera felt her heart constrict painfully in her chest, their connection going dim.

"Say something, please," she pleaded, her voice trembling.

"I..." Maverick paused, running a hand through his tousled hair. "I'm not sure what to say, Zera. You lied to me. And after everything I told you, about my past and your demands for the truth..."

He trailed off, his gaze dropping to the floor. Zera could see the hurt in his eyes, and it was like a dagger twisting in her gut. She'd begged him to be honest with her, and he hadn't even lied. Not directly. He'd only withheld information, which had hurt her ability to trust him. Now, she'd just severed their recent foundation of trust by lying to his face. To say she felt beyond guilty was an understatement.

"Please, I was only desperate to save Cole." Tears brimmed her eyes, and she blinked them back. She missed her son so much that she would do anything. Maverick had to at least understand that.

Maverick's jaw clenched, his hands balling into fists at his sides. "You should have told me the truth from the beginning," he said quietly, his voice laced with hurt but also fear. "You put yourself in danger, and now, you're indebted to Kraven. You put another target on your back, as if we don't have enough as it is."

"I know that! It's all messed up," Zera cried. "And the worst of it is, I didn't have the guts to be honest with you. I'm so sorry for lying to you. I never meant to hurt you. I just wanted to finally make progress on getting my son out of Pixie Hollow and back to our normal, ordinary, non-spy life."

Zera's shoulders slumped as she struggled to meet Maverick's piercing gaze. She knew she had betrayed his trust, and the weight of her poor decision left her utterly defeated.

Maverick remained silent for what felt like an eternity but finally let out a long exhalation. "I need some time to process this," he finally said, his voice tight. "Time can't be wasted, since we're running out of it, so get dressed and meet me downstairs in ten minutes for training."

Zera nodded, swallowing hard against the lump in her throat as he left her alone. She shook off the emotion that bubbled up from their growing bond. It had taken so much to get where they'd been last night, and now, because of one stupid decision, she'd risked everything. She'd risked their lives.

She grabbed her faestone, selecting Jade's image. She needed to see her son, to remind herself why she was doing all of this.

The screen blinked, the white dots flickering across her face. The faestone rang multiple times until a message saying they were not picking up popped up. Jade was probably busy with the morning routine. Zera sighed, the disappointment weighing on her. She would have to try again later.

She quickly threw on her workout clothes and met Maverick in the living room, her nerves on edge.

The training session started quietly, both avoiding eye contact as they went through warm-up stretches. The silence between them was deafening, filled only by the occasional grunt or shuffle of feet on the mats.

As they began sparring, Zera struggled to find the words to explain herself. "Maverick, I know I made a mistake," she started, dodging his punch while throwing one of her own, which he blocked with ease. "I was just desperate to get at Gareth, to ruin his plans so it's easier to take him out. I thought I could handle it on my own."

Maverick's expression remained stoic as he aimed a kick at her midsection, which she narrowly avoided. "You should have trusted me," he said gruffly. "We're partners. Mates. We have to have each other's backs."

The way he said mates sent an arrow through her heart. It wasn't said with the love they'd expressed to each other last night but dripped with sarcasm and disbelief. Zera bit her cheek. She had jeopardized not only their lives but their relationship. As they continued to spar, all she could do was vow to never break Maverick's trust again. She would do whatever it took to make things right. She'd follow Maverick's instructions to a tee, destroying Gareth together, and she'd replant the everfrost blossom, and this time she would succeed. She had been so close last time. It had lasted longer than the first seed. She needed more elevation for it somehow.

Zera focused on throwing her weight into a series of punches, channeling her frustration at the whole situation into each strike.

Jab. Cross. Right hook. Left uppercut. The sequence Maverick had drilled into her was beginning to feel like second nature. He still blocked them effortlessly, his expression unreadable. She had to prove to him and to herself that she was capable, that she could fix her mistakes and learn from them.

"I know I upset you," she said, dodging a roundhouse kick. "But I can make this right. Don't worry."

"'Don't worry'?" he mocked, and her anger flared. "Gareth already wants to harvest you. Now you owe Kraven, the most dangerous type of fae, and you can't even deliver."

She swung. He dodged.

"And may I remind you of what he does to those who cross him?" he growled, dodging her hit again. "The fae bodies left in the Shadowood Forest that not even the police will question him about?"

Of course she remembered. How could she forget when she had him to remind her? She sent a diverting kick to his left, sending him dodging as she grounded herself, loaded her left side, and struck.

He grunted when she landed a blow to his shoulder, and he laughed. He actually *laughed*.

"I will figure... it... out!" she gritted out as she fought even harder, throwing punch after punch.

He didn't move, didn't even try to defend himself. He just stood there taking her punches to his impeccably hard abs, which were, fortunately this time, covered by a shirt.

"Zera, I know why you did it," he whispered when her tears finally fell. "You did it for your son. But I wish you'd trusted me sooner. I could've helped."

"How?"

"I... I don't know, honestly, but we could've figured it out." He held her as she finally stopped fighting. She didn't have any more in her.

"I feel like a part of me is missing," she said, her voice barely a whisper. "I'm lost without Cole. I need to end this and get back to my son."

"I know," he said reassuringly.

Zera pulled back from Maverick's embrace, wiping the tears from her eyes. She took a deep, steadying breath as she met his gaze.

"Again, I'm so sorry I didn't tell you the truth sooner," she said. "I was scared of ruining things, and I thought for sure this time the everfrost blossom would survive. I was wrong."

Maverick nodded, his expression still reserved but no longer cold. "I understand why you did it. I just wish things could have been different between us."

Zera felt a pang in her heart at his words. She had hoped that after last night, after being so close and intimate, he would be more forgiving. But the hurt was still there in his eyes. She had scratched at old scars, wounds that had probably taken him decades to get over.

"Me too," she admitted softly. "I didn't want our first time together to be tainted by lies. It meant a lot to me."

Maverick looked thoughtful, as if weighing her words. "It meant a lot to me too. I don't regret it, Zera. I need some time to wrap my head around everything. But we're going to figure this out, I promise. We'll get you back to your son."

Relief washed over Zera. He was still there, even after she had betrayed his trust. There was hope for them yet. She offered him a small, grateful smile.

"Thank you, Maverick. That means more than you know."

He gave a single nod, the barest hint of a smile touching his lips. "Want to break to eat?"

She arched her brow. "Is that a serious question?"

Of course she would take a break from training to eat. Her stomach rumbled, as if in response.

Maverick chuckled, shaking his head as they moved to the kitchen.

"Do you have any idea what might've happened with your plant?" He opened the fridge, rummaged through the shelves, and pulled out containers of food.

She tugged on her ponytail, a nervous habit. "I don't know. I thought maybe it's elevation, but this penthouse is almost at the lowest point that the flower is known to bloom."

He skewered chicken and peppers, dipping them into one of the containers of some kind of marinade before tossing them into a black box with a grill option.

"How close is it?"

"Maybe fifty feet or so."

He nodded, opening the box, the chicken kebabs sizzling as he moved them onto two plates. "I may have an idea for that."

"Oh?" She leaned over the counter, her eyes hungrily taking in the kebabs.

"Yeah, come on. I want to show you something." He dusted his hands on a kitchen towel before grabbing his plate.

She took the other plate and followed him, curious to see what he had in mind.

He led her up the stairs, back into the bedroom, and into the closet.

"This is what you wanted to show me?" she asked, eyeing a room large enough to have a center island filled with shelves of neatly organized clothes and accessories.

He just gave her a look that told her to wait and motioned for her to keep following him to the back of the closet.

"This penthouse was made specifically for my alias, Dane," he said, balancing his plate in one hand while using his free hand to shove aside a row of garment bags. "And because I'm a spy, I naturally have two alternate ways to exit this place other than the elevator."

She blinked in surprise when he found some secret trigger behind the clothes, making the whole rack collapse inward to reveal a small staircase beyond. He motioned for her to go in first, and she carefully stepped over the ledge that had once been the back of the closet onto the winding staircase, which had steps barely the width of Maverick's broad shoulders.

Zera cautiously ascended the narrow staircase, the light overhead growing brighter. She gripped the rail with her free hand while keeping her plate of kebabs upright. She didn't want any of her food plummeting down the metal stairs.

She reached the landing and gasped. The whole city stretched out around them from every angle. She stepped onto the rooftop of the penthouse sixty stories above the ground, the air somehow warm and windless. The breathtaking view of the city skyline made her heart skip a beat. Maverick stood beside her, his gaze fixed on the horizon. The sun painted the buildings in hues of gold, casting long shadows over the bustling streets below, the faint hum of the city life filling the air.

"Wow," she gasped.

"It's probably the best view of the city," Maverick said before turning to her with a soft smile. "And now a plant sanctuary for your terrarium. This should get you closer to elevation."

"It's perfect," she said, a flutter of hope rushing through her veins.

He took her plate and moved to a little table with two chairs pushed against a wall. She followed him, taking in the cozy rooftop setup—potted plants, a rustic firepit surrounded by mismatched chairs, and a small grill in the corner. A stark difference from the posh furniture throughout the penthouse below.

"This is amazing," she said as they sat down and Maverick set her plate in front of her.

"I'm glad you think so," he replied with a grin. "This is the only place in this penthouse that actually suits me."

"Really?" She hardly believed that. Judging from the fancy restaurant where they'd met and the clothes he wore, she didn't take him for one who enjoyed the simpler things like picnics and sitting around a fire.

Maverick chuckled, the sound low and rich. "I'm a spy, Zera. There are so many things I keep buried in this line of work."

"So, where do you actually live?" she asked, savoring a bite of chicken that nearly melted in her mouth.

"If I told you that, then I wouldn't be a very good spy, now, would I?"

A smile tugged at the corners of her lips. It felt good to get back to a normal conversation. To distract herself from all the bad that happened, if only for a moment.

"You said this was a secret exit," she said, checking the surroundings. Though it seemed to be one of the tallest buildings around, anyone who could fly could easily see his patio setup. Also, she didn't see a way for a werewolf to get down. Someone with wings, perhaps, but not Maverick.

He smirked, tilting his head to the side. "You don't think I had everything about this penthouse spelled and shielded from those who don't know how to find it?"

To be honest, she hadn't even thought about it. Not even Sloane was powerful enough to shield a whole penthouse from everyone. That required a lot of counter-defensive magic. Or at least she assumed it would to counter everyone else in the Fae Realm.

Zera glanced around. "You mean this whole place is hidden? No one can see or sense that we're here?"

Maverick nodded, his smirk growing wider. "And the exit is a long dive that I'd take only if the penthouse were taken under siege."

She gulped. "You'd just jump off the side of a sixty-story building?"

He leaned against the hard back of the folding picnic chair. "I had the ledge spelled so that when I stepped over it, I'd float to the ground."

"But only you, I'm guessing."

He shrugged, as if that was a given. "I'm a spy. Don't want enemies who can't fly getting a boost."

She shook her head in disbelief. She didn't even want to know about the second exit. The height alone would make that fall a death wish even for the strongest of fae. Whatever witch or mage had done all this was probably expensive but worth every penny. But she guessed a rogue spy for hire could afford it.

At least there was hope that the elevation would help. It would get her closer to her goal, at least. She sighed and took another bite of her chicken, chewing slowly as she mulled over all the steps she'd taken when planting the last seed and what she would do differently this time. She could only change so much, but she wanted to be sure she hadn't missed anything. That it was, in fact, the elevation issue that had triggered the plant to die. She had gotten further than before. The plant had just gotten stuck in the middle stages.

Lost in thought, Zera barely noticed as Maverick spoke up.

"You know, Zera," he said, his voice low and husky, "there's something incredibly seductive about watching you savor every bite like that."

Zera choked on her bite. "What?"

"You heard me." He continued to smirk at her. At least he hadn't lost his arrogance entirely after her blunder. He grinned at her, as if he was a good catch, which he was, but she would never utter those words to him for fear of his head growing to double its size.

But that wasn't what made her nearly cough up bits of chicken and grilled peppers.

"Say what you said again," she said, putting down her sandwich and brushing off the grease on a napkin.

Her heart fluttered with excitement as a memory from the night of the gala took shape somewhere in her mind. It was distant, but something Maverick just said had jostled it free, and if she could catch hold of it, it might provide some answers. Maverick raised an eyebrow, clearly amused by her sudden interest.

"You really need me to repeat it? That the way you eat makes you all the more enticing? That it makes me forget about our first fight as a couple?" he teased, his voice dripping with playful innuendo.

"Ugh, no. Not that." She didn't have the brain capacity to think about his use of the word "couple" right now. Were they one? Even after her lie? Had last night coupled with their bond really changed everything?

No, she couldn't think about that.

"Repeat what you said exactly," she prodded.

He frowned in confusion. "That it's seductive to watch you eat like that?"

"Yes, that's it." She nodded, suddenly remembering the incubus's strange farewell at the gala. "Remember when you asked me if there was anything strange about my conversation with Kraven?"

He nodded, taking a healthy bite of chicken.

"That reminded me of something he said. It was really weird, but then I found you on the balcony and forgot all about it."

Maverick leaned in as understanding swept across his face. "What was it?"

"It was when I was leaving," Zera began hesitantly, unsure of how much importance to place on it and hoping she could remember precisely what was said. "He told me... something like, 'I'll be watching like a seductive shadow under a...' Oh, what was it?"

She tapped her foot, trying to remember. Then she snapped her fingers. "'Like a seductive shadow under a steel titan's gaze,' or at least that's what I remember."

Maverick's eyes widened in surprise, and he nearly choked on his kebab. He dropped it onto his plate, the intensity in his gaze returning. "Are you sure?"

"Yeah, I'm positive. Does it mean anything to you?"

"It's a location. One I'd totally forgotten." Maverick let out a growl.

Zera looked at him, bewildered. "Seriously? It's a location?"

Maverick nodded. "The Steel Titan is what Gareth used to call one of his many homes, but this one is different. It's not just a home. It's his stronghold along the Mystic Rapids. A heavily fortified fortress."

Zera's heart raced as the implications set in. Could it really be that simple? Had Kraven given them the key to tracking down their dangerous adversary?

But why?

"So Kraven was helping us find Gareth?"

Maverick nodded. "Seems that way. Why, I couldn't tell you."

Zera pushed her plate away, suddenly not hungry anymore. If they had found where Gareth was hiding, then they were one step closer to ending this nightmare. But she couldn't shake the fear that came with it. They were going against a dangerous elf with immense power—both magical and political. She'd witnessed that at the restaurant. And whatever reason the incubus had for giving Gareth up to them, she was sure it wasn't good. Perhaps he had an ulterior motive for helping them, even before he'd known she was working on a synthetic competitor to the pixie-dust drug Gareth was flaunting.

Whatever it could be, they didn't have time to consider it.

"What are we waiting for?" she asked. "We need to go there. Now."

Maverick shook his head. "It could be a trap."

"But what if it's not? What if it's our only chance at getting the upper hand on Gareth on our terms?" She couldn't believe he was hesitating after he'd been so quick to head out on leads with far less weight.

Maverick sighed, the wariness evident in his eyes. "I understand your urgency, but we can't rush into this blindly. I made that mistake several times already, and look where it's gotten us."

She chewed her bottom lip. She could see how much that had hurt to admit.

"Now," he continued, "I'm usually all about solo jobs, but each time we've gone in after a lead, he's been a no-show. I find that suspicious. If Kraven's lead is legit, we need to have the upper hand."

Zera thought for a moment. "Wouldn't us not acting right away on Kraven's hint at where Gareth's base is be enough of a surprise? I mean, it's been weeks since the gala."

"Yes, it would be," he agreed. "I never said we wouldn't go. The stronghold is most likely where he'll be. But we can't go in alone. He'll have an army there waiting for us, even if he doesn't know we're coming."

"Then who'll go with us?"

Maverick's lips curled into a sly, satisfied smile. "My network of spies."

"I thought everyone was icing you out because of the bounty Gareth put on our heads," she said, trying to hide the impressed lilt of her voice.

"These aren't those people," Maverick replied confidently, as if that didn't sound absolutely ridiculous.

She would just have to find out what he meant by that. A spark of hope ignited within her. With Maverick's network of spies on their side, they might have a fighting chance at finally taking down Gareth and his stronghold. She couldn't wait to see the look on his face when they did it too.

"One request," she said.

He cocked his brow in question, and she fixed him with a determined look. She had to see this through, and even though out of the two of them, he was the trained spy, she had to be the one to do it.

"Gareth is mine," she said firmly. "My son's life was threatened by his hand. It'll be mine that obliterates him."

Pride flickered across his face, but he only nodded. It was all she needed. Gareth was going down.

CHAPTER 18

ZERA

Maverick's network of spies proved to be reliable as they assembled at the penthouse within a few hours of being contacted. Felice, the boutique owner and mastermind behind every inch of breathable leather Zera wore, was the first to arrive. Zera sat perched on a stool at the kitchen island, waiting for the rest.

"So, this is where the happy newlyweds live," Felice said when she entered, wearing a broad smile as she took in the living room turned training room.

"Welcome to our humble abode," Maverick said with a smirk that told Zera he was back to his arrogant self.

Zera had almost forgotten about their ruse. She guessed they'd still have to play a married couple for a little bit longer. The idea sent a pang of guilt through her chest. She still couldn't get a read on where Maverick was. She regretted the lie, but she didn't regret the night they'd shared or the bond that had grown between them. She just wished she could do things over again, to be open and honest with him like he had been with her—despite Maverick acknowledging that he understood. That almost made it worse.

"Dane, are you teaching your new bride to fight?" Felice asked, motioning to the training mat that took up most of the room and the rack of weights and weapons that lined the window wall beyond.

"Well, she is my wife, so learning to defend herself is a given," Maverick said, his voice dripping with amusement as he continued their charade. "And who better to teach her than the most skilled man she knows?"

Zera rolled her eyes at his theatrical display. It was such a faeboy thing to say. Well, if he could pretend there was no issue between them, then so could she. She squared her shoulders, obliterating any thought of Maverick or their connection. She had to focus on the mission. Her shot at finally bringing Gareth down and reuniting with her son depended on it. The topic of arrogant, hot werewolves and any potential romantic future could wait. Possibly forever.

Felice took a spot next to her at the kitchen island. Quill arrived shortly afterward, making himself at home as he plopped down on one of the couches shoved against a wall.

The next to arrive were two that Zera didn't recognize—a slender, black-haired vampire Maverick introduced as Cillian, who Zera would avoid at all costs, and the Kobold goblin who was supposed to have been Maverick's date at the Crystal instead of Zera. The tall woman with high cheekbones, full lips, shoulder-length brown hair, and cunning eyes barely acknowledged Zera's presence. From the nasty smile Felice shot at the spy turned agent for the Faen Bureau of Investigation, Zera got the feeling there was some history between them.

Irdeel solidified this suspicion with the equally dirty looks she shot at Felice while pretending to be interested in the weapons Cillian was studying from the array of knives and magical devices secured on one of the shelves. There was definitely some bad blood there.

The spies all cluttered around the living room and kitchen, as if this was home, and perhaps they had been here together at one time. From what Maverick had told her before they arrived, though, it would have been years ago.

"Now that we're all here, why don't you get on with it?" Quill said, breaking a silence that bordered on awkward. The demon yawned lazily as he draped his legs over the arm of a love seat, his wild blond curls pulled back into a ponytail at the nape of his neck.

Zera's gaze darted to Maverick, who took point at the top of the training mat. His expression held a mixture of anticipation and irritation with the others. If he had any thoughts about Zera or their future together, he didn't let them show on his face. His walls were up, so she couldn't even get a read on him through their bond.

Maverick cleared his throat, and all eyes turned to him. "Thanks for coming on such short notice. I know some of you have gone straight, so I appreciate you being willing to help me and... my wife, Charlotte, out with this mission." He motioned toward Zera, who forced herself to cover her nerves with a look of sincere admiration for her fake husband. It was the part she had to play, but she wanted to grit her teeth every time he looked at her with his cocky eyes while wearing a self-important smile.

"We've got a lot to cover before we can infiltrate Gareth's stronghold," Maverick continued. "Quill, I believe you've got some floor plans for us to look at?"

"I thought you'd never ask," Quill said, flashing a devilish smile. He snapped his fingers, and a holographic image of what looked to be a six-story fortress appeared in a puff of smoke.

The floor plan hovered in the air in the center of their group so that they all could see exactly what they were up against.

"As you can see," Maverick said, "Gareth's stronghold is not something to scoff at. It's a highly secure, state-of-the-art fortress that's nearly impenetrable."

"It's not 'nearly impenetrable,'" Quill said, sitting forward in his seat. "It is utterly and totally impossible to break into."

Zera winced. That wasn't good news. This was supposed to be their in, the breaking of the last straw keeping her from returning to her quiet life with her son in Havenwood.

"But if it's not possible to break in, then what are we doing here?" Felice asked, crossing one long leg over the other. The siren's blue silk jumper swished with the movement.

"We're not going through the front door, obviously," Maverick answered, his tone confident and daring. "I have a plan."

Zera's heartbeat quickened. From the architecture of the stronghold displayed for all of them to see, it was clear this wouldn't be an easy feat. A steel-and-stone wall surrounded the structure built into the side of the mountain, thick enough that no grenade could penetrate it. And if the wall wasn't obstacle enough, the raging rapids that ran in front of it were enough to deter even the most powerful of fae. It would take more than a plan to get past all of the obstacles that stood between them and wherever Gareth would be holed up in the belly of the stronghold. She now understood why it'd been nicknamed the Steel Titan. Even if they were able to get in, find Gareth, and kill him, it was going to take every bit of their wits, cunning, and magic to make it out of there alive. Zera could feel the weight of the challenge pressing down on her, but failure was not an option.

"Now," Maverick continued, "each of you have been chosen for your unique abilities, and together I think our plan might work."

Felice flashed a smile, her siren beauty almost distracting enough to make one forget her dangerously enchanting voice. The designer twirled a lock of her fiery red hair between her fingers. "I assume I'll be playing the seductress in this little game of yours?" she purred, her eyes glinting mischievously.

"Of course she is." Irdeel snorted from where she stood near one of the cabinets of weapons, her slender body nearly towering over the vamp beside her. The four-inch heels on the boots she definitely didn't need for height made her even taller.

Zera bit back a laugh at the look Felice shot the goblin. Whatever was between them, it was a feud they'd been fighting for a while. Maverick seemed to ignore it, probably to keep the peace. Zera hoped it wouldn't cause a problem with their mission.

"What was that?" Felice asked, daring the goblin to say something to her face.

Irdeel just flashed her a vicious smile before returning her attention to the vampire and her fellow FBI agent, clearly more interested in the collection of weapons than the conversation at hand.

"Focus, people, please," Maverick said, shooting Irdeel a look of warning. "We will have to act as a single unit—one team—if we're to succeed in our goal to locate and kill Gareth inside his own stronghold along with anyone else who would fight to avenge him."

Zera gulped. When he put the plan that way, it sounded reckless. Only a fool would hunt someone on their own ground.

The goblin's ears twitched, but she gritted her teeth to cut off the apparent retort she wanted to throw back at him. She made a crude gesture directed at Maverick and Felice before returning her focus to the next weapon the vamp was studying.

"Each of you are masters of your own crafts," Maverick said, ignoring the crabby goblin. "First, Felice, you will act as the infiltrator and use your siren abilities to manipulate the guards surrounding the stronghold. Persuade anyone you need to, in whatever way you must, so we can have a clear path to the only potentially weak point in the wall of the stronghold."

Maverick nodded at Quill, who snapped his fingers. The floor plan shifted so they were now looking at a small door in the wall that was heavily guarded. And that was the weakest part of the wall. Dread and nerves settled in Zera's stomach, as if they were there to stay.

Maverick nodded to the diagram of the door and to where guards were stationed on either side of it as well as on top of the wall. "The stronghold is designed to become a sealed tomb if even a single scratch occurs to the wall. This doorway is our only entrance."

Zera didn't like the sound of that. What if their plan went sideways and they were stuck in that place and left to rot? She shuddered at the thought.

"But with Felice taking point during this first half," Maverick continued, "these guards won't know what hit them."

The siren nodded, an approving glint in her eyes.

"Next up, we have Irdeel," Maverick said, nodding to the goblin who was still inspecting the weapons with an unnerving interest. "Irdeel is a Kobold goblin with a specialty in alchemical sciences. She'll be our saboteur."

Irdeel barely looked up, her face a mask of boredom.

"She'll use her goblin nimbleness and shape-shifting abilities to blend in and infiltrate secure areas undetected," he said to no one in particular. "She'll also use her alchemical specialty to create and set traps to create distractions for our team."

"It'll be a blast. I'm sure nothing will go wrong," Felice chimed in, winning another dirty look from Irdeel.

Maverick folded his arms across his chest. "If this is going to be an issue, you two working together, tell me now because if we head out on this mission with beef between each other, then we're as good as dead."

Felice huffed. "The only issue I have is that we haven't heard a single word from her since she moved to the FBI. I don't trust her, and I have no idea who this Cillian is with her."

"Working with your lot was always just a side gig," Irdeel hissed through gritted teeth.

"You're welcome for that, by the way," Quill piped in and pressed the bridge of his nose between his thumb and forefinger. "If it weren't for me, you, Miss Irdeel, would never have had an alias to keep your nefarious 'side gig' from the FBI's radar. They probably wouldn't have even accepted your application."

"Don't think I owe you anything, demon. You were well paid for it," the goblin FBI agent spat as she shot him a glare that could curdle milk.

"Not everything's about money, goblin." Quill snapped his fingers, and a piece of black licorice appeared in a puff of smoke. "A thank-you card would've been nice. But my point is, I'm not sure we can trust the FBI traitor." The demon proceeded to peel the licorice and eat it at a leisurely pace, seemingly unfazed by the tense atmosphere that surrounded him.

"Who are you calling a traitor?" Irdeel asked, her tone as sharp as a blade.

Zera was certain that, if things didn't get under control soon, a full-on fight would break out among all of them, and then the mission would be off. She balled her hands into fists. That couldn't happen.

"You responded, so..." The demon's voice trailed off.

The squabbling spies might as well have been children, but it was Zera's child they were fighting for, and they didn't even know it. They were totally unaware of the full picture and urgency of this mission, and they were letting their personal issues get in the way.

Irdeel jumped to her high-heeled, boot-clad feet. "You conniving little—"

"Stop it," Zera said, her voice soft. But the bickering didn't stop, so she repeated it much louder and in her mom voice. "Stop this right now!"

Everyone froze. Mouths dropped as all eyes turned to Zera, who was now standing, though she didn't quite remember when she'd gotten off the stool at the kitchen island.

"Just so you know what the stakes are," Zera began, her whole body shaking with a mix of fear, anger, and determination jumbled together, "I have a son."

The room grew even more still, as if all the air had been sucked out of it.

Maverick's eyes went wide, and she knew he probably didn't approve of her sharing her personal story or any facts about her true identity, but she didn't care. She needed these people to be on the same page, to fight together, and she hoped that they were at least the types who would defend an innocent child.

"Gareth sent men to kill me and my son," she continued, avoiding Maverick's gaze. "He's a baby. And they nearly succeeded in both. Gareth must be stopped so that I can finally be reunited with my child without fear of people hunting me."

"That means we must all put our knives, claws, and fangs away,"

Maverick cut in, probably so she wouldn't share any more personal information and ruin their cover—even if it was a moot point, since all the spies must've known they weren't actually married. Not even their fake wedding bands could convince these seasoned spies, but no one had questioned it. "Gareth must be killed but not before we get him to remove the bounty on our heads. Those are both crucial to our plan and to help Charlotte and her son."

Maverick paused to give each one of them a look that said if they accused one more person of being a traitor, he would gut them with his wolf canines, which peeked out from under his top lip.

"Now, even though I haven't heard much from Irdeel since she left because she's been on a mission in the Human Realm, I can personally vouch for her integrity."

"And what about the vamp?" Quill asked, brows raised.

Maverick rolled his eyes. "Yes, I vouch for him too."

Felice stepped closer to Zera, her brows furrowed. "Did Gareth really send hunters to kill you and your son?"

Zera nodded, the memory of being powerless as the druid dangled her son above her still fresh in her mind. "Yes, a druid who worked for Gareth came. Nearly killed us all," she admitted softly, her voice barely above a whisper. She hadn't talked about that night in the kitchen until now. She'd shoved it aside, not wanting to think about it. But now, on the cusp of finally ending all of it, she had to tell them.

The heaviness of the truth settled in the room like a thick fog.

Felice turned toward Maverick, a determined fire blazing in her eyes. "Going after a fae child goes against our sacred rules. There's a line, and Gareth crossed it. We will all get along, setting aside our differences for this mission."

Zera held her breath, hope filling her as she watched the others nod one by one. A small crack in Maverick's mental wall opened, and a trickle of confidence that matched her own whispered through their bond. She couldn't help the grin that followed as she realized it was happening. Gareth would be gone, and within a few hours, she might be able to see her son, together again and free from this fear of being hunted. That was all she wanted. The bond that was growing between her and the faeboy couldn't compare, even if they could resolve things. Her kid would always mean more to her. Perhaps others would think that was wrong or unhealthy. Zera didn't care what anyone else thought on that subject. She would always be there for her child, and it killed her not to be with him now. This mission had to work. It meant everything.

When it was clear they were all on the same page and would put their personal issues aside, Maverick continued assigning everyone a position. Quill would be the forger, of course, as well as a backup illusionist if Zera's pixie dust dwindled. Cillian, the vampire and Irdeel's fellow FBI buddy, was not only a trained assassin but an expert in magical tech systems and would act as their hacker. Maverick, with his werewolf senses, would be the scout and help with navigating the difficult terrain. The stronghold was built into the side of a mountain along the Mystic Rapids with special spells that restricted anyone from shimmering in. Zera had a feeling they would definitely need Maverick's skills. But there was one role that hadn't been explicitly mentioned.

"So, if Cillian is the assassin and the hacker, what will I be?" Zera asked, hoping to still be the one to take the final shot at Gareth.

Sure, it couldn't hurt to have a backup plan, but this was her fight to finish.

Maverick locked eyes with her, the intensity of his gaze sending a jolt of electricity through the bond.

"You will also be the assassin," he said, moving toward Cillian and taking a case Cillian had just picked up from him. Zera recognized it as the box containing the Whisper's staff, and she stiffened.

Even from within the box, the staff hissed and groaned for her to touch it, to unlatch the box and free the weapon from its cage. A sliver of her was tempted by it, seduced by the passion of her ancestors and the pixie blood and dust that flowed through her.

But it wanted death to all, and Zera only wanted Gareth gone. She was a one-and-done kind of assassin.

"For our plan to work," Maverick continued, unlocking the case to reveal the staff, its double blades on either end reflecting off the lights above them, "you must use the Whisper's staff."

There were murmurs among the group of spies, but to Zera's surprise, no one protested.

Maverick closed the case to remove the distraction, but everyone's eyes were still on the reflective case. "It's the only weapon that will ensure Gareth and his elven powers die with him."

Zera's mind reeled. The last time she'd held the staff, she'd nearly killed Maverick. If she did that at Gareth's stronghold, she would never forgive herself, and worst of all, their chances of escape would be next to nothing. She couldn't do it. It was too much of a risk. Zera's heart thumped loudly within her rib cage as she met Maverick's gaze, her eyes pleading for another solution. The weight of the staff in that room felt suffocating, its power humming at her even to where she stood at the kitchen island.

Zera. Maverick's voice filled her heart, their bond strengthening and muting the seductive thoughts the Whisper's staff breathed in her mind. *You can do this. Remember, you are stronger than it. It will heed to your desire and yours alone. I wouldn't have formed this plan if I didn't think so.*

Her mind and heart raced as one. Maverick's familiar voice was a flicker of resolve amid the storm of doubt that threatened to consume her. In this moment, she knew she couldn't doubt herself. This was the moment that would define everything else. If she believed it, she'd do it.

She finally nodded. "I'll do it."

Maverick offered her the case. The Whisper's staff of gleaming wood and the symbol etched into it seemed to glow when she finally reached in and freed it from its bed. It was a silent offering of trust and belief in her power. She knew that. But she couldn't shake the uneasiness that still settled in her stomach as she held the ancient weapon.

Maverick gave her a proud smile before turning back to the rest of the team to finalize the details of their mission. They spent hours poring over the floor plans, discussing entry points, escape routes, and potential challenges they might face. Zera was impressed by the level of detail and attention they were able to give this mission in such a short amount of time, but she couldn't shake the lingering fear that something could go wrong. On a mission like this, anything could happen.

Finally, as they wrapped up their preparations, it was time to gather their weapons, magical items, and other necessary equipment. All members moved efficiently around the penthouse turned training room, collecting gear and strapping it to their vests and harnesses, readying themselves for the dangerous mission ahead.

Quill was to shimmer them one at a time to the edge of the Mystic Rapids, just far enough that it wouldn't trigger any wards to detect trespassers. The faster they got there, the better. It was already getting late in the day.

Dressed in black fighting leathers, Zera shrugged into the protective vest she was given. It took her some time to strap all the various weapons, along with the Whisper's staff, into their designated places within reach at each side of her vest, but she found it therapeutic. This was it. The final battle. She was ready physically to do what she had to do, but her heart kept rebelling against her resolve, and her traitorous eyes darted to Maverick as he buckled his own harness. She couldn't go into battle without telling him how she felt.

"See you all on the other side," Quill called, shimmering the last of them out, leaving her alone with Maverick.

Taking a deep breath, Zera approached Maverick, who was meticulously checking his gear. His focus was intense as he inspected each weapon in their holsters, but when Zera's shadow fell over him, he looked up with a raised eyebrow.

"Hey, I wanted to say thank you," she began, mustering the

courage to say what she needed to. "You've done so much for me—saving my life, the training, and helping me with finding a new location for the everfrost blossom."

"Zera," he said, his expression softening.

She shook her head. "It's okay, Maverick. You don't need to say anything. I wanted you to know how grateful I am that you were there for me and my son. I know you're still processing whatever this is between us, but I needed you to know that I'm beyond grateful."

They stood within arm's reach of each other on the edge of the training mat. This could be the last time they were in this penthouse together, and the thought sent a pang through her heart. All the memories, the struggles, and the passion that they'd shared ran through her mind, threatening to break through her resolve for the mission. But she wouldn't let it. She would say her peace and go into battle, knowing she'd said everything she needed to.

She folded her lips over her teeth, contemplating her next words. They were harder to utter than she thought. "I know we're about to run into the unknown, and I... I need you to know that I love you." Her voice cracked slightly, betraying her emotions, but she didn't care.

She pressed on. "You're an amazing man, and I'm honored to have met you. I wish our circumstances were different, but I hope you will one day forgive me. I can't stop thinking about the way you were with Cole, how you played with him, the way he grew attached to you, I know he loves you too. If we make it through this and if you're ever able to find it in your heart to forgive me, know that you'll always have a place in our family. If you want it. You don't have to say anything. I just needed to tell you that."

Maverick's eyes widened at her implication, as if he might not believe her. She hoped that he did, that he knew that she was sincere. A slew of emotions flickered across his eyes, and he opened his mouth to say something, but Quill shimmered in at that moment. Zera wasn't sure she wanted to hear the rejection she was certain was coming. It would be okay. She would be okay regardless of what happened next for them. She had said enough, and now, they needed to face the battle.

"All right, let's do this. Try to keep up, faeboy," Zera said, masking her emotions with a teasing wink at Maverick, who couldn't help but crack a surprised grin.

"I like this one," Quill said to Maverick, who merely chuckled before Quill took Zera's hand and shimmered her out. There was no turning back now.

CHAPTER 19

ZERA

It was nearly sunset by the time Quill finally shimmered all of them to the woods lining the east side of the river. The Steel Titan, as it was nicknamed, stood like a towering beast carved right into the cliffs along the most dangerous part of the rapids. The last bit of light reflected off the churning waters of the Mystic Rapids, located southwest of Mystic City. There was no going around it—the only way was through, and then they'd climb the side of the mountain.

Zera tried not to think about that just yet. A shiver ran down her spine every time she looked at the rocks that jutted out of the rapids like jagged teeth, ready to devour anything foolish enough to get too close. She clenched her jaw, focusing on the group huddled in the shadows of the trees. The thunder of water as it crashed against the rocks filled her ears, drowning out all other noise.

She couldn't help but notice that Maverick hadn't said anything to her since her confession at the penthouse. She tried not to take it personally. She knew better than anyone what was at stake if they lost their focus on the mission, but she couldn't help but wonder what he was thinking or if he'd even given their future any thought.

"Remember," Maverick said to the group hiding behind the tall oaks, his voice barely audible above the rapids, "once we've broken through the wards, we'll still have to limit our use of magic to keep the element of surprise."

They all nodded.

"When we get inside," he continued, "our primary objective is to lure Gareth into the dining hall, the belly of the stronghold, and surround him. When he's checkmated, Zera will come in with the final kill."

"Got it, boss," Felice said with a smirk, winning her an impressive eye roll from Irdeel.

Zera sent another prayer to any fae god that whatever beef they had with each other wouldn't cause a problem. Once they breached that stronghold, anything could happen, and they needed to stay united if they were to take down Gareth.

She rested a hand on the Whisper's staff, tucked into her protective vest. It hissed in response, and she quickly dropped her hands to her side. When it came time, she would use it, but she prayed she was strong enough to wield it.

Once Gareth was out of her way, she would be able to see her son again. That was the only thing that mattered to her right now.

She adjusted her vest, the weight of her gear digging into her shoulders. Zera checked her faestone, but there was still no call back from Jade about Cole. A twinge of worry gnawed at her, but she pushed it aside, focusing on the mission ahead.

With a deep, calming breath, she centered herself. Regardless of where she and Maverick stood, she would see her son again. That was a promise to herself. She had hope again now that the final everfrost seed had been planted. The wintry terrarium hovered at the perfect elevation, thanks to Maverick's rooftop garden. In a few more days, she'd have her precursor to create her synthetic pixie-dust drug. She just knew it. To get there, she had to focus on the here and now—infiltrating the stronghold and taking down Gareth.

She turned her attention to where the rest of the team was assembled, near the break in the trees. The ominous fortress loomed menacingly across the choppy waters, its stone-and-steel walls towering high and casting a dark shadow over everything in its path. Zera couldn't help but feel a shiver run down her spine at the stark contrast to the lush greenery surrounding either side of the Mystic Rapids. One wrong move, and it would devour them.

Maverick, Quill, and Felice were engrossed in discussion. Zera couldn't really hear them from where she leaned against a huge bald cypress between its many exposed roots. Irdeel and Cillian stood closer to the water's edge but far enough away to not be spotted or, ideally, smelled by any of the fae guards across the waters. They both scanned the perimeter of the stronghold, no doubt looking for weaknesses in the magical wards that supposedly protected it yet were invisible to them. By Irdeel's harrumphs and Cillian's furrowed brow, it wasn't going well.

"What's the verdict?" Maverick asked, moving to stand next to the vamp as he used whatever technical power he had. Zera chose to keep her distance from him. Who knew when the bloodsucker would need a snack? "Are you able to crack whatever wards they have surrounding the stronghold?"

Cillian shook his head, his hands extended out, but he dropped them and muttered curses under his breath.

"What's wrong?" Zera asked, pushing off the cypress. A snap of purple energy singed a piece of bark in the process, and her pixie senses hummed in overdrive. She had drunk extra water to ensure her pixie dust was at full capacity, but it would need an outlet soon. It snapped and sizzled under her skin, and the heat of it put her on edge.

Cillian ignored her question, still focused on their wolf leader. Perhaps the vamp could smell her distaste for his kind. She didn't care if he did. He could drink pixie blood just as easily as a human's, which put him in the predator category, despite him tagging along on this mission.

"I've never sensed anything like it," the vampire told Maverick, who she noticed stood with his back to her. He hadn't looked at her since they'd arrived at the river. She tried not to take his silence personally.

"But can you crack them?" Maverick prodded, the tone gaining the attention of the others.

"From what I can tell?" Cillian shrugged. "They're virtually impenetrable. I don't know what they used, but I can't get a read on what was used to make the wards."

"Is it even warded, then?" Quill asked, now tuned in to what the agents were doing.

"It's invisible, even to my powers," Irdeel said with a nod. "But there's definitely something there."

"There's an energy to it," Cillian added, "but it's imperceptible to the untrained eye."

Quill scowled at the subtle jab. The vamp breezed right by it.

"It's as if it's both there and not there," Cillian continued without paying the demon any heed. "Whatever magic this is, it's beyond my technology. At least from this distance."

"Then we get closer," Maverick said with a tone of finality. "Quill, can you shimmer us across the rapids?"

"That's a definite no," Quill said. "When I tested my shimmer, this was as close as I could get. Anything beyond that river is like running into a brick wall."

"I could perhaps use my siren song to persuade the rapids to slow enough for us to cross," Felice suggested.

Maverick shook his head. "That would be too noticeable and alert any number of those guards to our presence."

Zera followed his gaze across the rapids that ran into the side of the cliff wall and Steel Titan. The smooth stone shot upward and stopped at a ledge, where a slew of guards patrolled the wall that lined the modern stronghold built into the rock. Each guard was armed to the teeth and moved with unnerving precision, steps practiced and efficient. That didn't even take into consideration what other types of powers they could wield.

The team finally settled on moving farther upstream to find a way to cross. If they could shatter the wards, then they would climb to the top of the mountain to attack the stronghold from its only visible weak spot—from the top. Zera cringed inwardly at the idea, even though there seemed to be a clear path once they were at the top. Heights weren't her thing.

The group kept to the trees and out of the guards' line of sight, in search of a way to cross without using magic in case it would set off any kind of alarm. The rapids frothed and swirled in the wind, picking up mossy water droplets that sprayed her cheeks. If the team members were without the ability to use their powers, they would have to brave the treacherous waters and approach the stronghold head-on.

Zera set her jaw, her resolve hardening. They would find a way in. Failure was not an option when everything she cared about hung in the balance. She would see this through, no matter what it took. Gareth's time was running out.

After a tense search and after they had backtracked several times, they found a more manageable crossing to the stronghold. A series of large rocks jetted out from the water like stepping stones, deceptively stable against the raging current. Without the ability to use her pixie dust, Zera was certain she'd slip and fall, only to be swept away downstream. She shuddered at the very real possibility. Even the water on the wind stung her cheeks like little icicle pinpricks.

"We'll do this one by one," Maverick instructed, his eyes scanning for any potential threats. His canine ears shifted to enable him to better hear over the water. "Be careful, stay low, and remember your training."

Zera nodded, though she wasn't sure their training sessions had included anything helpful for this situation, aside from strengthening her calves and core muscles. Quill went first, nimbly leaping from rock to rock like it was a Riverdance. His hands weren't even out for balance but still shoved into the pockets of his leather jacket. The nonchalant approach he took was inspiring.

When he was successfully on the other side, it was Felice's turn.

Her ability to navigate waters and her control aided her in getting to the other side even faster than the demon. Irdeel and Cillian made quick use of the rock crossing as well, leaving just the two of them.

Zera's heart beat so hard she knew Maverick could hear it. She looked up at him standing next to her, the golden rays of sunset hitting his strong jawline that hinted at a shadow of dark scruff. His mussed hair whipped wildly in the wind, and her hands itched to run through and tame it. Or tangle her fingers in it again while he ravaged her as he had last night.

Maverick hissed a breath. "If you keep staring at me like that, I'll be tempted to whisk you into these woods and do just that."

Heat flared within her core. He'd heard her thoughts through the bond, but she still couldn't hear his. Perhaps it was a wolf thing. She didn't know—it had never been that way with her ex. They'd never shared the level of closeness that she'd felt, heard, seen, and accepted wholeheartedly last night. Her chest ached that she might've ruined that, but this little sliver of hope that he still felt the same way about her gave her some relief.

Or perhaps it was pure distraction because when she looked into Maverick's eyes, she didn't see desire or even the usual arrogance that danced in his expression. No, it was something else entirely. A deep-rooted fear as he watched the frothing waters in front of them.

It was a fear she recognized in herself, and her heart ached for him. She looked at the water, and then a thought struck her. Now that his team was on the other side, the arrogant armor he wore cracked. He felt comfortable enough around her to let her see the demons he truly faced. The water. Endless, lapping, and whirling water that threatened to consume them both.

She feared that the Whisper's staff was so powerful that it might consume her if she wielded it, and if someone saw her use her true power, they'd hunt her for it. Water was that fear for him.

She didn't say anything. Didn't even utter the words of confidence she wanted to tell him. The fact that he allowed himself to be this vulnerable in front of her in a way that he wouldn't even with his closest allies meant something. Even if he never forgave. It meant something. She took his hand in hers, the warmth of their mutual touch sending a binding energy that snapped through their bond.

He had been there when she'd faced her worst fear, when she'd used her power and now was hunted. He had never once left her side, and she wouldn't leave him now.

His hand closed around hers, and she rubbed gentle circles against his palm. It was a calm moment between them. A moment in which she could reassure him, giving him strength when he'd given her so much, as he was about to go into the viper's den with her.

"You don't have to do this if you don't want to," Zera said, knowing he was trying to build up enough gumption to cross. "You've already done so much. I can end this."

He glanced in her direction, and he didn't hide his fear when he trained his eyes back on the river in front of them. In that moment, she knew he'd just shared a rare piece of vulnerability that he hadn't ever shared before. Fear of the water wasn't uncommon among the werewolf species, but it was rare for werewolves to let anyone see it, so she vowed to keep this to herself. She knew in her heart that Maverick knew it, too—even with the unknown of where their relationship stood.

A laugh loosened his chest. "I think I can manage one little river."

He turned those piercing, storm-filled eyes on her with an intensity that made her stop and truly look at him. She saw his strength, his wolf power, but more importantly, she saw him in the same way that he did her. Two souls, two hearts. Beating as one.

"And I won't leave your side," he whispered. The sorrow in his voice and the longing in his eyes revealed what she knew he couldn't bring himself to say. Not yet. Not while they were standing on the edge of fear and the unknown. She felt it in her heart. Love. Pure, unadulterated love.

"And I yours," she said with a sad smile, knowing that this could be the last time they'd have a moment like this. "Go now. You can do this. I'll be right behind you."

She squeezed his hand, hoping it brought him the same confidence that settled within her as she turned toward the roaring waters. Fear still gnawed at her gut, but it wasn't the same. It didn't devour her like it had when she was trapped in her house. This was a fear that equipped and secured her from deep within her soul.

Maverick's grip tightened on hers for a moment longer before he let go and moved toward the rapids. The hiss of water snapped at his ankles like snakes, but he took a running start and lunged for the nearest rock.

Something stirred within her as she watched, a foreign energy that was both new and ancient, but she shrugged it off.

He crossed to another rock, and he was two rocks from the violent river's center. She copied his movements and landed on the first rock. She took deep, controlled breaths as she kept an eye out for Maverick while keeping her footing.

Each step, each jump was a leap of faith that they would cross and make it to the other side to face the chaos and settle things. That they'd be able to bring Gareth to his knees as he had threatened to do to them.

The next stone in Maverick's path was nearly half his height, and Zera had never seen a man who was otherwise so strong, so firmly grounded, balk at the water that rushed between the rocks.

Just breathe. She sent her thoughts through the space between them. She watched his whole body go rigid before his shoulders squared, and she knew he'd heard her. It brought her comfort to be able to help him through this.

He'd shown her patience during each day of training, walking her through a fighter's stance, showing her how to dodge and punch with the techniques of a spy. He'd taught her everything he knew, opened his heart, and confessed his darkest past. He'd held nothing back from her, and when it mattered most, she hadn't trusted him enough to tell him the truth. Hadn't trusted what they'd built.

Helping him now was the least she could do even if she never saw him again. The thought of that brought an ache to her heart.

She landed on the damp rock right behind him. Her hands scraped against the coarse stone as she crouched, keeping low to counter the unforgiving winds that blasted down the rapids.

The wolf spy balanced on the final rock. It was too narrow to get a running start, and so he swung his leg back and propelled his body forward toward the grass and rock and rubble that waited for him on the bank.

Zera held her breath.

He arched over the water, his boot-covered toes dipping into the rapids.

She loosened a breath when he made it the rest of the way, joining his team on dry land.

Zera didn't even give herself a second to think about the distance before hurdling after him.

Step. Leap. Plant foot on solid stone.

That was all she could think about as she launched herself between rocks that were farther apart than she'd ever jumped before. But now that Maverick was across, she didn't have to worry. He knew what he had to do. He was the only one who knew where Cole and her sister were, so if anything happened to her, he would take care of them. She knew that.

She drove her foot into the side of the rock and launched herself into the air toward the final stepping stone.

Time stood still. She soared over the water. Wind whipped past her ears, the only sound louder than her thunderous heartbeat. She couldn't even see the rock anymore. She didn't care. Whatever happened was out of her hands now.

A breath. An exhalation. A moment later, her foot finally planted on the rock, followed by her other foot. Success. She let out a breath of relief. It was a breath too soon. She stepped again and slipped on wet moss, pitching forward headfirst into the raging rapids. She flailed her arms, searching for purchase.

Wrong move.

White liquid teeth hissed at her, and then she was falling deeper into the water. Ice-cold talons gripped her. She gulped, choking down water. Her nails clawed against rock that ripped by as the current whisked her away. The ice broke away. Air. She gasped. Water engulfed her again. Something hard slammed into her side. A rock in the water. Her ribs seared with pain a second later. She had to get out. Spinning. She was spinning through the water as it twisted her like a wet rag. She had to find the bank. This couldn't be her end.

Her eyes still squeezed shut, she searched by touch for anything to grab hold of. A tug within her chest was all she had to keep herself moving. Maverick. It was him keeping her focused. Searching. He was searching for her.

That ancient tug, not from the Whisper's staff but from something deep within her, coiled again. She didn't have time to take notice of it, though, when a second later, she crashed into a hard wall. Her hands ripped at the smooth surface, and she cursed the water when she found nothing to grab hold of. The force of the current sucked her down deeper.

Cole's sweet face, round cheeks, and tousled curls flashed across her mind. Air. She needed oxygen.

She willed her arms and legs to keep moving despite how much they ached. Her heartbeat slowed, but she knew she couldn't give in to that deep black void that called to her from the back of her mind.

For her child, she would survive. For her son, she would do everything in her power to see him one more time. To make sure he was safe.

A prayer escaped her to any fae gods who would listen. Finally, her hands, still scratched, battered, and bruised, snagged on a crevice in the stone, and a whoosh from behind her sent an unfamiliar spark of energy through her body.

Then her head broke free from the river, choking out the water. She coughed and sputtered from her nose. Everything burned, even when she finally inhaled greedily, taking in the sweet, decadent air that brought with it a tang of vomit.

Her stomach roiled, but she held on tight to that sliver of hope etched into the side of the stone—the smooth wall of the stronghold. She blinked, looking up and up until the top of the wall was in view. It hit her then that she'd slipped right through the barrier. Whatever ward Maverick and the others had sensed hadn't kept her out, and she'd washed through it without a scratch. Without alerting the guards. This was her chance, her opportunity to take them down by surprise. But how had she gotten through those wards the vamp called "impenetrable"?

She scrubbed water droplets from her eyelashes. Where were the others? Probably frantic at the edge of the barrier. She blinked. A cobweb of purple light reflected around her in the setting sun. It rose from just a foot away from her and surrounded the stronghold, an intricate web of interwoven cells that glowed with the faintest spark of purple. The wards. They were made of pixie dust. That was how she'd been able to slip right through unnoticed. It was a trap meant to snare the weak. Gareth had no idea his trap would quickly become his own prison.

Thunder beat at her back, and a rage consumed her that she'd only felt once before—when she'd defended her child. Her people had died so that this monster could hide himself. A coward. She would tear him apart from the inside out. Everything he had, she would take from him as he had done to the countless souls that glimmered around her.

A whisper from the staff that somehow was still attached at her side told her it approved and would help her.

She didn't need it. Her power would be strong enough, but she wouldn't turn the voices of her ancestors down. They would come with her. She would give herself up for the cause to not only avenge her son—her blood—but also the women, men, and children who'd been tortured and consumed by this heinous man not worthy of his own skin.

Her body burned with rage, the heat of it sending another whoosh and wisp of power surging through her veins. That was when she noticed the empty hole in her chest. The bond that was once a tether to Maverick had gone cold.

Maverick. She sent the call out into the ether, but only silence returned. *MAVERICK!*

Her mental shields stretched far and wide, but it was like he'd fallen off the face of the realm. Frantic voices above her sent her pressing her back up against the side of the wall. Someone had alerted the guards.

"There! Get them," a guard from overhead called, and her breath froze.

They'd found her hiding spot. They must have. But she would be ready for them. Anger filled her. She was power and might. She was a pixie and would no longer be fearful if someone saw her use magic. No fae or fear could control her now. She was free from it. No more would she hide in the shadows, cowering like a dog to keep from being seen. Let them see. Let them see what eons of keeping her kind powerless and afraid could do.

She shot a glance over shoulder, and a sly grin spread across her features that looked more wolfish than pixie-like. Purple wings sparkled and flapped behind her in the oranges and pinks of dusk. Their veins were almost blue as they wound around behind her, supporting the near-sheer membranous wings that wisped into sharp, jagged lines at the ends—not quite like a butterfly's wings but also not quite angelic. It was both foreign and ancient to her, yet somehow familiar. Her wings, no longer dormant, flapped behind her with a power she'd never felt before.

Free. She was free from the shackles she'd developed to keep herself safe. What a stupid way to live. She was worthy of this power. Worthy of living as an equal with the rest of the faen world without fear. Her son was worthy of a life where his mother didn't cower or bow to others. He deserved someone strong enough to run into the viper's den and protect the world from its poison.

She would do that and more.

A familiar growl shook the wards around her. Maverick. He'd

somehow broken through the shield. Or perhaps he'd been forced to. She flapped her wings harder, forgetting how high above the rocky rapids she was, and carefully rose up the side of the stone wall. The main building was built over a waterfall that rushed with white water. She inched toward the top of the wall and paused to look over the edge. All the guards had either moved to the far-right side or had completely disappeared.

Angry growls and voices came from the other side of the wall. She inched her way through the air, flying closer to get a view. She flapped her wings once. Twice. She finally reached the edge of the wall and peeked around the side of it.

She cringed at the view that met her. A giant troll armed with a whip slashed at Maverick, who shoved and fought to get away, but his powers were subdued. The rings that circled his ankles and wrists, siphoning his powers, glowed each time he attempted to shift into his wolf form. He was powerless.

Irdeel and the rest of the team were being dragged by sharp-nosed elves and donned matching bracelets and anklets. They were all prisoners, leaving only Zera to save them.

Zera ground her teeth. This was not going according to plan. Her fall into the Mystic Rapids had gotten her team caught, and now she had a rescue mission on her hands.

CHAPTER 20

ZERA

A gust of wind whipped through Zera's brown hair, and her pixie wings shimmered with iridescent colors as they held her at the edge of the stone wall. Her heart raced wildly, determination coursing through her veins like fiery lava. She narrowed her lavender eyes, scanning the scene below.

"Damn it," she muttered under her breath, her hands balling into fists. The sight of the troll and elves capturing Maverick's team—her team that would help her finally put an end to Gareth's miserable existence—sent shivers down her spine, her blood running cold with horror and urgency.

She had to think. Her mind raced with possible plans of action. As she hovered, she focused on the intricate details of her surroundings. Her keen observation skills kicked in, her pixie senses heightened now that the weight of fear had been taken from her. As if the river itself had washed it away. She searched for any weak spots or opportunities.

A door in the side of the jagged mountain appeared far below the fortress, and three guards emerged while the troll and seven armed elves made a show of shoving Maverick and the others through it.

She glanced at the wall behind her. Guards patrolled every inch of it, and when she counted, even more appeared out of the stonework. Entering through the roof would be suicide. She would have to find a way through that invisible door in the mountain.

Maverick's eyes slid to hers, and she shuddered. His eyes widened at the sight of her wings, but he quickly jerked his gaze downward and winced with pain at the crack of the whip that ripped down his back. The troll followed his gaze, and she darted out of view.

She held her breath. Another smack of the whip made her flinch. She peeked around the corner of the wall again as everyone disappeared behind the huge door into the belly of the stronghold. She had to follow them, somehow slip in behind them before that door closed.

Her pulse raced. She made quick work of flying close to the wall, making sure she didn't cast a shadow on the guards below. The steel door that appeared in the stonework began to fade. She had to move faster.

Zera's heart thundered in her chest, adrenaline fueling her every move as she darted toward the fading entrance. She was right on top of the entrance that was now nearly invisible. With a burst of speed, she stabilized herself in midair then halted the flap of her wings. Wind rushed up, blowing her hair and clothes upward as she went into a free fall. She bit her cheek to keep from crying out at the sensation of her stomach flipping as she fell. The ground flew toward her, and she released her wings once again with a whoosh. She halted in the air, just above the entrance and behind the three guards. They whipped around when they felt the air move.

"Stop right there!" one of them shouted. Zera didn't have time to give him any attention before she slipped through the entrance as it closed and vanished. She had barely avoided being trapped outside.

The door slid closed, shutting out the setting sunlight. Darkness drenched all around her, save for the red glow of the wings orbiting around her team, trapping their magic. The elves and troll guided them around the corner. She had to keep up. Her feet trod lightly as she raced after them, making sure to keep a healthy distance. The last thing she wanted was to be trapped without her magic. Then their mission would really be dead.

She followed the group down another long tunnel and then a winding stone staircase, deeper and deeper into the mountain. It felt like heat never reached this part of the stronghold. Zera made note of each turn they made, counting her steps so that she could find her way out again. After she killed Gareth, of course.

"Lock them up in here," hissed one of the elves with a deep baritone voice. "He'll want to know we've got company."

Zera's back stiffened against the edge of the doorway. She only spared a glance around the corner to see that the elves and troll had stopped the procession in front of a row of cells made of iron that glowed faintly purple. She shuddered. Pixie dust would keep prisoners in the cells and trap pixies who dared enter the area.

Kill them, the Whisper's staff called to her, itching to be held.

Soon enough.

Her wings fluttered with anticipation, her body aching to spring into action, but she had to strike at the right moment. Otherwise, she'd risk everything.

The cell door clanged open, and grunts echoed as each of her team members was shoved inside the cell. The door squealed shut, followed by a click of a lock. Zera held her breath, waiting for the troll and elves to pass her on their way out.

"Well, look who we have here," a cold voice said, much too close to her face.

She jumped, and fear claimed her heart and iced over every nerve. Gareth, preening, looked down at her, baring his teeth in a grin that didn't reach his eyes.

"Don't—" She backed away from him right into one of the elves.

"Don't what?" Gareth tilted his head to the side, his clear irises roving over her, making her stomach clench. She wanted to punch the smug look right off his face.

"Oh, I thought I smelled a pixie." One of them chuckled, as if he had a mouth full of saliva.

Zera cringed and pressed her back against the cold stone wall. She was surrounded by Gareth and a beady-eyed elf holding a key ring of glowing red rubies that resembled the orbs that restricted magic.

"Contain her, and put her with the others," Gareth ordered.

The air rushed out of her lungs. A demon lunged for her from the shadows behind the elves. Pixie dust surged through her, the heat of it shooting out from her palms, sending the demon flying back in a powder of purple dust. She reached for it again, but before she could slam Gareth or any of the elves with the same power, the elf with the key ring spat at her hands and feet.

Matching glowing red orbs locked into place around both her ankles and feet. The pixie dust, though warm and within reach, froze inside her veins, as if the essence of her power had been caged. Panic struck her as she lashed out, swinging at any elf close enough for her to land a punch as she tried to fight her way out of this.

Gareth's taunting laughter chased her. "You think you could enter my stronghold without me knowing? Or even land near the vicinity of it and not realize I was already a hundred steps ahead of you?"

A punch to her face followed by a kick to her gut sent her stumbling back. Her head knocked against the stone wall behind her. She held her hands in front of her for protection, but the damage had already been done.

A ringing in her ears drowned out the elves and their sickening laughter as they yanked her forward. She stumbled into the cell that had the scent of old blood mingled with fresh droplets from her cellmates. She shook off a dizzy spell that threatened to take her under. She felt searing pain in her jaw, and the skin at her side and stomach was tender where the elves had struck the bruises that were forming from her trip down the rapids.

"Zera!" Maverick rushed to her side.

"No talking," Gareth barked.

They both jerked their gazes to the bald elf. A snide grin spread across his face, as if the sight of them together—bruised and battered—brought him some kind of sick pleasure.

"Now that you're here, you should behave," Gareth crooned, taking a cocky step closer to the cell bars. If Zera had the energy, she would've reached through and strangled him. "My investor will be so pleased that I now have my mare along with her offspring. With the pair of you, I shall be able to rebuild my empire—the one this wolf took from me."

Maverick's jaw dropped, but Zera could barely notice anything else as what Gareth said was still processing. Had he said her *offspring*?

"Oh, did you think I would forget?" Gareth chuckled, a dark sinister laugh that made Zera's skin crawl. "Or just let you run around with my bounty without my spies knowing your every move?"

Then it finally clicked. Cole. Gareth had her baby.

"What have you done?" she rasped, choking on the words. "Where's my son?"

"Your son?" Gareth taunted. "He's no longer your son. He's *mine*, and once my investor sees what I'm building, he will fund everything. I will be on top of the realm once again, no thanks to this wolf trash."

He snapped his fingers, and suddenly Maverick's wrists were bound and he was yanked against the wall at the back of the cell. He bellowed as silver liquid oozed from the ropes.

"Wolfsbane is hard to come by but so necessary when you're expecting a traitorous wolf," Gareth hissed before turning to her. "I won't kill you. Not yet. Not until I've bred enough pixies out of you to fulfill my supply chain."

She shook with a rage she'd never felt before and lunged for the bars. Fire and ice melted the skin of her palms on impact, and she cried out, stumbling backward. Gareth laughed at her shock as the skin on her palms bubbled with a heat that felt icy hot.

"You think I wouldn't know how to keep a rat like you inside a cage?" Gareth chuckled again, and Zera had every intention to smash his lips into his gums after plucking each tooth out of his mouth. "You don't survive in this business as long as I have without the one thing everyone pays for. Knowledge."

"Where's my son?" she repeated, her heart thundering at the thought of her baby being anywhere near his slimy hands.

"My property is being cared for until his pixie dust emerges, though him being a half-breed does make him significantly less profitable," Gareth said, and Zera's lip curled upward.

"I will gut you if you even touch him," she promised.

Gareth simply shook his head and threw a sadistic laugh her way. "It's unfortunate for you that you won't be there to stop it. You'll be unconscious, in a state of slumber until you've been entirely used up."

A shudder ran down her spine. She flung her fists at him again, not even caring that the bars were molten and her skin burned on impact. She screamed through the pain, grabbing his face hard, and her nails found sensitive skin and dug in deep. Gareth yelped, prying himself free and stepping back just out of reach.

His eyes were red, his skin marked with her nails. His eyes flared with anger. "You'll pay for that with your life."

With that, he spun on his heel, leaving her and the rest of them caged and helpless. She had to find her son. She didn't care what happened to her. This was exactly what she had feared, and it had happened. Her heart clenched as tears stung her eyes. She cried out, smashing her hand against the rough rock wall that lined the back of the cell.

She could sense the others staring at her, and she turned to them. They didn't speak for fear of what other tricks Gareth would pull on them if he heard them. From the cameras that blinked around them, she was certain he would hear every word.

Batting at the tears that threatened to spill, she let the anger wash over her and fill her entire being with the emptiness she'd felt since leaving Cole for his own protection. Felice's eyes widened—at what, Zera couldn't figure out. Maverick even looked startled, along with the vamp whose bloodred eyes were dim, due to the bracelets they all donned.

That was when she realized what was wrong.

"It was him," she gasped.

"Who?" asked Felice, whose wounds looked the least gnarly. The troll had definitely taken it out more on the others. Even Irdeel lay unconscious on the vamp's lap.

"The demon. Your forger." The one who'd attacked her outside the cell moments before. Maverick stiffened, and Zera knew he'd also put the pieces together. "He's how Gareth knew where to find Cole. He sold my son out to that ugly piece of elven shit!"

She took a steady breath, and as she exhaled, she let out a wail that shook her entire core. Bones cracked. Perhaps they were hers. She couldn't feel anything. All she saw was blood. Gareth's blood, which she would use to paint these walls. She was no one's prisoner. She'd lived as though she was trapped for long enough, trapped with fear from the expectations pressed upon her from others. She was done conforming to what others wanted or needed from her.

The blood in her veins chilled, and suddenly that familiar warmth of magic moved an inch. The siphons orbiting her wrists and ankles quivered, but still her magic froze, and her wings flattened farther into her back before melting into her spine, dormant once again. But she felt the give in the binds that locked her magic. She would keep pressing, pushing them until she was free.

Breathless, she panted and stared at everything and nothing at all. A primal energy hummed beneath her skin, and she knew she was close. The siphons would give, and she'd save her son. Cole would be free. She would give anything to kill Gareth and get her son to safety. That wasn't just a wish. It was a promise. She balled her hands into fists as her heart hummed to the beat of the vengeance that prowled inside her heart.

"Whoa." Felice's eyebrows shot up. "That puts even my siren call to shame."

Maverick choked on a laugh, sweat beading across his brow before he turned serious at the look in Zera's eyes.

"Did you know it was Quill?" she asked.

Something in his gaze broke, and a muscle in his temple quivered. "I swear on my life I didn't."

Zera trained her gaze on the siren and vamp, who both shook their heads adamantly.

"Irdeel wouldn't have known either," Cillian said, the tightness in his eyes proof enough for Zera to believe him.

"That bastard," Maverick said, spitting on the floor where Gareth had stood.

"How long do you think Quill was spying on us?" Zera asked. Sweat beaded across her forehead. "From the beginning?"

"No," Maverick said firmly. "I believe he wasn't interested in the bounty, but Gareth must've sweetened the deal later. Which is why he gave us that tip about Kraven. Shit."

The guilt in his voice and expression was palpable even through the pain of the wolfsbane burning through his skin. The silver liquid crusted where the rope held him bound.

He slumped against the restraints and fixed Zera with a pleading gaze. "I'm so sorry, Zera. I should've known. Should've—"

"Don't." She shook her head. She couldn't hear another apology. He'd done enough for her. He'd given up everything to protect her and her son. She knew that. He wasn't to blame for this. He wasn't the one who should be begging for her forgiveness.

Judging from the change in his eyes, he knew what she meant. Even without their bond—she got emptiness when she reached for his mind—he still understood her in a way that no one else could.

"He will pay," Maverick choked out. "Both of them. But not until your son is safe."

It was all she needed to hear to fuel her. Her son was out there in this stronghold somewhere. Scared, alone, and in the arms of that hideous man who would use them, drain them for their pixie dust. A pit formed in her throat at the thought of what Gareth might do, what he would have already done to her baby.

"Yes, he will," she hissed. The siphons quivered again as her rage flared in a rush of fire and ice through her bones.

"But how?" Felice asked, motioning to Irdeel, who was just now beginning to stir. "We're already one fae down, we don't have any magic, plus we're trapped in this cell for who knows how long."

Zera was opening her mouth to respond when a metal door clanged open. At least she wouldn't have to wait very long to get out of here.

The elven fae with the red key ring marched down the hall, the keys rattling with each of his massive steps. His nose scrunched up, and his bloodred eyes flickered over each one of them.

"Filth," he muttered before unlocking the gate. He focused his hateful gaze on Zera. It took all of her power not to cringe back. "The master will see you in the dining hall. The investor wants to see his product."

Her lip curled upward at the corners, and she snarled as the elf grabbed her with a death grip. The siphons were weakening. If she could break free of them by the time they reached the dining room, she would destroy each and every one of them.

"Do it," Maverick said, as if he'd read her thoughts. She looked back and met his eyes filled with determination. "And don't you dare come back."

Tears sprang up when his eyes bulged as he silently pleaded for her to get far away from them once she got her son. She blinked the moisture away. She couldn't manage a response. He was prepared to give up his life so that she and her son could be free. She ground her teeth and forced her legs to move down that hallway, farther away from the one man who truly loved her the way she deserved to be loved. The one man who she knew in her heart would be the only one she would ever feel this way for. Her mate.

She swallowed hard, but her heart remained elsewhere. Despite her love for Maverick, her son would always be her priority. Cole deserved a long and happy life, and it was her duty to ensure that happened. It was an honor, and when she got her baby out of here, she would be eternally grateful for each person who made it possible.

That was the future. She wouldn't let herself doubt it.

The elven fae shoved her through the endless halls, past even more metal doorways. Scratches lined the stones around them, as if something massive had been dragged past them. She wouldn't think about what that might be. The stagnant air smelled more of rotting blood and feces the deeper into the mountain they went. It took all of Zera's willpower to keep her empty stomach from retching.

Finally, the narrow halls opened into a giant room carved out of the stone itself. A massive rug with threads of blue and green covered the center, stained with dark blood that a fairy clothed in rags scrubbed with a hard-bristle brush. A red collar circled her neck. A prisoner to the elves. Like they all were. It wasn't right. These were crimes against the Fae Realm. Did the Fae Tribunal even know? Were they aware of Gareth and what he did in the dark?

The fairy's sad eyes lifted, and Zera tensed. She had to look away so she didn't run to the poor fairy to break her chains. Soon. She would save them all. This was more than just about herself and her son, though he would always be her top priority. She would get him out first, but the others didn't deserve this either. The FBI should've saved them, and yet Gareth was here, living only a short flight from the capital.

Zera couldn't ignore the faint screams that echoed through the halls as she forced herself to move forward. She had to rescue these innocent fae. She didn't know how, but she would find a way.

Double doors groaned open as two heavily armed elves met them.

"He will see the pixie now," the elf with onyx-black hair and pallid features said, nodding toward Zera.

She rolled her eyes, not even bothering to hide her contempt. What else could they do to her? They already had her child captive, and who knew what conditions her sister and her wife were in? Might as well make a show of getting under their skin.

The elven fae bared his teeth at her as she was pushed into the dining hall.

Chandeliers made of bone hung above dark tables laden with food—a severed bear head on a platter, bowls of blood broth, and even more dishes of unsavory things with too many legs. A meal fit for a monster.

Gareth's bald head gleamed in the dim light, and a victorious sneer was upon his lips. "Ah, our little sprite is finally here."

He rose from his throne-like chair. No weapons were in sight, and he wore a crisp navy tunic with golden accents. Zera glared at his costume and the food reminiscent of the old age, the age of the thousand-year war she'd learned about in school. It had been a chaotic time when wars raged between the faen species for land, glory, riches, and slaves. It was the modern age now, and Gareth was nothing more than a lunatic in a costume.

"You like it?" Gareth asked when he noticed her staring at his tunic.

She forced her lips into a smirk. "It looks like you're ready for Phantom's Feast. Where'd you get it?"

Gareth preened beside the meat-laden table. His eyes gleamed, his iridescent pupils making her skin crawl. "Bring in the animals."

Her heart clenched as chains slapped the ground behind her. She craned her neck, and her heart stopped when her eyes met Jade's. Her half sister's eyes bulged, but her split lip didn't move an inch as she marched behind the fae with elven ears who held the red key ring and yanked the shackles connected to the rings around her ankles.

Both Jade and Sloane were gagged, and identical red bracelets decorated their wrists, siphoning their powers. Where they had gone, Zera didn't know. Perhaps back into the universe from wherever they came.

Sloane limped behind Jade, one of her eyes swollen with dark purple-and-black bruises. Zera's tears sprang forward at the sight, and her heart clenched. Then she spotted the head of brown curls in the bundle in Sloane's arms that she struggled to hold. Cole's eyes were closed, and his face was pale. A fear like Zera had never known gripped her, tightening her chest. The air rushed from her. Was he...

She couldn't even bring herself to form the word in her mind.

"No," Zera gasped, making a move to her son.

Fear struck Sloane's face, and she shook her head to stop Zera from running over.

"My son... What did you do?" Rage roiled within Zera's gut, and she exerted her will against the siphons that held her power, but there was only a small give.

It was enough give, though, that she knew that if she kept at it, she would shatter the siphons. Free. She had to free herself. She had to get her son out of here. She didn't even want to think about what his ashen cheeks meant. He had to be alive. She had to get out.

"Oh, my bounty's alive," Gareth said, a hint of joy in his voice that made Zera's lip curl. "The others won't be for long once my investor sees what a prize catch I've found."

"Let me go, and I'll show you exactly what you've found," she hissed, her gaze promising death, but she was met only with laughter from the three other fae seated at the table with Gareth.

Including Quill, who sat smugly next to the monster himself. The traitor sat casually back in his seat, smirking, his stupid curls pulled into a bun.

"I hope it was worth it," she spat at him.

He merely shrugged. The casual air in which he admitted to deceiving an old friend sent a pit forming in her stomach.

"Enough," Gareth said with a scowl. "The investor approaches."

She didn't even bother to turn around. She already knew who it would be. Her eyes locked on her son, the only thing that mattered. Her chest constricted at the sight of him. She only wanted to hold him. He deserved better than this. Cole had his whole life to live, and now it was at risk of ending before he'd even had a chance because of the monster staring her down. Gareth didn't deserve the air he breathed. She flung everything she had at the shackles, but they held true. She let out a scream, falling to her knees.

Laughter surrounded her, harsh and ugly. She couldn't tell and didn't care who it came from. She slammed her fists on the stone floor so hard her skin broke.

"Is this the pixie?"

Zera froze at the familiar voice, soft as velvet yet firm. She breathed in gulps of air as heat washed over her and warmed her frozen bones.

"Yes, and her offspring," Gareth said with pride. "Though he's in a state that I can't evaluate his pixie dust, thanks to a no-good witch."

Gareth spat toward Sloane, whose chin remained high. Zera whispered a prayer of thanks before her eyes jerked up to meet the gray fox's piercing blue ones, which were vacant of all emotion. The curiosity and amusement in them she'd seen before were gone. Despite this, a sense of hope filled her. She'd struck a deal with him. Surely, he wouldn't leave her here to die without even having a chance to make good on it, right?

Kraven turned away from her and toward her son. Zera lunged at him.

"Don't touch him!" Her body was flung back by an invisible force thrown out at her by Gareth before she could even reach the incubus.

Her back slammed against the rock-hard floor, and searing-hot pain ripped up her spine. She blinked through the tears in time to witness Kraven taking Cole in his arms. Her whole body shook with anger. Any hope she'd had before was gone, vanishing the moment the incubus crime lord had crossed that boundary. All the lies he'd told her at the ball came flooding back to her, including how he'd said he pitied her for what Gareth had put her through when Kraven was the reason the elven piece of shit was doing all of this to begin with.

Kraven's greed was as bad, if not worse, than Gareth's, and she'd been a fool to strike a deal with him. He was venomous, and she was now feeling his sting.

"I said don't touch him," she said with more calm than she felt, throwing herself against the siphons one last time.

The air rippled with energy as she fueled her rage, the pixie dust within her stirring and throwing everything against the rings that bound her magic within. She balled her hands into fists and squeezed out every bit of power. It churned and surged until the rings at her wrists and ankles melted from the heat of pixie dust that flooded her veins.

She was power itself, and nothing could stop her. Kraven stared at her blankly, his grip still on her son, and she screamed, her outstretched hands reaching for her child. Cole vanished in a puff of purple smoke and reappeared in her arms. She felt his heartbeat the minute she held him. Her heart thumped in time with his. Cole was home, next to her where he belonged, but not yet safe.

"Grab them!" Gareth bellowed.

The trolls and elves who'd stood in shock, watching the spectacle of pixie-dust-fueled fury that now swarmed the room, raced for her. But Zera was too quick and dodged all of them.

They stumbled into the tables that lined the dining hall, their curses like music to her ears.

She glanced at her son—his eyes were still closed, and a small smile was on his lips—and could smell the sleeping potion on him, and her fear lessened. He was alive and sleeping. When all this was done, she swore she would hug Sloane so hard. The witch had kept her son alive and at peace, even though it had probably given her that black eye.

"There's nowhere for you to run," Gareth hissed, flinging his power at her. She caught sight of it at the last second and shielded herself with a wall of pixie dust before flinging the energy back at him.

Gareth's own power knocked him back, and he tumbled over his chair. Kraven didn't move to help and remained in the center of the room. His hands were in his pockets, as if this was exactly how he'd expected this meeting to turn out.

With her son safe on her back, Zera grabbed her Whisper's staff. The minute her fingers touched the staff, the wood extended, releasing the knives on either end. She took a deep breath, focusing on the rage that fueled her every movement. The staff pulsed with energy, the blades flickering with an eerie glow. Zera knew she was a formidable force, a pixie armed with her weapon and the unleashed power of her people.

A fae with a scarred face and elven ears shrieked, opening her mouth. Before the flurry of thorns could escape the fae's lipless mouth, Zera flung the staff's blade at the fae's scalp.

It sliced through with a satisfying thud. Fae came at Zera from every angle, creating a wall between her and Gareth. She would kill them all. She would have her revenge, and her son would survive, even if it took everything she had to get out of there.

She propelled her body into a run and pulled the staff from the fae's head. It fell back at an odd angle. She didn't give herself a second to think about what she'd done. The whispers of her ancestors echoed in the air, guiding each step. Each kill. This was as much for them—every pixie these people had taken to feed their greed, every innocent life they'd ended to further their own lifestyle—as it was for her son and family. It ended tonight.

With blow after blow, she took them down one by one. An elf with a large bear snout and claws slashed at her, and she jumped out of its path but not before it struck her exposed skin at her shoulder. She glanced at the flesh wound as it oozed with blood and snarled.

"You'll pay for that." She threw herself into the air, her pixie dust carrying her up, and she plunged her blade between the elf's shoulder blades.

A growl shuddered through him as he tumbled onto a table. It collapsed under his weight, sending a flurry of her pixie dust into the air, as the fae crashed. Dead.

The room reverberated with her magic, leaving a trail of shimmering dust in its wake. A shuffling noise from behind her reached her ears, and she whipped her head around. Quill's lips bled, and his ponytail was drenched in sweat. He shoved at a giant limb of one of the dead fae that blocked the exit.

"Going somewhere?" she asked, cocking her head to the side.

The smug look had been wiped off his face, replaced with pure, unadulterated fear. It made her smile.

Take us to him, the Whisper's staff breathed into her ear.

Quill opened his mouth to speak, but Zera didn't give him a chance to answer before she threw the staff with all she had. The hilt of the top blade struck deep into his temple, sending him sprawling across the wood floor. It made a satisfying crack, and his body went limp.

A smile curled her lips. The traitor was dead, and now, she had to take care of the rest of the mess.

Zera marched over to her staff, not even giving the dead a second thought as she yanked the staff free. She turned and sneered at Gareth, who cowered behind an overturned table. Her eyes flashed with a sadistic glint, daring him to make a move. Only one thought was on her mind—she wanted him to see the monster he'd created before she took her final blow. The way he cowered behind the table, shaking with fear, fueled her resolve.

She panted, trying to catch her breath, and swiped at the sweat that beaded her brow. For a moment, the air was still, save for the soft whisper of pixie dust as it swirled around the room. She twirled the bladed staff in her hands, the feel of it like her own skin. Like it had become one with her body.

Gareth looked around the room at all of his dead soldiers then at Kraven, who hadn't moved from his spot in front of Jade and Sloane, who were crouched in the corner for protection. Zera had almost forgotten about him.

"What are you doing?" the elven drug dealer asked. "Stop her before she kills us!"

Kraven's blue eyes stilled on Zera's, and the feeling she'd had at the ball swept through her again. A calm that somehow conveyed he wouldn't touch her. But why? He could've used his powers of persuasion to keep her from doing all of this. Yet he just stood there entirely unfazed, as if this fighting was beneath him. He was the crime lord, the one everyone orbited, who controlled every pixie drug deal in the city.

If he wished for it, they'd all be dead.

CHAPTER 21

ZERA

Zera remained as still as a statue under Kraven's intense gaze. His muscular body tugged against his black suit, his silver hair a dull shade of gray under the dim lights. Gareth trembled behind the overturned table. Severed animal heads and battered critters littered the floor.

"Why won't you kill her?" Gareth bellowed. "Will it, and she will use that weapon on her own neck."

Jade and Sloane sobbed in the corner, still shackled with matching red bracelets that restrained their powers. Zera wished she could free them right then and there, getting them and her son as far away from this as possible. They weren't involved in any of this. Then there were Maverick and the others, still in the cell somewhere in that labyrinth of halls. His warning not to come back still rang heavy in her ears. She couldn't leave them there to rot in this place, but she would ensure her son was out first.

"Do it!" Gareth pressed the incubus, his pallid face reddening. "Slip into her mind, and end this."

The incubus stared at her, tilting his head to the side as he considered Gareth's words. Zera held her breath. She didn't dare move. Not yet. She wouldn't go near the incubus until she knew he wasn't in her mind.

"The truth is, Gareth," Kraven said finally, "I've been wondering about your tactics of acquiring a new supply of pixie dust."

Zera hesitated, not knowing who to strike first. The incubus was dangerous, but there was something within her that told her he wasn't going to hurt her.

She watched the drug dealer sputter, as if all words failed him.

"And now that I've seen your sources, I doubt they'll be able to provide me with enough volume fast enough to meet my demands."

"This is the only way the demands get met," Gareth said, gaining enough courage to finally stand. He dusted his costume off with a manicured hand. "Pixies with the dust are dwindling. Your suppliers have all gone dry. *I* am the only one who can supply you with any."

Kraven's smirk deepened as he finally turned on Gareth. "Your way seems rather... tedious and, if I'm truly being honest, archaic."

The drug dealer's jaw slackened, and Zera mimicked the motion.

"You don't have any other option. You need me," Gareth pressed, which only made the incubus laugh. His white teeth glistened much too brightly.

Zera's grip on the Whisper's staff tightened.

Kill them. Kill them all.

It whispered to her, but something encouraged her to pause her magic. It wasn't so much a voice as it was a feeling, one she knew from experience belonged to the incubus. But one wrong move and her pixie dust would sweep through that entire hall and destroy them all. She knew her strength now, knew what she was capable of, and no one—not even the incubus and his persuasion—could stop her.

After what felt like an eternity, the incubus finally said, "Because I need her."

She blinked. Shock must've reflected on her face because Kraven's crooked smile deepened as he kicked at a boar's severed head lying in a pool of blood.

"I knew you were a wicked thing the moment I met you. I just didn't know you were also a mother."

He studied her child cocooned behind her—still spelled, since he hadn't yet made a sound, but his heartbeat reached her pixie ears.

She stepped back, angling her body to keep herself firmly between Kraven and Gareth. The incubus's eyes jerked down to hers again at the movement. Zera's whole body tensed under his stare.

He chuckled and shook his head in total dismissal of her.

She gritted her teeth. If she was truly being honest, she was more worried about the incubus than the elven drug dealer, whose power paled in comparison. Not an inch of fear or feeling was in Kraven's eyes. She gripped her Whisper's staff harder, preparing to kill them all once she caught her breath and found a way out of whatever persuasion Kraven had put in her mind.

"It makes your offer make much more sense," Kraven continued, studying his own fingernails before flicking some invisible speck off his forefinger with his thumb. Then he looked her dead in the eyes. "And more enticing."

"What offer?" Gareth blurted.

Kraven ignored him and nodded. "Kill him."

The air crackled with a tension so thick, Zera could taste the metallic tang of the carnage on her tongue. Kraven's order was clear, his deep voice resonating with an undercurrent of dark power that sent a shiver down her spine.

"Come on. Do it," Kraven said, his eyes burning into her with an intensity that made her pixie blood simmer.

The blood rushed from Gareth's face.

It might've been a trap, but Zera had waited too long for this to even consider doing anything else. She turned slowly to face the man who had turned her world upside down, who had threatened her family—her own *son*. The elven drug dealer had threatened everything she held dear. Gareth's bald head gleamed under the dim light, his razor-sharp nose twitched as if he sensed the imminent danger, and those clear irises of his reflected nothing but malice.

"You can't let her do this!" he scoffed, his eyes boring into the incubus who kept his gaze firmly on Zera. "I'm your supplier. All your other options have dried up, and if you want to stay in the game, you'll stop her."

Kraven didn't even give the drug dealer a second glance when he said with a lazy shrug, "As it so happens, Gareth, I've found a new supplier who's far less expensive. Let's hope she's worth it."

Zera gulped. She felt the weight of her son's future, the safety of her family and friends, all resting on her slender shoulders. Perhaps it was a fool's mission, but if she played her cards right, she could take them both out with one swift movement. Or two.

First, the drug dealer and then the incubus, and then she wouldn't have to worry about her everfrost blossom problem. Though she did pray it had blossomed so that she could further her experiment. Getting rid of the drug dealer and crime lord would do nothing to stop the actual problem, and as long as pixies existed, there would always be another drug dealer and crime lord to take their place. She would just have to worry about her little supply problem later.

Determination hardened her jaw, and something feral and fierce uncoiled within her—a power she had always possessed but never fully embraced until now.

"This is for my people," she said, her voice steady despite the turmoil inside her, and she unleashed the fury of her rage upon them. She launched the Whisper's staff at Gareth, but he ducked, and it missed.

Her lips curled as she called upon her pixie dust, letting it simmer once again under the surface of her skin. It prickled her fingertips. "And this is for my son."

With a swiftness born of necessity, she flung her hands into the air, fingers flexed and shimmering with the remnants of her pixie dust. The dust surged forth in a wave of purples and blues, sparkling violently as it sought its target.

Gareth attempted a sneer, but it was cut short as the pixie dust enveloped him before he could dodge her again. He let out a stran-gled gasp, his telepathic abilities useless against the sheer force of Zera's unleashed wrath. There was no charm or spell that could save him now, not from the raw elemental power of a pixie protecting her kin.

Zera watched, almost detached, as the dust sparked and burned into Gareth's flesh, burrowing into every exposed crevice with an insatiable hunger. It was as if her anger had given it a life of its own, a need to eradicate the threat that had loomed over her long enough. And eradicate it did—his flesh caved in, melting around his bones, until Gareth was nothing but a heap of charred remains.

Her chest heaved with exertion, and even her wings ached beneath her skin. The room was silent but for the sound of her breathing and the fading echoes of Gareth's final cries. Zera closed her eyes briefly, allowing herself a moment of relief. But she knew there was no time for rest. Not yet.

A slow clap reminded her of that. Her eyes rose to Kraven's, who still had yet to move, and her spirit was ablaze with resolve. She would put an end to all of this, once and for all.

"Well done, my dear," Kraven said, amusement touching his lips.

Zera strained to get a grip on her heart rate, the adrenaline from what she had just done setting in. She watched as he meandered over to where Gareth had once been and kicked his ashes, the ones resulting from her incineration of him. Something hollowed out in her chest. Not from grief of the loss, because the realm was better off without him, but from what she'd had to do. What her actions had taken from her. Though there was none, she had blood on her hands, and the stain it left on her stung.

"You've taken care of a huge problem for me," the incubus continued, crouching to sift through the soot. His fingers brushed against the wooden staff, and Zera stiffened at the sight of it. "And I was surprised to see this old thing again."

She frowned. "Again?"

His eyes locked on hers as he straightened. "You really have no idea who I am, do you?"

The sound of her swallow was the only response. He rose and crept toward her, and she made every attempt to draw on her power, but again, that silent resolve to keep him alive—the one she knew she wasn't in control of—slammed against her power like a bucket of ice water, keeping her frozen.

Zera's eyes jerked to Jade and Sloane, who hadn't moved from the farthest corner of the room. Jade's protective arm was in front of her wife. Zera shook her head, her eyes begging her half sister to stay quiet. Jade nodded silently.

Kraven's humorous laugh echoed off the barren stone walls. "Who do you think the pixies came to with their little Lunar Brotherhood problem? Who gave them the knowledge to fashion such a weapon?" He caressed the smooth wood, his thumb brushing over the interlocking circles carved into it. "I've been alive much longer than you and lived through darker times than you could ever imagine."

He stopped mere inches from her, the Whisper's staff between them. The double-edged staff seemed to purr in his hands.

"My kind are rare because we've been alive since the gods and goddess who made this realm created us. We were the first they forged from the shadows—the incubi and, unfortunately, our female equivalent." He pursed his lips, a darkness washing out the blue of his eyes, as if the mention of the succubi drew up a memory he would rather forget. "Our kind were too... deviant. Too needy, they deemed us. And so they vanquished us just to start again."

Zera sucked in a breath. This wasn't what she'd been taught in school. In fact, the knowledge of the ancients was shadowed in mystery, but Kraven, he actually *knew*. Because he'd lived it.

"They didn't know that I still breathed," he said, his eyes distant. "That my heart kept beating, holding on to that magic they left behind. They created every kind of beast from the blood of our kind but separated our power—kept you broken so that your magic remained diminished. They would never let those with my power live, so I hid until they deserted our realm, leaving their new creations to their own devices."

The age of the thousand-year war. She'd read the accounts that had been recorded in history books during a required course she'd never finished but she was certain hadn't covered the incubi.

Perhaps she would go back to school after all, if only to find out what knowledge she might be missing. But faeology still called to her, and if she couldn't kill Kraven tonight, then she knew she would need that degree more than ever.

"Where did they go?" It was the only question she could manage.

He gave a simple shrug. "They grew bored of you. Perhaps they left to start anew. Whatever it was, I thank the bloody fae that they left. It allowed me to come out of the shadows, only to find out that darkness had taken over this realm. An insatiable greed that couldn't be quenched until it took claim to everything and everyone. But fortunately for me, I was the one thing it couldn't claim.

"I kept the darkness leashed, and when your ancestors came to me, begging for a way to stop being the prey because the gods had given them the short end of the stick, I happily obliged."

He pointedly eyed the staff he caressed in his outstretched hand. "It's yours. Take it."

The gray fox watched her take the staff back like a predator watching its prey fall into its trap.

"Why?" She couldn't keep the question from tumbling out as the staff shuddered and moaned, as though it wanted to be back in the hands of the incubus who'd stepped out of her reach.

She ground her teeth, regretting that she hadn't taken the shot when she'd had it, but there was something about him beyond his persuasion that had kept her from killing him. Perhaps it was the extent of his power, which absolutely terrified the shit out of her.

"Because equilibrium is important to survival." His jaw twitched. "And when the gods and goddesses of old realize I'm alive and return for me, I want power on my side. All of it."

"But—" She took a step toward him but froze when his body started to billow into a mist of gray that hadn't been there before.

"Don't forget our agreement, my dear." He winked as he withered into gray smoke and vanished.

She whirled around in search of him, her hand clutching the Whisper's staff that hummed with ancient power, but he was gone, as if he'd been sucked into the smoke itself. Her gaze settled on the spot where he'd stood, cold and empty. Kraven was gone.

"Damn it," Zera muttered under her breath, disappointment souring her mouth when her eyes darted around the room in search of him, but there was nothing.

Her one shot at getting out of this mess had vanished. But how? That wasn't his power. At least it wasn't one that had been recorded as belonging to an incubus, no matter how powerful the incubus was known to be. But if he was one of the few who had lived as long as he claimed, then she supposed he could've written whatever information existed about his kind.

It was a question that meant nothing now, though. She raced across the debris and skidded to a stop in front of her sister.

"Are you okay? Are you hurt?" She checked her sister for any injuries. The only ones she could see were the bruises caused by the gag. She carefully untied the piece of cloth, and Jade sputtered, gripping her jaw with her free hand.

"Thanks. Just a bit bruised. I think Sloane hurt her ankle, though," she said with a grunt as she flexed her jaw, now free from the gag.

Zera glanced down at Sloane's ankle and the skin that swelled around the shackle.

Jade carefully removed her wife's gag. Tears welled in Sloane's eyes, but she nodded in answer to an unspoken question from Jade. The moment was intimate but fleeting as Jade turned back to Zera. "We need the key. Our powers won't work to wake up Cole until we have our *lovely* accessories removed."

"Right." Zera stood and glanced around the mass of broken tables and limbs.

Jade joined her to help sift through the bodies for the red key ring, stumbling once on the chain that connected the shackles at her ankles. "Zera, I'm so sorry this happened. I don't know how they found us. We were so careful. Even stayed at an inn."

Zera clamped down on the side of her cheek to keep the tears at bay. It pained her to think Jade thought that any of this was her fault. If it was anyone's, it was her own. "It's okay. We had a mole, but I took care of it."

She caught the shocked blink from her half sister and smirked. "You didn't think I had it in me?"

"Of course I did," Jade said with a shocked laugh. "You've had to deal with your share of close encounters at the tavern. I just didn't think you'd have to."

Zera nodded in understanding. Then her heart clenched when she caught her son's reflection in a broken piece of glass. "Is he... safe?"

"The safest one of us all," Jade said, and Zera's nerves eased. "Luckily, Sloane sensed the danger before they crashed into our motel room. Placed the spell that kept Cole fed, nourished, alive, and untouchable. Thoroughly fae-proofed the baby."

"Yeah, and it wasn't easy either," Sloane added from where she finally rose to stretch her limbs. "Took most of my magic to do so. Not that it mattered because as soon as Gareth's men arrived, they siphoned our powers."

"Same here," Zera said, waggling her wrist. The red loop hummed.

"It's weird that it didn't shatter when the fae was killed," Jade said with a frown.

"Or maybe he's not dead yet," Zera said, picking up an overturned chair, her eyes locking on bloodred eyes. "You."

She gripped the fae by the collar and yanked him to his feet. Blood oozed from a gouge at his side. He snickered. His teeth were speckled with even more blood. His laugh was cut short when he reached toward her shoulder, where Cole was still safely snuggled in a wrap and strapped to her back.

The fae rasped, eyes wide. He looked down at the knife jabbed into his other side.

"Wanted to ensure they matched," Zera said snidely and watched as the fae's eyes rolled into the back of his head. He sagged against her, and she shoved him to the floor.

"What?" she asked when she caught Jade staring at her, jaw practically rolling on the floor.

"You really are vicious. You know that, right?" A hint of pride touched her sister's eyes.

Zera shrugged. "When my family's threatened, you know I'll do whatever it takes. Even if it means being trained by an arrogant faeboy."

She grabbed the glowing key ring, making quick work of removing it from the dead elven's belt, and freed Jade from her magical restraints. Not that they did much, since Jade's pixie gland hadn't ever developed, much like the rest of their pixie kind.

"Where is that spy anyway?" Jade asked, rubbing her wrists. "And who was that other guy? The gray-haired one?"

Zera rolled her eyes. "The faeboy got himself locked in the cell. Guess we'll have to go save him after this. And that other guy… That's a problem for another time. Come on, let's free Sloane so I can finally see Cole again."

They turned to head back to where Jade's wife sat, but Jade placed a hand on Zera's shoulder as she asked, "What's that?"

She followed her sister's line of sight to the exact spot where the gray fox had stood. There, perched on top of splintered wood and rotting meat, was a satchel that had definitely not been there before.

Zera frowned. "I don't know."

She stepped over the dead fae and picked up the small bag, the rough leather creaking in her grip. It was surprisingly heavier than expected. She untied the strings, revealing a single envelope, an iron key, and a small box.

"It's a letter," Zera said, her tone a mix of curiosity and alarm.

She removed the letter and quickly read it, gleaning that Kraven had given her the keys to the stronghold and an address to a safe lab to reproduce the synthetic pixie dust she'd promised him. It was also a warning that if she didn't live up to her part of the bargain, there would be consequences. She shuddered. She didn't want to find out what those were.

But despite the threatening tone of the letter, Zera didn't get the sense that it would involve the death and destruction Gareth had rained down on her life. From her very limited experience with Kraven, in tandem with his story of his strife for power against the gods and goddesses who promised destruction if they learned he was alive, she felt that they had a commonality. Survival.

Why would he have divulged such a secret to her if he was going to kill her? If what he said was true, then she was certain he wanted her to succeed as much as she did. The thought gave her a hint of comfort.

"What does it say?" Jade prodded, but Zera quickly pocketed the letter, keys, and mystery box that was barely larger than her palm. She tossed the satchel in with the rest of the ruins.

"It's nothing." She gave Jade a reassuring smile. "Just the keys to this place. Guess that other guy doesn't have use of it, but I'm not sure I want to set up shop here."

Jade grimaced. "Yeah, it's not exactly kid friendly."

"I want to go home," Zera said with a heavy sigh. Her bones ached to the very core, and she could use a shower *and* a bath. And a glass of wine.

"Too bad our home's been burned," Jade said glumly as they walked back to where Sloane had managed to prop herself against the wall.

"Yeah, I know." Zera grimaced. She'd almost forgotten about that. "Guess that's the end of an era."

They had shared so many memories in that home, but perhaps it was time for something new.

"You're not upset?" Jade furrowed her brow.

Zera let out a sigh. "Not really. I'm mostly relieved to not have to go back to that house with all those memories lingering around. Perhaps this is a chance at a fresh start."

A look of awe and pride washed over her sister.

"And at least we're all safe. That's what matters most to me."

They approached Sloane, and Zera gently unlocked her bracelets.

"Finally," Sloane said with a deep inhalation once her bracelet was off and her magic came rushing back. She whispered a spell, and the shackles at her ankles snapped in two with a wave of her hand.

With a few more muttered spells, the swelling in her leg vanished along with the bruise under her eye.

"Let me see the boy," Sloane said, nodding to Zera's little baby, who was still strapped to her back.

"Here," Zera said, carefully unhooking the fabric and setting him in her lap.

The little bundle of cheeks and light curls was so still that Zera had to keep reminding herself he was alive. Sloane crouched in front of them, her corkscrew curls tumbling over her shoulders and her hands extended over the sleeping baby.

"Wait," Zera said suddenly, glancing around the room. "Not here."

She didn't want this to be what her son saw when he first woke up. He'd never remember it, but she would.

As if Jade had read her mind, she paved a path through the carnage to the dining hall doors and out into the vast network of halls leading off to various levels of the stronghold. Zera didn't know who else lurked in them, but she didn't want to be here to find out. The hall to her left she knew led down into the cellar. Once she ensured that Sloan and Jade were safe with Cole, she would return to save Maverick. Again. Her lips curled upward. She would be sure to remind him of that.

Jade shut the doors to the dining room, and once they were safely out of sight of the horrors that had taken place within, she breathed a sigh of relief.

"We made it."

Zera smiled weakly, her lavender eyes scanning the halls just in case.

"Here's good," Sloane said, motioning to a surprisingly soft rug placed in front of a steel armchair. Cold with hints of comfort was the overall theme of the place.

Zera carefully placed her son on the carpet and sat back to give Sloane room to work. She watched the witch's fingers dance with a subtle grace as they wove threads of magic in the air. The warm glow emanated from her palms, enveloping Cole in a tender luminescence. It was a gentle undoing, a spell unraveling, as each thread of protective enchantment rose with care not to wake him.

"Come on, baby," Zera whispered, her voice laced with both urgency and comfort. "Time to wake up."

Sloane finished with a final flourish, and the magical light dissipated back into the darkness. Cole's little chest rose and fell more deeply, and his eyelids fluttered. Zera held her breath as she waited for those tiny eyes to open, to look into hers and see the world they'd inherited—a world she would move the sky and earth to make safe for him. In fact, she already had, and she would do it all over again to ensure he grew up without fear. Safe. Secure.

"Is he..." Jade began, but the question hung incomplete as they all watched in silent anticipation.

"Shh," Sloane hushed gently, a knowing smile touching her lips. "The spell is broken. He'll come around when he's ready."

And then, at long last, Cole opened his eyes—big, bright, and bewilderingly aware. They fixed on Zera, and it was as if an entire ocean of love crashed over her. Her heart swelled so fiercely that, for a moment, she feared it might burst right out of her chest.

"Hi, baby," Zera cooed, cradling Cole against her. His tiny hand reached out, fingers curling around a lock of her hair. She pressed her lips to his forehead, inhaling the sweet scent of innocence and warmth that only a child could possess. Her world narrowed to this single, perfect point in time. Nothing else mattered—not the danger, not the chaos, not even the letter or mysterious box burning a hole in her pocket.

"Thank you," she mouthed silently to Sloane, who nodded with a soft, empathetic smile.

Cole's excited laughter echoed off the stone walls, his eyes lighting up when he beheld his mom, and they all laughed.

"Looks like somebody missed his mama," Sloane teased lightly, brushing a thumb across Cole's chubby cheek.

"Can't blame him," Jade chimed in, stretching her limbs. "With a mom who kicks ass and takes names? This kid's going to have stories for days."

"Let's hope it's a while before he understands any of them," Zera replied, a laugh bubbling up despite the weariness that clung to her bones. Her arms tightened around Cole, and she gave a silent promise that she'd never let harm befall him again.

Shouts sounded from down the hall opposite them, and they all froze.

"Where is he?" a deep voice filled with rage growled.

CHAPTER 22
MAVERICK

MAVERICK HISSED AT THE WOLFSBANE THAT DUG DEEP INTO HIS WRISTS. Sweat beaded his brow as he strained again and again to shift. If he could just break through the bracelet that siphoned his magic and give in to his wolf, then he could escape.

Zera was probably already in the dining hall with Gareth by now, and Maverick's window was closing. If he got out, he could save her. He wouldn't allow himself to think about the alternative. Because to think she would die at the hands of Gareth because of his own stupid carelessness would be unbearable.

She didn't even know what she meant to him or how what she'd said by the river had affected him. He hadn't even gotten a chance to tell her that he did love her, too, and that he'd been an idiot to let something so small ruin what they had. He would give everything to have that time back, to say the things he'd kept inside his heart. He'd been a coward.

But not her. She was the bravest woman he'd ever known, and he would do everything in his power to get to her. To save her. To kill anything and everything that threatened to take her or her family.

Even if she never accepted his apology, she was alive, and that was all that mattered to him.

The desperation clawing at Maverick's chest intensified, and he pushed against the magic-restricting bracelet, gritting against the searing pain of the wolfsbane-drenched ropes.

"It's no use," Felice said after trying over and over again to break her bracelets by using her voice. She winced. They had tightened with each attempt until circulation was almost cut off.

Even Irdeel, who was still rubbing a bruised head and ego from getting knocked out, shot Felice a glance filled with pity.

"We can't keep straining like this," the siren pressed when Maverick didn't respond.

A ferocious look flickered across his face. "Are you saying we should just sit back and wait for Gareth to finish whatever twisted plan he has in store for Zera? For her *son*?"

Maverick gazed at each of them, from the siren to the vampire who stayed glued to the goblin's side. Felice's throat bobbed as she swallowed.

"To put it in terms I think you'll understand," Maverick began, his expression darkening with guilt and duty, "Zera and her family are civilians. You, of all people, should understand what that means."

They were silent as the weight of his words settled around them like a heavy fog. The urgency of the situation was palpable, and each of them felt the gravity of the mission to rescue Zera and Cole from Gareth's clutches.

"I swear, if that bastard hurts a hair on their heads..." Maverick growled, letting the threat hang in the air.

"We'll make him pay if he does." It was Cillian who spoke up. The vampire's bloodred eyes were dim, his power drained by his bracelets.

"Yes, but what do you expect us to do with our magic siphoned and us trapped in this cell?" Felice asked. Her wild red locks clung to her shoulders in a damp sweat. The stagnant air of the cell barely provided enough oxygen for them all.

The ground shuddered above them, and their eyes rose to the ceiling. Dirt and pebbles sprinkled down from the cracks in the ancient mountain, a telltale sign of the chaos unfolding outside. Maverick's jaw clenched.

"We're running out of time," he hissed.

The stone walls seemed to press in on them, the air was thick with tension, and the distant sounds of battle raged above. Maverick balled his hands into fists, his heart pounding with a primal urgency to protect Zera and Cole. Nothing else mattered to him except their safety.

A sharp pang shot through his chest, like a tug on an invisible tether—a connection to Zera that transcended the physical barriers separating them. In that moment, he could feel her fear and her desperation, and it ignited something deep within him.

Maverick's eyes flashed with an alpha fire that promised retribution to anyone who dared harm his mate or her son. A guttural growl rumbled from his throat, and the others recoiled, instinctively sensing the raw, untamed force radiating from him that no siphon could quell.

Even Cillian licked his fangs nervously and shrank back in surprise.

With a surge of adrenaline, Maverick felt his muscles ripple beneath his skin as he strained against the wolfsbane-soaked ropes binding his wrists. All he saw, all he felt was her. Her warmth and compassion for those she held close. Her unwavering dedication to her son and deep sense of responsibility were just a few of the things he admired in her. She was a beacon of good in a world of darkness, and he would give everything to protect that light.

His whole body shook against the restraints. Droplets of sweat stung his eyes. He bellowed as another tug down the bond sent him into a fury he'd never known before. The magic bracelets that circled his wrists dimmed then cracked and shattered, falling from his arms in a clatter of red fragments.

Felice gasped, her eyes wide with disbelief. Irdeel clutched her goblin dagger, her knuckles whitening as she gripped the hilt tightly. Cillian extended his fangs and coiled his body with a predatory tension.

Maverick snarled, ripping through the ropes as if they were made of paper. His nostrils flared as he caught the scent of Zera's distress like a beacon guiding him forward. With a primal roar, he slammed his shoulder into the cell door, the reinforced steel buckling under his supernatural strength. But it wasn't enough. His stormy wolf eyes glowed with flecks of gold lightning.

He reached within himself to shift, but his wolf was weakened by the wolfsbane. What he wouldn't give for one of Irdeel's well-placed alchemical traps or even his belt of grenades. He would blast right through this place to get to Zera and to keep her safe. He knew she could handle herself, but not being able to get to her when that fear ripped down that bond would be the death of him. Another desperate plea from her was all he needed. A growl ripped through him again, and he shoved the bars with everything he had.

The steel groaned and creaked under his force, but it held strong. He gritted his teeth, feeling the blood oozing from his raw knuckles as he pounded on the metal. His wolf was howling in agony, desperate to break free and protect his mate.

Maverick's primal instincts surged through him, a tempest of power and desire that threatened to overwhelm him. The connection to Zera pulsed with an intensity that fueled his resolve, igniting a fire within that burned brighter than anything he had ever experienced.

With a mighty roar that echoed through the confines of the cell, he sent all of his alpha power crashing into the bars, his muscles straining and bulging with the effort. The force of it knocked the reinforced steel from its hinges, sending the bars clattering across the floor amid a shower of sparks.

The others watched in stunned silence as Maverick stepped out of the crumbling cell, his alpha wolf energy sending a clear message—bow or be crushed. The guards outside the cell stumbled back, their weapons drawn but their faces ashen.

"Let's go," Maverick growled to the others, his eyes blazing with determination.

"Guess we're fighting out of this the fun way," Irdeel said with a smirk, dusting her hands off on her maroon leathers.

Felice only grumbled something about wearing the wrong fashion armor for a prison breakout but followed them out of the cell, where the four guards waited for the ambush.

"It's been a while since I had the taste of elven blood." Cillian flicked his tongue across one of his fangs.

The guard closest to them was the first to turn his back and run for the door to cut off their escape. Wrong move.

Maverick lunged at him with all the force of an alpha, and the rest of the group sprang into action. The sounds of tearing and ripping of skin off bones, like cleaning a deer, echoed off the shallow ceiling. They would no longer be prisoners of this cell, trapped by magic or anything else. Nothing could stand in his way of freeing his mate and her family from the evil that roamed these halls.

Once the guards were taken care of, Maverick and his team grabbed any weapons off their bodies and sprinted down the dimly lit corridor, the echo of their footsteps a rhythmic drumbeat urging them forward.

Maverick led the charge, his muscular form a blur of motion, his storm-filled eyes fixed on the path ahead toward the sugary blend of lilac and determination—the undeniable scent of his mate. He could taste her fear and adrenaline on his tongue and feel that the weight of Cole's safety pressed heavily upon her. If only he could get to her. *Find her.*

He knew these halls, had navigated them many times when he worked undercover for Gareth, but he'd never known the rage he now felt. The pure panic of knowing what the elven arms dealer turned drug dealer was capable of.

"This way!" he called, leading the way to the left and up out of the darkness toward the open foyer to the dining hall.

He prepared himself for the worst.

As they approached the foyer, Maverick's heart pounded in his chest. Each step heightened his anticipation. What would he find? Zera was still alive—he could feel it—but he couldn't tell what state she was in, and that unknown made it hard to breathe.

Maverick's boots skidded to a halt as he reached the double doors. With a deep breath, he nodded to his companions before bursting through, ready for whatever lay ahead.

The scene that greeted him made his heart stop.

Zera knelt in the center of the room, her arms wrapped protectively around Cole. Her lavender eyes were locked on the small child who clung to her with his face buried in her shoulder.

Relief flooded through Maverick, washing away the tension that had coiled in his muscles. Zera and Cole were safe. Alive.

Without hesitation, he rushed toward them, his steps quick and purposeful. The distance between them seemed to stretch on forever, but he pushed forward, driven by an overwhelming need to hold them in his arms.

Twin sets of lavender eyes met his. Cole's crinkled with a smile as Zera's went wide with surprise. A silent communication passed among them. In that moment, the world around them faded away. It was just the three of them, together at last.

Maverick's heart swelled with a mixture of love and relief as he finally reached them. He engulfed Zera and Cole in a tight embrace, his strong arms encircling them.

"You're okay?" he whispered, his voice rough with emotion.

She nodded and melted against his chest, the intimacy of the movement making his heart sputter.

He pulled back to take them all in, checking for any signs of injury, but there were none.

"Of course you're okay," he said, his lips ticking upward ever so slightly. His heart swelled with pride. "You had a good teacher."

"Ha! You wish, faeboy." She shoved him lightly.

He winked at her, and her answering blush only deepened his wolfish grin.

"Okay, time to break it up, you two," Jade said with an exaggerated eye roll.

Maverick smirked at her before turning to Cole, who clapped his hands and giggled at the sight of Maverick. "And look at you! You've grown twice as tall since I last saw you. Thanks to your good aunties, no doubt."

Sloane smiled, rising to stand next to her wife, who was busy giving the other three fae who tailed him an appraising look. Irdeel remained unfazed, picking some invisible dust out of her nails as she went back to shooting Felice nasty glares. Cillian kept an eye out on all the exits for any sign of danger.

"I'm glad you're here." Zera nudged him again, and her lavender eyes danced with humor. "Saves me the trouble of having to save your ass."

Maverick chuckled as her playful jab hit him right where it counted. He leaned in and breathed in her sweet lilac scent. "You can save my ass any time."

Zera's cheeks flushed at his flirtatious remark, but she didn't back down. "Don't tempt me, wolf boy," she retorted, her lavender eyes sparkling with mirth.

Her fight and spunk were two of his favorite things about her. He was relieved that Gareth hadn't had a chance to smother that fire in her.

Before he could respond with another cheeky comment, something dawned on him. "Where is he? Where's Gareth?"

"Dead," she said without even batting an eyelash.

Zera's blunt response about Gareth's fate hung in the air for a moment before she continued. "I took care of him and his men while you were breaking out. They won't be a problem anymore."

There was a flicker of something dangerous in her lavender eyes that both impressed and broke something in Maverick. He knew she was more than capable of handling herself, but the thought of her having to face Gareth's cruelty made his blood boil.

He jerked his gaze to the dining hall doors, which were shut like a sealed-off tomb. He didn't have to look to know she'd left Gareth and his men in a bloody mess. The message on her expression was clear—never cross a mother or her child. The loyalty and devotion of this woman astounded him. She tugged on his alpha heartstrings, but it was more than just his admiration of her primal need to protect her young that captivated him.

It was her independence, her humor, her fire, and her unyielding strength that made him know he loved her and would love her with everything he had—if she gave him the chance.

What did you say? Zera's voice whispered to him through the bond.

He blinked. He hadn't even realized he'd lowered his shields. *What did you hear?*

Zera raised a brow in challenge. *You first.*

A smile played at his lips. I didn't say anything, but what you may have sensed is that... I love you.

Their hearts raced in tandem at Maverick's confession, but he didn't stop there. He couldn't, not after she'd left him speechless at the river without him getting the chance to say...

I'm sorry for how I behaved. He pushed the words through the bond, and by the way her eyes shuttered in reaction, he knew they meant something to her. *I was a fool. An utter fool for how I acted. For doubting you and blowing everything up. You didn't deserve that, and I will never shut you out like that again.*

Zera's breath caught in her throat, her lips parting in surprise, yet a glimmer of joy and hope settled between them.

Say it again.

It took all of Maverick's self-control not to claim her lips at the sound of her whisper through the bond—straight to his very soul.

I'm sorry, he murmured back to her, and he would say it as many times as she needed to hear it.

She shook her head. They ignored the incredulous looks from the others standing around them. *Not that.*

He smiled, realizing what she meant, and leaned into her. *I love you.*

The bond between them pulsed, strengthening with each passing second.

Zera's smile grew, and she whispered back, *I love you too.*

His eyes flickered to her lips—soft and delicate and kissable. Everything in him yearned to claim them, to worship her whole body as he'd done the night before. Only this time, it would mean so much more. Their bond was so much stronger, and if she would have him, he promised to honor her in every way she deserved. There was nothing that compared to the union between mates. Or so he'd heard.

If only they didn't have an audience. Perhaps it was for the best, though, since he knew they had more pressing matters at hand. Like finally getting out of this place.

"Oh," Zera exclaimed, pulling back as if she'd had a sudden realization. "And I have something for you."

Not if I have something for you first, he whispered through the bond.

She shot him an incredulous look, but his devilish grin only deepened.

Come on, I'm serious.

All right, you've got my full attention, he said through the bond and pushed those thoughts aside for now, giving her a respectful nod. "What is it?"

She reached inside her back pocket and pulled out a set of keys. A familiar box the size of a ring box tumbled out, too, but she quickly tucked it back into her pocket. He hoped that box wasn't what he thought it was.

"The keys," she said, handing the iron set to him. "To this place. They were given to me, but I figured, since you are already familiar with the stronghold, that you might want them."

He stared at the keys for a long while. They represented a past he wanted to forget. This place reminded him of an evil that had almost taken the most important things from him. A fact he would rather forget, but he took the keys nonetheless.

"Hmm. Thanks, I guess." He took the keys but barely gave them a second glance as he pocketed them. Cole giggled and reached out to Maverick, who laughed, "Oh, you want to come here?"

He looked to Zera for permission. She nodded and handed Cole off before rising to her feet. Maverick wasn't sure what he'd done to win such affection, but he wasn't about to question the little guy's taste.

I heard that, Zera shot back at him, and he had to stifle a laugh.

Maverick stood up, bouncing the boy on a hip and shuffling from foot to foot before casually nodding toward the imprint of the box, still obvious in the pocket of her black leathers that were ripped and frayed from battle.

"What else did you loot for us?" He hoped his playful smirk was enough to cover his concern.

She scowled. "Nothing."

Yet guilt trickled down their bond, an unintentional admittance of her lie.

"Zera," Maverick pressed, "what else is in your pocket?"

"Ugh, can't you two newlyweds save your banter until after we're back home?" Felice asked with an exaggerated huff.

The magic Sloane performed on Irdeel's concussion faltered for a second.

Jade glanced up as she unlocked the last of the bracelets from the others, her protective gaze lingering on her half sister.

"We're not actually married. That was only a cover, so don't worry," Zera said to Jade before fixing Maverick with a glare.

The words hit him harder than any blow. He knew he wasn't actually Dane Brown and she wasn't truly married to him, but there was something comforting about their cover. Something that felt like it might've been real.

Perhaps she only wanted him as a mate—to love but not to share a life with. He would be okay with that. He'd lived alone, afraid to trust, for far too long to let her slip away. That was why he needed to know about the box. He wanted her to know that she could trust him fully and not push him away because she thought she had to figure things out on her own.

Zera's eyes softened when she saw the pain in his, the regret whirling like a tempest in the storm.

"What's going on between you two?" It was Cillian who spoke up, and they all turned to look at the vamp, who just arched an onyx brow in return.

"Fine." Zera loosened a breath before reaching into her pocking and pulling out the box and chucking it at Maverick. He caught it with a single hand at the last minute. "It was a... gift from Kraven before he left. After he let me kill Gareth. I think he wanted him dead."

Irdeel watched like a hawk as Maverick opened the box. Her goblin claws poked out through her fingertips in anticipation.

"I haven't opened it yet," Zera added.

Maverick held his breath as he undid the hook and opened the top. A bloodred ruby cut into a giant baguette took up the center of the gold band. Even in the dim light of the foyer, it gleamed.

He reached in and pulled it out, a muscle ticking in his chiseled cheek as he studied the gaudy thing.

"Oh no." Felice shook her head, recognition washing over her face. "What did that crime lord ask of you?"

"Who's Kraven?" Jade asked, her back straightening a little at the concern in Felice's tone. "And what does that ring mean?"

"It's a debtor's promise." Maverick clenched his jaw. He knew all too well the weight such a promise carried. A deal made with the cunning and ancient incubus crime lord was no trifling matter.

"He wants to work with me." Zera's chin rose a little. "He's given me a lab to replicate the synthetic pixie-dust drug I've been working on in order to manufacture it at scale. A competitor to protect pixies, since our government's efforts have fallen short. No offense." She shot Irdeel and Cillian a look of sympathy that wasn't returned.

All the color drained from Irdeel's face as she said, "I'll pretend I didn't hear any of that."

Maverick smirked. He knew the agents wouldn't be telling anyone of anything they learned or gleaned from this trip. If the FBI discovered that their two agents ventured into Mystic City territory on an unauthorized mission, especially while collaborating with a pixie intent on creating a synthetic version of an illegal drug, there would be severe repercussions.

Zera continued, her voice gaining a steely edge, "I made a deal with Kraven to keep my son and my family safe. He provided me with protection and resources after Gareth threatened us. But more than that, I believe a synthetic drug is the key to keeping my people from being hunted for their pixie dust."

"If you can't keep the drugs off the street, keep the street from hunting us," Jade muttered, her pixie ears twitching at a phantom sound. "It's not a bad idea."

"Except for the part about working with the incubus," Felice said with a warning look. "He's dangerous. Perhaps even more than Gareth."

Zera shrugged. "Well, we'll just have to hope my everfrost blossom has bloomed because that's the only way I'll be free. If I can make good on my promise, then perhaps I can live a normal life with my son and make the streets a bit safer in the process."

"We will make it happen," Maverick said, finally stepping up beside her and taking her hand in his free one. Cole was still propped up by his other and played with a button at the collar of his flexible fighting leathers.

Felice's eyebrows nearly vanished into her fiery red hairline. "You're getting into this business too?"

Maverick held Zera's gaze for a heartbeat, his piercing eyes intense yet soft at the same time. "I'm in this with you," he said, giving her hand a gentle squeeze. "Whatever comes our way, we'll face it together."

A rush of gratitude swept down the bond, and her affection for him reflected in her eyes. For a moment, her emotions collided with his and her heart fluttered as she fell further in love with him for his unwavering loyalty to her despite his tough exterior and sometimes shady profession. He would have to fix that if he were to be her mate, but he would never ask her to do the same.

He wanted her to experience everything she hadn't been able to and desired to be the one to take care of Cole while she pursued her passion and went back to school—or whatever it was that she wanted. He'd lived in the shadows and played with fire, so he knew how to work the world that Zera was dipping her toes into. They would face this challenge and everything else together. That much they both knew, thanks to their newfound connection.

"Of course you all will have to vow to secrecy, but there's no reason any of you should be involved," Maverick said with a shrug. "The debtor's promise was addressed to my mate."

Sloane and Jade gawked at his use of the word "mate," but from Zera's answering smile and the way her eyes glistened like a field of lilacs, he knew she claimed him too. She was utterly radiant.

Cole cupped Maverick's face and tugged on the dark beard he desperately needed to shave. The boy's giggles were contagious, and the whole group laughed along with him.

Maverick chuckled along with them, delighted to see such genuine mirth and happiness in their midst. Then he turned to the rest of them and said, "I'm sure you all have questions, but we should probably leave before this one decides to eat my beard for a late-night snack."

He leaned down to pass Cole back to his mom.

Zera leaned into Maverick as she whispered, "Thank you for trusting me, for believing in us." Her voice carried a mix of relief and adoration that tugged at his heartstrings.

"Anytime," he said, and he meant it.

The motley crew fell into formation. Zera and Maverick took the center position. Cole giggled excitedly in Zera's arms as they set off down the dimly lit halls and out into the brisk night air. Maverick couldn't help but steal another glance at Zera. Her beautiful eyes lit up with a passionate fire and the determination of a mother that he knew would burn brighter and longer than the night sky.

He took a deep breath, savoring the moment and knowing that he was in uncharted territory. But one thing was certain—with her by his side, nothing seemed impossible. They would make it through this and any other challenge. He was sure of it. And maybe, just maybe, he had finally found the love and family he'd always longed for.

Putting the stronghold behind them and the wild unknown future ahead, they all stood in front of the roaring rapids, waiting for Sloane to finish her spell that would create a portal back to the penthouse.

Maverick sighed. He couldn't believe it. They had actually made it through all the obstacles and challenges with their lives. Well, most of them, at least. The air was thick with anticipation as they all knew what this meant—if the everfrost blossom bloomed, Kraven would make his appearance, and they would officially be in business with the leader of all the organized crime in the city.

He glanced down at Zera, who now fed her son from some packet her witchy sister-in-law had conjured up. He knew that, no matter what happened, Cole would always be Zera's top priority.

Zera, he whispered through the bond, and she glanced up at him. *Once you've developed this... synthetic drug of yours, perhaps it'd be good for all of us to find a place away from all of this.*

Are you thinking about going straight? She arched a skeptical brow.

I've been thinking about it for a while. He chuckled at her surprise. *I'd do it for you. And to help raise Cole. Perhaps we could live near your family, for him to grow up in a safe and normal environment. That is, if you want and, of course, want me there with you.*

A caress through the bond and across his heart was all he needed to feel to know that she felt the same, but he still wanted to hear the words, just as she had wanted to.

You'd give up your life as a spy?

He shrugged. *I've been trying to find a way to retire from this business. This seems as good as any. Perhaps I'll become a security consultant.*

Her lips parted in a transcendent smile, and she leaned into him to whisper, "I want you by my side."

Always. The promise echoed through the bond.

His eyes fluttered shut for a mere moment as he savored the words from her beautiful mouth. He cupped her face and brushed his thumb gently over her cheekbone, a soft smile playing at the corners of his lips.

"I love you," he whispered to his mate as the witch finished the incantation and the portal to the penthouse whirred to life and whisked them away on a phantom wind.

CHAPTER 23

ZERA

THE FAMILIAR STREETS OF HAVENWOOD OPENED BEFORE ZERA LIKE A WARM embrace, instantly easing the tension from her shoulders. After months of working on her synthetic pixie-dust drug using the precursor she'd extracted from the everfrost blossom, she'd finally done it. She'd created what she called pixels, and with Kraven's stamp of approval, she was ready to bring it to her old boss, the alpha to the Haven Moon pack.

She hoped for everyone's sake that this meeting was a success.

"Are you ready?" Maverick asked from beside her in the parking lot of the tavern she'd last set foot in when that druid had nearly killed her and her son.

The memory still made her heart stop when she thought of what might've happened had she not called Maverick and accepted help. If that experience had taught her anything, it was that sometimes calling someone for help was okay. She didn't have to do everything alone.

A whisper of love and affection melted through their bond, as if he'd heard every word coming from her heart and confirmed them to be true. Maverick's large, smooth hands found hers and gave them a gentle squeeze.

She finally nodded and managed a soft smile at the simple gesture. Who would have thought she would crave the affectionate touch of a faeboy spy? That her mate would wind up being a were-wolf—once her enemy but now her fiercest confidant? It wasn't what she'd imagined would happen when she went on that blind date. When she first met Maverick, she'd sworn to hate him, but now she couldn't imagine her life without him.

And neither could Cole, for that matter. The two of them were inseparable. and it warmed her heart to see her son grow and thrive with Maverick's guidance. Despite the odds against them, they had found a way to make their unconventional family work.

But with the meeting with the Haven Wolf alpha and everything that they stood to lose looming over her, she couldn't help but worry. What if Ryker didn't agree to the deal? What if she couldn't get the Havenwood territory for Kraven as a distribution point for pixels after she'd promised to deliver it to him? Would the crime lord come after her? Would her family be in danger yet again?

She had to remind herself that Jade and Sloane lived next door and that Sloane had built impenetrable shields around the entire property and the home that Maverick and she had built together. A safe haven where Cole could grow up away from all of this. They were protected in the Havenwood mountains. It was their own little piece of paradise, close enough that they could keep tabs on things in the Havenwood territory as well as have weekly check-ins with her lab, given by Kraven, on the outskirts of Mystic City.

That was, when she wasn't in class at the city's university, where she now attended. It was about time she finished that faeology and alchemical science degree, and it was all thanks to a little encourage-ment from Maverick and his assurance that he'd be happy to watch Cole, when her half sister allowed him to, so Zera could go to her classes. Sloane had also made the whole property hidden from the outside world, a world Zera was working to fix to make safer, not only for her son or herself but for the rest of her pixie kind.

That was the main reason this meeting was so important.

Maverick squeezed her hand once more before releasing it, bringing her back to reality. She looked up at him, and his expression was serious as he met her gaze. "No matter what happens," he said firmly, "we will face it together."

His resolve through the bond was a salve to her fears and worries. A peace washed over her, one she wasn't sure she had ever felt in her whole life, save for that brief and tender moment when she'd first held her son.

She smiled gratefully at him and placed a hand on his cheek. "Promise? Even if all of this goes south?"

Maverick's storm-filled eyes flickered wolfish gold as he said through the bond, With everything I am.

A flicker of confidence raged through her, and she knew they were an unstoppable force. Mates and partners for life.

"Let's do this," she said with a determined nod, and together they hopped out of his old, bare-bones truck—a much more practical vehicle than she'd imagined him having.

She'd joked that, after taking in his penthouse, she expected Maverick to own something much more glamorous or expensive. He'd laughed and reminded her that his cover identity's tastes and his own were very different. He enjoyed the occasional outing into the city, but what he enjoyed most was being in nature.

It was a sentiment she shared with all her heart, and seeing him in his own element on their little piece of land in the mountains had been like coming home. They had come from two very different backgrounds, but their hearts were truly the same, and by a twist of fate, they had found each other in the least-expected way.

The gray clouds hung low above the surrounding oaks, barren for the winter. A light snow had fallen the previous night, but it was just cold enough for the mist to hang over the ground. Their boots crunched against icy asphalt that was marred by cracks and potholes.

"Zera! You're alive!"

A whirlwind of energy and pink smacked into her before she could process the voice. Long, slender arms engulfed her as Quinn, Ryker's werewolf-pixie cousin, engulfed her in a tight hug.

"Hi, Quinn." Zera laughed despite herself, returning the embrace.

"I tried your faestone so many times!" Quinn cried, her face showing a flurry of emotions that made Zera question whether Quinn was about to laugh or cry. "Where were you? Oh!"

Her eyes finally landed on Maverick. His arms were folded across his muscular build as he took a wide stance. The sleeves of his army green jacket over his white T-shirt strained against his biceps as he regarded Quinn with a mix of amusement and wariness.

Zera couldn't hold back a laugh. "Quinn, this is Maverick, my..."

"Mate," Maverick finished for her, a smirk playing on his lips as he extended a hand to Quinn. "Pleasure to meet you."

A surge of raw emotion crackled through the bond between Maverick and Zera, pulsing with the intensity of something unbreakable. It rippled through the air so that even Quinn must've felt the truth of their connection.

"You didn't mention how hot he was," Quinn whispered as she looped her arm around Zera and led the way inside the tavern.

Zera felt a flush of heat rise to her cheeks as she elbowed Quinn playfully. "I had other things on my mind besides dishing the details."

Maverick slid his hands into the pockets of his jeans—it was a miracle that he wasn't wearing his fighting leathers—as he fell into step beside them, his piercing gaze locked on Zera with an intensity that made her shiver. His subtle smirk hinted at the thrill he took in their newfound intimacy.

They truly had come so far.

Quinn chuckled, tucking her chin-length pink hair behind a

pointed ear. "Come on, I'll show you to Ryker's office. Careful, though, he's in a mood."

"I'd be worried if he wasn't." Zera rolled her eyes with a knowing grin as they entered the dimly lit tavern.

"Do tell me about this new project of yours," Quinn said.

The bar wasn't open just yet and was empty of patrons, save for a couple of Haven Wolf Pack members playing darts in the back corner. Several muscular wolves sprawled in chairs around a wooden table, nursing tankards of ale and discussing whatever pack members talked about.

Quinn led the way past the bar, where she shared a meaningful look with her cousin Vinny—the half brother to the alpha. He gave her a nod and jerked his head toward the door labeled Pack Members Only.

"Ryker's in his office. This way," she said, her rune tattoo on her muscled right shoulder glowing as they passed under the protected door.

Zera couldn't help but smile at the familiar sights and sounds of the tavern. The smell of woodsmoke and fresh pine filled the air, and the low rumble of conversation mixed with the occasional clink of glasses. She'd spent many nights working here, and though that life was a distant past now, it brought back some fond memories. She'd met Quinn here—the only half pixie other than her son she'd ever met—along with Ryker, who was half demon and half werewolf, which wasn't a common combination, let alone for an alpha.

Yes, it had been a beautiful part of her life. They'd made her feel at home despite everything her ex had put her through. Moving to a place where she knew no one hadn't been easy, but these were the people who had made it just a bit easier. And when Cole came along, they had been there to support her and help her navigate being a single mom.

But now, as she took the narrow stairs down to the pit—the pack's lair with pool tables, a private bar, and, of course, Ryker's office—she knew it was a past best left there.

She would leave behind every tear she had shed for her ex, every long shift she had taken to support her child, the late nights rocking him to sleep—all of it.

She would do it all again, knowing that it had brought her here, to her life now. Finding her fated mate had just been the glaze on the winter-spiced Bundt cake Maverick promised to bake her in a few days on their first winter solstice.

But it wasn't only that that had made her life so much better. Now she was making a difference, creating a world where it was safe for her—and eventually her son—to use their powers out in the open. A world where she pursued her passions and her desires without anyone holding her back. And with her degree in the works and this amazing career that allowed her to work in a state-of-the-art lab, there wasn't anything she couldn't accomplish.

Even her powers were stronger for it, and she knew that the future of pixies would be forever changed for the better, thanks to her synthetic drug—pixels. She just had to get Ryker on board.

He sat across from them, his stoic face revealing nothing after they finished carving out their plan. Quinn stood behind where Ryker sat in his high-back armchair, like she was his bodyguard, her face a mask as well. Zera had no doubt that she could totally be his bodyguard if he, in fact, needed one. He didn't.

Maverick remained standing as well behind Zera, a pillar of strength if she needed him.

You won't, he whispered through the bond, and she smiled inwardly. *I've seen you in a fight, Zera. You don't need anyone to protect you.*

She couldn't argue with him about that. Despite her small stature, she was a fierce fighter, thanks to her continued training. But still, it was comforting to have Maverick by her side.

She felt Maverick and Ryker posturing, but she kept her focus on her old boss.

"So..." Ryker began. He tilted his buzzed head, which caught the light of the single bulb that hung above the metal desk between them. "You want me to allow Kraven into my territory and invest in this... drug of yours, a supposed synthetic to pixie dust—"

"Pixels," Zera interjected. "And yes. As you can see, Kraven is prepared to make it worth your while."

Ryker pressed his mouth into a thin line, a quirk of his lips his only response.

Quinn stepped in, as if she sensed her cousin's mood, and said, "If a synthetic is a possibility, it could present a better alternative to kicking out the riffraff dealing around here. Perhaps it could help with the violence and overdoses."

Zera nodded eagerly. "Yes, exactly. With a synthetic, we can control the purity and dosage. It could potentially save lives and decrease the hunting of my kind. Of our kind."

She said that last bit while eyeing Quinn, who smiled in appreciation. Though Zera didn't know if Quinn had pixie dust, as a half pixie, she was still a potential target. Being an honorary member of her cousin's pack could protect her from only so much.

Ryker leaned back in his chair, lacing his fingers together behind his head. He studied Zera for a moment before speaking again.

"And what do you get out of it? Besides money, that is." His sharp demon-violet eyes bore into her, searching for any ulterior motives.

Zera met his gaze without wavering. She knew Ryker was a shrewd businessman and wouldn't make this easy for her, even if she was a past employee. Transparency was everything.

She lifted her chin and stated plainly, "Other than making a world where I and others like me, including my son, don't have to live in hiding or fear being hunted, I get to uphold my part of a debtor's promise."

Ryker arched one of his dark, scarred wolf brows but remained silent. The Haven Moon alpha had a way of getting people to talk, and she was discovering why. He didn't say anything, waiting for her to continue. Zera took a deep breath, deciding to reveal only what was necessary.

She shrugged. "It's a long story, but at the time, I did what I had to do to keep my son and myself alive."

Ryker was quiet for long moments, his piercing gaze on both her and Maverick, looking like the deadly demon wolf he was. It took all of her self-control not to shift in her seat. Somehow, she kept her eyes trained on him. She hadn't endured so much only to succumb now.

His throat bobbed, and the Haven Wolf alpha tattoo on his neck rippled briefly as he swallowed audibly.

Finally, Ryker leaned forward, his hands resting on the desk in front of him. "I can appreciate the desire to protect one's own. I, too, have my own to protect," Ryker began, his tone measured. "Which is why I must know if your wolf knows what you'll both have to sacrifice if I say yes."

A flicker of doubt rushed through her. Maverick had said it was possible that Ryker would uphold the pack law this time. One could bend the rules only so many times as an alpha. Otherwise, he'd risk losing even more of his pack. Ryker wouldn't agree to enter a deal that impacted his whole pack without Maverick and Zera becoming pack members. Which meant Maverick would have to acknowledge Ryker as the alpha.

Zera understood that, but she hadn't expected Ryker to come to the decision so quickly.

Maverick's reassurance rumbled through the bond like a caress on her cheek. *There isn't anything he could take that I'm not ready to give right now.*

She swallowed hard. *Even if it means giving up alpha?*

I never wanted the title anyway, he replied, and the answering rumble in her heart told her he meant it.

"He does." She'd never sweated so much as she stared down the alpha, not even in one of Maverick's toughest training sessions.

Ryker's gaze sharpened as he studied her. "And what exactly are you offering me in exchange for risking my pack's safety? The safety of this town we're sworn to protect?"

Zera took a steadying breath. This was the crux of the deal. "Kraven authorized me to secure whatever terms are necessary." She held Ryker's stare. "Name your price."

An uncomfortable silence stretched between them. Zera could sense Maverick's sudden unease, but he remained still and silent, allowing her to negotiate.

Ryker leaned back in his chair. "Sixty percent—of all synthetic sales in Havenwood territory." His mouth curved into a lupine grin. "Plus I want a direct line to Kraven for... added security."

Zera's heart jolted. A sixty percent cut would mean Kraven wouldn't make a penny in this territory because she and Maverick were getting forty percent. But Kraven hadn't said anything about wanting to make money from the territory, and something told her he didn't want a foothold in this town for profit.

Without a second thought, she lifted her chin. "Done. You have a deal."

Ryker's grin widened as he stood, extending his hand. "Then welcome to the Haven Moon Pack." His violet demon eyes shifted to gold as they rose to Maverick's eyes. He now stood by her side. "To both of you."

As she grasped the alpha's hand to seal the pact, Zera couldn't deny the thrill that coursed through her. They had taken a massive step, but she was ready to embrace this new path, wherever it might lead.

Maverick's pride washed over her through their mate bond. Not only would her debt to Kraven be paid, but she would be making the realm a safer place. Something she was excited about, even if it meant delving into the criminal underworld. She knew that whatever happened, they would be safe.

"It's an honor to be part of your pack," Maverick said when he shook Ryker's hand and bowed his head to the alpha.

He meant it too. He had grown up as heir to a pack full of blood thirst and prejudice, so joining a pack that accepted others with open arms seemed an honorable choice.

The alpha nodded, his eyes flickering with respect before he rounded the desk to the exit. "We'll be in touch to get you your"—he made a gesture with a slender hand over his toned shoulder—"marks and pack ceremony. Quinn will take care of it."

Taking the hint, Maverick and Zera left.

"Oh," Ryker said, stopping them before they made it past the pool tables lining the foot of the stairs. "I don't suppose, Zera, you'll still be interested in moonlighting as a bartender?"

She smirked. "Not a chance."

"Yeah, boss, you're just going to have to hire a better replacement," Quinn said with a grin, folding her arms across her chest.

Even if she was half pixie, the werewolf in her was obvious, since she stood even taller than the alpha, who grumbled something about how tedious it was to find good help these days.

Zera chuckled and glanced up at Maverick. His eyes held a gleam of mischief as he leaned in closer to her, his lips hovering near the ear.

"I can think of a better way to celebrate," he murmured, his warm breath sending a shiver through their bond.

Her breath hitched, and she leaned in to whisper, "Lead the way."

She tossed a quick goodbye to Quinn, who waved them off with a knowing smile, and headed up to the tavern.

They emerged into the dimly lit bar above, and the smells of stale beer and polished wood filled Zera's senses. The room was now deserted, with no sign of Ryker's men, as if he'd called on them to settle pack business. The tables were neatly lined up, and chairs were turned over on their surfaces.

Zera glanced around one last time, taking in the familiar surroundings. This place had been like a second home to her for years. She'd tended bar, joked with the regulars, and found solace in the rhythmic motions of mixing drinks. A nostalgic pang tugged at her heart, but it was quickly overshadowed by the thrill of their recent victory. She would finally have more time for Cole, among other things, and it was all she'd ever wanted.

But perhaps she would pour one more for old times' sake.

"Look at this place," she said with a grin, giving Maverick's hand a squeeze. "Empty as can be. Perfect for a celebration drink."

Maverick's lips curled into that roguish smirk that accentuated his sharp cheekbones she found so irresistible. "You read my mind."

He guided her to the bar, his hand drifting to the small of her back. The mere touch of his fingertips on the bit of skin exposed between her cropped sweater and high-waisted jeans sent shivers down her spine.

She rounded the bar while he grabbed a barstool, and their eyes never once wavered from each other's.

"What'll it be, faeboy?" she asked with a wink. "The usual?"

He slid into the seat with an effortless grace. Even simple actions looked devastatingly suave when he performed them.

"Surprise me." His eyes danced with devilish amusement.

Zera pondered her options for a moment before she started plucking bottles from the shelves, moving about the familiar bar with fluid familiarity. She palmed the mixer and prepped the ingredients in no time at all. It was a recipe she'd been thinking up for a while now, and this seemed as good a time as any to test it out.

As the liquid swirled and mixed within the shaker, Maverick observed her every move with a look of intense interest. His eyes didn't even leave hers when she set a glass in front of him and poured the pink liquid into it. A sugary citrus aroma filled the space between them as she slid the drink over to him. She matched the mischievous glint in his eyes with one of her own.

"I call it the Pink Pixie." She shuddered when his fingers grazed hers as he took the glass.

Her gaze lowered to his lips as he lifted the glass and took a slow, sensual sip.

He took his time savoring the taste before he set the glass down.

"Well?" She arched her brow.

"Well, it's a little tart," he purred, leaning over the bar to trail his fingers along her neck, "but sweet—just like you."

His touch electrified her skin, sending a rush of warmth through her veins. Zera's breath hitched as she felt the intensity of his gaze locking on hers. The air crackled with an unspoken tension, a magnetic pull drawing them closer.

"But I do wonder," he said, breaking the spell for a moment, "why is it called the Pink Pixie when it's the same shade of lavender as your eyes?"

A smile broadened across Zera's face. "Because, you smart-ass faeboy, it's not just lavender. Take a closer look."

He frowned, but his smirk remained as he lifted the glass up into the light. There it was, the magic of the vodka that Pixie Hollow was famous for, called Lumicitrus. Under the light, it transformed the lavender shades of the other liquors into a delicate pink.

"I named it for Quinn and me," she said, waving her fingers at the bar menu and watching as her pixie dust printed the drink at the top of the list. "A couple of pixies in a den of wolves." She winked. "And it's the last cocktail I will be adding to the bar menu."

"I'm sure it'll be a huge success," Maverick murmured, and their eyes locked once again.

Maverick rose and set the drink down, closing the remaining distance between them. With a seductive gleam in his piercing, storm-filled eyes, he brushed a stray lock of hair from Zera's face. "Perhaps we should celebrate our success in... other ways now?"

A delicious shiver ran down Zera's spine at his suggestive tone. Her breath caught in her throat as she met his smoldering gaze. He didn't give her a second to respond before his lips captured hers in a heated kiss, sending a surge of desire coursing through her veins. Zera melted into the kiss, her hands finding their way to Maverick's strong chest, feeling the steady beat of his heart under her touch. His scent was a heady mix of citrus and earth and something uniquely his own.

She let him see through the bond all the things she wanted to do, and his answering rumble of approval resonated in her mind.

He broke off the kiss to meet her gaze. The intensity of their mate bond and the raw longing in his eyes sent every nerve in her body tightening in anticipation.

Her lips parted, and she wished his lips, which hovered just above hers, would return. But instead, he brushed her cheek with the backs of his fingers before sliding them behind her neck while his lips tugged at her earlobe. A shuddering gasp escaped her as she arched into him as he made deathly slow work of trailing kisses from the soft skin below her earlobe down her neck.

Who's your faeboy? Maverick smirked down the bond, taunting her.

Her heart stuttered. *You are.*

Yes, I am. He nipped at her lobe again. *Now, why don't you shimmer us home so I can show you just how good a faeboy I am?*

Zera's eyes shuttered for a moment before she pulled back, breathless. "I... I haven't really mastered shimmering yet," she admitted, chewing her lip nervously. Teleporting from place to place with pixie dust was possible, according to what she had learned in an elective course on rare faen species that included pixies. Since then, she'd started working on it and had been able to teleport herself to town from their home. Yet she'd never attempted to shimmer someone else.

Maverick lined his lips against the shell of her ear, his hot breath sending tingles down her spine. "I believe in you, Zera. Take me home."

The low timbre of his voice made it difficult to focus, but she cleared her mind and reached deep within herself to that wellspring of magic shimmering down her spine. She visualized their bedroom —the giant king-sized bed with its plush comforter, the bay windows framing the majestic vista of Havenwood Forest. Focusing all her energy, she felt the familiar warmth of her pixie dust swirling around them, and she opened her eyes.

Iridescent sparkles of purple whipped around them on a phantom wind and swept them up as if they were weightless. The tavern vanished around them, and they rematerialized right on top of their bed, tumbling amid the cotton sheets in a fit of breathless laughter. Zera landed half on top of Maverick, and their bodies entangled. She pushed herself up slightly, scanning his face with poorly concealed awe.

"I did it," she breathed out in disbelief. She'd actually shimmered them both successfully and, as far as she could tell and feel, with all of their limbs.

Maverick's hands slid sensually up her sides, sending tingles where his fingers touched. "I never doubted you for a second, my mate." His voice had dropped an octave and was thick with pure masculine desire.

Zera felt the heat of their connection intensify tenfold as she drank in the sculpted lines of his face and the sharp angles of his jaw. Strands of sun filtered through the windows and painted golden hues across his chiseled features. In that moment, the world around them fell away until there was only the two of them—two destined souls bound by a love deeper than either of them could have ever imagined.

Maverick's fingers tangled in her hair as he guided her lips to meet his once again in a searing kiss. Their mate bond ignited into an all-consuming blaze, setting every nerve ending alight with inde-scribable ecstasy. Zera gasped against his mouth. She had never experienced anything even remotely close to this level of intimacy and raw passion.

As if he'd read her thoughts, Maverick rasped through the bond, This is only the beginning, my love. He growled wolfishly with unconcealed hunger and devotion as he lowered her gently onto the soft comforter. She tugged at his shirt, not wanting anything between their naked bodies.

She made to unbutton his shirt when she heard a peal of childish giggles outside their bedroom door.

"Cole! Where are you going?" Jade's voice filtered in.

Maverick and Zera turned their heads as a tiny blur of brown curls came barreling through the half-open door. Cole crawled at full speed to the bed, his round face alight with mischief and his big lavender eyes sparkling with innocence.

Zera shot Maverick an apologetic look laced with longing. Through their bond, his affectionate amusement washed over her in reassuring waves before Maverick hopped out of bed and scooped Cole up to join them.

"Hey, little guy," Maverick said as he swung Cole in the air, eliciting a burst of giggles and squeals.

Zera couldn't help but smile at the sight of her son's joy and Maverick's effortless way with him.

"Oh, sorry!" Jade said, poking her head into the room. "I didn't know you all were back. You want me to take him?"

She arched a brow at Zera with a knowing look.

"It's okay, Jade," Zera said with a wave. "Go be with Sloane. I've got him."

Her half sister hesitated but then waved her goodbye.

"Thank you!" Zera called after her before Cole nosedived toward her with open arms. "Hey, baby!" She caught him with a laugh, hugging his tiny body close as she nuzzled her face into his soft curls. His sweet, powdery scent filled her senses.

"You're okay with just hanging out and playing with us?" she asked, gazing up into Maverick's piercing, stormy eyes that smoldered in response.

"I'm more than okay with that plan," he whispered, his voice low and husky as he wrapped his muscular arms around them both. Cole giggled and clapped his hands, clearly enjoying the attention from both his mother and Maverick.

Zera leaned into his solid warmth, her heart overflowing with love for her new little family. This was everything she'd ever wanted and more—a profound bond, unconditional love, and a life full of laughter.

As Cole babbled happily between them, Zera met Maverick's tender gaze once more. She knew then that no matter what challenges lay ahead, they would face them together, united by an unbreakable connection that would only grow richer with each passing day in their forever after.

BONUS CHAPTER
A FEW YEARS LATER...

Zera stood at the doorway of their back patio, her heart thrumming like her own wings as they fluttered behind her. The purple glow of her wings cast shadows against the glass pane—the only thing between her and her destiny that lay beyond. Today, underneath the dwindling light of the sun as it set behind the mountains, she would marry her bonded mate. Her love that she had found when she'd least expected it.

A flurry of butterflies swarmed her insides, but it only made her smile broaden because there in the backyard, at the end of the white carpeted aisle lined with white garden chairs filled with her closest friends, a few family members, and Ryker and the rest of the Haven Moon Pack, stood her forever faeboy.

Zera couldn't keep her gaze off of Maverick as he fidgeted with a cuff or readjusted the blue rose pinned to his lapel. The wolf looked nervous, and Zera's cheeks hurt from smiling so hard. In all the time she had known him, she had never seen him look truly nervous.

Everything was perfect. Except...

Her smile faltered. A pang of sorrow swept through Zera as she thought about the family that were missing. Her parents wouldn't be among the guests. She knew that, though her eyes still swept over every chair visible to her from this angle.

Zera wasn't by any means traditional and didn't need a man to walk her down the aisle. She had asked her half sister Jade to do the honors, and Zera couldn't imagine anyone else better for the job. But the desire to have one's parents beside them on such an important day still tugged at her heart. At the same time, she knew better than to think the queen and king of Pixie Hollow would grace her with their presence. Not after the way she left things. The fight she'd had with her parents all those years ago still echoed in her mind. When Their Royal Highnesses found out that Zera—their firstborn daughter and heir to the pixie kingdom—was a traitor, allowing her heart to fall for a werewolf, they forbade her from ever seeing him again, and if Zera ever did see him again, she would never be welcome back to Pixie Hollow. Of course, Zera had been young, and the threat hadn't seemed like that big of a sacrifice at the time.

But that was before she got pregnant and the werewolf she'd fallen for left. Now, though? Things were different. Sometimes she longed for home, and the blossom-scented wind called to Zera's pixie wings. She was glad Cole, at least, had been welcomed there when Jade and Sloane had taken him while she went hunting with Maverick. It had been a terrifying moment in her life but one she wouldn't trade for the world. Though, she would've taken Cole's life not being put in danger at all if she'd had the choice.

Perhaps one day, Zera would try to make amends with her parents and the kingdom of Pixie Hollow, though she didn't think marrying a different werewolf—and not just any werewolf, but an ex–Lunar Moon Pack alpha—would help her odds of reconciliation. But Zera's heart still yearned to share this moment with her parents, yearned for them to know their grandson better and, hopefully one day, their future grandchildren.

Zera blinked back the tears. She wouldn't cry. Not on her wedding day and especially not when so much hope and beauty lay before her. Truly, Sloane had outdone herself transforming the backyard into a true fantasy. From the bouquets of flowers to the white flickering candles dancing in the air and the sparkling fairy lights strung up between trees, it was like stepping into a scene from a fairytale.

Even the Haven Moon pack had contributed to the ceremony, providing the altar, made of wood that a pack member had intricately engraved with little pixies and werewolves frolicking among ivy leaves as a symbol of their united truce—thanks to Pixels, Zera's synthetic pixie-dust drug that was now on the market and doing very well. So much so that she'd fulfilled her debtor's promise to Kraven the crime lord in record time.

Though she still supplied him pixels now, it wasn't out of fear of him collecting payment. Maverick and Zera rarely saw him anymore, as he'd moved on to other projects, and that was the way they liked it. Neither of them trusted the incubus, but at least he was helping them stop the hunting of pixies thanks to her synthetic drug. It was a victorious achievement in the Fae Realm.

And yet, even though the hunting of pixies had nearly become extinct due to the popularity of her synthetic pixie dust, Zera hadn't received a single word from the pixie nobles. Not even Jade, who was still on relatively good terms with their parents even after declining to inherit the throne, had heard from them about anything except for surface-level pleasantries. It wasn't like Zera thought things would go back to the way they were before she'd run off with the wolf. She wasn't naive enough to think they'd give her firstborn right back, to announce her the heir to Pixie Hollow. Zera didn't want the title anyway. It was too much of a responsibility, and she'd always wanted her own life.

But she wanted her family, and she wanted her son to know his grandparents.

"Here. Wear these," Jade said, pulling Zera's attention back to the present by thrusting a box into her hands

"What's this?" Zera asked, opening the box to reveal a pair of elbow-length lace gloves so delicate and fine they looked to have cost a fortune. She gasped at the gorgeous fabric, how the diamonds that dotted it glittered in the light.

"It's your something old," Jade said with a wink, sliding her hands into the black tux she donned. "Our grandmother wore them to her wedding."

"But how... how did you..." Zera trailed off, her heart stuttering as she whirled back to face the backyard. "Does this mean they're here?"

"You mean mom and dad? Yup." Jade grinned. "They arrived just a few minutes ago. They didn't want to bother you, but wanted you to have it. Guess they figured out what you did."

Zera swallowed back a sob. Tears again welled in her eyes, but this time, they were tears of joy. Her heart had never felt so full as she watched her parents gracefully take two seats near the front that magically appeared. Her stepfather sat tall and proud next to her mother, who shared Zera's same lavender eyes and purple wings. With his noble brow, lavender hair, and golden wings, he stood out in his navy tux complete with a purple pocket square. Though he wasn't her biological father, who had died before she was born, Zera considered him her true father, as she'd never known anyone else.

"I can't believe it," Zera gasped, turning back to face Jade just as the front door swung open and a woman cursed.

They turned in time to see Quinn stumbling in, yanking off a work shoe and shoving on a lavender high heel that matched the silk bridesmaid dress she donned.

"Don't worry! I'm here," Quinn said breathlessly, tossing strands of pink hair out of her eyes. "The blasted Ryker had me work the last shift before closing for the evening. Can you believe it?"

Zera chuckled, and Quinn froze, gasping as she took Zera's appearance in.

"You look gorgeous, Zera!" Quinn exclaimed, finally with both heels on, and pulled Zera into a hug. "I'm so happy for you. And I'm especially happy to have a new outsider as a member in the pack."

They all laughed, knowing it was a huge step. For too long had the werewolf packs been ruled under archaic laws. Now, Ryker was leading the Haven Moon Pack into a new age, one that would honor those who had been marginalized or ostracized altogether. Zera couldn't help but worry what the recourse would be from the surrounding packs, but for now, she would revel in this victory.

Cole suddenly shimmered into the room in a puff of purple sparkles with Sloane hot on his heels. He had come into his half-pixie magic quicker than Zera had anticipated, and it made this stage all the more entertaining and challenging.

"Momma!" He shouted, his brown curls framing his face. He donned a half-buttoned-up shirt, a diaper, and his shoes.

"My baby!" Zera called, kneeling down and opening her arms for her son, who had grown so much over the last two years. She really needed to start his potty training, but she would tackle one problem at a time.

"Sorry, Zera," Sloane said with a soft chuckle, donning a matching dress to Quinn's. "He just won't put his pants on and only wants to eat crackers."

"Is this true, my little one?" Zera grinned, encircling her arms around Cole as she hoisted him off the floor and spun him around even though he was over thirty pounds.

Cole's laughter was infectious as he squealed in delight. Zera sat him down and kneeled in front of him. "Now, is everything okay?"

The toddler nodded, stuffing a peanut butter cracker in his mouth.

"Then can you please put your pants on?" Zera asked.

"Why?" Cole asked between bites.

Zera smiled, knowing he was testing his boundaries and wanting to practice his newfound independence. It was a trying season for her as well as her sister and sister-in-law who helped take care of Cole, but Zera tried to face every season from a nurturing perspective. Zera knew she didn't get it right all the time, but Cole was her son, and she only got one chance to raise him to be the kind of man he should be.

"Because you know that when you do, we can go outside and see daddy," Zera said, and Cole's eyes instantly lit up.

Since moving in with Maverick, the two had become almost inseparable. Cole and Maverick adored each other, and Zera could see the fatherly love only bloom further as time passed. So when Maverick asked if she ever thought about him adopting Cole as his own son, Zera knew then that their little family was falling into place. It was a moment Zera would never forget. The only time Cole's biological father ever reappeared was to sign the paperwork, and then he vanished into the ether again.

Good riddance, Zera thought. Cole deserved a father figure who prioritized him, who would put everything on the line just to save him, who would show Cole what a true man was. Maverick was all of this and more. Sometimes it wasn't about the family you were born to but the one found in the least-expected places.

"Yay! Daddy!" Cole nearly dropped his cracker as he ran back to his aunt Sloane to get his pants.

Zera rose, smoothing out the gossamer fabric of her A-line gown that fit her perfectly at the waist, embroidered with vines, tiny flowers, and dewdrop-like crystals, accentuating her figure before flaring out in a pool of skirts behind her.

"Are you ready?" Jade asked, taking the rings out of her jacket pocket and looping them into the pillow that Cole would take down the aisle. The gold bands caught the light, a symbol of Maverick's unyielding loyalty and love for her that, in turn, spoke to her own promise to stand by his side in all the adventures and trials life would bring. Zera gazed at the rings, feeling a surge of gratitude for the love she had found in Maverick.

Zera drew in a deep breath, squaring her shoulders. "I've never been more ready in my life."

Jade gave her a knowing smile. Her sister always could see more than she let on.

"Ready, Auntie!" Cole called, diving out of his aunt Sloane's arms to jump up and down in front of his auntie Jade. His lavender tux matched Sloane's silk dress and Jade's bow tie. Zera couldn't help but think how fantastic they all looked. And now with her parents in the crowd? Perhaps everything was falling into place.

"You are?" Jade asked, kneeling down so her face was at Cole's height. "Okay, your aunt Sloane and I have a really important task for you. Do you think you can handle it?"

Cole nodded emphatically, his brown curls bouncing.

Jade handed the pillow with the rings to him. "Do you think you can take this pillow to Maverick? You see him standing at the end of the aisle with all those twinkly lights?"

"Uh-huh," Cole replied, taking the pillow.

"Awesome!" Jade applauded him. "Okay, I'm going to open the door, and you go right to Maverick. But no shimmering. Got it?"

"Got it." Cole grinned, flashing his werewolf fangs, and nearly flew out the back door at inhuman speed when Jade slid it open.

"Wow, he's fast. Even without shimmering," Jade commented.

"That he is." Sloane shook her head with a loving smile, her beautiful brown skin standing out against the lavender straps of her dress.

"You look gorgeous, babe." Jade placed a kiss on Sloane's lips before turning back to Zera. "Alright, Quinn, you're up. Sloane and I will follow you, and then I'll be back for you, Zera."

Zera watched as Quinn led the way, followed by Jade escorting her gorgeous wife down the aisle, the soft strains of music filling the air as the two reached the end of the aisle. The soft orange glow of the sunset filtered through the canopy of leaves above. The magical ambiance of the forest seemed to intensify as Zera took a deep, contented sigh, her heart swelling with love for her sister and Sloane. As she waited for her cue to make her own entrance, she couldn't help but steal another glance at Maverick.

He stood tall and proud, holding Cole in his arms with the ring bearer pillow in tow, his eyes fixed on the glass door Zera stood at that Sloane had enchanted so those outside couldn't see in. Moisture brimmed Zera's eyes again, but they were tears of joy as she watched the two most important men in her life. This was her family, and she wouldn't trade it for the world.

Jade soon returned and reached for Zera's arm. Zera took it without hesitation. With a grace that seemed to make the very air around her quiver, Zera took her first step down the aisle. The hem of her dress whispered over the white carpet, a cascade of fabric that shimmered like moonlight on water. Each stride was an affirmation of her strength and love.

All eyes turned as Zera neared, escorted by her sister. The music changed to a lilting melody, the string quartet playing with as much passion and love for the song as Zera felt in her own heart. Everyone rose to stand, even her parents, who gave her an encouraging, diplomatic nod. It was more than Zera could've asked for, and she was grateful to have her family, especially her sister, by her side today.

But then it all faded away as Zera reached the end of the aisle and Maverick's eyes met hers, a silent exchange passing between them that spoke volumes. Finally, mere steps away from Maverick, Zera reached out with slender fingers that held not just the power to enchant but to touch the deepest recesses of the soul. Maverick, holding Cole in on arm, took hers in his, his warmth enveloping her, and as their fingers entwined, it was as if two disparate melodies had converged into a harmonious chord.

Jade took Cole and guided him to a seat reserved for them while Sloane took her position as the officiant. Zera and Maverick stood facing each other, hands clasped, their gazes locked in a dance of unspoken promises and shared dreams. The forest around them seemed to hold its breath in reverence.

Sloane's voice, soft and soothing, welcomed honored guests and invited Maverick and Zera to say their own vows.

"From the moment I became a mother, every day has been a wonder and a battle, a chance to rise and protect the magic within us." Zera's voice grew richer with each word, an echo of her once-solitary struggle. "But, Maverick, you entered our lives so unexpectedly, fierce and unyielding, yet beneath it all, you bore the calm resilience I didn't know I was missing. You never sought to tame the wildness of my heart; instead, you fought beside me, your faith unwavering. You are my forever faeboy."

Zera winked, her words eliciting a knowing chuckle from Maverick that made his eyes dance. As she finished, her vows hanging suspended like the final note of a symphony, Maverick's eyes glistened, not with sorrow or coldness but with a warmth that radiated love. He took a deep breath, the habit of running his hand through his hair absent in this sacred moment, replaced by stillness.

"Zera, the moment I first saw you, I was struck," he said, his voice deep and sincere. "Not only by your beauty but your strength. You not only saved my life on our very first date, but you took charge and didn't let your fear take control of you. And after playing the part of your fake husband, it didn't take long for me to realize I wanted to be yours. For real and for always."

Maverick brought her hand up to his and kissed the top of it before murmuring, "Today, I vow not just to protect but to cherish you and Cole, to be the shield against any storm and the laughter within these woods."

If Zera's heart could melt, it would be a pooling mess all over their dressy shoes. The raw honesty in his words was more than she could ever have hoped for. Zera's hand trembled ever so slightly as Maverick slipped the ring onto her finger. It was a simple band but glittered with the hidden magic of the bonded promises they'd made to each other.

Maverick's eyes flickered from stormy gray to wolf gold as she did the same, securing his ring on his finger, his hands engulfing hers as soon as it was secured.

"And now that we have witnessed these promises," Sloane said, her voice rising above the soft music that played in the background. "By the authority given unto me by the Fae Realm, I now pronounce Zera and Maverick ma—"

A loud thud cut Sloane off, causing Zera's heartbeat to stutter. The guests collectively turned and murmured in surprise when another guest emerged from the sliding back door. But this wasn't just any guest. Zera recognized the silver-haired man with the deadly blue eyes in an instant.

Kraven, known to Zera and Maverick as the notorious incubus crime lord, sauntered down the aisle, commanding attention as he took a seat next to Zera's parents as if he knew them. Zera could only stare and gawk as her own mother smiled at him. She actually *smiled*. Zera couldn't remember a time when her mother showed that much emotion, but Kraven's arrival seemed almost welcome to her parents. How did they know each other?

"Apologies for my tardiness," Kraven said smoothly, adjusting his silver tie with an air of nonchalance. His piercing blue eyes flicked between Zera and Maverick, their gazes briefly locking before he leaned back in his seat.

The moment of tension hung in the air like a thick fog, causing Zera's breath to hitch. She hadn't thought Kraven would come. She hadn't seen him since she gave him her last payment and the debtor's promise was lifted. Zera had only sent him an invitation because of formalities, but the fact that he actually came sent a sinking sensation through Iris. Why was he here? Did he want something else from them?

Zera didn't know much about the nearly extinct incubi, but there was always a price paid by those around them. Would that price be paid now? Would something jeopardize her and Maverick's marital plans?

Maverick's grip on Zera's hand tightened, offering a silent reassurance as he said, "Let's not let this dampen our joy." His storm-filled gray eyes met hers, and the warmth in his gaze seemed to chase away the tension.

Zera nodded, trying her best to push aside her worries. She couldn't let the crime lord's presence ruin their special day. With a deep breath, she focused on the officiant, Sloane, who was waiting for them to continue.

"Then, by the power vested in me," Sloane said, her voice steady and filled with emotion. "I now pronounce you husband and wife."

Maverick's crooked grin sent Zera's insides fluttering as he wrapped his massive arms around her waist and drew her against his chest. His scent of citrus and caramel with a hint of oak enveloped Zera, and she breathed in the intoxicating aroma as his lips touched hers. A soft sigh escaped from Zera's throat, accompanied by the sound of guests cheering and clapping in celebration. Maverick drew a hand up and caressed her cheek, the light touch soft and tender but filled with the promise of a lifetime of love.

Zera forgot about all of her fears and troubles because she knew that with Maverick at her side, they could face any obstacle.

The reception began shortly after, with music playing and the scent of delicious food wafting through the air. The lively atmosphere seemed to chase away any lingering tension, and Zera found herself swept up in the celebration.

As Zera and Maverick danced and mingled with their guests, laughter and stories flowed freely. They shared heartfelt moments with friends and family, both old and new, who offered congratulations and well-wishes for their future together.

"Zera," Jade said as she hugged her sister tightly. "We're so happy for you both."

"Thank you, Jade," Zera answered, her lavender eyes shimmering with unshed tears of happiness.

"And don't worry while you're off on your honeymoon," Sloane said when it was her turn, hugging Zera tightly. "Cole is in good hands here with us. I'll have my strongest wards up, though I should've put them up this evening."

Jade grunted her agreement. "It might've kept out some of the riffraff."

Zera followed their gazes to Kraven as he mingled with the more noble guests in attendance.

"Could've used it to keep him out too," Quinn chimed in,

nodding to Ryker as he tried to have a conversation with Maverick, who was too distracted by tossing a giggling Cole up into the air.

Zera chuckled, barely restraining a grin. Those two were inseparable.

"Congrats again," Quinn said, pulling Zera into another hug, her pink hair catching the light of the flickering candles and faelights that bobbed above the dance floor.

"Well," Maverick's deep voice said, interrupting the moment. "I think this one's ready for bed."

Cole erupted into a fit of giggles as Maverick flipped him and placed the toddler on his feet in front of them. Soon, Zera's little boy would be too big for that, but Maverick, being a werewolf and having enhanced strength, would probably be able to keep tossing Cole around for years to come.

Zera said good night to her son, hugging him close for as long as possible. She had to remind herself that Sloane was right. This time, Zera would be leaving a for a week to visit the Spire Alps, the very place that her Everfrost Blossom originated and the reason that her synthetic pixie-dust drug even became a thing. She couldn't wait. But she couldn't help the tinge of sorrow that struck, reminding her of when she last had to leave Cole with his aunts. But now would be different. They were safe, and there was no one else in the world Zera would trust with Cole besides Maverick.

After Jade and Sloane left to go put Cole down for bed, the night continued on with music and dancing, food and drinks flowing freely. Maverick raised a glass in celebration, toasting to their beautiful little family and all the adventures that lay ahead. As they danced together under the stars, surrounded by loved ones and laughter, Zera knew that she was exactly where she belonged. Her lavender eyes sparkled with delight, but a hint of unease lingered within them. She couldn't shake the feeling that something was off.

Her gaze wandered across the gathering, eventually settling on Kraven as he conversed with her parents, the king and queen of Pixie Hollow. The sight of the incubus crime lord chatting with her parents in such a friendly and familiar way sent a shiver down her spine. Not only had Kraven arrived late, but he seemed to be chatting up anyone and everyone who had connections, and now her parents? What could he possibly want with them? Zera was certain whatever it was, it couldn't be good.

"Is everything alright?" Maverick asked, noticing her distraction.

"Take a look over there," Zera murmured, nodding subtly towards Kraven and her parents. "I don't like him being so close to them."

Maverick's gray eyes narrowed as he observed the scene before them.

"I mean, what could they be talking about?" Zera asked, distracted as Maverick whirled her around in a spin before twirling her back into his arms and dipping her back.

"I could use my wolf hearing to listen in, or we can do one final recon? This time as a real married couple?" Maverick waggled his eyebrows conspiratorially.

Zera couldn't help but laugh at his comical expression. She'd never seen him so happy. "I thought you gave up all that shady spy stuff years ago?"

"Of course," Maverick said with a wicked grin. "But what's one more mission for old times' sake?"

A thrill of excitement raced through Zera at the thought of indulging in a bit of espionage for the sake of nostalgia.

"Let's do it, but let's be discreet," Zera agreed.

"Oh, I think we both know I can be discreet," Maverick said huskily against her ear.

Zera could only laugh as they shimmied their way across the dance floor and closer to Kraven and her parents. They pretended to be distracted with each other, completely enthralled with the music. As they approached, Zera overheard her stepfather, King Theo, asking Kraven how the queen of Obsidia was faring, his tone laced with an underlying threat.

"Obsidia remains in good hands, I assure you," Kraven replied smoothly, casting a knowing glance at them.

Did her parents know that they were talking this way to an actual crime lord? Zera had to keep her eyes glued on Maverick to keep from breaking her cover and gawking at them. It wasn't a bad view, though. In fact, she couldn't wait to get this strong male wolf alone and...

Don't tempt me, Maverick growled through their bond.

Zera's smile turned devilish. *I can't make any promises.*

"As the grand advisor, I'm sure you're aware of the unrest we've been hearing about along our borders," her stepfather, the king of Pixie Hollow, said, his voice jarring them back to the task at hand. "Drudges running amuck? It could start a war."

Who was her father calling the grand advisor? It couldn't be Kraven, could it?

The song came to an end, and so did their ruse when her parents greeted her, pulling Maverick and Zera from the dance floor. Zera hadn't had a chance to talk with her parents after all these years and, truth be told, she hadn't been sure how to approach them. There were so many unsaid things between her and her parents that needed to be addressed. But not tonight.

"Zera, dear, have you met Kraven before?" her mother, Queen Everly, asked as if no time had passed at all. As if Zera hadn't been banished for falling for a werewolf and her mother wasn't now celebrating Zera's marriage to another.

But Zera could let it go. The fact that they were here meant something, and for the sake of making things better, Zera refused to allow her inner pride to jeopardize things.

"Only briefly," Zera answered cautiously, not wanting to divulge the pack's involvement with the likes of him. "And how do you all know each other?"

"Oh, we go way back," King Theo said proudly. "As he's the grand advisor to the vampire Queen of Obsidia, we are well acquainted."

Zera's eyes widened, betraying her shock at this revelation. She had known Kraven as a criminal mastermind but not as a political figure in the Fae Realm. The matching look of astonishment on Maverick's face told Zera he was surprised by this news as well. What other secrets did this man hold?

"Congratulations to you both. Excuse me," Kraven said, offering a polite smile before slipping away into the crowd. Zera couldn't help but feel a sense of relief as he left.

Now alone with her parents, Zera attempted to bridge the distance between them. They exchanged stiff pleasantries, but Zera sensed it was a step in the right direction. She hoped that one day, they could mend their fractured relationship.

"Things are brewing in the south," King Theo said with a harrumph, his pixie wings fluttering with the motion. "We will have to be vigilant about our borders as unrest builds."

"Oh, enough of this shoptalk," Queen Everly said, swatting her husband lightly on the arm. "You both look dashing."

"Thank you, Your Grace," Maverick said, taking the queen's hand and placing a kiss atop it.

"Queen Everly will do," Queen Everly said with a soft smile before turning to Zera. "Enjoying the festivities, my dear?"

Zera had to fight to roll her eyes. Her parents were always so formal.

"I am," Zera replied, smiling genuinely. Her happiness was palpable, and she reveled in every moment of her wedding day, but now that it was coming to its conclusion, all she wanted was to curl up into Maverick's arms.

Sensing Zera's desire, Maverick wrapped his arm around her waist. "May I steal my new bride for another dance?"

"Certainly," her mother said with a stiff nod.

As Maverick led Zera back to the dance floor, she couldn't help but feel a mixture of emotions. The revelation about Kraven's position as the grand advisor to the queen of Obsidia, along with her father's rather ominous warning of the unrest along the vampire border, left her with lingering questions.

Questions that can wait until after our honeymoon, Maverick's inner voice purred down the bond, making heat coil within Zera's core.

Maverick swayed her gently to the music, his gaze fixated on hers. "Did you have a good time today?"

"It was... unexpected" Zera said, a small smile playing on her lips. "I never imagined myself getting married, let alone to a werewolf."

Maverick's lips twitched. "Well, I never thought I'd end up with a feisty little pixie—"

"Careful, faeboy. Don't forget I have the Whisper's staff and I know how to use it," Zera teased.

"Point taken," Maverick said with mock surrender. "But seriously, I couldn't be happier. You and Cole are my everything."

"Mine too," Zera breathed, her eyes misting over.

Maverick leaned in, nipping at her earlobe, his citrus-and-bourbon scent mingling with her own sugary blend of lilac and spice. "So, about that honeymoon," he whispered, sending a shiver down her spine.

Zera blushed but couldn't help the thrill of anticipation that coursed through her veins. "I couldn't agree more. Let's go."

Maverick smirked and took her hand in his, and together, they bid their farewells to their guests. Once they were finally alone, Zera leaped into Maverick's arms before shimmering them off to the Spire Alps in a cloud of purple smoke. The crisp wind of the mountain air greeted them as they materialized outside a quant log cabin nestled at the foot of a range of mountains and framed with evergreens.

White snow blanketed the ground, glittering under the soft moonlight that bathed the alpine landscape. To their right, beyond a frozen pond, lights from the small dragon-shifter town twinkled in the distance where they planned to dine and shop. To the left stretched towering slopes, lined with lifts and gondolas designed for fae unable to fly. It was there that Zera and Maverick planned to take ski lessons alongside the dragons. But neither of them could think about skiing right now. Not with the carnal need to claim each other pulsing through their bond.

The light smoke that puffed through the chimney of the cabin promised warmth and shelter, and as Maverick carried Zera across the threshold, his lips crashed into hers with passion and need.

Her hands tangled in his hair, eliciting a moan from Maverick, his wolfish instincts kicking in as he carried her over to the large four-poster bed draped in white linen that dominated the far wall across from the roaring fireplace, setting her feet down on the plush bearskin rug.

Maverick's gentle but urgent kisses trailed down her neck, his hands deftly at work undoing the buttons of her wedding gown. Zera's skin tingled beneath his touch as his fingers continued to explore her curves, memorizing every inch of her. Her breath hitched when the last button snapped free and the dress fell in a pool of skirts at her ankles. Maverick's heady gaze roamed her body before he pulled her against him. Zera wrapped her legs around his hardened body, pulling him down onto the bed and on top of her with a squeal.

The air between them crackled with electricity and need as they tangled limbs and lips, their love burning hotter than any fire could provide.

"Maverick," Zera moaned, arching into his touch when his fingers touched the sensitive nerves at her core.

He growled low in his throat, pressing his hardened length against her and sending delicious shivers through her body. "You have no idea how long I've waited to make you mine."

"Then stop teasing me and claim me," she said, nipping at his lips.

With a feral growl, Maverick obliged, his mouth and hands roaming her body at once. Zera ripped his shirt from his shoulders while he unbuttoned his pants in between kisses to her lips, neck, and nipples. He trailed kisses down her stomach, stopping to twirl his tongue over a very sensitive spot, and she moaned, her hips bucking.

Maverick's deep chuckle taunted Zera even more as he took his hand, pinning her hips to the bed. She fisted the sheets, her eyes rolling back as his tongue swept across her in one long, slow lick, his breath sending goosebumps raising on her heated skin.

Zera gripped the sheets tighter, her nails sinking in as she arched against his until she reached the top and his fingers sent her over the edge.

"Please!" She begged, pulling against him. She needed him inside her. Now.

Maverick's eyes blazed with desire and the primal need to claim her. When she felt like she couldn't take it anymore, he positioned himself at her entrance, throbbing with the need to be inside her. Zera lifted her hips, and Maverick's restraint broke with a growl as he thrust inside her, filling her up with every inch of him.

Zera gasped and wrapped her arms around his shoulders, her nails digging into his skin as their bodies meshed together. It felt so right, like he was made for her. Maverick groaned, his hips flexing as he plunged into her, his movements slow and leisurely. Maverick gazed into her eyes, his hand caressing her face as if he couldn't believe this was real. A teasing gleam flickered in Zera's eyes as she brought his thumb into her mouth and licked it as she would the length of him later.

Maverick licked his lips, his eyes flickering with desire as he read her dirty thoughts. *Trying to tease me, are you?*

Who, me? She responded through the bond. *Never.*

Zera grinned even wider, and Maverick growled, suddenly pulling out and flipping her onto her hands and knees. She giggled in pleasant surprise as she braced herself on the headboard, his hands gripping her hips as he plunged into her again and again, his hand sneaking around her waist to tease her while he took her from behind. Zera moaned loudly, her magic swirling under her skin as Maverick pounded into her, chasing her orgasm.

Gods, you're gorgeous, he growled through the bond. *And you're mine.*

Another wave of ecstasy crashed through her, and she met his thrusts with urgent desperation, her wings trembling in passion as she came apart in his arms, and at the same moment, he spilled himself inside her.

They collapsed together on the bed in a heap of limbs. For several moments they remained there, panting and spent, their heartbeats pounding in their ears. Zera relished the feel of his hot breath against her skin.

That... that was... Zera started through the bond, unable to form words.

Amazing? Maverick finished for her, his voice a low rumble even through their shared bond.

Zera laughed, turning her head and catching his lips in a searing kiss. She would never get tired of this. Lying with the man of her dreams, her mate, and now her husband. She reveled in the feel of him, his lips against hers, his tongue swirling against hers as he deepened the kiss. She could feel him hardening again, and she giggled into the kiss. *Greedy, aren't we?*

She could feel his smirk in his kiss, even as he rocked his hips against her. *Takes one to know one.* Maverick chuckled, and she playfully slapped his chest. He captured her hand in his, placing a tender kiss on each of her fingers. *As much fun as that sounds, I think refreshments are in order. And perhaps a hot bath?*

Zera let out a soft breath, his words music to her ears. "That sounds perfect."

After finding soft robes, Maverick went in search of sustenance while Zera started the bath. A claw-foot tub took up most of the bathroom with a giant window overlooking the mountains and the stars. She filled it with hot water and a sprinkle of pixie dust, which caused the water to bubble like a hot tub. The steam began to rise, and she felt her muscles relax at the sight of it.

Maverick's footsteps neared from the kitchen, and he entered with a tray of assorted cheeses, fruits, and two steaming cups of tea. It was a honeymoon made of dreams, and Zera couldn't imagine herself anywhere but here.

After everything they'd been through, all the hurdles they had battled, they were finally safe and together. For real this time, and for always.

The End

Loved Zera's story? Want to find out more about the unrest in the south and Kraven's involvement with the vampire queen?

Get ready for the next in the Midlife Adventures of the Fae Realm: *Blood & Bordeaux*. A hunter with a midlife crisis, forced to play consort in a deadly game. She will have her revenge.

www.TabiSlick.com/books

DON'T MISS THE NEXT MIDLIFE ADVENTURE!

BLOOD & BORDEAUX

A hunter with a midlife crisis, forced to play consort in a deadly
game. She will have her revenge.
Available at www.TabiSlick.com/books

Acknowledgments

I would like to extend my heartfelt gratitude to the incredible team at Red Adept editing for their meticulous copy editing of this manuscript. Your expertise and dedication have truly refined and enhanced my work.

A special thanks to Darlene at Red Adept Editing, your insightful feedback and attention to detail have been instrumental in shaping this novel.

Also, to Virge B. at Red Adept Editing for your thorough proofreading. Your keen eye for detail ensured that every aspect of this novel was polished to perfection.

I am also deeply grateful to Stephy Draws Art for designing the stunning character artwork. Your artistic talent has brought my characters to life in a way that words alone could not.

To Deranged Doctor Designs and their team who created such a beautiful cover that it literally made me cry.

To my son, Logan, who was born just a few months before I began writing this novel. I cherish all the sleepless nights rocking you to sleep. I would battle an elven drug lord for you.

To my husband, Devin, who has been my rock and biggest supporter throughout this journey. Your encouragement and belief in my dreams have given me the strength to pursue this passion. You are my forever faeboy.

To the advanced readers who took the time to read this manuscript and leave a well-thought-out review: your feedback has been invaluable, and your support means the world to me. Thank you for your time and thoughtful insights.

Finally, to all the readers: thank you for embarking on this journey with me. Your enthusiasm and love for stories fuel my passion for writing. I am immensely grateful for your support.

Thank you all for your invaluable contributions. This book would not have been possible without you.

Thank you for joining Zera on her journey. If you're ready for another midlife heroine facing magic and danger, don't miss Iris's story in *Blood & Bordeaux*! Grab your copy at **www.TabiSlick.com/books**

ABOUT THE AUTHOR

Tabitha Slick (aka Tabi Slick) is an enchanting fantasy author who masterfully explores paranormal romance, dark fantasy, mysteries, and the magical world of the fae. Her imaginative storytelling and beautifully crafted characters grip readers from the first page. Within the Transitioned Universe, she has penned numerous books, including the exhilarating Tompkin's School (A Supernatural Academy) series and the eagerly awaited Beast Hunter from the Fae Romance Realm. With a background in linguistics, Tabitha has a passion for language and literature that drives her captivating narratives. When not writing, she enjoys exploring new destinations, cherishing loved ones, and devouring novels and coffee while learning how to sew clothes from scratch.

Read More from Tabitha Slick

www.TabiSlick.com

WHO'S YOUR FAE BOY?

9 798991 509671